NUMBER **11**

· NUMBER ·

11

Jonathan Coe

ALFRED A. KNOPF

NEW YORK · 2017

THIS IS A BORZOI BOOK
PUBLISHED BY ALFRED A. KNOPF

Originally published in hardcover in Great Britain by Viking,
a division of Penguin Random House Ltd., London, in 2015.

www.aaknopf.com

Knopf, Borzoi Books, and the colophon are registered trademarks of
Penguin Random House LLC.

Library of Congress Cataloging-in-Publication Data
Names: Coe, Jonathan, author.
Title: Number 11 / Jonathan Coe.
Other titles: Number eleven
Description: First Edition. | New York : Alfred A. Knopf, 2017.
Identifiers: LCCN 2016019484 (print) | LCCN 2016026352 (ebook) |
ISBN 9780451493361 (hardback) | ISBN 9780451493378 (ebook)
Subjects: | BISAC: FICTION / Literary. | FICTION / Contemporary
Women. | FICTION / Family Life.
Classification: LCC PR6053.O26 N86 2017 (print) |
LCC PR6053.O26 (ebook) | DDC 823/.914—dc23
LC record available at https://lccn.loc.gov/2016019484

Jacket photograph based on Vulture Labs / Getty Images (digitally altered)
Jacket design by Oliver Munday

Manufactured in the United States of America
First American Edition

In memory of

David Nobbs,

who showed me the way

"Because there comes a point, you know, Michael"—
he leaned forward and pointed at him with the
syringe—"there comes a point, where greed and
madness become practically indistinguishable. One
and the same thing, you might almost say. And there
comes another point, where the willingness to tolerate greed, and to live alongside it, and even to assist
it, becomes a sort of madness, too."

Jonathan Coe, *What a Carve Up!* (1994)

CONTENTS

The Black Tower
1

The Comeback
67

The Crystal Garden
121

The Winshaw Prize, or
Nathan Pilbeam's Breakthrough Case
169

What a Whopper!
219

Acknowledgements
335

Tony Blair, addressing the U.S. Congress, 17 July 2003:

"In another part of our globe,
there is shadow and darkness."

The Black Tower

1

The round tower soared up, black and glistening, against the slate grey of a late-October sky. As Rachel and her brother walked towards it across the moor, from the east, it was framed by two leafless, skeletal ash trees. It was the hour before dusk on a windless afternoon. When they reached the trees, they would be able to rest on the bench that stood between them, and look back towards Beverley in the near distance, the neat clusters of houses and, rising up in the midst of them, the monumental, answering greyish-cream towers of the Minster.

Nicholas flopped down on the bench. Rachel—then only six years old, eight years his junior—did not join him: she was impatient to run up towards the black tower, to get close to it. She left her brother to his rest and scurried onwards, squelching her way through the cow-trodden mud that surrounded the foot of the tower until she was right up against it, and could lay her hands upon the gleaming black brickwork. The flat of both hands upon the tower, she looked upwards and could not comprehend the size and scale of it, the perfect, lucid curve as it arched itself, like a sway back, against a threatening sky through which a pair of rooks were now skimming, cawing and circling endlessly.

"What did it use to be?" she asked.

Nicholas had joined her now. He shrugged.

"Dunno. Some kind of windmill, maybe."

"Do you think we could get inside?"

"It's all bricked up."

There was a circular wooden bench running all around the base of the tower, and when Nicholas sat there, Rachel sat beside him and stared up into his pale, unresponsive blue eyes, which for all their coldness only made her feel how lucky she was, how blessed, to have an older brother like this, so handsome and confident. She hoped that one day her hair would be as blonde as his, her mouth as shapely, her skin as downy and clear. She nestled against his shoulder, as close as she dared. She didn't want to be a drag upon him, didn't want him to become too aware that, in this strange and unfamiliar town, he was the only thing that made her feel safe.

"You cold or something?" he asked, looking down at her.

"A bit." She inched away slightly. "Will it be warm where they are, d'you think?"

" 'Course it will. There'd be no point going on holiday somewhere where it's cold, would there?"

"I wish they'd taken us with them," said Rachel feelingly.

"Well, they didn't. So that's that."

They sat for a few moments in silence: each of them, once again, trying to wrestle as best they could with the conundrum of why their parents should have chosen to go away for half-term without them. Then, as soon as the cold started to bite, Nicholas jumped to his feet.

"Come on," he said. "Are we going to look at this cathedral before it gets dark?"

"It's a minster, not a cathedral," said Rachel.

"Same difference. It'll just be a big old church, whatever you call it."

He set off quickly, with Rachel running up behind him in an effort to keep pace, but before they had got very far along the path back to the main road, they were halted in their tracks by the sight of two people approaching them in the distance. One of them was in a wheelchair: it appeared to be an old, old woman, swaddled against the afternoon chill by layer upon layer of thick woollen blankets. Her features were scarcely visible: her head was bowed, drooping tiredly, and she was wearing a silk headscarf which screened most of her face from view. In fact, the longer the children looked at her, the more likely it appeared that she was fast asleep. Her chair was being trundled roughly along the path, meanwhile, by a young-looking man wearing motorcycle leathers and balancing something on his left forearm as he pushed. The something could not, at first, be identified: but as the figures came closer, it looked as though it might—however implausible this seemed—be some sort of bird; a suspicion which was then suddenly and dramatically confirmed when the creature spread its wings to an amazing width, and flapped them languidly, in black silhouette against the grey sky—looking, at that moment, more like some fantastical hybrid creature from mythology than any real bird Rachel could remember having seen before.

Nicholas did not move, and as Rachel stood beside him she clasped his hand, relishing his weak responsive grip, sensing the coldness of his bare hand even through the prickly thickness of her woollen mittens. Unsure what to do next, they watched as the man in leathers settled the wheelchair in place and then spoke a few words to the bird, which reacted by hopping obediently from his arm to one of the chair's handles. With both arms free now, the man busied himself making sure the old lady in his charge was warm and comfortable, adjusting her blankets and tucking them in around her ever more snugly. Then he turned his attention to the bird.

Rachel inched forward, trying to pull her brother with her.

"What are you doing?"

"I thought you wanted to get on."

"I do. But I'm not sure that it's safe."

The man had taken out a length of twine with something attached to the far end, and had begun to swing it around his head in long, slow, circling movements. There was no traffic on the main road at the moment, and the afternoon was so still that the two children could clearly hear the regular heavy *SWUSH* of the twine as it swept through the air. They could even hear the beating of the kestrel's wings (it was clear that it was a kestrel now) as she took off in pursuit of the lure, training herself on the lump of meat at the end of the twine with lethal accuracy, and yet always just missing it, as the man swung it out of her reach in glorious, repeated feats of strength and timing. Every time the bird missed the meat she would dip, swoop lower and then climb steeply again, pushing swiftly up into the sky until she reached the limit of her parabola, hung suspended there for the briefest of moments, whirled and then dived again, rushing down towards the coveted lump of meat with preternatural speed and precision, only to have it snatched from her questing beak at the last possible instant.

After this exhilarating ritual had been performed two or three times, Nicholas and Rachel began to move forward cautiously. The man was standing slap in the centre of the path as he swung the lure about his head, so that they found it necessary to deviate from the track a little—at least far enough to stay out of the way of the circling twine. But this was not good enough for the falconer, who, without taking his eyes off the bird for a second, shouted at them in a voice filled with fury:

"Keep out of the way, can't you? Keep out the bloody way!"

But it wasn't the note of anger that surprised the children. It was the pitch of the voice: high, shrill and unmistakably feminine. And now that they were only a few yards from the taut, concentrated figure in motorcycle leathers, their mistake was obvious. It was a woman: a woman of around thirty-five, perhaps, although neither of them was very good at guessing the age of grown-ups. Her face was pale, her cheeks pinched and sunken, her hair shaved down to a severe and uncompromising crew cut. Her ears and nose were pierced and decorated with multiple silver rings and studs. A livid, dark blue-green tattoo of some indeterminate shape seemed to cover most of her neck and throat. She was the most terrifying woman, without a doubt, that Rachel had ever seen. Even Nicholas seemed taken aback. And if her appearance was not startling enough, there was the rising note of rage in her voice at the temerity, the insolence of these children for encroaching upon what she must have felt to be her own and the bird's territory. "Go on! Piss off!" she shouted. "Keep out the way! Use some bloody sense!"

Nicholas tightened his grip on his sister's hand and turned a sharp left, so that they were heading directly away from the danger zone. They sped up until they had practically broken into a run. Only when they were at twenty yards' safe distance from the scene did they stop and turn to take one last look. It was a tableau, a moment in time, that would remain forever stamped on Rachel's memory: the Mad Bird Woman (as she would always be called from now on) twirling the lure around her head with ferocious energy and concentration; the unimaginable swiftness and sureness of the bird as she plunged towards her prey and then soared upwards again, thwarted but dauntless; in the background, the black tower, tall, implacable and lowering; and in the foreground, the old lady in her wheelchair, fully alert now, her eyes bright and shining as they followed the movements of the bird, her vividly rouged lips parted in a rapturous smile as she called out to the plunging kestrel: "Come on, Tabitha! Come and get it! Dive for the meat! Dive, Tabitha, dive!"

Rachel did not like the look of the Minster at all. As they approached the main entrance from Minster Yard North, it was almost a quarter past four and dusk was already beginning to settle on the town. The thin shreds of mist which had been creeping along the streets and between the houses all day were turning bluish in the fading light, coiling and twining around the streetlamps with their blurry yellow coronas. And now a darker, more muted, blue-black light was starting to descend and spread itself, so that the walls of the Minster, as Rachel dragged her reluctant feet towards them, became hard to make out: no more than a whisper, an intimation, of the church's looming and ominous bulk. The cold which had first begun to grip her out on Westwood pasture, as she sat at the foot of the black tower, had now entered her bones, and taken such a pitiless hold that it felt as if these very bones were themselves made of ice. However tightly she pulled her duffel coat around her shivering body, however deep she plunged her hands into those sweet-wrapper-filled pockets, nothing could protect her from that cold. Soon the mixture of cold and apprehension had slowed her footsteps to a halt, only a few yards from the Minster doorway.

"Now what's the matter?" said Nicholas, crossly.

"Do we have to go inside?"

"Why not? We've come all this way."

Still Rachel held back. Inexplicably, her unease at the prospect of stepping through the Minster doorway was intensifying, mutating into something like dread. Nicholas took her by the hand again but there was nothing comforting about the gesture this time; he was pulling her towards the door.

In a moment they had passed through, into the darkness. Or at least, they were through the doorway, and into a small vestibule, but before they could get any further a startling thing happened. They had assumed they were alone in this narrow space but suddenly, quite silently and without warning, a figure stepped out from somewhere: from one of the pools of shadow, presumably, in its furthest corners. He appeared before them so unexpectedly, his footsteps so absolutely noiseless on the flagstones, that Rachel could not help but let out a scream.

"Sorry," he said, to the little girl. "Did I frighten you?"

He was a small man of somewhat striking appearance: his hair was albino white, his complexion so fair that his skin was almost transparent, and he had no eyebrows that Rachel could see. He wore a shabby fawn mackintosh over a light-grey suit, with a very wide brown tie of the sort that might have been fashionable about twenty-five years ago, back in the 1970s.

"Can I help you?" he asked. His tone was friendly but somehow intimidating. He spoke with a slight lisp which made Rachel think he sounded like a snake.

"We just wanted to go inside and have a look round," said Nicholas.

"Minster's closed now," said the man. "It closes at four o'clock."

The warmth of relief flooded through Rachel's body. They would not have to go inside. They could turn, and go home; back to the relative sanctuary of her grandparents' house anyway. She would be spared the nightmare.

"Oh. OK then," said Nicholas, disappointed.

The man hesitated a moment or two.

"Go on, then," he said, with a smile and a sinister wink. "You can have a wander around for a few minutes. They won't be shutting up just yet."

"Are you sure? That's ever so kind of you."

"No problem, son. If anyone asks, just say Teddy told you it'd be all right."

"Teddy?"

"Teddy Henderson. The assistant warden. Everybody knows me here." He watched as the children continued to hesitate. "Go on, then. What you waiting for?"

"All right. Thanks!"

Nicholas was off through the main door in no time, leaving Rachel with two options: to follow him, or to remain in the vestibule with the smiling figure of Mr. Henderson. It was no choice at all, in fact. Without glancing once at the discomfiting stranger, she took a deep breath and followed her brother.

It had seemed quiet outside the Minster, and inside the vestibule; but once Rachel had stepped inside the church's actual, vast interior, she found herself enveloped by quiet of an entirely different order. The silence was overpowering. She paused for a while, listening to it, absorbing it, holding her breath. Then she took a few steps forward towards the central aisle, and even those gentle, tentative footsteps sounded intrusive in that vaulted and silent space. She looked around for Nicholas but couldn't see him. The cold and the dark pressed down upon her. Dim electric bulbs threw feeble light over some of the walls, and there were a few candles flickering in the candelabra up towards the pulpit. But nothing could really palliate the sense of overwhelming gloom and unearthly silence. Where had Nicholas gone? Rachel walked quickly up the aisle now, looking anxiously to her left and right. He couldn't have gone far: she would see him in a second or two, surely. She had walked almost as far as the choir stalls when a sound suddenly made her freeze: a crashing sound, long and reverberant and horribly loud. The sound of a door being closed. She wheeled around. Was that the main door? Was that Mr. Henderson, locking up and going home? This was one of her keenest, most primal fears—the fear of getting locked in somewhere, after dark, and having to spend the night in a strange and lonely place. Was that what was happening now? She wanted to run towards the door to see, but stayed rooted to the spot. Indecision paralysed her. Tears sprang to her eyes and her body began to contract, turning in upon itself, seizing up with terror.

She sensed a movement behind her; she heard voices, murmuring. Turning round sharply, she thought she could make out two figures, talking in the shadows beyond the choir stalls. She took a breath and, in an act of desperate courage, called out: "Who's that?"

After a couple of seconds the voices stopped and one of the figures stepped forward. It was Nicholas. It was all Rachel could do to stop herself from letting out a yelp of happiness. She ran towards him and threw her arms around him. He embraced her, too, but there was something cold, preoccupied about the gesture. He did not look down at her, barely seemed to notice that she was clinging to him. Soon he eased himself away—pushing her from him—and then he glanced back towards the spot where he had been talking, a frown upon his face, as if something he had been told there was still puzzling him.

"Where have you been?" said Rachel, her voice loving, accusing. And, when he didn't answer: "And who was that? Who were you talking to just now?"

"She's one of the wardens here." Nicholas continued to stare back towards the rear of the church. Then he shook his head, and in a tone both brisk and nervous said: "Come on, I think we should go. This wasn't a good idea."

He hurried on towards the main door, Rachel padding along behind him, struggling yet again to keep up.

"Nick, wait! Slow down, can't you?"

The door of the vestibule was still open, but the main door, the door leading to the outside world, was now locked.

"It's shut!" Nicholas said, unnecessarily, after twisting the handle a few times.

"I know. I heard him close it. That man with the funny hair."

"Come on."

He strode off again, back in the direction of the choir stalls, and she scurried after him.

"Where are we going now? How are we going to get out?"

"There's another way. A little door down a passageway here. The lady told me."

Even for Rachel, now, there was no mistaking the note of panic in her brother's voice; and this was what scared her more than anything. She knew that if Nicholas was frightened, something must be very wrong.

"Can't you find her again? She could show us the way."

"I don't know where she is."

The candles had been snuffed out, and now with a click which itself echoed around the Minster walls, stretched and amplified a hundredfold, most of the lights were abruptly switched off. Darkness engulfed them. There was just one pinpoint, glimmering faintly, on the northern side of the nave.

"Come on," said Nicholas. "That must be it."

She tried to grab his hand again but he was already on his way. This time she broke into a sprint in order to catch up. In a matter of seconds they had reached a little arched doorway that led into a narrow, low-ceilinged corridor, at the end of which was a door marked "Exit only in emergency."

"Phew—this is it," said Nicholas. "We're going to be OK."

She followed him as he entered the tiny corridor, but instead of opening the door he leaned against the wall for a moment or two, breathing heavily to calm himself down.

"What's wrong?" Rachel asked. Her brother didn't answer and so, following a hunch, she made the question more specific. "It was something that lady said, wasn't it? What did she say to you?"

Nicholas turned to her, and his voice sank to a conspiratorial whisper. "She asked me what I was doing here, and I told her Mr. Henderson had let us in and said it was OK for us to have a look around. But she said that wasn't possible. She said . . ."

He tailed off. Rachel herself was too petrified to speak, but her eyes, fixed unmovingly upon her brother, demanded that he finish the explanation.

At last Nicholas swallowed hard and concluded, in a whisper that was softer but more urgent than ever: "She said, 'It can't have been him. *Teddy Henderson died more than ten years ago.*'"

He looked down at her, waiting for her reaction. She returned his gaze, her eyes steady and without expression. It was clear that she did not, at first, understand the full meaning of what he had just told her. It was too terrible for her to absorb. But slowly it began to happen. Her eyes widened and she put her hands to her mouth in horror.

"You mean . . . You mean he . . . ?"

Nicholas nodded slowly and then, without another word, he grabbed the handle of the exit door, pulled it open and was off: away, out into the freezing October air, down the path which led towards Minster Yard North and then back to the shops and safety.

He outpaced Rachel easily and it wasn't until he stopped to recover his breath in a sweetshop doorway that she was able to catch up with him. Her own sprint through the streets had been, up until that point, a thing of panic, confusion and heedlessness; already she could remember nothing about it. Now she stood and watched as Nicholas doubled over in the doorway, his shoulders heaving. As usual she wanted to hug him, to cling on to him, but this time something held her back. Some creeping element of suspicion. She looked at him more carefully. Her capacity for rational thought started to return as the pounding of her heart relaxed into something more measured and regular. And then the realization hit her. It wasn't the fear, it wasn't the exertion that was causing his shoulders to heave like this: it was laughter. Nicholas was *laughing*—silently, helplessly, unstoppably. Even then, she could not think what was making him laugh like this. It seemed an inexplicable reaction to the experience they had just been through.

"What is it?" she asked him. "What's so funny?"

Nicholas straightened himself up and looked down at her. He was laughing so much that his eyes were running with tears, and coherent speech was almost impossible.

"Your ... Your face," he spluttered finally. "Your face when I told you that story."

"What story?"

"Oh my God. God, that was priceless." His laughter subsided, and he became aware that his little sister was still staring at him in bewilderment. "The story," he repeated. "About that guy who let us into the church."

"You mean the ghost?"

At which Nicholas burst into laughter again. "No, you *dumbo*," he said. "He wasn't a ghost. I made that up."

"But that lady you spoke to said—"

"She didn't tell me anything except how to get out."

"So what about ... ?"

And then, finally, she understood. She understood, and she saw the full cruelty of the joke he had played on her. The boy she had trusted, the one person from whom she had thought she could seek comfort, had only wanted to upset and torment her. Of all today's horrors, this was the worst.

She did not scream, though, or burst into tears or shout at him. Instead, a sudden numbness overcame her, and all she said was:

"You're horrible and I hate you."

She turned and walked away, not having a clue where she was heading. To this day, she has never been entirely sure how she found her way back to her grandparents' house.

2

The paradox is this: I have to assume, for the sake of my sanity, that I am going mad.

Because what's the alternative? The alternative is to believe that the thing I saw the other night was real. And if I allowed myself to believe that, surely the horror of it would also make me lose my mind. In other words, I'm trapped. Trapped between two choices, two paths, both of which lead to insanity.

It's the quiet. The silence, and the emptiness. That's what has brought me to this point. I never would have imagined that, in the very midst of a city as big as this, there could be a house enfolded in such silence. For weeks, of course, I've been having to put up with the sound of the men working outside, underground, digging, digging, digging. But that has almost finished now, and at night, after they have gone home, the silence descends. And that's when my imagination takes over (it *is* only my imagination, I have to cling to that thought), and in the darkness and the silence, I'm starting to think that I can hear things: other noises. Scratches, rustles. Movements in the bowels of the earth. As for what I saw the other night, it was a fleeting apparition, just a few seconds, some disturbance of the deep shadows at the very back of the garden, and then a clearer vision of the thing itself, the *creature,* but it cannot have been real. This vision cannot have been anything but a memory, come back to haunt me, and that's why I've decided to revisit that memory now, to see what I can learn from it, to understand the message that it holds.

Also, I'm taking up my pen for another good reason, quite an ordinary reason, and that's because I'm bored, and it is this boredom—surely, this boredom and nothing else—that has been driving me crazy, provoking these silly delusions. I need a task, an occupation (of course, I thought I would find that by working for this family, but it has been a strange job so far, quite different from my expectations). And I've decided that this task will be to write something. I've not tried to write anything serious since my first year at Oxford, even though Laura, just before she left, told me that I should carry on with my writing, that she liked it, that she thought I had talent. Which meant so much, coming from her. It meant everything.

Laura told me, as well, that it was very important to be organized when you write. That you should start at the beginning and tell everything in sequence. Just as she did, I suppose, when she told me the story of her husband and the Crystal Garden. But so far, I don't seem to be following her advice very well.

All right, then. I shall put an end to this rambling, and attempt to set down the story of another visit to Beverley to stay with my grandparents, in the summer of 2003. A visit I made not with my brother this time but with Alison, my dear friend Alison, who at last after so many years' mysterious distance I have found again, picking up the threads of our precious friendship. This is our story, really, the story of how we first became close, before strange—not to say ridiculous—forces intervened and drove us apart. And it's also the story of—

But no, I mustn't say too much just yet. Let's go back to the very beginning.

3

The body of Dr. David Kelly, the United Nations weapons inspector, was discovered by Oxfordshire police at 8:30 on the morning of Friday 18 July 2003. The body was found in the woodland on Harrowdown Hill, less than a mile north of the village of Longworth, in a spot accessible only on foot, where Dr. Kelly had sometimes been known to take his afternoon walks. A verdict of death by suicide was quickly announced by the authorities.

His death was a matter of huge public interest. In preparation for Britain's supporting role in the U.S. invasion of Iraq, Tony Blair had been trying to persuade the British people that Saddam Hussein's regime presented a significant threat to British security. A government dossier had been prepared which included the claim that Saddam Hussein possessed weapons of mass destruction, and that these could be targeted at the UK within a timeframe of forty-five minutes. After an interview with Dr. Kelly, a BBC journalist had broadcast a report suggesting that this claim was unrealistic, and that the dossier itself had been "sexed up" in order to bolster the case for war. The widespread belief that the source of this report was Britain's leading international weapons inspector suddenly made Dr. Kelly a controversial and politically inconvenient figure.

I don't really know why I think so often about David Kelly's death. I can only suppose it's because, at the age of ten, it was the first national news story that made any impression on me at all. Maybe, too, because it evoked such a strong and chilling image: the loneliness of his death, the body discovered so many hours later in that remote woodland, silent and unvisited. Or maybe because of the way Gran and Grandad reacted: the way they made it clear that this was not an ordinary death, that it would have consequences, send ripples of unease and mistrust throughout the country. That Britain would be a different place from now on: unquiet, haunted.

The first I heard of it was on the six o'clock news, the day that Alison and I arrived in Beverley. We'd not been there long. Grandad had driven over to pick us up from Leeds and we'd both said rather teary-eyed, apprehensive farewells to our mothers, who would be heading off to catch a plane together that evening. On arriving back at my grandparents' house, Alison and I had gone upstairs to the bedroom in which I'd stayed so many times before, sometimes alone, sometimes with my brother. Unpacking took only about two minutes; then Alison went out into the garden, and soon afterwards I went downstairs to follow her but I must have looked into the living room first to ask Gran and Grandad something, and that was when I got waylaid by the news. They were both totally absorbed by the television, and normally when I saw grown-ups like that I would just have left them to it, but this time there was something about the news item they were watching that drew me in. I stepped further into the living room and sat down on the sofa next to Gran, who barely seemed to notice that I was there. On television the reporter was talking in a portentous voice over helicopter shots of a verdant and wooded patch of English countryside. On the screen and in the room, there was an atmosphere I had never encountered (or at least noticed) before: charged, expectant, filled with shock and apprehension. I sat in silence and watched, not really understanding any of it except for the fact that a man had died, a doctor who had lived in Oxfordshire and had something to do with Iraq and weapons and everyone was very upset and worried about it.

When the report was over, Grandad turned to Gran and said: "Well, that's that, then, isn't it? He's got blood on his hands now."

Gran didn't comment. She rose to her feet—quite a slow, effortful process—and shuffled into the kitchen. I got up and followed her.

"What does that mean?" I asked.

She was reaching up into the cupboard, looking for tins of something.

"What, lovey?" she said, turning.

"What Grandad said. Who was he talking about?"

She tutted and went back to her task. "Oh, you don't want to take any notice of him. He's always getting on his high horse."

This was not exactly a satisfactory answer, but before I could ask her to be a bit clearer Grandad came hurrying into the kitchen, muttering words of reproach: "Now why didn't you tell me you were getting tea ready? You know I'm supposed to be the one who does that. You're not to let these girls tire you out."

She rounded on him and said: "How many times do I have to tell you? I'm not feeling tired."

"I don't care," said Grandad. "You should be taking things easy. Let me do it."

I left them to their squabble and went to call Alison in from the garden, and then the four of us sat around the kitchen table eating sardines and tomatoes on toast. Grandad seemed moody and didn't talk much. I was still thinking about the story on the news, the dead doctor who had been found sitting up against a tree in Oxfordshire, wherever that was. And Grandad's remark about the other unknown man, the one who had got blood all over his hands. It was all very disturbing and mysterious. So that just left Gran and Alison talking together. Gran asked her what she wanted to do for the next week and Alison said she hadn't really thought about it and she didn't especially mind. "I hope you don't find it too quiet here, that's all," Gran said. "You're not in the big city now, you know." By "the big city" she meant Leeds, which she always seemed to imagine as a teeming metropolis, even though the part Alison and I lived in was not like that at all.

A few minutes later, when we were out in the garden together, Alison asked me, "So what *are* we going to do here for a week? No offence to your grandparents, but they seem a bit . . . old?"

"I don't know," I said, shrugging my shoulders. "We'll find stuff. There's a big moorland near here with woods and trees and stuff." Alison did not look impressed. "Ooh—and there's a library."

"A library? Great. A week reading books."

"I bet they have CDs and stuff as well."

Alison was making me cross. We were doing her a favour by inviting her here, after all. It wasn't even as if she was one of my best schoolfriends.

"What's in that shed?" she asked.

"Let's go and look."

We spent a few minutes rummaging through the contents of Grandad's little lean-to shed, but our pickings were slim. We found a cricket bat and a couple of very old tennis balls, and I was on the point of retrieving what we thought must be a skipping rope from one of the furthest corners when I saw something and gave a little scream and ran back out on to the lawn.

"What's the matter?" she asked, joining me.

"It's full of spiders back there. I can't stand them."

"Really? What's so scary about spiders?"

"Haven't you heard of arachnophobia?" I asked.

I don't think Alison had. She just said: "You're as bad as my mum. She goes bonkers if she sees a spider, especially a big one. Once she actually fainted. Really."

Clearly she regarded this as pathetic behaviour, although I was very much in sympathy with her mother, as it happened. Not caring to think about it anymore, I looked around and said: "Do you think we could climb that tree?"

We walked to the back of the garden to take a look at it. I realized, as we did so, that although my grandparents' house did not look very impressive from the front, the back garden was actually quite large. The lawn was in two tiers, each with a slight incline, so the patch of soil from which the tree grew was itself quite high up, almost on a level with the first floor of the house.

I don't know why I had suggested climbing it. At home, I liked to borrow quite old-fashioned children's books from the library, the sort of stories in which middle-class kids ran wild in the countryside, having picnics, building dens and apprehending local criminals while they were at it. Trees, in this universe, were there for climbing. So Alison and I might as well climb this one. It was a plum tree (Gran told me this later) and there were plenty of sturdy-looking branches close to the ground, but even so, for two townies like me and Alison, who both lived in places with no gardens to speak of, it was a daunting prospect.

Alison went first, and seemed to make pretty short work of shimmying up to a branch about three-quarters of the way to the top of the tree. After a few seconds' hesitation I clambered after her.

"This is cool," she said, as we sat on the branch together and surveyed our new domain.

From here we had a good view of the adjoining gardens and indeed the whole neighbourhood. Neatly kept gardens similar to my grandparents' were spread out on every side: trimmed lawns, lily ponds, patio furniture—all speaking of the same modest, comfortable, unadventurous life. Next door, a couple about the same age as Gran and Grandad were sitting at a white plastic garden table, drinking glasses of white wine and nibbling from a Tupperware bowl filled with Pringles. They looked up at us and Alison waved back cheerily, calling out, "Hi there!" The man just stared back but the woman raised her hand in cautious reciprocation.

I don't know how long we sat there. It was fun. It was a long, warm, mellow July evening and we could have stayed in the tree for the whole of it. After a while Alison looked at her watch.

"Our mums'll be taking off in a minute," she said.

"Do you two girls want some cake?"

It was Gran, calling from the back door of the house. I climbed down from the tree first, taking it fairly slowly and warily. Alison, though, attempted to jump from about five feet above the ground, and she landed heavily on her left leg.

"Ow! Fuck! God dammit!"

I stared at her in amazement, blushing. Never in a million years would I have dared to use the F-word, even with no grown-ups around. But it wasn't the time to dwell on niceties of speech. She seemed to be in real pain. She couldn't even get up at first.

"I'll get Gran."

I ran indoors and came back with both my grandparents. Between us we helped Alison to her feet, and then she limped down towards the house, resting on our shoulders.

"Off with those jeans," Gran said, as Alison sank down, wincing, into one of the kitchen chairs. "Let's have a look at you." Grandad was hovering in the background, but she glanced at him and made a "Get out!" gesture with her eyes. When he still didn't take the hint, she said: "Go on, Jim—make yourself scarce."

Seeing Alison peel off her jeans, Grandad finally understood. "I'll go and . . . take some air, I think," he muttered.

Gran took a good look at Alison's leg but couldn't see very much wrong with it. "Well, there's no bruise," she said. "And I can't see any scratches either. Bit of a swelling here, though." She laid a finger on Alison's leg just above the knee and applied some gentle pressure.

Alison winced again. "That's been there for a while," she said. "I don't think it's anything much."

Gran rubbed some cream on the swelling and after that Alison decided she'd had enough of the great outdoors and stayed inside to watch TV. I wandered out to the garden again and found Grandad talking over the fence to his next-door neighbour: the one whose wife had waved at us.

"Hello," said this red-faced, white-haired man, beaming down at me. "It's Rachel, isn't it?"

"Yes."

"I remember you from the last time you came. Goodness, but you've grown up a lot since then."

"Thank you," I said, since it seemed to be intended as a compliment.

"And this time," said the man, "you've brought a little black friend with you, I see."

Now this really flummoxed me. It would never have occurred to me to describe Alison in this way, and in fact I'd never heard anyone mention the colour of her skin before. All I could do, rather stupidly, was to say "Thank you" again, and wonder why this peculiar man was smiling at me so kindly.

4

Death is final. I know that's a banal observation but what I'm trying to say, I suppose, is that this week in Beverley was the first time I had really understood it. And yes, *that* must be the real reason I've never forgotten the death of David Kelly. It was the first time the reality of death had been brought home to me. It was, if you like, the first death in our family.

Up until that point I'd known almost nothing about the war with Iraq, but now I could tell that something had changed; a line had been crossed. A good man had died, and could not be brought back. And our Prime Minister (I realized now that this was who Grandad had been talking about) had blood on his hands.

"Whatever else you say about her," he told me, "Mrs. Thatcher would never have allowed anything like that to happen. She was a great lady."

"Has he been going on about that woman again?" Gran said, as we did the washing-up together. "I wish he'd change the record."

She was always criticizing Grandad for something or other, I noticed, and yet they seemed far more devoted to each other than my own mother and father had been. (Mum and Dad had split up by now. That holiday they'd taken without me—the time my brother and I had been sent to Beverley together—had been a last-ditch attempt to patch things up, I think. Needless to say, it hadn't worked, and they'd gone their separate ways soon afterwards.) It struck me that Grandad would rarely let Gran out of his sight and did not like her to carry out any tasks that were remotely strenuous.

"Has Gran been ill or something?" I asked him, one day near the beginning of our visit.

"What makes you ask that?" he asked, not looking up from his *Telegraph* crossword.

"I don't know. You never let her do anything. Mum was the same with me after I had chicken pox last year."

He glanced up at me now. "A few weeks ago, she had a bit of a . . . funny turn. So the doctor asked me to keep an eye on her, that's all."

I realize now that this way of speaking was completely typical of Grandad. What he referred to as a "funny turn" had in fact been an epileptic fit, following which Gran had been sent to hospital (after a wait of four weeks) for a brain scan. Now they were waiting for the results, but both were aware that the news could be bad. A brain tumour was the most likely explanation for the fit, and many patients die within a few months from cancerous gliomas.

Of course, I didn't understand any of this at the time. I did not know that the shadow of death, in all its terrible finality, had arrived so suddenly, without invitation, and was hanging over the two of them. But I noticed something, at least: I noticed that Gran and Grandad seemed closer to each other than any grown-ups I had ever seen before, and this closeness manifested itself, not only as a constant need to be in physical proximity, a refusal to let each other out of their sight, but also as a perpetual state of—for want of a better phrase—loving irritation. Almost every word that the one spoke to the other would touch some nerve, provoke some petulant spasm in response; but this was testament only to the state of near-unbearable anxiety in which they were both living, to the renewed awareness of love that had been kindled by the prospect of losing each other.

As I said, I didn't understand any of this; but I was aware of its outward manifestations. What really annoyed me about Alison, over the first few days of our visit, was how insensitive she seemed to be to what was happening around her. Seeing my grandparents sitting in the garden one afternoon, sipping from their mugs of tea and holding hands lightly across the space between their plastic chairs, she said, "Look at those two. Let's hope we never get to be like that, eh?" and she never missed an opportunity to remark on how old and decrepit they appeared to her.

We had little in common, I soon realized: the significant friendship was between our mothers, not between Alison and me. At school we were not together often enough to irritate each other; here, sharing a house and indeed a bedroom, our relationship was already under strain. Another thing that had started to annoy me was the way she picked up on everything I was feeling and tried to make it her own. The death of David Kelly was a typical example.

"What are you doing?" she'd asked me on Saturday morning, when she found me in the living room after breakfast trying to make head or tail of Grandad's *Daily Telegraph*.

It was pretty obvious what I was doing. "I'm reading the paper."

"Since when have you cared about the news?"

"Did you even know there's been a war in the last few months?"

" 'Course I did," said Alison. "But there are always wars. My mum says war is stupid and people are stupid."

"Well, we had no choice this time. We had to go to war, because Iraq had nuclear weapons aimed at us and they could have nuked us in forty-five minutes."

"Come off it. Who says?"

"Tony Blair."

For the first time, Alison seemed to be showing a flicker of interest. She pointed at the front page of the newspaper. "So who's this guy, then?"

I explained who David Kelly was—to the best of my knowledge and ability—and something of the circumstances in which he'd died. Halfway through my somewhat garbled explanation I could tell that Alison was losing interest again; but she could sense that I was troubled by this story, and she wanted to share in this disquiet, either as a way of getting close to me or in order to appropriate it for herself, to claim it as hers. So she seized upon one detail: the discovery of Dr. Kelly's body, propped up against a tree in that lonely patch of hilltop woodland.

"Wow, that's scary," she said—missing the whole point, as far as I was concerned. "Imagine that. You're out for a stroll one morning, walking your dog or something, and suddenly . . . you find that, smack in the middle of your path."

"Nobody really knows *why* he did it, though," I said. "Grandad says it's Tony Blair's fault, but he hates Tony Blair anyway . . ."

Alison didn't care. All she wanted to talk about was this single image, which seemed to play in her mind like some scene out of a horror movie.

"Fuck," she said. "That would so freak me out. Finding a dead body like that. Right in the middle of nowhere."

I stared at her, feeling a sudden wave of hatred. She was using that word again—*inside* my grandparents' house. I wanted to say something and was furious with myself that the words wouldn't come. I was a coward. A scaredy-cat.

5

Alison owned a device which seemed to me, at the time, to be literally magical. It was called an iPod and even though it was not much bigger than a matchbox it was apparently capable of storing thousands and thousands of songs so that you could take them anywhere with you and listen to them any time that you wanted. It was a beautiful clean white colour and had a little wheel in the middle which clicked when you turned it with your finger.

Nevertheless I thought it rather sad that, with all this storage capacity, Alison only ever seemed to listen to one album. She listened to it over and over and when she wasn't listening to it she made me listen to it instead.

"Your mum's got a nice voice," I assured her, easing the slightly waxy earphones out of my ears and handing the machine back. In truth I hadn't cared much for the song she'd played me for the umpteenth time. Precociously, I was more interested in classical music in those days, and my favourite CD at home was a recording of Fauré's *Requiem*.

"She sang that song on *Top of the Pops*, you know," said Alison.

"Yes, you told me."

"She's pretty famous."

"I know. You said. Only . . ." (I had been meaning to say this for some time, but hadn't been able to think of a way of putting it tactfully) ". . . only, this was a few years ago, wasn't it?"

"So?" Alison pouted, and put the iPod away in the little satchel she was carrying with her. "She still sings, you know. Makes demos and stuff. You can always get back in the game."

It was quite late in the evening, and we were sitting at the foot of the Black Tower, our backs against its glistening brickwork. We had become quite fearless, over the last few days, about exploring by ourselves and staying out until it was almost dark. Most times we would head for Westwood, which we knew well by now, although as children of the city we could still not quite get used to the idea that this sprawling tract of moor and woodland was ours to roam, freely and at will. We liked to come here because we were hoping to get another glimpse of the Mad Bird Woman, whom I had described to Alison in some detail, her image having been stamped indelibly on my memory ever since that one transient encounter four years ago. According to Gran and Grandad she still lived in Beverley, in a big house which had been left to her by the wheelchair-bound old lady when she died. Her real name, it seemed, was Miss Barton.

"It sounds as if people don't like her very much," I told Alison. "They say she shouldn't have been given the house. Gran said there was something fishy about it."

"Fishy? What does that mean?"

"Don't know."

"Maybe . . . Maybe she murdered the old woman. To get her hands on the house."

Typical Alison, I thought. Silly and over the top. "Don't be daft," I said, at which Alison fell silent. Worrying that I might have offended her, and wanting to keep the conversation going, I added: "She doesn't have the bird anymore either."

"Probably doesn't come up here much, then," said Alison, getting to her feet. "Come on. Let's go."

"All right." There was a television show I wanted to get home to see, one of my favourite comedy programmes. "It's nearly nine o'clock anyway."

"Eleven o'clock in Corfu," Alison said, failing to quicken her pace so that I had to slow down in order to fall back into step beside her. "Almost bedtime. I wonder if either of our mums has got lucky yet."

"Lucky?" I didn't understand. "I don't think they've gone on holiday to gamble, or anything like that."

Alison laughed a nasty, superior sort of laugh. "Come on, Rache. Even *you* can't be that innocent." And, when I still looked bewildered: "Why d'you think they've gone away together, then?"

"I don't know . . . Everybody needs a holiday now and again."

"They're both single. They've both been single for years. Don't you get it? They've gone looking for men."

This idea horrified and enraged me. "Don't be disgusting," I said.

"What's disgusting about it?"

"Shut up, Alison. I've just about had enough of you."

"You need to get real."

"You don't even know what you're talking about." I was fighting back tears now.

" 'Course I do. And I don't see anything wrong with it either. If your mum wants to go abroad for a week and spend her time shagging the arse off a Greek waiter, why shouldn't she?"

For a few seconds there was nothing but appalled silence between us. Then I slapped her, hard, across the cheek. She shouted out in pain and put her hands to her face and while she was like that I pushed her to the ground. Then I burst into tears and stormed off in the direction of the house. I looked back once and she was still sitting there, on the yellow sun-baked grass, nursing her cheek and staring after me.

I never did get to watch my TV comedy show, because when I got home Grandad was watching a political programme on another channel. It seemed to be making him very angry, but the angrier he got, the more he seemed to want to carry on watching it. It was a report about people-trafficking and forced labour in modern Britain. Of course, I'd never heard either of these expressions before, and when the narrator started talking about migrant workers enduring conditions of "slavery" I was very puzzled, because to me the word "slavery" conjured up images of Roman galley slaves being held in chains or whipped by muscular guards with their shirts off. But the subject of this programme, in a way, seemed just as horrifying: I was soon distressed by the litany of tales of builders and agricultural workers being made to work long hours and live twenty to a room in horrible bedsits.

"Disgraceful!" Grandad kept saying, but before I could agree with him he made it clear that he was talking about something else entirely. "Week in, week out, the BBC gives us this left-wing propaganda. If these Latvians and Lithuanians don't like doing British jobs, they should go home and get better ones. Did you know there's a shop in Selby that only sells Polish food now?"

I think this question was directed at Gran, but she had left the room some time ago. As Grandad didn't seem to need an audience I quietly slipped away, too, and went upstairs to bed. Alison was not back yet, and normally this would have worried me, but I was still too angry with her to care.

I must have fallen asleep straight away. The sky around the edges of the curtains was still only dark blue when I felt myself being shaken awake by a hand on my shoulder. I opened my eyes drowsily. It was Alison, of course.

"What? What are you doing? I was asleep."

"I know, but this is important."

With some reluctance I raised myself into a sitting position. My eyes opened further and the first thing I noticed about Alison was that she was shaking.

"What's happened?"

"I saw one, Rache," she said, her voice quivering. "I saw one just now, in the woods."

"Saw what?"

"I saw a body. A dead body."

Our eyes met. I said nothing.

"Just now," she added, as if that somehow made it any more believable.

I lay down again and turned away from her, facing the wall.

"Alison, you're pathetic."

"I *did*, Rachel—really."

I turned back over and glared at her.

"A dead body, yeah? In the woods. Just like that man in the paper. Was he sitting up against a tree?"

"*Yes*," said Alison, and now there was such a note of distress and insistence in her voice that for the first time it crossed my mind she might be telling the truth.

"I don't believe you," I said, all the same. "No way."

"It was bloody terrifying. His head sort of . . . flopped over when I came up to him, so it was like he was looking at me. His eyes were open. He had all this grey hair, long and tangled. His skin was yellow—and all stretched and wrinkled. He was so *thin* . . ."

I sat up again, and looked at her carefully. I had an unfortunate history of being gullible when people played practical jokes like this on me.

"What's that in your hand?" I asked, glancing down.

Alison was clutching a single playing card.

"I picked this up in the wood," she said. "There were loads of them, scattered all around him."

I took the card from her hand. On the back was a pattern of yellow and black diamonds. Turning the card over, I found a drawing of a spider. It was a grotesque and horrific thing, standing upright on two of its legs, and raising the others fiercely in the air as if challenging someone to a fight. Against the glossy black background of the card, the pale green of its underbelly shone out with queasy clarity. The artist had dotted dozens of coarse hairs all over its distended belly, at the bottom of which, in a detail which made me feel particularly sick, there hung some sort of fleshy sac filled with God knows what. Although the drawing was crude and cartoonish, it somehow managed, at the same time, to be far too realistic.

As I handed the card back to Alison with a shudder, she threw her arms around me, buried her head against my neck and held me tight. She was still trembling all over and I had no choice, from that moment on, but to believe everything she had told me.

6

"This is the tree," she said. "Just here."

"You're sure?"

It was the next morning, a gloriously warm and sunny one. As we explored the little patch of sunken woodland at the eastern end of the Westwood, sunlight streamed through the leafy canopy above us, and by the time it reached us the light was a delicious, cool lime-green. The air was fresh and the only sounds were the occasional chirrup of birdsong and the distant hum of traffic. It was the kind of spot you would come to for a picnic, or to lie beneath a tree reading a book. Instead, we were looking for a corpse.

"There's nothing here," I pointed out, after we had stood for a few seconds looking at the bare patch of grass. It does no harm to state the obvious every now and again.

"It's gone," Alison agreed.

What were we supposed to do now? I had read enough kids' adventure stories and Sherlock Holmes mysteries to know that there was a procedure to be followed in these circumstances. I knelt down and began to stare intently at the ground.

"What are you doing?" Alison asked.

"Looking for clues."

Alison crouched down beside me. "What sort of clues?"

"I don't know." I thought about mentioning footprints or finger-prints but that seemed rather old-fashioned. Then I remembered something I'd seen on a TV show recently. "DNA," I said, with an air of confidence. "You always find DNA at a crime scene."

"OK."

We both started to examine the area minutely, parting the very blades of grass with our fingertips.

"What does DNA look like?" Alison asked.

"Kind of . . . slimy, I think." I didn't have the faintest idea what I was talking about. "Slimy and see-through."

"Well, I can't see anything like that."

Alison was not as patient as me. Before long she was standing up again, looking around vaguely, without any clear intention. I tutted and continued with my search. Perhaps I would find something else significant—a lost button, or a fragment of torn clothing. Or perhaps this was, after all, a complete waste of time: just part of some malicious joke on Alison's part, her revenge for the slap I'd given her last night, which she hadn't mentioned since and for which I was yet to apologize.

Soon she had wandered off altogether. I didn't know where she'd gone; I only knew that the wood had started to feel quieter than ever. Even the birds seemed to have stopped singing, and I couldn't hear a single car even though the road was only a couple of hundred yards away. So when I heard the sound of a branch or twig snapping nearby, it was almost as if a gunshot had rung out. I jerked upright and looked around sharply in every direction. But there was no one there.

"Alison?" I said.

No answer.

I stayed like that for another minute or two, still kneeling. The silence was absolute once again. Of course it had only been some bird hopping from one spot to another; or perhaps a rabbit (we had seen one or two of those over the last few days); or Alison playing some tiresome game of hide and seek. There was no need to be jumpy about it. I would continue looking for clues.

The second noise was louder than the first, and seemed to come from a point about ten yards away, to my left. Louder than just the snapping of a twig this time, it sounded unmistakably like a footstep in the undergrowth. At the same time I saw—or thought I saw—the shadowy movement of some object or figure in the bushes. A whisper of motion, nothing more. Then everything was silent and still once again.

Alison. It had to be. What was she playing at?

"Alison?" I called. "Alison, where are you?"

This was getting really annoying now. Or rather, I was doing my best simply to find it annoying, while trying to ignore the way my heart had started to thump and a sheen of sweat was breaking out on my brow. I rose to my feet, slowly and cautiously, feeling it important to make as little sound of my own as possible. I looked again towards the bushes where I thought I had heard a sound, and seen a fleeting movement. The temptation just to bolt, to make a run for it, was getting very powerful. But I decided not to do anything sudden. In a careful and studied movement I turned through 180 degrees, heading directly away from the bush and whatever danger my fevered mind had decided lurked inside it. Another dozen of these steps would take me away from this dense cluster of trees and bushes and out into more open woodland. Then, and only then, I would start running.

But after only a few more steps, something caught my attention and stopped me in my tracks. Caught between the branches of a bush, above my eye level, was another playing card: just like the one Alison had found, only this time the illustration showed a fish, not a spider. A blue-and-yellow-striped fish against a shiny black background. As with the spider, there was something disturbing, even repulsive, in the cartoonish simplicity of the drawing: the way the fish's eyes bulged and its mouth drooped open stupidly. Was this the clue that I had been, subconsciously, looking for? I had no idea what these playing cards might have to do with Alison's macabre encounter in the woods last night, but it seemed of overwhelming importance, now, that I should retrieve this piece of possible evidence. I stretched out my hand but the card, maddeningly, was just out of reach. I stepped forward and stood on tiptoe. If I stretched any further I would surely fall over. But now I could almost touch it. Another half an inch and I would just about be able to hold it between two fingers.

And then, another hand—a grown-up hand—appeared out of nowhere, was thrust towards the card and snatched it.

I gasped and wheeled around: and there she was, right behind me. Her face was red with anger. Her cropped hair, piercings and tattooed neck and throat were just as before. Her grey eyes bored into me.

The Mad Bird Woman.

"This is mine, thank you very much," she said.

I don't know where she came from, but now—somehow or other—Alison was standing beside me. Terrified, we faced the apparition together. We stared at her, and she stared back, none of us uttering a word. It was like a staring competition. The silence of the wood pressed down upon us.

"Are there any more of these around here?" she said at last.

"I . . . don't think so, miss," Alison faltered.

"They must be returned to me. *All* of them. And you're not to tell *anyone* about this."

"Yes, miss," we said in rough unison.

"Good. Now clear off."

We didn't move. We were too stunned.

"*NOW!*" she shouted.

And then we were gone, out of the woods as fast as we could run, back across Westwood in pursuit of safety, our tiny bodies a whirl of spinning legs and pumping arms, our fugitive figures shrunk to nothing by the ageless, impervious bulk of the Black Tower behind us.

7

My grandparents' house did not provide quite the sanctuary we were expecting. We returned to find that the living room was full of people. Full of old people, to be precise: nothing but silver hair and cups of tea wherever you looked. After one glance at this lot (Grandad and his next-door neighbour being the only ones I recognized) we beat a rapid retreat to the kitchen, where Gran was standing at the table laying chocolate biscuits and custard creams out on serving plates.

"What's going on in there?" I asked.

"The local Conservative Club," she said. "It's our turn to be the hosts."

"They look like a right bunch of old relics," said Alison.

"Never mind that," said Gran. "Take these in, will you? I'm going to have a bit of a sit down."

She gave us a plate of biscuits each, and we set off nervously to make a tour of the room. When we made our entrance, Grandad's neighbour (whose name, I discovered later, was Mr. Sparks) was holding forth on the subject of vagrancy, another word I'd never heard before.

"Vagrancy," he declaimed, "is becoming a serious problem in Beverley and its *environs*. The council should be dealing with it but frankly they seem to lack both the will and the means." He noticed, at this point, that I was holding a plate of custard creams under his nose. "Ah! Is one of these for me? How very kind."

"As usual," said a lady with alarmingly pointy horn-rimmed glasses, who was sitting in Gran's armchair, "Norman has hit the nail on the head. My evidence is only anecdotal, but at Saturday market

I have personally noticed a marked increase in the presence of . . . *undesirables.*" She practically sang the word out, in a deep, throbbing alto, stretching the third syllable to a semibreve at least. "Many of them, needless to say, belong to the *ethnic minorities.*" Precisely as she whispered these last two words she became aware of Alison, standing right in front of her and offering her a chocolate biscuit with the sweetest of smiles. "Why, thank you, dear," she said, thoroughly flustered. "Of course, I didn't mean . . . I wasn't trying to say that *all . . .*"

We returned to the kitchen with the plates still half full of biscuits and set about working our way through them.

"What are they blathering on about in there now?" Gran asked. She didn't seem to think much of Grandad's friends.

"I wasn't really listening," I admitted. "Something about vacancies at the Saturday market."

"They called me an ethnic minority," said Alison, in a tone of bemusement but also pride.

"How rude."

"I don't think she was being nasty," I said. "She just noticed that you were from a different . . . culture, I suppose."

"What nonsense. Alison's from just the same culture as all of us. Aren't you, lovey?"

"Well, not really," said Alison. "I'm from Leeds." She took the last custard cream and popped it in her mouth in one go. "Anyway, it's my dad who's black and I hardly ever see him. My mum's as white as they are, so I don't really see what they're on about."

"Quite," said Gran, and we all fell silent.

"What is a Conservative, anyway?" it now occurred to me to ask.

"Well, I suppose a Conservative," said Gran, "is someone who likes things the way they already are. They think that the world is essentially how it should be and we shouldn't mess about with it too much."

After reflecting on this I said: "That sounds OK. I like things the way they are, too. Doesn't Tony Blair?"

"Mr. Blair is the leader of the Labour Party," said Gran, "which in days gone by used to believe in a thing called socialism. Socialists think that the world could be made much more fair for everybody, but in order to do that, you have to change things and sometimes scrap things which are traditional and perhaps a bit out of date."

"But he doesn't believe that anymore?"

"Well . . . nobody is quite sure what he believes."

"And what about you, Gran? Which one are you?"

She let out a heavy sigh. "Frankly, Rachel, right now I think I'm one of those people who's starting to believe that none of it matters in the slightest."

She turned away from us, perhaps, even, because she was trying not to cry, although neither Alison nor I was likely to notice. From our point of view, this conversation was getting a bit boring, and we had far more exciting news to tell her.

"Ooh, Gran, guess who we saw up in the wood?" I said. "The Mad Bird Woman. She gave us a terrible fright."

Alison glanced at me, a silent reminder that we were not supposed to have told anyone about this. But since the secret was out now, she added:

"We were just walking around, minding our own business, when she sort of popped out from behind a tree. It was almost like she wanted to scare us. Nearly gave us both a heart attack."

"Oh dear," said Gran. "How horrible for you both. She really is the nastiest, most difficult person . . ." She pursed her lips. "If she deliberately scared you then I suppose I should really—one of us should really go and speak to her about it . . ." She tailed off, clearly not relishing the prospect of such a confrontation. I felt sorry for her, and said:

"Don't worry, Gran. There's no need to do that. Is there, Ali?"

I looked to my friend for confirmation but all she said was: "Where does she live?"

"There's a tiny little road," said Gran, starting to rinse the biscuit plates under the hot tap, "which runs off Newbegin. It's called Needless Alley, because it doesn't go anywhere. That's where Mrs. Bates used to live. And when she died, she left the house to Miss Barton."

"Why did she do that, I wonder?"

"Yes, a lot of people wondered that," said Gran. "In fact, they did more than wonder about it. They got very angry about it, which was a bit stupid of them."

"Yes," I agreed. "Because it was none of their business really, was it?"

"Exactly. But people can be very . . . judgemental."

"What's the number of the house?" Alison asked. She was try-ing to sound casual but I could tell there was some secret purpose behind these questions.

"I can't remember, offhand," said Gran. "But you can't miss it. It's the one that's covered in ivy and laurel bushes and goodness knows what, and the whole thing is covered in netting and behind that she keeps birds."

"Birds?"

"Oh yes. A regular aviary, it is. Budgerigars and canaries and all sorts."

"No kestrels?" I asked hopefully.

"No, she doesn't have a kestrel anymore. I don't know what became of it."

It seemed that we had exhausted Gran's knowledge of this topic now, but in the process she had stretched our curiosity to breaking point. When we went upstairs to discuss our plans for the rest of the day, I knew exactly what Alison was going to suggest.

"We don't have to go inside," she insisted. "I just want to see what it looks like. Don't you want to see all these birds and everything?"

It was true, I was desperate to see where the Mad Bird Woman lived, even though she scared me almost to death. And so later that afternoon Alison and I set out to find Needless Alley.

It didn't take long to get there. Newbegin was a long one-way street leading from Westwood down towards the town centre. The Alley peeled off from it towards the left, running at first between the walls of two very tall houses: this part of it was so narrow that there was barely room for the two of us to walk abreast. Soon, how-ever, it widened into a short cobbled street with large, venerable, eighteenth-century houses on both sides. The one we were looking for could not have been easier to spot. It was set quite apart from the other dwellings, being separated from its nearest neighbour by a long, low wall running around an expanse of unkempt, not to say chaotic, front garden. On the front door was the house number in rusty silver numerals. It was Number 11.

Presumably the house was built of brick, but you would never know it, looking from the front. The entire façade was covered in foliage of one sort or another—mainly ivy, although there were also many other climbing plants which I couldn't identify, all mingling and interlocking and twining themselves around one another in a thick jungle of greenery. In the midst of all this, dozens of little birds were hopping, fluttering or resting: a few of them were exotic and brightly coloured but mostly they were your regular songbirds—sparrows, thrushes, that sort of thing. Dark-green netting was stretched over the whole front of the house, preventing them from flying away to freedom. They were basically trapped in a huge verdant open-air cage, but they seemed perfectly happy about it, and kept up a pleasant chorus of chirruping which contrasted with the otherwise sinister ambience of the Bird Woman's house. I couldn't help noticing how thickly the ivy creeped over the walls, trespassing on the windows as well, obscuring half of them almost entirely so that it must, I imagined, be quite dark all day inside most of those rooms. I was glad that we'd found it and seen the birds, but still, it was the kind of house you immediately want to run a mile from, the sort that gives you bad dreams. Only a crazy person, I thought, would want to live in it; or even go inside; or stand any closer, for that matter, than the two of us were standing now.

At this point Alison cheerfully pushed open the gate and walked into the garden.

"What are you *doing?*" I hissed. "I thought we were just going to look at it."

She turned and gave me a challenging smile. "Are you coming?"

"Coming where?"

"Go on, let's have a look through the downstairs windows at least."

"Why? What would be the point? What are you looking for?"

Without realizing it, I had taken a few steps forward myself, and was now standing beside her in the front garden, my heart thudding inside my rib cage with a violence that was actually painful.

"Have you forgotten what I saw in the woods last night?"

"*Thought* you saw," I muttered, under my breath. I was still suspicious of the connection between David Kelly's death and this convenient sighting of Alison's.

"The point is," said Alison, picking her way through a pile of fallen rockery that lay strewn in the garden path, "this woman probably has something to do with it."

"How do you work that out?" I asked. It seemed like quite a leap of the imagination to me.

"Why else would she want to scare us off from the woods like that?"

Just now, as we were getting close to the front door of the house, Alison stumbled on an especially large stone in the pathway and almost fell.

"Fuck," she said. It looked like rather a minor stumble but she still had to sit down and start rubbing her leg.

"Are you OK?"

"My leg still hurts from where I fell out of that tree, you know."

"In the same place?"

"Yeah."

I looked around anxiously, prey to a growing, irrational sense that we were being watched. Then I noticed something.

"What are you sitting on?"

"Eh?"

Alison realized, for the first time, that she had sat down on some kind of metal armchair, surrounded by overgrown bushes, some of which had tangled themselves around it, tethering it to the ground. It was, in fact, a wheelchair. She rose to her feet quickly, as if she had come into contact with something contaminated.

"Woah! What's *that* doing here?"

"It must have been Mrs. Bates's," I said, trying and failing to pull a rope of ivy out from between the spokes of one wheel. "It must have been here since she died."

"God, that's freaky. Come on, let's take a look through the windows and then get out of here."

We crept nearer to the front of the house. We now had our noses up against the netting, and one or two of the bolder, more inquisitive birds hopped from their leafy perches to take a look at us. They might have been hoping for crumbs of bread but we had nothing to give them. Peering through the thick tendrils of ivy, we could just about see into one of the downstairs windows, but the room beyond seemed to be empty and was in any case so dark that we could make nothing out, except that there appeared to be a large, gloomy picture hanging on one of the walls. The second downstairs window looked into the same room. Once we had done this I felt that honour had been served and we could beat a dignified retreat.

Alison, however, had other plans.

"*Now* where are you going?" My voice was tight with panic.

"Oh, come on, there's no one around."

"How do you *know* that?"

I hurried to catch up with her as she made her way down the little alleyway at the side of the house.

"What are we looking for anyway?"

"I don't know," said Alison, in a preoccupied way, glancing from side to side. The alleyway was strewn with rubbish, besides containing three green wheelie bins which were also full to overflowing. I noticed a lot of old brushes and paint pots. "I just wanted to get an idea . . . a feel for what this—"

She stopped in mid-sentence. Froze, would be a more accurate way of putting it. Her gaze was fixed on a long, thin window at the back of the house, just above ground level, beneath the level of the room we had just been looking into. A basement window, in other words. Behind the dust- and dirt-streaked glass was the bright yellow glow of a powerful lightbulb. It was the glow that enabled us to see, quite clearly, the shadow of a human figure in sharp outline.

The figure was in profile. He (or she) was standing (or more likely sitting) perfectly still. We could see the suggestion of a face in silhouette: a short, flat nose, a pointed chin with skin hanging loosely beneath it, straggles of thin, uncombed hair reaching almost down to the shoulders. That was about all we could make out, but it was enough for Alison to exclaim, in an awestruck whisper:

"That's him! I mean—that's her—it—whatever it was . . ." And finally, just to spell it out for me: "*That's who I saw yesterday in the woods.*"

Our eyes met as the reality of the situation began to sink in. Neither of us could explain things, neither of us knew what was going on, by any means, but we were both convinced, now, that we had stumbled upon something huge: something sinister and secret and potentially explosive. This was the biggest, most shocking thing that had ever happened to either of us.

Suddenly, high up in the house, a sash window was yanked open and a woman's voice shouted:

"OY! YOU TWO!"

We did not even look up to see her face glowering down at us. We turned and ran: out through the front garden, back down Needless Alley, faster than we could have believed possible.

8

It was late that night, when the lights were out and I was almost asleep, that Alison had her brainwave.

"Oh. My. God," she said, sitting up in bed slowly. "I think I've got it. I know what's going on in that house."

I sat up, too, and waited for the explanation. "Well?"

"Have you seen *Psycho*?" Alison asked.

"*Psycho*? The film? Are you serious? Of course I haven't seen *Psycho*."

"You've heard about it, though, right?"

"I've heard that it's the scariest, most horrible film ever made. Why?" I couldn't stop myself asking the question, even though the answer was pretty predictable. "Don't tell me that *you've* seen it?"

"'Course I have. My babysitter brought it round and I watched it with her, about three years ago."

"Your *babysitter*?" Every time I got these little insights into Alison's life I was torn between horror and envy.

"Sure. She was cool. Anyway, you do know what the story's about?"

"Can you remind me?" I said, not having a clue.

"There's this mad guy—he's the psycho—who lives in this big old house by the side of the road. Next to the house is this motel that he runs, and when this woman comes to stay there for the night he kills her while she's having a shower. So then her sister comes looking for her and meets this man and straight away she can tell he's some kind of psycho, so she goes into the big old house to look for his mother, 'cause she thinks he might be keeping his mother captured there or something. So she goes down to the cellar and finds his mother sitting there in a chair. Only she's dead."

"Dead?"

"Yeah. Turns out she's been dead for years and he's been keeping her body in the house with him all that time. Sometimes he keeps it in the cellar and sometimes he takes it upstairs and lies it down on the bed."

I thought about this, and a practical difficulty occurred to me. "Don't people start to . . . smell a bit, after they've been dead for a few days?"

"He's been pickling her," said Alison, matter-of-factly.

I pictured an old lady's body being squeezed into an enormous jar, filled with the same horrible-tasting liquid I'd seen in Mum's jars of pickled onions. How on earth this would be feasible was quite beyond my imagination; but right now that seemed the least of my problems.

"You don't mean . . ."

"Why not? Didn't your gran say there was something fishy about the old lady dying and leaving her the house?"

"Yes, but . . . If you killed someone to get their house, why would you keep their body? You'd want to get rid of it, wouldn't you?"

"A normal person would, yes. But this is the *Mad* Bird Woman, remember?"

The objections to this theory were numerous, I thought.

"But you saw the dead body in the *woods,* not the house."

"Yes. She'd taken it there."

"Why?"

"I don't know. To give it some exercise and fresh air. Rachel, she's *mad.* Totally crazy. Who else would live in a house covered with birds?"

"How would she carry the body into the woods? It'd be too heavy."

Alison was silent, and for a moment I thought that I'd actually scored a point. But the victory was short-lived.

"Of course—the wheelchair! That's why she's still got the wheel-chair in her garden."

I wasn't convinced by this for long, either. "But it was covered in ivy and stuff. It looked like it hadn't been used for months."

Alison ignored this objection, and played her trump card. "Never mind that. In the film, do you know what the psycho's name is? Norman Bates. His mother's name is Mrs. Bates. *Mrs. Bates.*"

I couldn't tell you, now, why it was this argument—the silliest and most irrational argument of all—that finally clinched it for me. Perhaps Alison had just worn me down. But from now on, without agreeing that every feature of the situation corresponded with every detail in the film (besides which I was, in any case, still very hazy on most of those details), I was more persuaded than ever that we had stumbled into the very epicentre of a mystery; that the Mad Bird Woman was the key to it; and that if we wanted to solve it, we were going to have to find out more, somehow, about the person—or the thing—whose silhouette we had glimpsed that afternoon through the window of Number 11, Needless Alley.

In other words, we would have to go into that cellar.

9

Alison's second brainwave broke upon her late the following morning.

When she came to tell me, I was sitting by myself up near the top of the plum tree, trying to get some peace and quiet.

It had been a stressful morning. At breakfast, Gran and Grandad had seemed unusually tense. Gran was fussing around making toast and tea in a very absentminded sort of way, and Grandad was hiding behind his newspaper. The front-page headline, as usual, was about the war in Iraq. "Saddam Hussein's Sons Captured and Killed," it said. (Or something like that.)

Buttering my toast and sugaring my tea, I was unnerved by the silence between them. It was most uncharacteristic.

"Grandad," I said, timidly. "Can I ask you something?"

"What?" he said, in a tone that was far from encouraging. But I pressed on.

"Are we still at war with Iraq?"

"It's complicated," he said, without putting the paper down.

"Oh."

Gran noticed my tone of disappointment, even if he didn't.

"Nobody really understands what's going on," she said. "The good thing is it's all happening a long way from here."

"Saddam Hussein's going to be pretty angry, isn't he, now that his sons have been killed?"

"I think he was quite angry already, what with one thing and another."

"But does this mean he might start attacking us now? Because I know that before he died, David Kelly said—"

Before I had a chance to proceed any further, Grandad slammed down his paper with an angry snort.

"Your gran's got more important things to do than answer your stupid questions," he said. He stood up, and fished his car keys out of his pocket. "I'll go and get the car out of the garage," he said to Gran. "She" (meaning me) "can do the washing-up when we're gone. And the other one, if she ever gets up."

He left the kitchen and in the cold silence that followed Gran laid her hand on my shoulder and gave it a squeeze.

"Take no notice," she said. "He's all worked up this morning."

I was glad of the gesture: Grandad's behaviour had startled and upset me. "Are you going out somewhere?" I asked.

"Just to the doctor's. We'll have to leave you two girls alone for a couple of hours." She pursed her lips doubtfully. "Perhaps I should ask Mrs. Sparks to come round and keep an eye on you."

"There's no need," I said, wanting to quash this idea at once. "We'll be good. We won't even leave the house."

"Well, if you're sure . . ." said Gran. "I suppose it's all right. If you need anything, just go next door."

About half an hour later Gran and Grandad drove off, both looking as pale as ghosts. I realize now, of course, that they had been waiting for this morning for many weeks; that this was the meeting where they would be told once and for all what had caused Gran's "bit of a funny turn"; would be told, basically, whether she was going to live or die. But I guessed nothing of this at the time, and had little more serious on my mind, as I wandered through the garden, than my shock at the way Grandad had spoken to me, and a more pressing—though shapeless—anxiety about how Alison would propose to continue with our investigation into Number 11, Needless Alley: something which I was beginning to think had already gone quite far enough.

At the top of the garden, once again, I climbed up the plum tree and found my favourite spot among its branches. I had already come to love this tree. There was nothing nicer than sitting here by myself, amidst the soft rustle of its leaves, looking down on the surrounding gardens, watching the little fragments of suburban life being played out there, or tilting my face towards the sun, feeling its gentle heat on my closed eyelids. I could have sat there forever. This is what my week with Gran and Grandad should have been like, all the time. Instead, Alison was ruining it with her silly, selfish fixation on this weird narrative she had constructed around the Mad Bird Woman, the body in the woods, the mystery of Number 11 which might not even be a mystery at all. And here she was now, trotting up the garden path towards me, that familiar mischievous glint in her eye, doubtless bursting with some unwelcome new suggestion or foolish piece of information to torment me with. The shocking truth revealed itself to me suddenly: I was beginning to hate her.

"OK," she said, clambering onto the branch beside me, causing it to sway and judder, clumsily breaking off a blameless twig as she settled herself. "I've got it all worked out."

"Oh yes?" I said, keeping my voice flat, trying to convey as little interest as possible.

"The thing is—what's stopping us from going round there, knocking on the door, and walking into the house?"

I sighed. "Well, that's obvious. She'd never let us in."

"True," said Alison. "Not unless we had some excuse. Like, for instance, if we had something that she wanted."

"But we don't," I pointed out.

"Ah," said Alison, proudly, "but we do." She held up the playing card, the one with the really revolting, brightly coloured picture of a spider. "Remember what she said to us in the woods? 'They must be returned to me—all of them.' But we haven't given her this one."

My heart sank. Alison was outwitting me again. It was true: the Bird Woman had insisted that every one of those cards be returned to her, so we would only be doing what she had asked.

"So you think we should take it round?"

"Yep."

"When?" I had been so happy sitting here. And now I was less inclined to move than ever.

"No time like the present," said Alison, brightly. "Come on, let's get it over with."

We locked up my grandparents' house with the spare set of keys and set off into town. We were breaking my promise to Gran that we would stay at home, of course, but Alison was no longer to be swayed by thoughts like that. She strode on ahead of me so quickly that we reached Needless Alley in little more than ten minutes. When we arrived, it was getting on for noon and the fierce July sun was high in the sky. Beverley appeared placid and friendly that morning, but as soon as we turned into the narrow opening between those two tall houses, shadows started to encroach, the temperature seemed to drop, and Number 11, as we approached it with increasingly reluctant footsteps (on my part, anyway), looked more threatening than ever. A thick, blanketing silence covered the street, as it had yesterday, and it wasn't until we had penetrated the front garden and almost reached the front door that it was broken: first of all by the sound of our footsteps scuffling against the stony obstructions in our path, and then by the melancholy chirping of the birds trapped in the leafy aviary that made up the house's bizarre façade.

At the foot of the four steep steps that climbed up to the front door, we paused. This was it. Our last chance to think better of the adventure, and turn back.

Alison's eyes met mine. I saw at that moment something I had not suspected before: she was as apprehensive as I was. But she was also, at heart, much braver: and without any more dithering she now marched boldly up the steps, grasped the heavy iron knocker (in the shape of some contorted gargoyle) and let it fall three times against the door's thick oak panelling.

There was a long pause: long enough to allow me the luxury of some sweet relief, a few moments' precious hope that the knock would not be answered at all. But finally we heard shuffling footsteps behind the door; and then it was pulled open.

Already dark with suspicion, the Mad Bird Woman's face hardened still further when she saw us.

"You! What do *you* want?"

"Please, miss," said Alison, "we've got something that belongs to you, and we've come to give it back."

I looked at her full of new admiration: her tone struck just the right balance between insolence and wheedling politeness. She held up the spider card, and as soon as she saw it, the Mad Bird Woman reached out a demanding hand.

"Ah, yes. We were wondering where that one had got to. Come on, pass it over."

But Alison kept the card back. "Please, miss, we've walked all the way across from the other side of town to bring you this, and now we're thirsty. Can we have something to drink, please?"

The Woman's eyes narrowed at the audacity of the question. She licked the studs on her lower lip, thought for a few seconds, and said: "All right. Come in."

We squeezed past her into a hallway which was gloomy enough already, but was plunged into even greater blackness when she promptly slammed the door behind us. Now she was just a shadow, a mannish bulk looming indistinct against the dun-brown background of the wall. We had all become shadows.

"I'll get you some water," she said.

"I'd rather have a cup of tea, please," said Alison. "With milk and two sugars."

The Woman gave an incredulous grunt, and said, "Would you now?" But she threw open a door, all the same, and held it wide for us. "In here, then."

We stepped into a room which was slightly—but not significantly—brighter than the hallway we had just left behind. Most of the noonday sunlight was held at bay by the thick screen of ivy which covered much of the window, in the midst of which a couple of dozen birds were hopping and nesting and looking in at us with bright eyes and curiously inclined heads. This was the same front room we had peered into the day before. It was dominated by a long, narrow dining table in dark wood, with massive wrought-iron candlesticks at either end; and by a large, murky oil painting, half abstract and half landscape, which took up most of the wall opposite the windows. The walls must once have been white, I supposed, although now they were closer to grey. Cobwebs sprouted from every corner and dangled down from the flaking cornices. It was a singularly cold and cheerless room.

"Are you going to give me that?" the Woman asked again, holding out her hand.

"Tea first—card later," said Alison, in a defiantly sing-song tone.

The Woman glowered at her and left the room, closing the door behind her with a firm slam.

I rushed to the door and tried the handle, fruitlessly.

"Now look what you've done," I wailed. "We're trapped! She's locked us in!"

Alison strolled over and opened the door in a relaxed and easy movement.

"Calm down, can't you? You were turning the handle the wrong way. We can leave any time we want."

"Then let's leave *now*," I said. "She doesn't want us here. She looked like she was going to murder us. Did you see those . . . things all over her face? And those tattoos!"

"Lots of people have tattoos," said Alison. "And if she didn't want us here, she wouldn't be giving us tea." Now she wandered over to a second painting, a smaller one, some sort of still life, which hung next to the door. "What do you make of this?" she said.

"For heaven's sake. We're not here to look at paintings. What did you want to come inside for? Why couldn't we just have given her the card and gone home?"

"Because that wasn't what we came for. Now look—when she comes back, I'll slip out and go down to look in the cellar, so you'll have to keep her talking."

I was horrified. "What? I can't keep her talking."

"All right, then—I'll keep her talking, and you go down to the cellar."

"No! I can't go down to the cellar either."

"Well, there are only two of us. You've got to do one or the other. Is that meant to be a tennis racket, do you think? And what about this? It looks like a football."

I tugged her away from the painting, maddened by the insouciance with which she now seemed to be accepting this desperate situation. I was convinced that we were never going to get out of this house alive.

"By the way," Alison added, "did you notice what she said?"

"When?"

"Back on the doorstep, when I showed her the card. She said,

'We were wondering where that one had got to.' Not *I* was wondering. *We.*"

She gave me an emphatic, meaningful nod, seeming happy at this apparent confirmation of her theories. As for me, this further proof—if proof it was—of the Bird Woman's madness sent my heart plummeting even further. The thought of being alone in the room with her made me want to be sick. In fact, I couldn't do it: there was simply no way. I was going to have to choose what now seemed (incredibly) to be the lesser of two evils.

"Look, Ali—I'll go down to the cellar. You stay here and keep her talking."

"Are you sure?"

I nodded miserably, and just then the door was opened again and our terrifying host reversed into the room, carrying with her a tea tray rather than an axe or a carving knife. This was some consolation, I suppose, although it still left open the possibility that she intended to poison us.

"Here you are, then," she said. "Two nice mugs of tea." She put the tray down on the table and then swirled the teapot around a few times before starting to pour. "Aha!" (She noticed that Alison had wandered over to the larger of the two paintings.) "Admiring my artwork, are you?"

"Did you paint this?" Alison asked, evidently impressed.

"All the paintings in this house are mine."

"Cool. So where is this?"

Still carrying the teapot, the Woman came over to stand beside Alison and look more closely at the canvas. Despite everything, my gaze was drawn towards it, too. Now that I looked at it properly, I could see that it showed a bleak swath of moorland, beneath a stormy and cloud-covered sky rendered in such brutal strokes that it appeared at first to be a mere chaos of grey and black shades.

"North Yorkshire," said the Woman. "You see this house?"

She laid her finger upon a patch of canvas. Perched almost on the crest of a vast, forbidding ridge, overlooking a large expanse of dismal and featureless water, was a gaunt mansion rendered in the blackest of blacks. It took up very little of the painting but somehow seemed to dominate it: a mad conglomeration of gothic, neo-gothic, sub-gothic and pseudo-gothic towers which collectively resembled nothing so much as a giant hand, snatching at the clouds as if in the conviction that, despite their vaporous insubstantiality, they could be pilfered from the sky itself.

In the bottom right-hand corner of the picture, two words had been written: "Winshaw Towers." They were followed by the initials "P. B." and the date "1991."

"That's a real house," the Woman continued, "where I used to work for a while. As a nurse. Until one night, twelve years ago . . ."

She fell silent, lost in a memory—and not a very pleasant one, by the sound of it.

"Twelve years ago . . . ?" Alison prompted.

"Something bad happened."

We waited, but clearly no further explanation was forthcoming. Not wishing to talk or even think about it any more, the Woman went back to the table and the tea tray. "Milk and two sugars, wasn't it?" she said. "Is that the same for both of you?"

"Yes please," I answered; and then—aghast at my own courage—I began to set the plot in motion. "Can I use your toilet?"

She threw me a look full of mistrust, but after weighing the request briefly she seemed to relent. Turning away from me to concentrate on pouring the milk, she muttered: "All right then. There are three doors at the end of the hallway. It's the one on the left. Don't touch either of the others. And come straight back."

"I will. Thank you."

I began to back out of the room, slowly and unwillingly. Now that the deed had to be done, I was still not sure that I was capable of it. Alison glanced at me, her eyes eloquent with the command to hurry up and get on with it. But still I lingered, gripped by some sort of absurd inertia. In desperation, Alison turned back towards the Woman and began to babble at her about the other painting.

"Can I ask you something about this?" she said. "I just wondered what you were trying to do when you painted it. I mean—this is a football, right? And this is a tennis racket . . ."

Upon hearing these words, the Woman made a noise we had not heard before—something akin to a growl—put down the milk jug and came storming over towards the picture. This was my cue, at last, to beat a final retreat, and this time I actually managed to slip out through the door and back into the hallway, staying within earshot just long enough to hear the disgruntled artist say:

"Why does *everybody* get this painting wrong? It's Orpheus, for God's sake! It's the lyre of Orpheus and his disembodied head being carried along by the waters of the Hebrus. How many times do I have to *explain* this . . . ?"

I left her to her rant and stole quickly through the shadow-filled hallway, past a steep and thinly carpeted staircase ascending to the first floor on my right, until I had reached the three doors at the corridor's very end.

The first door, to the left, opened on to a small bathroom containing toilet and hand-basin. The second door, in the middle, was solidly locked. The third door, which led under the staircase, was obviously the one that would take me down to the cellar. Before putting my hand to the doorknob, I prayed that this one would be locked as well. Then all I would have to do would be to go back to Alison and report failure. I would have done my duty, at least. Please God, I prayed silently, let this be what happens. Don't make me go down there. Don't make me go down into the darkness.

Then I grasped the doorknob, turned it . . . and the door swung creakily open.

The first thing that hit me was a strange, damp, stale smell wafting from somewhere in the depths. It had elements of dry rot, rotting fruit and fried onions—or fried food of some sort, at any rate. It was not quite as off-putting as I had expected.

What was off-putting, certainly, was the profundity of the darkness that greeted me as I stepped forward and peered down the stairs towards the cellar. It was almost impossible to make out anything at all. With my left hand I reached out and found that there was some sort of rail or bannister to hold on to. The steps beneath my feet were concrete. I took one more glance towards the room where the Mad Bird Woman had served us tea—half expecting her to be looking out through the doorway, checking on me—and then started my descent.

As I got closer to the foot of the stairs, the silence became heavier and the smell grew stronger. Surprisingly, too, it became slightly easier to see ahead of me. This, I realized, was because the staircase ended in a closed door, and from behind this door, visible around its edges, a soft yellow glow was emanating. And so, whether the cellar was occupied or not, there was certainly a light on in there. Just like we'd seen yesterday, through the window.

I stopped outside the door. In the silence I could hear my heart beating, my breath coming and going, the blood ringing in my ears. Nothing else. Not another sound.

I laid a hand upon the door, and pushed. It began to swing open.

Again, it creaked: much louder than the door at the top of the stairs. But the noise was still not loud enough to disturb the figure sitting at the table in the centre of the room.

From where I was standing, it was evidently the dead body of an elderly lady. Her back was towards me, illuminated by the harsh glare of a lightbulb hanging directly above her. I could see straggles of thin grey hair hanging off the skull, down as far as the prominent shoulder blades. She wore a blouse which was torn, decaying, almost in tatters; what was left of the yellowing flesh peeped through in patches underneath. I took a few reluctant, appalled steps towards her, my head swimming, my stomach tightening with nausea, and even though I knew that she was dead, stupidly, irrationally, I could not help myself saying, in a tiny voice:

"Mrs. Bates? Mrs. Bates?"

But the corpse remained quite motionless. I came closer, and realized that she was sitting—or had been placed, rather—in front of a table. A green baize card table. Laid out on the table was a game of Pelmanism. The cards featured those by now familiar crude, slightly sickening pictures of animals, and had all been paired off, one with another: fish with fish, tigers with tigers, snakes with snakes. There was only one that was lacking its partner: the card showing a single, giant spider, standing upright on two of its legs, raising the others fiercely in the air as if challenging someone to a fight, the pale green of its underbelly shining out with queasy clarity. It was waiting to be paired off with the missing card, the one we had come here to return.

Tearing my eyes away from this horrid but compelling image, which I could see from behind the dead body by peering over one bony shoulder, I raised my hand slowly, wondering if I actually dared to touch the thing. Would it crumble and decay the moment I laid my hand on it, however careful I tried to be? Would an arm fall off in a cloud of powder and dust, the bones clattering to the floor? How long had she been here? What sort of state was she in?

My hand came closer, closer to the brittle, angular shoulder blade.

"Mrs. Bates?" I whispered, again.

And then, at the moment of contact . . .

. . . at the moment of contact something truly astonishing happened. The corpse jerked abruptly and violently into life. It swivelled around in its chair and instead of being confronted by a fleshless skull I found that I was looking into a pair of wide-open, startled, madly staring eyes. And then the mouth opened, too, and a terrible sound came from inside it. A long, animal monotone: a single-note scream of fear and incomprehension which, the moment it started, felt as though it was never going to stop. Which meant there were two screams, of course, because I was already screaming, too, at the top of my voice, and it must have been the pitch and volume and suddenness of my scream that made the figure raise its painfully thin arms up in the air, crashing into the lightbulb and sending it swinging, back and forth, back and forth, so that now his crazed, distorted face (because it was a man, after all, there could be no doubt about that) was bathed in light then shadow, light then shadow, as the bulb above it swung like a pendulum, and the two of us locked eyes and continued to scream as long and loud as we could until there were footsteps on the stairs and the next thing I knew . . .

10

. . . the next thing I knew, I was sitting in the most comfortable arm-chair in the world, in a room flooded with natural light, where one of the walls was made entirely of glass and looked on to a beautiful, manicured, walled garden, filled with fountains and rose bushes. A lovely piece of gentle classical guitar music was playing in the background. Alison was sitting on a footstool beside me, holding my hand. On a little table next to my chair was a fresh mug of tea, from which I took a sip: it was strong and sweet and deliciously reviving.

"Where am I?" I murmured.

"This is Phoebe's studio. Great, isn't it?"

I felt so tired, it was an effort to get even one more word out. "Phoebe?"

"The Mad Bird Woman. Only I don't think we should call her that anymore. Her name's Phoebe."

I managed to turn my head and look around the room. It was indeed filled with canvases, easels, paint pots and brushes. There was also a dining table—about half the size of the one in the front room—at which the man from the cellar was sitting, wrapped in a blanket, still playing his game of Pelmanism.

"Who is he?" I faintly said to Alison.

"We don't know. But we think that his name's Lu, or something like that, and he comes from China."

A door opened and Phoebe herself came in. Glimpsing a view of the hall through the open doorway, I realized that the door to this wonderful, light and airy studio must have been the second one that I had tried: the one that had been locked. At this memory, images of my horrific descent to the cellar began flooding back for the first time. I drank some more tea eagerly.

"How are you feeling now, Rachel?" Phoebe asked.

"OK, thank you," I said. Was this the same woman I'd been frightened of for the last few days? She seemed so gentle and kind.

"You shouldn't have gone down there, you silly girl. You must have given each other a terrible fright."

I smiled. "Yes, we did."

Over at the table, Lu gave what seemed to be a cry of satisfaction. Going over to look at the progress of his card game, Phoebe put her hand on his shoulder and said: "There you are—brilliant! Not a single card missing. You did it." To which she added a few broken words in (I suppose) Chinese. Lu turned and grinned at her. At least a third of his teeth were missing, but it was still a nice smile.

"*Wǒ zuòdào le,*" he said, in a harsh and cracked voice.

"He's been playing that game for more than a week now," Phoebe explained, drawing up a chair and coming to sit between us. "I gave it to him because he seems to have lost his memory and I thought it might help him to get it back. The cards are very old—they belonged to my parents. They're kind of horrible but pretty easy to remember, at least."

"So . . . what were they doing in the woods?"

"I can't keep him here," Phoebe said. "I can't hold him prisoner. That's not the idea. It's just supposed to be somewhere he can feel safe for a while. He's free to come and go as he wants. So one evening he went off to sit in the woods, and he took the cards with him. He takes them everywhere, in fact. But I expect he got confused, and forgot them, and left them all behind." She smiled at us, and must have seen the confusion on our faces, because now she launched into a fuller explanation:

"It was in the woods that I found him, about ten days ago," she said. "It was early in the morning and he was sitting up against a tree and he was so weak that he could barely move. He looked as though he hadn't eaten for weeks. He wouldn't come with me so I went home and fetched him some food. Even after that, he was still scared of me and it didn't help that I couldn't understand a word he was saying. But I wanted to get him to some sort of safety. I didn't want to get the police involved because I didn't think they'd be sympathetic. People in Beverley are pressuring them to crack down on vagrants, and I thought that was the category they'd probably put him into.

"After a while I realized that he did understand a bit of English, and by the end of the morning, I'd managed to persuade him to come home with me. I told him that he was welcome to sleep here for a few days—my guess was that he'd been sleeping rough, I don't know how long for—but he didn't want to be in any of the bedrooms, for some reason. The place he really seemed to like was the cellar, so I fixed it up for him as best I could, put in a camp bed and a few rugs and chairs and bits and pieces to try and make it more cosy. He seemed happy down there. That was where he wanted to be. Maybe because it made him feel safe."

"Why was he so scared?" Alison wanted to know. "What's he running away from?"

"Well, unfortunately, I haven't been able to get much sense out of him," said Phoebe. "The language that he speaks is Mandarin, I'm pretty sure of that, so he's come to this country from China. He's probably come here looking for work, and my guess is that he *has* been working here, for quite a while. Working very hard, which is why he looks so worn out. I don't think he's anything like as old as he looks."

I had a sudden inspiration. "Has he been trafficked?"

Alison and Phoebe both looked at me, equally impressed. I did feel rather proud of myself for being so worldly and knowledgeable.

"I saw this programme on the television the other night," I explained. "Apparently there are *slaves* in England. Real slaves. Most of them come here from other countries and they have to work, like, twenty-four hours every day and if they try to run away they get beaten up or attacked by dogs."

"I don't know if he's been trafficked," said Phoebe, "but I think he has been doing some kind of forced labour. There aren't many clues, because he doesn't have a passport with him or anything like that. Probably his employer's got it. But he did have this in his pocket."

She showed us a slip of paper. It was a handwritten payment slip, scribbled out on cheap blue headed notepaper. The name of the company at the top was "Sunbeam Foods."

"Sunbeam Foods?" said Alison. "Who are they?"

"I did some research on the Internet," said Phoebe. "They're a food-processing company, based down in Kent. Outfits like this send cheap labour to farms all over the country. So it looks like Lu's been working for them. And I've got a pretty good idea what he might have been doing. There was one word that, when I mentioned it to him, completely freaked him out. It was *chickens.*"

At the mere sound of the word, Lu turned sharply towards us, panic etched on his face.

"Chickens?" he said. *"No. No chickens."*

Phoebe got up and comforted him, rubbed his shoulders, soothed his brow. "No chickens," she kept saying, until his agitation had subsided. "It's all right, Lu. No chickens. No chickens for you."

"What's his problem with chickens?" Alison asked.

"We did factory farming in school, don't you remember?" I said. "It was horrible. Some of the class had to leave the room. Isabel and Anunya have been vegetarian ever since. Was it something like that, do you think?"

"Considering that Sunbeam Foods is one of the suppliers for the Brunwin Group, yes, I think it probably was," said Phoebe. (But she did not explain what "the Brunwin Group" was, and I did not—at this stage—know.) "They market themselves now as being free range and humane and all that sort of thing but . . . well, that can cover a multitude of sins. And it still means there are people like Lu working some way down the supply chain in terrible conditions."

"So what are you going to do now?" asked Alison, drawing the conversation back to practicalities.

"I don't know. Just wait and see, I suppose. I got some Teach Yourself Mandarin tapes from the library, so every day we understand each other a tiny bit more. And every day he seems to be remembering a little bit more as well. He keeps saying this one thing, which for a while I thought was a word I didn't understand, but now I think it's somebody's name: 'Xiang.'"

At the sound of these two syllables, Lu turned again, and stared at Phoebe intently. His eyes blazed with urgency.

"Xiang," he repeated. *"Xiang!"*

"That's right," said Phoebe. "You want to find him, don't you? I'm going to help you."

"Find Xiang," he answered, nodding furiously.

"My theory is this," Phoebe explained. "And it is only a theory. But, supposing he and this Xiang came over from China together—either legally or illegally, but in any case probably paying some dodgy character a small fortune to help them. At some point they get separated, maybe before Lu starts working for Sunbeam Foods, maybe after. Perhaps they both worked there together. Who knows? But obviously, if the company is based in Kent, and Lu has ended up here in Yorkshire, he and the other workers were being driven long distances all over the country to work on different farms. Supposing Lu decided he couldn't take any more of this. So one night, maybe they were parked in some lay-by and getting a few hours' sleep or something, he just slipped out and ran away."

"But he wouldn't have gone without Xiang," I insisted.

Phoebe thought about this for a moment. "No, you're right," she agreed. "They must have got separated ages ago. Maybe when they first arrived in the UK."

"Well, I do hope that he's all right," I said, sitting up and finishing the last of my tea. There was a clock on the wall of the studio and I'd noticed that it was almost 2:30. Gran and Grandad would be home by now, and would be wondering where on earth we had got to. "Thank you very much for the tea, and for looking after me so well. But Alison and I should really be going home."

Phoebe saw us to the front door.

"Call again if you want to," she said. "I'm sorry we got off on the wrong foot. I didn't mean to scare you in the woods, only I was a bit paranoid about finding those cards. I don't think it would be a good thing if the police worked out that Lu's here, so . . . do keep it to yourselves, won't you?"

"Of course we will," said Alison.

And then, just before leaving, I thought to ask: "What happened to your kestrel, by the way?"

Phoebe seemed taken aback. "How did you know that I used to have a kestrel?"

"I saw you flying it once," I said, "up on Westwood. A few years ago."

"Tabitha . . ." said Phoebe, musingly. Her eyes were briefly glazed with sadness. "I used to keep her in a shed out in the garden. But one night somebody got in. I never found out who it was. They strangled her."

We both gasped. "Oh, that's awful," Alison said. "Why would anyone do something like that?"

"I don't know. They were angry with me, I suppose, because Mrs. Bates liked me, and left me this house. People are strange, very strange." She smiled now, and held out her hand for us to shake. "But now *you've* met me, and you know that I'm not as bad as people make out. Tell your grandparents I'm not this mad scary woman who goes round murdering old ladies. Spread the word."

"We will!" I promised.

Then we both shook her hand vigorously, and I knew for the first time that I was not frightened of the Mad Bird Woman at all. But I also knew that I would never get used to the piercings all over her face, or the tattoos all over her neck and throat and around her eyes. Why would you disfigure yourself like that? What had inspired her to do it? I had a vague but deep-rooted intuition that it had something to do with the painting in her front room, that wild stormy wasteland and the menacing black house that overlooked it. But I was not brave enough to ask her, either then or later.

11

In fact we only ever saw Phoebe one more time.

When we got back to the house that afternoon, Gran and Grandad were already home, and didn't even ask us where we'd been. I had never seen them looking so happy. Only now did we learn of the cloud that had been hanging over them that week. But all was well, in any case: Gran had been given the results of her brain scan and the doctor had told her that she did not have cancer after all. She had something called a meningioma, apparently: a benign tumour that was not too difficult to operate upon. The sense of relief, of thankfulness and lightheartedness, that pervaded the house from that moment onwards was so sweet and strong that we felt we could almost touch it with our fingers and taste it on our tongues. The house and garden seemed drenched in light.

On Thursday afternoon, our last full day in Beverley, all four of us went up to Westwood with a picnic. Gran and Grandad sat on the wooden bench that encircled the foot of the Black Tower; Alison and I laid out a couple of rugs in the sunshine, and gorged ourselves on fish paste sandwiches and Gran's homemade chocolate cake. Afterwards, Alison lay flat out and closed her eyes and seemed to have fallen asleep. I sat upright and let the thoughts course through my head. I was looking forward to seeing my mother again, but also felt prey to a gentle, pressing melancholy at the prospect of leaving this place, which had come to feel so welcoming and familiar, so much like home. I remembered the first time I had sat here with my brother, some years ago, on a cold and grey afternoon in late October, the same afternoon on which, as dusk descended, he had played that nasty joke on me in the Minster. And then, just as my memory was calling up images of Phoebe pushing Mrs. Bates's wheelchair across the moorland, with her kestrel Tabitha perched on her arm, Phoebe herself appeared in the distance; approaching us, it seemed, from exactly the same spot, but now waving cheerfully in recognition. She came and crouched down beside us on the rug and I introduced her to Gran and Grandad, who (having already been given a carefully edited account of our visit to her house) half rose from their bench with instinctive politeness, and extended their hands to give hers a cautious shake, but never stopped looking uncomfortable in her presence.

Phoebe had come to say good-bye, but she couldn't stay for long. She had something on her mind.

"Lu disappeared," she told us. "I'm not sure when. I went down to find him yesterday morning and he was gone."

"We have to find him," I said. "Alison and I can help you. He won't have gone far, surely."

Phoebe shook her head. "I spent all of yesterday looking. I took the car out and drove for miles. But it wasn't any use. There's nothing much I can do now. I don't think he would have gone unless he felt ready for it. He has some money, and he's a lot stronger than when I found him last week. We just have to hope for the best."

"We're going home tomorrow," Alison said. "You will write and tell us, won't you, if you hear from him again?"

"Of course," said Phoebe. But she never did.

Strangely enough it was Alison, out of the two of us, who kept in occasional contact with her after that. Phoebe's paintings—in fact not just the paintings but the studio, the atmosphere in her house, her whole way of life, everything about her—seemed to have inspired Alison, and from then on art became her passion. When her mother came back from holiday the next day she brought a new boyfriend with her, and before long Alison and her mother had moved down to Birmingham in order to live with him. From then on, of course, we hardly saw each other at all; but the events of that week in Beverley had created a bond between us which was not easily broken. I had begun by feeling indifferent towards Alison; then at one time, briefly, I had hated her; finally, we had come to be friends, and that friendship has strengthened and endured, now, over many years, despite absence and distance, despite the ways in which we have grown up and grown apart, and sometimes misunderstood each other.

Those few, intense and mysterious days in the early summer of 2003 continue to haunt me. The memories are strong. I remember how the discovery of David Kelly's body was reported on the news, how it had shocked and angered my grandparents, and how it made me realize something about the finality of death. I remember the shadow of death that hung over their house during that time, and the tingling euphoria that seized us all when it miraculously lifted.

There is another thing I have no trouble remembering. I have no trouble remembering it because I have it in front of me, right now as I write these words: the Pelmanism card with that loathsome picture of a giant, brightly coloured spider. The afternoon of our picnic, Phoebe had the pack of cards with her, and she gave me and Alison a spider each, as a souvenir of our adventure, and as a token of our friendship, which she told us we must never neglect because it was one of the most precious things we would ever possess. I never spoke of the cards to Alison again; I don't know whether she kept hers, or whether she lost it. But mine has always stayed with me: first at home, in a special drawer of my bedside cupboard; then at Oxford; and now . . .

Now it sits in front of me on my desk. It has never been a pleasant thing to look at it, it has always filled me with dread, and tonight, in the deathly stillness of this house, it poisons my mind once again with strange imaginings, and I can't help walking over to the window, one more time, pulling back the curtain and looking into the garden. Peering into the shadows at its furthest depths.

There is nothing there. Nothing at all.

Such silence. Such darkness. It is no wonder that in a world like this, things can disappear. Even people. People like Lu, whose existence seemed so precarious, so unrecognized, that there was nothing to stop him slipping away into that woodland at dawn and simply evaporating, blending into the mist. Did he ever find his friend? I've wondered about that, many times, over the years. The men who drowned in Morecambe Bay the next year, picking cockles for their gangmaster as the treacherous tide rushed inwards ... they were Chinese, most of them. Just the other day, I read once again about their terrible deaths on the Internet and my stomach tightened when I saw that one of them was called Xiang. But I expect it's a very common name in China.

Dodie Smith, I Capture the Castle *(1948):*

"Perhaps watching someone you love suffer can teach
you even more than suffering yourself can."

The Comeback

1

From: Susan Wells
To: Val Doubleday
Subject: Re: Dilemma
14/09/2011 22:17

Dear Val

You asked me for advice. You are not going to like what you hear.

First of all—very sorry to hear that things are so tough at work. You won't be surprised to learn that the situation up here is much the same: libraries, if not closing, then having their opening hours reduced and being told to cut down on staff. I'm sure your job is safe but I can see how hard it must be, managing on less and less money every week. It's happening everywhere. Even at our chambers, people are being laid off. A lot of our work was for legal aid clients, and there's not much available for legal aid these days— more people are choosing to represent themselves instead. The results are pretty disastrous as you can probably imagine.

It's so depressing. Everything seems to be going to pot at the moment and we have another four years of this lot to put up with. Sounds like you are at the sharp end of it as well. When I think of all the time our daughters used to spend at the library, and all the wonderful things they got out of it, and now our grandkids are going to have none of that, at this rate. It's enough to make you howl.

But come on, Val, however desperate things are . . . Steve??

You want to get back together with Steve? Oh, I know you didn't say that straight out, but, reading between the lines, that's what you're thinking of, isn't it?

It's grim, sometimes, being a single middle-aged woman. I think that's something we can both agree upon. But just remember what he did to you . . .

And ask Alison for her opinion, if you haven't already!

Lots of love
Susan

"Guess who I sat next to on the bus the other day?" said Val.

"What are these?" said Alison, fishing inside the shopping basket and bringing out a bag of carrots.

"They're carrots."

"I can see that. But they're not organic."

"So?" said her mother, defensively. "They're still carrots aren't they? I sat next to Steve, since you're so interested."

Alison frowned. It was a name she never wanted to hear. "I thought we always got organic. They put all sorts of pesticides and chemicals into these, you know. That's why they all look the same."

"Yes, well, they cost about half the price, so that's what we're going to be eating from now on. You'd better get used to it." Val snatched the carrots from her daughter, slit open the bag with her fingernail and tipped them into the fridge's chill compartment. "We had a really good chat."

"That's nice."

"He's struggling a bit. The college made him redundant and then took him on as a freelance. So now he's on half what he was for the same work. It's terrible, isn't it, how they can do that?"

"Four bottles? Really?" said Alison, lifting out one bottle of Pinot Grigio after another.

"They were 50p off," said Val.

"Oh I see, so by getting four of them you've saved even more money."

"Oh shut up. The thing is, I thought I might invite him round here for dinner."

"It just seems silly to be saving money on vegetables when you're wasting it on wine."

"It's not a waste. You drink it too, don't you?"

"Sometimes."

"So what do you think?"

"About what?"

"About having him round for dinner."

"Nothing to do with me," said Alison, still unpacking, and not looking up.

"Of course it's something to do with you. He was practically your stepfather for a while."

Alison rounded on her. "He was *never* my stepfather. Never anything like it. OK? He was the bloke you . . . shacked up with, for a few months. He was the bloke you met on holiday and then changed cities to come and live with, and got dumped by as soon as life started to get difficult."

"That is *so* unfair," said Val, her voice already tearful.

"Have you forgotten already, Mum? When I went in for the operation? What he was like?"

Val glared at her for a few seconds, and then said, through a half-sob: "I never get a bit of support from you anymore, do I? Not one *fucking* bit." She grabbed one of the wine bottles from the kitchen table, and a tumbler from the shelf, and stormed off in the direction of the living room.

Alison stood still for a moment, stunned by the speed with which this quarrel had blown up. Then she shook her head and resumed her unpacking. She heard the television being switched on in the next room, and a few seconds of each different programme—local news, quiz show, sitcom—as her mother flicked between channels. She imagined her unscrewing the cap of the bottle fiercely and filling the tumbler three-quarters full with wine, drinking it like it was lemonade, which was how she always seemed to drink it these days. Three or four sips, one after the other, without taking her mouth from the rim of the glass.

After thinking about it for a minute or two, she decided that she was the one, as usual, who would have to do the apologizing. Her mother's capacity to sulk had become pretty much inexhaustible, and Alison didn't want to spend the entire evening in silence with her. So she went and stood in the living-room doorway and said:

"Mum? I'm sorry."

"That's OK," said Val, not turning around or turning the television down.

"Did you hear me? I said *I'm sorry.*"

Val glanced back towards her. "Yes. I heard you. All right. Apology accepted. But maybe you should just think a bit more carefully before you say hurtful things."

This was monstrously unfair, but Alison let it pass. There was no point in carrying on these fights anymore. "I listened to your song," she said instead.

These words, by contrast, had an immediate effect. Val muted the television and turned round, a beseeching smile on her face.

"You did? What did you think?"

And answering this was easy. However much her mother's behaviour annoyed her, Alison had always enjoyed her music, never tired of listening to it, never had any trouble sharing her conviction that one day, with luck, with persistence, she would catch the public's attention again and have another hit. And this new song, which she had listened to ten or fifteen times during the course of the day, was easily one of her best.

"I loved it," she said. "It's beautiful."

"Really? I mean, you're not just saying that?"

"No, Mum. I'm not just saying that. It's brilliant. You know it is."

"Come and sit here." Val patted the place on the sofa beside her, and as soon as Alison had sat down gave her an impulsive hug. "What did you think of the arrangement?"

"It's fine. I mean, you know, it's . . . getting there."

"Well, it's the best I can do at home, obviously. Do you think it's good enough to send to people?"

"I don't know, Mum. I'm not in the music business."

"Maybe if I bought some studio time. Just three or four hours' downtime somewhere . . . Then I could record the vocal properly."

"Sure. Good idea. If you think you can afford it."

"Then I could send it to Cheryl."

Alison nodded. She never knew what to say when her mother mentioned her so-called "agent," who hadn't returned one of her calls or messages for about ten years.

"Do you like the title?" Val asked now. "'Sink and Swim'? Is it catchy enough?"

"I like everything about it." Finding herself caught up in another swift, clinging embrace which threatened to last for some time, Alison pushed her mother gently away and stood up. "OK, I'm going upstairs. I've got to finish writing to Rachel."

"That's funny," said Val. "I just got an e-mail from her mother."

"Yeah? How's she?"

"OK. Depressed about work, like everyone else."

"You should ask *her* what she thinks about you seeing Steve again."

Val turned back to the television screen and unmuted it. "Oh, we don't really discuss that sort of thing any more."

The conversation was over, apparently. Leaving her mother to watch adverts for financial services she would never use and holidays she would never take, Alison went upstairs to her room, took her half-written letter out from the clutter of her desk drawer and began reading it through.

Nowadays, when it came to ways of keeping in touch, she and Rachel were spoiled for choice: they e-mailed and texted, and they talked on Facebook and WhatsApp. In the last few weeks, they'd even started using a newly launched app called Snapchat, which allowed them to send pictures and brief messages which were only visible for a few seconds before being wiped from the screen forever. But every so often, when one of them had something special to say to the other, only a real, old-fashioned letter would do. And what Alison had to tell Rachel now was as special and as personal as could be imagined.

So far she had written two pages and not even started to address the subject. Her last paragraph read:

So, I started at college two weeks ago (yeah, this isn't *Oxbridge*, honey, we actually have a term that starts in September) and it's looking pretty cool so far. Not sure if the course is going to be quite what I want but it's such a relief to be hanging out with other students and teachers who just want you to do *art* and nothing else. The pressure to tow the line is off at last!

That was all very well, but Alison was cross with herself for not having come to the point yet. And so, nervously, she took up her pen, nibbled on the end of it for a minute or two and then wrote:

Anyway, none of that stuff matters, really. That's not why I'm writing to you. I'm writing because there's something you need to know, something I haven't told any of my other friends yet. I wanted you to be the first, because . . . well, for all sorts of reasons. But mainly because you're my oldest real friend and your reaction is incredibly important to me.

So. Can you guess what it is? Of course not. Why should you? (Deep breath.) I'm gay.

On Saturday afternoon Rachel, wanting to add a few things to her wardrobe before she left for Oxford in a couple of weeks' time, went shopping with her mother. There was a recession on, but you would never have known it from the crowds in Leeds town centre, drifting sluggishly from shop to shop, hungry for consumer durables. Miss Selfridge and Monsoon were milling with customers. Primark was packed. H & M, Topshop, Claire's Accessories, and Zara were too full to get into. River Island and Lush were turning people away. Rachel and her mother were both hot and exhausted by the time they got home.

As they approached the house, they saw that there was a car parked outside: a bright-red Porsche. Leaning against it, smiling smugly at them as they trudged up the street with their shopping bags, was Rachel's brother, Nick.

"Bloody hell," his mother said, "what are you doing here?"

"Hello, Mum. Hello, little sis." He kissed them both. "Try to look a bit more pleased to see me."

"Of course we're pleased. I just wish you'd give us a bit more warning."

"Flew in from Hong Kong this morning. Can I help you with those?"

"Hong Kong?" said Rachel, handing him the bags. "I thought you were in Cuba."

"Oh, you're way behind."

Nick hadn't been home for more than a year. Now twenty-six, he looked, if anything, younger and more beautiful than ever. Essentially, Rachel's feelings about him had not changed since the time, twelve years earlier, when they had stayed together at their grandparents' house in Beverley, and he had played a cruel joke upon her while they visited the Minster at dusk: in other words she worshipped him, disapproved of him and, deep down, feared him a little bit. This unspoken wariness had not diminished at all since Nick had reached adulthood and teamed up with a "business partner" called Toby. Their work meant that he now enjoyed a peripatetic lifestyle, which seemed to involve unspecified dealings in several different continents, hopping from one country to another at will and treating international airports the way that most people treated suburban railway stations. Whatever it was that he and Toby did for a living, it was clearly very lucrative, and beyond that Rachel felt it was probably best not to enquire.

Inside the hallway, Rachel saw that the post had finally arrived.

"Ooh—a letter from Alison," she said, excitedly.

"Never mind that now," said Nick, taking it from her and tossing it onto the hall table. He and Alison had never liked each other. "I'm only here for one night. Kindly make me the centre of attention for once."

"All right," Rachel agreed, smiling. "What have you come home for anyway?"

"Your eighteenth birthday, of course. You didn't think I'd miss that, did you?"

"It was three months ago," she said, laughing.

"I know. You probably thought the celebrations were all over. That's what's going to make tonight so special."

"I might not be free tonight," said Rachel, playing hard to get. "What did you have in mind?"

"A surprise," said Nick, taking her in his arms. "And a pretty good one, if I do say so myself."

It turned out that he was not exaggerating. After a few minutes' chat with their mother, he bundled Rachel into the Porsche and soon they were driving north out of Leeds along the A61, until they reached Harewood House. By then, it was almost six o'clock.

"What are you doing?" Rachel asked, as Nick swung the car into the serpentine driveway. "This place'll be closed now, won't it?"

"To most people, yes," he answered.

How did he manage to arrange these things? Rachel suspected that it was less to do with having money to spend, and more with his network of contacts in the most unexpected places. In any case, he had arranged for them to enjoy a private tour of the Terrace Gallery, followed by champagne on the terrace itself, and then a private dinner for two in the State Rooms.

The Terrace Gallery was especially impressive, with two new pieces by Antony Gormley on display in addition to the permanent collection. Rachel could not help thinking how much Alison would have enjoyed this privileged view. She took a picture of one of the sculptures on her phone and, while she and Nick were waiting for their champagne to be served on the terrace, sent it to Alison via Snapchat.

Soon afterwards a picture of Alison's bedroom in Yardley popped up.

Hi Rache, did you get my letter?

The words were only on the screen for ten seconds or so, before dissolving into nothingness. By way of reply, Rachel took a quick picture of the parkland laid out in front of them, bathed in evening sunlight, and then wrote with her forefinger on the screen:

Yes, will write back soon.

Alison replied:

That looks good! Where are you?

Rachel took a picture of the house itself, and wrote:

With my brother. We're doing the nicest thing tonight!

There was a longish pause before Alison's reply came through. It said simply:

W T F??

Had she misunderstood, somehow? Rachel took another picture, this time with the Terrace Gallery itself in the background, and wrote:

Right up your street I would have thought.

There was no reply from Alison after this, but Rachel didn't think anything of it. A waiter approached them from the main house to announce that their table for dinner was ready.

The next day, Rachel read Alison's letter, and was profoundly moved by it. She replied at once. She wrote a heartfelt message of support, saying that Alison was not to feel shy, let alone ashamed, of what she had realized about her own identity. She promised that they would always be friends, whatever happened. She hoped that it would not be long before they saw each other again, and could discuss these things face to face.

She was surprised, at first, not to receive a reply. She put it down to the fact that Alison had just started college and must be busy. Then she, too, had the beginning of her first term at Oxford to think about, but although that distracted her, she was still puzzled to have heard nothing at all. She called Alison on the phone and texted her, posted messages on her Facebook timeline, but never got any response. She began to wonder if there had been something in the letter which had offended her. Had she not sounded supportive enough? Had she made Alison's announcement sound more like a problem than a cause for celebration? As the weeks went by, and turned into months, her puzzlement dwindled, receded but never quite went away. It mutated, eventually, into a low-level hum of resentment. She had done the right thing, after all. She had responded just as a good friend should. She deserved something better than silence.

The Number 11 bus route, which follows the whole of Birmingham's outer circle, makes a complete circuit of the city in about two and a half hours. Most passengers stay on it for only a fraction of that time. Alison and Selena, new students together and already new friends, were sitting on the lower deck of the 11A, the anti-clockwise version, heading from Bournville in the direction of Hall Green. They were on their way home from college, having dozed through a ninety-minute lecture on "Mapping the Historiography of the Para-Architectural Space," which had failed to catch their imaginations. Well, never mind. They couldn't expect everything on this course to be brilliant.

It was late September, and a low sun was still washing the city in pale golden light, glinting off the windscreens of cars and the panes of allotment greenhouses. Alison glanced at her phone to see what time it was, as the bus shuddered to a halt at a pedestrian crossing. Almost six thirty. This was proving to be a slow journey.

"You going straight home now, then?" Selena asked.

"No. I'm meeting my mum for a drink. With her new boyfriend. Well, she calls him 'new.' He's her old boyfriend, in fact. But he seems to have popped up on the scene again."

"How do you feel about that?"

"Whatever makes her happy, I suppose," said Alison, without much conviction. Then: "Your folks are still together, right?"

"Yeah." Selena laughed, and said: "I don't know why, sometimes, but they've stuck it out. For the sake of us kids, I think, as much as anything else. Good on them. I've seen most of my friends having to deal with their parents splitting up. I know how tough it is. You an only child?"

Alison nodded.

"That's even worse, isn't it? So it's just you and your mum at home, and I bet half the time it's you looking after her, not the other way round."

"Yeah, there's all of that. Plus, you know, it just gets so fucking *lonely* a lot of the time. Sitting at the kitchen table, having dinner together, just the two of us. If you don't put the radio on or something you can hear the clock ticking on the wall."

Selena's wide, hazel eyes were full of sympathy: "Look, any time you want to come round and have a meal at our place . . . Just say the word. There's five of us and it gets pretty loud and, you know, we have a good time. It might take you out of things."

Returning Selena's gaze, Alison took a long breath and said, in a tone of voice suddenly nervous and confiding: "Look, Selena, we only met a couple of weeks ago, but there's something I want you to know about me. Something you really *have* to know, actually."

Selena was startled by the change in her manner. She waited for some passengers to jostle past them on their way to the exit door, then said: "OK. What is it?"

Saying nothing, her eyes still locked into Selena's, Alison took hold of her friend's hand with a gentle grip. She lifted it, and now, moving it slowly, unobtrusively, so as not to attract the attention of the other passengers, she laid it on her own left thigh, just above the knee. She squeezed Selena's hand, so that Selena herself was encouraged—even compelled—to respond by giving Alison's thigh a reciprocal, questioning squeeze.

Selena's eyes, not leaving Alison's for a moment, flickered with surprise. There was a long silence between them: a silence charged with confusion and uncertainty. Selena's hand did not leave her friend's thigh; in fact it was still being held in place there. Gradually, her lips widened into a smile; the smile became broader, revealing her teeth; and at last, unable to contain her feelings any longer, she burst into laughter.

"What the *fuck*!" she said, and Alison started laughing as well.

"What the *fucking fuck*!" Selena repeated, and neither of them seemed to mind now that some of the passengers were turning to look at them. "Have you got a false leg?"

"Yes!" said Alison, barely able to get the word out, as she was by now doubled up with laughter herself. "Oh my God, the way you looked just then!"

"My God, I didn't know what you were doing! And now this . . . It's like . . . What is it like? What's it made of? It's like plastic."

"Of course it's plastic. They don't make them out of wood anymore, you know. I'm not bloody Long John Silver."

"But . . . what happened? How long have you had it?"

The bus staggered its way through Kings Heath and along Swanshurst Lane as Alison told her the story. Passengers came and went, the bus changed drivers at Acocks Green, but the two students were wrapped up in each other, and took no notice.

"When I was ten," said Alison, "I kept getting these pains in my leg for no reason. Really bad pains that wouldn't go away. We moved to Birmingham round about then, so I was going in for hundreds of tests at the Queen Elizabeth, and in the end they diagnosed me with this very rare thing called Ewing's sarcoma, which is a really aggressive kind of cancer. I was on chemotherapy for months but in the end that wasn't enough and they told me they were going to have to cut the whole thing off."

"Shit, that's terrible."

"Well, the alternative was kind of worse, wasn't it? Here I am, after all. Alive and kicking."

Selena couldn't work out at first whether this was a joke or not. When Alison's smile made it clear that it was, she gave a relieved laugh of her own.

"Do you want to see it?" Alison asked now. "It's very realistic."

She rolled the left leg of her jeans almost up to the knee to expose a section of prosthesis which did indeed have the convincing look of flesh and bone.

"The knee doesn't look quite so good—I'll show you that later," said Alison, rolling her trouser leg down again, "but otherwise it's all right, isn't it? They even matched my skin colour. When they're ready to make the leg they give you a book of samples and you have to flick through all the different skin tones, just like you were choosing a carpet or something."

"You're kidding."

"No. I could have had one white leg, if I'd wanted to. How cool would that have been? I could have been a living example of ethnic diversity."

Alison explained that the cancer had been so aggressive that the surgeons had had to perform a transfemoral amputation, above the knee. This meant that her left leg was lacking all the motor power of the knee joint—one of the strongest joints in the human body—so she could still only take stairs, for instance, step by step, one stair at a time. Nonetheless, on level surfaces, where there were not too many people around to impede her progress and get in her way, she was able to walk with perfect confidence.

"How long did it take," Selena asked, "before it started to feel . . . you know, natural?"

"Oh, it never feels natural," said Alison. "Never has, never will. But learning to feel—I don't know—comfortable with it didn't take too long. I worked with a physical therapist: in the hospital at first, and then after that she started coming to our house. That went on for a few months. Stressful time for everyone, very stressful. This guy I was telling you about—Steve—my mother's boyfriend, he was around at this time. In fact that was when he showed his true colours."

"Was he not very supportive, you mean?"

"Not really. He started shagging the physical therapist."

After a second or two they both started laughing again at that, it sounded so ridiculous. In any case it was easier, for Alison, to laugh about it than to remember the real agony of that time, when all her own hopes had seemed to lie shattered around her, and in the face of Steve's betrayal her mother turned into a wreck who drank herself to sleep most nights and seemed to age ten years in as many months. She really, really didn't feel like seeing him again tonight.

"Hey, look," she said to Selena, quietly now, "you couldn't come with me to the pub tonight, could you? Safety in numbers, and all that. Only it'll be the first time I've seen him in about seven years, and I could do with having a friend there, to stop me doing something stupid."

Outside The Spread Eagle, Alison laid a warning hand on Selena's arm and said: "She's white, by the way."

"Who?"

"My mum."

"So?"

"Some people are surprised, that's all."

"I think I can handle it. As long as she doesn't have two heads or something."

"You know what I mean. I just thought you'd probably be expecting . . ."

"Alison—stay cool. Everything's cool. You need to calm down a bit."

"I know. OK."

Alison nodded her head, and took a few deep breaths, composing herself, trying to find her centre of gravity. She held out her hands, palms downwards, and pushed down as if on a pair of invisible parallel bars.

"Right," she said, after a few moments of this. "I'm ready."

They went inside.

Steve seemed to have lost most of his hair since Alison had seen him last, but apart from that, he looked very much the same. He kissed her on the cheek and gave her a big hug and she had little option but to put up with both of these things. When he went to the bar to get their drinks she could not help noticing how her mother's eyes followed him appraisingly, longingly, and yet she was probably the only person in the pub who would have given this balding, pot-bellied figure a second glance. Alison did her best not to betray her feelings, but inside she was letting out a long, deep sigh of resignation. It was going to happen all over again. Life was all too predictable sometimes.

Another example of this sad truth presented itself just a few minutes later. Her mother went to say something to the girl behind the bar. She was pointing at the little shelf of CDs that were kept there to use as background music, and Alison knew exactly what was coming next. Val's sole top-twenty hit (from twelve years ago) was included on any number of compilation CDs, and sure enough, before long she had persuaded the girl to slot one into the CD player and search forward for the relevant track. Over the pub's PA system the familiar keyboard riff soon blasted out, broken up by an offbeat drum pattern, providing an angular but catchy backdrop to Val's strong, plangent melody, with her three fellow bandmembers oohing and aahing behind her in competent close harmony.

With an apologetic but proud smile at her companions, Val wandered back over to their table. Just in time to hear Selena say:

"Ooh, I *love* this song."

"Really?" Her surprise was obvious. "You know it?"

"It's one of the first things I can remember hearing. My mum used to have it on in the house all the time."

"I wrote it," said Val, and watched thirstily as a respectful amazement transformed Selena's face.

"*You* did? You wrote this?"

"Yeah. That's me singing. I'm *that* Val Doubleday."

Selena didn't actually recognize the name; it was the name of the band that was remembered by those who remembered the song at all. All the same, she was impressed; more impressed than even Val could reasonably have hoped for.

"You sang this on *Top of the Pops,* yeah? I remember the little dance routine."

"Oh, God ... We practised that for *days.*" She set off down a well-worn path of reminiscence, recalling how Louisa, the fourth, blondest and prettiest member of the group, had developed a mental block about their simple dance moves and they'd had to spend the best part of a week in a London dance studio with an increasingly exasperated choreographer. Alison had heard the story many times before, and recognized by now that it took the form of a classic humblebrag: the underlying message being that the four of them may have been ditzy and naive but at the same time, they had been serious players, with the resources of a powerful record company behind them. It was dull having to listen to all of this again, but still, it gave her mother pleasure to tell the story, so she listened with a patient smile on her face and didn't interrupt.

"So what are you doing now?" Selena wanted to know. "Are the four of you still together?"

Val laughed. "No. We split up ages ago. Straight after we did our first album."

"But you're still in the music business, right?"

"Of course. I can't stop writing and singing. It's in my DNA."

"Val's an incredibly creative person," Steve said, sliding a proprietorial arm around her shoulders.

"And guess what?" said Val, looking pointedly at her daughter, whose scepticism remained unspoken but, to everyone around the table, palpable. "Cheryl e-mailed me today about the new song."

"Really? That's great. What does she think?"

"She hasn't had a chance to listen to it yet. But she said she was really looking forward to it."

"Oh, OK. Wow. Well, that's a real breakthrough . . ."

The sarcasm was cruder and more bitter than she had intended. Val looked down, unable to meet her daughter's gaze, and took three or four rapid sips from her gin and tonic.

"Your mother doesn't need that kind of cynicism right now," Steve said.

Alison's eyes lit up angrily. "Why does it matter to you?"

"Because Steve cares about me and my career," said Val. "He's going to get me some downtime in the studio at college, so I can do a better version. You know—he's doing something constructive. Something helpful."

"About that, love," he said, leaning in closer to her. "I've been having a word with Ricky, the engineer, and he reckons that Tuesday evenings would be the best. If you could come in after nine . . ."

Alison only half listened to the rest of their conversation. She could tell that Selena was feeling restless and embarrassed; maybe it had been a selfish idea to bring her here, to thrust her into the middle of this awkward family situation. It angered her, too, to see that Steve was already well on his way to being reinstalled as her mother's confidant. Soon Val had taken out a letter she had been given at work that day—something about a reduction in her working hours—and was discussing it with him.

"The thing is," she was saying, "I can't support the two of us on anything less than I get at the moment. No way. It's just not possible. Especially not with the winter coming up, and fuel bills . . ."

"Don't worry, babes," he said—the arm never leaving her shoulders, staking its claim to ownership ever more tightly—"we'll sort something out. Just give me time to think about it."

Alison's glass was empty. So was Selena's. She didn't suggest buying another round.

"Come on," she said. "I'll walk you to the bus stop."

Selena rose to her feet with every appearance of relief.

As they walked along Warwick Road, bathed in the evening sky's final sunset glow, the smell of chips and kebabs and jerk chicken steaming out from the fast-food outlets, Alison took Selena's arm and said:

"Sorry. That was even more horrible than I was expecting."

"That's OK. But you should have told me you had a famous mum. That's just awesome."

"Well, she's not famous anymore, not by any stretch of the imagination. But she does write good songs still. I try to . . . hold on to that."

"What were she and Steve talking about just now?" Selena asked. "When she was showing him that letter?"

"Something to do with her work. She works in the library in Harborne."

"So that's what she is now, is it? A librarian?"

They had reached Selena's bus stop. They could see the bus in the distance, one set of traffic lights away.

"At the moment, yeah," said Alison. "But even that's not looking good. They're cutting her hours back. Libraries aren't getting the money anymore."

"I thought they were building a big new one in town. Spending millions on it."

"True, but . . . Well, I don't know. Don't ask me how these things work."

She spoke these words unthinkingly, formulaically, as the bus rumbled towards them and her conscious mind dissolved into panic at the thought of what form, exactly, her farewell to Selena should take. A hug, a friendly hand on the arm, a kiss on the cheek? In the event, it was a clumsy mash-up of all these things. The hug lasted longer than either of them had been expecting, and involved a certain amount of affectionate back-rubbing, and they touched cheeks rather than kissing; but in the process Alison's lips brushed against Selena's ear, and the memory of its texture stayed with her for the rest of that evening, along with her delicate, animal scent. As she walked home, she continued to savour them both, and realized that she was singing to herself, over and over, the chorus of her mother's new song:

Still I try to do my best, but I need your breath
As the moonshine controls the water,
I will sink and swim.

*Perry Barr—Handsworth—Winson Green—Bearwood—Harborne—
Selly Oak—Cotteridge—Kings Heath—Hall Green—Acocks Green—
Yardley—Stechford—Fox & Goose—Erdington—Witton—Perry Barr.*

The weeks went by, the days grew shorter and colder, until one day, in early November, a turning point came.

Val's hours had been reduced from four days to three mornings a week.

Her salary was cut in half and she was having to spend more time at home. The house was freezing. She started to worry about her next heating bill. And it was boring, sitting at home by herself all afternoon, watching daytime TV. Boring and lonely.

One Wednesday lunchtime she was coming home from the library on the Number 11 bus. She got on in Harborne and planned to get off close to her home in Yardley, a journey of some twenty-five minutes. But as she approached her stop, she changed her mind. The bus was warm; her house was cold. The bus was full of people; her house was empty. The view from her seat on the bus was ever-changing; the views from her house were monotonous. Suddenly she felt no inclination at all to get up from her comfortable seat and step out into the cold.

It was 1:15. A complete circuit of the city would bring her back to this same spot at 3:45. So that was what she did, and that was what she soon got into the habit of doing every day. Every working day, at first, but then, before long, she found that she was doing it on Tuesdays and Thursdays as well. Sometimes clockwise, sometimes anti-clockwise. Two and a half hours in which nothing was required of her, except to sit still, to watch the comings and goings of the other passengers, and to allow her thoughts to drift in spiralling patterns which mirrored the bus's slow, circular progress.

Yardley—Stechford—Fox & Goose—

Why was her house so cold? Because she couldn't afford to keep the radiators on all day. And even when they were on, she didn't turn them up to 5 anymore, the way she used to when winter came. Nowadays she never turned them higher than 2. Why not? Because the library couldn't afford to pay her properly. Because the government had drastically reduced its budget for libraries. Because we were now all living—apparently—in an age of "austerity."

—*Fox & Goose—Erdington—Witton—Perry Barr—Handsworth—*

This new buzzword—austerity—had only entered common currency about a year ago. What did it mean? In 2008 there had been a global financial crisis and some of the world's largest banks had been on the point of collapse. The people had bailed them out and now, it seemed, in order to pay for this, public services would have to be slashed and benefits would have to be cut. But it was worth it because we had been living beyond our means and we were "all in this together."

—*Handsworth—Winson Green—Bearwood—*

And this, essentially, was why Val was now being careful never to turn her radiators up higher than 2 and was choosing to ride round and round the outer circle on the Number 11 bus rather than go home to her chilly living room. But at the same time, she couldn't help thinking about the traders and fund managers whose activities had brought the banks to the brink of collapse: Were many of them, she wondered, being careful to keep their radiators turned down to 2? It didn't seem very likely.

—*Bearwood—Harborne—Selly Oak—*

The thought made her angry and depressed. The fact that she was angry and depressed made her feel guilty. It couldn't be much fun for Alison, living with a mother who was angry and depressed all the time. What could she do to stop herself from feeling angry and depressed?

—*Selly Oak—Cotteridge—Kings Heath—*

Last night she had watched a TV panel show where a popular comedian, Mickey Parr, had gone off on a satirical riff about bankers still getting bonuses even after the banks had had to be bailed out by the government, and the studio audience had been in stitches. They all seemed to think the situation was hilarious. Val had sat on the sofa with her glass of Pinot Grigio and watched the routine through a puzzled frown. Why did people think it was funny? Why did it not make them angry and depressed?

—*Kings Heath—Hall Green—Acocks Green—Yardley*

She was still pondering that one as the bus reached her stop at last, after a longer than usual journey of two hours and forty minutes. It was three o'clock in the afternoon. Before getting off she hesitated very briefly, wondering if she should stay on for another circuit, but even Val realized that would be a step too far. So she disembarked and went straight to the supermarket, to try and find something different (but cheap) that she and Alison could have for dinner. It was on the short walk home from there that her mobile rang, heralding the call from Cheryl that would transform her life.

Alison had been to the pub with Selena again, and was late home. It was after 9:30 when she let herself in. She went into the kitchen and found that her mother's shopping was still sitting unpacked on the kitchen table. From the living room she could hear the sound of the television.

She picked out the first thing she could find in the shopping bag. It was a small plastic packet, on the front of which were the words "HAPPEE CHICKEN BITES," accompanied by a cartoon picture of a purple chicken with a cheeky smile on its face, biting its own leg off. Alison turned the packet over and read the small print at the bottom. "Manufactured by Sunbeam Foods," it said. "Part of the Brunwin Group."

She took the packet into the living room. "What is this, Mum? Are you taking the piss or something?"

Val jumped to her feet. "Where the *hell* have you been?" she said. "I've been trying to contact you for hours."

"Sorry, my phone battery ran out." She was almost having to shout over the sound of the television, it was turned up so loud. "Can you mute that? Why are you watching that shit anyway?"

Val was watching a famous reality show in which a dozen celebrities were flown off to the Australian jungle and had to survive there for two weeks, while the viewing public voted them off the programme one by one. It wasn't the kind of show she would have bothered with in the past, but nowadays it seemed she would watch almost anything.

"Why am I watching it?" Val turned and pointed at the screen. Her face was flushed, her pointing finger was shaking. "You want to know why I'm watching it? I'm watching it *because I'm going to be on it.*"

Her eyes were wide with an excitement she was waiting for Alison to reciprocate. But the words she had just spoken made no sense to her daughter. Alison recognized them all, individually, but her brain could not put them together into a meaningful sentence.

"What are you talking about?" was all she could say.

"Cheryl rang up this afternoon. I thought it might be about the song, but . . . anyway, this is nearly as good. They want me to go on the show. *This show.*"

After opening and closing her mouth ineffectually a few more times, Alison managed to ask: "When?"

"The day after tomorrow," said Val, and laughed wildly. "I know. It's amazing, isn't it? They want to bring someone new in halfway through the series and the person they'd booked has dropped out. So they called Cheryl and said they were desperate to find someone and she suggested me."

"Desperate?"

"Well . . . no, that wasn't the word. Anxious, or something. It might have been desperate. I don't know. Anyway, that's not the point. In three days' time, I'm going to be in *that* camp. With *those* people."

Alison stared at her mother, utterly nonplussed. In fact neither of them could speak now: but the moment of release, when it finally came, was euphoric. It wasn't long before they found themselves shrieking with excitement, and dancing together around the room until Val lost her balance, fell heavily against her daughter's artificial leg and they collapsed on to the sofa in a heap, tears of joy running down their faces.

2

Val sat in the middle of her hammock, trying to get used to its wobble, trying to keep her balance. She looked around her at the camp. She didn't know what time it was: mid-afternoon, maybe. It was difficult to keep track, since none of them were allowed to wear watches. Most of her campmates were asleep, or trying to sleep at least. There was nothing much else to do in this heat. Edith, the elderly soap star, was flat on her back, one arm dangling over the edge of her hammock, snoring gently. Roger, the celebrity TV historian, was curled into a foetal position with his back to her, a river of sweat visible through his shorts at the cleft of his buttocks. Pete, the genial reality TV star from Manchester, had one hand on his crotch and the other behind his head. Only Danielle, the endlessly lovely, the beautiful Danielle, seemed to be keeping her composure and her dignity. She lay on her back, perfectly still, her hands folded on her belly, breathing evenly, the only traces of sweat being a few beads on the upper slopes of her breasts, which did nothing but add to her carefully tousled allure. Her tan was smooth and even and she seemed to have applied concealer to the two or three mosquito bites on her face and neck, despite the nominal ban on makeup in the camp. She had a way of getting around these things.

For her own part, Val felt like shit, and knew that she probably looked it as well. Before arriving here she had resolved always to look her best for the cameras, but had already given up on that idea. Really, would anyone care what she looked like? The important thing—as Alison had said—was to "be yourself, because then everyone will like you." That, and to make sure that she got to sing "Sink and Swim" to the show's ten million viewers at some point. Although the last thing she felt like doing, at this moment, was bursting into song.

It wasn't that she was jetlagged, exactly. The worst of the jetlag, she was told, would kick in after the journey back to England. This was simply a profound sense of disorientation. Five days ago she had been at home in Yardley, a place she had not left—apart from a few days' holiday here and there, always with Alison, always within the British Isles—for several years. But an incredible amount had happened in those last five days. So much so that now, already, she could hardly remember the events in sequence. There had been . . .

. . . the mad dash down to London for two emergency meetings. The first had been at the offices of the production company, Stercus Television. A young, brittle production assistant called Suzanne had met her at reception and led her upstairs into the Hilary Winshaw suite, named after the legendary executive who had joined the company in the early 1990s and transformed its fortunes by taking it in its present cost-efficient, populist direction, with 90 per cent of its output in the field of reality shows. Here she was briefed on her travel arrangements, given contracts to sign and told that Suzanne would be flying out to Australia with her and would not leave her side until the helicopter flight into the jungle itself. The second had been in the consulting rooms of a Harley Street doctor. He gave her a quick examination, and an even quicker psychiatric assessment. "You did tell them," Alison had asked when she got home that evening, "that you're terrified of insects?" One of the questions they had put to her, it was true, was whether she suffered from any phobias, but Val had said no, fearing that otherwise she would not be allowed to take part. "Well, that was bloody stupid," Alison had said. "What are you going to do when they start getting you to eat cockroaches?" "Why would they do that?" Val had asked, to which Alison said, "Have you ever *seen* this bloody programme, before last night?", leading to another tremendous row which went stratospheric when her mother had informed her that Stercus were paying for one companion to fly out to Australia with her, and she was taking not Alison but Steve . . .

. . . the taxi drive to Heathrow the next morning. Steve clasping her hand as she sat in the back seat, shaking with nervousness and expectation, the beige conurbations of Banbury, Bicester, High Wycombe, Hemel Hempstead swirling past on their way down the M40 . . .

. . . the sheer, unimaginable joy of flying first class, the pamperedness of it, the dry marzipan richness of the free champagne, the quantity and variety of the free food, the things they had never tasted before, the caviar, the foie gras, the carpaccio of bluefin tuna, the fillet of Kobe steak, the thin ribbons of pasta in truffle sauce, and finally the thirty-year-old single malt which had sent them into a deep, restful sleep, the depth and restfulness of this sleep being made possible by the welcoming embrace of the fold-down beds, and by the soothing ministrations of the cabin crew, who did pretty much everything but massage their toes, stroke their hair and sing them lullabies . . .

. . . the dazzling whiteness of the light as soon as they stepped off the plane at Brisbane, a light they had not experienced, had not even been able to imagine, while living in Birmingham, and then the excitement of having a cluster of young, enthusiastic people from the production company waiting for them in the arrivals hall, and a couple of dozen journalists and paparazzi. The thrill of being recognized again, of no longer feeling invisible . . .

. . . the wonderful, trashy opulence of the beachside hotel outside Brisbane, to which they were taken by limo. The mindboggling acreage of bedroom, sitting room and bathroom—altogether about twice the size of Val's house in Yardley—all done out with magnificent vulgarity . . .

. . . a vulgarity which was carried over to the poolside restaurant where they had their first dinner in this amazing new continent and met some of their fellow guests: Mr. and Mrs. Perry, the parents of Danielle, the gorgeous young glamour model who was favourite to win the competition this series; Mary Walker, the mother of Pete Walker, the reality TV star, and her younger sister Jacqui. "So Pete and Danielle were allowed to bring two people over with them, were they?" Val had asked Suzanne, and Suzanne had nodded but offered no explanation, giving Val her first intimation that perhaps there was a hierarchy among the contestants on this show, and she was not going to be at the top of it. But she had brushed this mildly troubling thought aside, and instead found herself enjoying the company of these people, enjoying the feeling of being part of a chosen few, an elite, transplanted from mundanity into paradise, and she soon warmed to Mary and Jacqui, who remembered her hit single and agreed with her that this show was just what she needed to reboot her career, and she didn't warm to Danielle's parents quite so much, in fact she and Steve agreed afterwards that they were rather strange, especially when Val ordered a Caesar salad and when it arrived Mrs. Perry burst into tears, because apparently Caesar had been the name of their boxer dog, and he had died just a couple of days before they'd flown out to Australia, after twelve years of living with them, and that was a bit weird, the way a salad made her burst into tears, but anyway, they both sympathized, and put it down to the champagne, of which they had all drunk about a bottle and a half each by the time they made it upstairs to bed . . .

. . . the helicopter ride the next day, which had been the real start of the adventure. She had kissed Steve good-bye and said—for the first time in seven years or so—"Love you" (which he had answered by hugging her and whispering "Good luck, babes"). Before she had climbed into the helicopter, a sound engineer had clipped a microphone to the lapel of her jungle outfit and Val was told that anything she said from this point onwards would be recorded and could potentially be broadcast. She tried not to swear, or to say anything too inane, or to scream too loudly as they took off. She had never been in one of these things before and it was, at first, predictably terrifying. But the journey, which she had imagined would take at least an hour, plunging ever deeper into impenetrable rain forest, turned out to be quite short—only ten minutes or so—because the camp was really only a few miles from the hotel, in what looked from the air like rather a tame stretch of national park. The pilot had made a lot of unnecessary swoops and dives, to get her screaming and to make their arrival look more dramatic, but then she was deposited safely in the middle of the forest and there was a guide on hand to walk her towards the camp . . .

. . . her entry into the camp. What had she been expecting? Whoops of recognition? Hardly. But something more, certainly, than the palpable sense of indifference when she walked into the clearing.

"Hi everybody!" she had cooed, embarrassed to hear how needy her own voice sounded already. It took about ten minutes to explain to everybody who she was, and then it transpired that only two of her campmates—the oldest two, as it happened—remembered her, her hit record or her fleeting appearances on *Top of the Pops*. Apparently there had been a rumour going around that the star of a hit sitcom from the 1990s was coming to join the camp, and they were all a bit deflated to discover that this wasn't the case. (Val guessed that this was the person she had been called in to replace, although she had been told to keep quiet on that subject.) After that it seemed there was nothing much she was expected to do except settle in. The prevailing atmosphere among the celebrities, she noticed, was one of intense boredom. Everyone seemed to be suffering from exhaustion, brought on by a combination of heat, humidity and hunger. All that anyone could think of, and talk about, was the evening meal, which consisted of ungenerous portions of unflavoured rice and beans: in fact tonight's portion would be especially small, as Edith, the elderly soap star, had failed dismally at today's "trial." The purpose of these trials was to entertain the public by torturing and humiliating the celebrities, making them perform various revolting tasks in order to obtain food for their campmates: tasks which usually involved being put into confined spaces with large numbers of insects, snakes or other jungle creatures which presumably found the experience just as distressing as the human participants.

Val had not thought too much about what would happen if she was made to perform one of these trials herself. The choice of celebrity was down to the viewing public, who usually picked on the most obnoxious and made him, or her, go through the ordeal day after day. Since she was determined to be cheerful, likeable and friendly to everyone, no matter what the circumstances, she was confident that it wouldn't happen to her. And now, in fact, was the perfect opportunity to put this resolve into practice: for Danielle had just glanced over towards her and offered her a weak smile and a tiny wave of the hand, a tentative but unmistakable invitation to conversation. With a slow, effortful heave, pushing against the humid air as if it was a cushion of dampness pressing down upon her, Val rose from her hammock and wandered over to chat with the exquisite young model. She was keenly aware, as she did so, of how flawless Danielle's beauty was, how ragged and dowdy she herself must appear by comparison. And the age difference between them was such that she could easily have been the girl's mother. Perhaps that, then, should be the keynote of their relationship: her attitude towards her should be motherly. She should try to be friendly, caring and protective, offering advice and wisdom as well as companionship. Val knew that she must already have made a good impression on the viewing public. This approach could only make them like her even more.

Back in Yardley, Alison sat at the kitchen table with a pile of newspapers in front of her, skimming through the early press coverage of her mother's arrival in the camp.

SHE'S A NONENTITY—GET HER OUT OF THERE was a typical headline.

"As the latest 'celebrity' makes her underwhelming entry into the jungle camp," the article began, "viewers up and down the country are asking the same question: *Who the hell is Val Doubleday?*"

AREN'T THESE PEOPLE SUPPOSED TO BE FAMOUS? another headline asked.

REVEALED, another one boasted: *JUNGLE "CELEBRITY" IS ACTUALLY PART-TIME* **LIBRARIAN**.

"In its heyday," Alison read, "contestants on this show used to fall into two types: has-beens and wannabes.

"But now ageing single mother Val Doubleday (or Crabs as she is already known to the production team) represents a whole new category: never-was-in-the-first-place."

Alison winced for the first time. "Crabs," her mother had once told her in a confiding moment, used to be her nickname at school: a cruel playground twist on the initials V. D. It was alarming to learn that it had been revived by people working for this programme, and had leaked to the newspapers already. This felt ominous, somehow.

Alison pushed the papers aside and turned to her laptop. Before her mother had left for Australia, the two of them had set up a Twitter account for her. They had discussed whether to use a recent photograph or one from Val's singing days, and had finally compromised by combining an up-to-date profile picture with a screengrab of her old *Top of the Pops* appearance, stretching across the top of the page as a banner photo. It all looked very smart and professional. For the first day or two the account had attracted no attention at all, but as soon as the first news of Val's participation was published, a trickle of followers appeared, and now the number had swelled to 4,752. Alison was keeping the notifications page permanently open, and she now noticed that there had been 319 new messages. Excitedly, she began to scroll through them.

The first one said:

Who the fuck are you bitch?

Followed by:

Never heard of you
U r well ugly
Yawn Bored with her already
I remember ur song it was shite
Vote her off! The campaign starts here #getridofVal
Your face makes me ill
U r well old
Ugh what a witch
Ha ha cunt

And so on, for tweet after tweet. After she had looked through the first one hundred messages or so, Alison decided it was time she started blocking most of the posters. It took a couple of hours to block all of the most offensive ones, not least because new tweets started appearing almost as fast as she could block them. At the end of it she felt somehow soiled, as if she had spent the morning scrubbing out a toilet without wearing rubber gloves. And still the new messages continued to appear. She was fighting a losing battle. For the time being she gave up, and went into college to check out the afternoon lectures.

A sense of unreality, of weightlessness, persisted for the rest of the day. Riding home that evening on the Number 11 bus, Alison struggled to understand that her mother was ten thousand miles away, on the other side of the world, probably asleep beneath an Australian sky in the company of a dozen people she had never met before. Her life for the last few years had been so circumscribed: how on earth would she be coping? The last piece of news she'd heard had been a text from Steve, saying "Just seen Val whisked off by helicopter, jungle-bound. That's it for a few days then!" To which she had not replied. So now she had only her own imagination to rely upon, and it was not equal to the task. Perhaps it would be best to put the whole thing out of her mind, if possible, until nine o'clock that evening, when the edited highlights of Val's first day in the camp would go out on national television.

By five to nine she was ready on the sofa, with a big plate of brown rice and stir-fried vegetables, waiting for the programme to start. The sound on the television was muted for the adverts and it was striking how silent the house seemed, how empty, without even her mother's subdued, untalkative presence. Alison missed her, more than she would ever have imagined possible. Would watching her on TV be the next best thing?

Sixty minutes later, she was not sure what she had just seen. Very little of her mother, that was for sure: her total contribution to the programme, including the footage of her arrival in camp, could not have amounted to more than two or three minutes. The moment when she turned up and called out "Hi everybody!" seemed especially lame: the cameras lingered heartlessly on the scene for what seemed like forever, revelling in the silence that followed her greeting, zooming in to pick up the eagerness in her eyes and then, seconds later, the disappointment that clouded them. She looked so small and old, Alison thought. How could she not have noticed that before? And had she always walked with that half-stoop? Her posture was terrible. After that, in any case, she more or less disappeared from the programme, most of which was devoted to prolonged shots of Danielle the glamour model and Pete the reality star showering in their swimwear. Val made only one more appearance. She was seen chatting with Danielle on her hammock in the afternoon, while the other campmates slept.

VAL: . . . I thought there might be a bit more of a fuss when I arrived, that's all.

DANIELLE: I think everyone's just a bit tired, you know? Don't worry about it.

VAL: For me, it was a bit of an anti-climax, after the helicopter and everything.

DANIELLE: A bit of a damp squid, yeah . . .

VAL: (*after a beat*) Squib, you mean.

DANIELLE: What?

VAL: That's the expression—"damp squib."

DANIELLE: Oh, I see. So you're correcting me?

VAL: Well, a lot of people get it wrong.

DANIELLE: I thought it was "squid" because, you know, squids live underwater, so they're probably quite damp.

VAL: Yes, you'd think so. But it's actually squib.

DANIELLE: Oh. OK. (*a beat*) Well, thanks for putting me right about that.

When the programme was over, Alison sat for a while on the sofa, staring at the blank TV screen. Watching the show had been one of the strangest experiences of her life. She knew her mother intimately: better—far better—than she knew anyone else in the world. And the woman on the television had recognizably been her mother. And yet, in the very occasional glimpses of her which the programme had afforded, it had also been like watching a stranger. She had seen her as the cameras had seen her, and as the people editing the show had seen her, and these perspectives, she thought, were unforgiving. They were unfiltered by love.

As for Twitter, there was not much love for Val to be found on there this evening.

Omg she is so dull
Get this woman off my fucking tv screen
Join the campaign #getridofVal
Fucksake what a bitch
How many blowjobs did you have to give to get on this show
Grammar nazi!

Lay off Danielle
Correcting Danielle who the fuck do you think you are
How dare you speak like that to Danielle you ugly old sow
Anvil faced mare #getridofVal
Get back to your library and leave Danielle alone
#teamDanielle
Fuck off back to ur libary
Squid squib who gives a fuck apart from some dried-up librarian
Fucking bitch the viewers are going to make you suffer for that

Again, Alison spent an hour or two blocking the most offensive people. Again, she felt as impotent as Canute trying to hold back the tide. Her mother's account had 6,111 followers now, she noticed. Not bad, except that Pete's had 314,566, and Danielle's was fast approaching one million.

The odds, she couldn't help feeling, were stacking up against her.

Beneath a dark-blue, starry sky, Val sat in the shadow of a eucalyptus tree, alone. Her hands were clasped tightly around her knees, and her knees were pulled up to her chin. In this position, curled into a ball, she rocked backward and forward, eyes closed, allowing herself a few cathartic sobs. She hoped that nobody would see her, although presumably there was at least one camera trained on her, somewhere or other. They were everywhere: hidden in hollowed-out tree trunks, or in secret cavities inside the rocks; mounted on retractable poles sprouting from within the greenery. There was no privacy, none at all. Of course, she had forfeited that when she had agreed to take part. But still, she had never imagined that it would be this hard . . .

Backward and forward she rocked, forward and backward. She tried to remember the meditation techniques her yoga instructor had once taught her, but that was a long time ago. They would be no use anyway. The images she was trying to purge were overwhelming, immovable, and made it impossible to call anything else to mind. They were banal images, at first, from earlier in the day: late morning, early afternoon, something like that. Daylight anyway. Bright sunshine. First of all, the clearing into which her guide had led her. The table at which she had been required to sit down. The perspex tank which had been placed on the table, and inside it . . . Oh God. The insect, the . . . *thing*, the . . . what was it called? A "Goliath stick insect," the programme's two chortling hosts had informed her. For Christ's sake, the thing had been at least six inches long. A vivid, sickly green. Six thin, gangly legs, a long torso carapaced in some hard matter, solid and unyielding, and at the end of it . . . the *head*, uncannily (save for the two antennae) like a little human head, the beady eyes staring up at her, alert, vital but inscrutable. (The expression of terror she thought she could see there being an example, presumably—at least, please God, let it be so—of pure anthropomorphism.) And then she had been obliged to put on a pair of plastic goggles (she was still not sure why), and then screw her eyes tightly shut, and then the "insect wrangler" (yes, there really was somebody with that job description) had taken the poor, revolting creature, and Val had opened her mouth wide, and then the thing was inside her, inside her mouth, she could *feel* it, feel it wriggling, struggling frantically, its obscenely long legs flailing against her tongue and the roof of her mouth, her mouth which had become a prison, a cage for this animal . . . Almost at once she could feel the gorge rising in her throat and she had felt an incredible urge to gag and open her mouth and expel the insect on to the table in front of her, but she knew that for every ten seconds she kept it inside her, her campmates would be given a portion of food, and she didn't want to let them down. Now it was wriggling and thrashing even more violently inside there, and trying to escape out the back by forcing itself down her throat, but Val just screwed her eyes even tighter—her eyes from which tears of distress were starting to leak—and closed her mouth ever more firmly. Even then part of the insect, one of its legs perhaps, must still have been protruding, because now one of the chortling hosts said, "Come on, Val, be a sport, you've got to get the whole thing in there," and his co-host had giggled and said, "Ooh, I bet it's been quite a while since a fella said that to you, eh, Val?" and the whole crew had started laughing, but it was only now, in retrospect, that she realized the leering offensiveness of what they had said, at the time she was just training all her energy on the task of not gagging, not vomiting, of keeping her eyes and her lips closed, trying to ignore the scrabble of long, angular, insectile legs kicking inside her mouth, until, suddenly, the creature became still. And then Val thought, Oh my God, have I killed it?, but this thought only lasted for a second or two because then she felt something else in her mouth, something liquid, and a taste—Christ—a taste fouler and more vile than anything she had ever tasted or imagined tasting, and she realized that the stick insect was shitting itself inside her mouth, literally shitting itself with fear, and as she felt the first trickle of liquid excrement sliding down her throat, her stomach heaved and her gorge rose and with a loud, choking gurgle she spat the insect out onto the table, followed by a thin trail of drool, after which she must have . . . if not passed out, exactly, at least lost all awareness of what was happening around her, because she did not remember the cheers and applause of the hosts or the crew, she remembered nothing until she was sitting up in a chair, wrapped in a blanket, drinking mouthful after mouthful of water and swilling it around and spitting it out in a desperate attempt to get rid of that taste, that hideous taste which was coming back to her even now and making her want to gag again . . .

Val rolled over on to her hands and knees, crawled towards a clump of ferns and vomited, as quietly as she could. Thanks to her failure at the trial, her dinner that evening had been meagre—just a handful of rice and beans—and now all of it had come back up. Still, she felt better for it. Another few minutes to compose herself, and she might be ready to rejoin the others. The sooner the better, because she needed to talk to Danielle. She had spoken too sharply to her after dinner. Made some comment about her not helping with the washing-up. Val had been in the right, no doubt about that— Danielle was lazy, she never helped out with any of the routine tasks around the camp—but it had sounded snappy, and she didn't want to upset her: or, of course, to alienate the viewers at home. As soon as she felt better again, she would go and apologize.

Danielle was not in the camp. She was lying with Pete in a clearing, about fifty yards away. They were both flat on their backs, staring up at the stars through the canopy of trees. Danielle's face, as so often, was without expression. Pete looked bored and restless.

"Oh, sorry, I didn't mean to intrude," said Val.

"That's all right," he said, sitting up. "Did you want a word?"

"Yes—with Danielle, actually."

"No probs," he said. "I need a dump anyway."

He got up and left. Val squatted down beside Danielle, and said: "Hello, lovey. I didn't break up a romantic moment, did I?"

Danielle inclined her perfect head a few degrees. "Don't worry. No chance of romance with him, as far as I'm concerned. He's a tosser. We were only doing it because the director keeps telling us to look more romantic with each other."

Val nodded, not really knowing what to say to this. She was surprised to hear that they had been getting instructions from the "director." She didn't even know that there was such a person.

"What did you want anyway?" Danielle asked.

"It's about the washing-up."

Danielle turned away from her again and looked blankly up at the sky. "Yeah? What about it?"

"I just came to say . . . I'm sorry if I was a bit rude to you. You're not angry, are you?"

"You didn't show me much respect in front of the others," Danielle said, pouting. "I know I'm younger than you, but, you know, I think I deserve to be treated in a certain way . . ."

"I *was* respectful, actually," said Val. "I mean, I could have said, 'Oh, come on, you lazy cow, when are you going to start pulling your weight around here?' Couldn't I? But I would never talk to you like that."

"I suppose . . ." said Danielle. She was softening.

"I mean, we've all got to do our bit, that's all, if we're going to get through the next couple of weeks. 'We're all in this together,' as our beloved Mr. Osborne would say."

"Who?"

"George Osborne. The Chancellor of the Exchequer?" Danielle's face showed no comprehension, and Val could not stop herself from laughing. "Oh, Danielle, you really are the limit. What planet do you live on? Eh? Don't you ever read the newspapers?"

"I don't have time."

"You should make time. Everyone should know what's going on in the world."

"I work hard, you know. I'm in the gym at six thirty every day. And then all day, I'm either on a shoot or in a recording studio."

"Recording studio?"

"Yeah. I'm a singer. That's what I really want to be. I'm making a record at the moment, but, you know, it takes a long time to get the notes right and everything. I haven't been trained, or anything like that."

"Do you play an instrument?"

"I can play 'Yellow Submarine' on the guitar. You know, the Beatles' old song."

Val felt a sudden wave of tenderness towards her. She looked so young; and not just young but lonely, and vulnerable.

"Bet you miss all that at the moment, don't you?"

"I miss *everything*," said Danielle. "It's horrible in here. They keep making me do tasks with Pete and everything because they've sold lots of stories to the magazines about our big romance, but we can't stand each other. I don't like any of the people in here. They're all old and boring. I want to go home. I miss my Mom and Dad. I miss my sister. And the one I miss the most—the one I *really* miss—is Caesar. Our boxer dog."

"Oh, I know, love," said Val, putting a sympathetic hand to her shoulder. "I heard about that. Your Mom told me just before I came in. It's awful, isn't it, when a pet dies. I had a cat called Byron, and when he passed away—"

"What?" said Danielle, sitting up and staring at her. "What are you talking about?"

Val put her hand to her mouth. "Oh my God. You didn't know."

"Has something happened to Caesar? What's happened to him? *Tell me!*"

After that, Val had no choice but to break the news to her, and, as soon as she heard it, Danielle burst into tears. She sobbed in Val's arms for a few minutes, and Val dabbed at her eyes with a tissue, which was soon soaked through.

"Sorry—I've spoiled your Kleenex," was the first thing Danielle said, when she was able to talk again.

"Never mind—I'll go and get some more," said Val. She gave what she hoped was a comforting laugh, trying to lighten the mood. "There's plenty more where that came from."

As she set off on this errand, she threw one glance back, and saw that Danielle was gazing after her, her face not quite as blank as usual. Her baby blue eyes were now limpid pools of sadness, her lovely young face streaked with tears.

"*Shit*," said Alison. "*SHIT!* Mum, you fucking idiot—what are you playing at? What did you go and do that for?"

She sat forward on the sofa, gripping the remote control so tightly that it might have cracked in her hand. Panic seized her; her breathing accelerated rapidly; she was starting to hyperventilate. Not wishing to listen to the show's closing theme tune, she muted the TV, rose to her feet and began to pace the room, doing her best to slow down her breaths. On the screen, telephone numbers for voting off the different contestants scrolled by silently. Finally Alison paused in front of the television, turned it off, put her head in her hands and said to herself, one more time: "Oh Mum, why did you have to *do* that?"

It had been bad enough watching her mother perform the trial, having to put that huge creature into her mouth and hold it there while everyone around her stood watching and laughing. She knew that Val was afraid of every kind of insect. The terror and revulsion had been written all over her face, but as far as the programme makers (and, Alison supposed, the viewers) were concerned, that just made the whole thing funnier. But then, after that, at the end of the programme . . . the conversation between her mother and Danielle: how had that happened? What the hell was going on there?

Val had spoken a little sharply to Danielle after dinner. She had asked her to help with the washing-up, and pointed out that she didn't do much work around the camp generally. Danielle had looked offended, and had wandered off to lie down with Pete, at some distance from the camp. Then a few minutes later, Val had interrupted them, apparently with a view to renewing her complaint. The conversation as broadcast had gone like this:

VAL: I didn't break up a romantic moment, did I?
DANIELLE: Don't worry. What did you want anyway?
VAL: It's about the washing-up.
DANIELLE: Yeah? What about it? You didn't show me much respect in front of the others. I know I'm younger than you, but, you know, I think I deserve to be treated in a certain way . . .
VAL: Oh, come on, you lazy cow, when are you going to start pulling your weight around here?

(Close-up on Danielle's face, shocked.)

VAL: What planet do you live on? Eh?

(Another close-up on Danielle, who now bursts into tears. Val immediately walks off.)

VAL: *(glancing back, laughing)* There's plenty more where that came from.

(Close-up on Danielle gazing after her, her face streaked with tears.)

Alison didn't dare check on Twitter that night. She went straight to bed, and after lying awake for an hour or two, wondering what demon could have possessed her mother out there in the Australian jungle, provoking such an outburst of rudeness and casual cruelty, she fell at last into a fitful sleep. But it didn't last long. She was awake by six o'clock, and after making herself a double-strength cup of instant coffee, she fired up her laptop.

The news was bad. Terrible, in fact. Her mother's account was haemorrhaging followers—she was down to just over 3,000—and the abusive messages now seemed to be coming in at the rate of four or five every minute. Most of them had the hashtag *#teamdanielle*, and it was fair to say that the model's million followers were not happy with what they'd seen on the television last night.

Bitch from hell
Fuck off I want to kill you
You are just a fucking big bully ugly cow
Hello Crabs I hope you get vd youself but that wd mean some1
wd have to fuck you 1st so not very likely haha
You made our angel cry we will make you suffer bitch
Have never hated someone like I hate u. Hope u die of cancer
Fuck you cunt
You big cunt bully. You deserve to be raped
till your dried out old gash is sore and bleeding

Alison felt physically sick when she read that: she had to go to the bathroom and kneel in front of the toilet for a few minutes, convinced she was going to throw up. Nothing came, though: just dry retching. After that, reluctantly, out of filial duty and nothing more, she forced herself to do some more quick searching. She looked her mother up on Google Images, and where once she would have found a few ancient publicity shots and grabs from her *Top of the Pops* routine, there were already hundreds of new pictures. Where had they all come from, and how had they been uploaded so quickly? Most of them were from yesterday's trial: horrid, grotesque close-ups of her mother's face, every pore and wrinkle showing, her eyes screwed up behind those plastic goggles and her face contorted in a mixture of terror and loathing as she took the stick insect into her mouth. Pictures from the last few moments of the trial, showing her bent double over the table while retching, with a trail of vaguely green-coloured drool dangling from her lips, seemed to be especially popular. But there was nothing that Val, or Alison, or anybody else, would be able to do about this. This was how her mother was going to be remembered online, from now on.

It was all too depressing to contemplate. Alison glanced briefly at Google News, where she learned that, according to a new poll, her mother was now the most unpopular contestant in the show's ten-year history, and then she went back to bed.

Val warmed her hands at the fire, smiled around at her fellow campers and felt a spreading glow of happiness. Today had been a wonderful day. Really relaxing and enjoyable. First of all, Dino, the handsome and relentlessly macho TV chef from New York who was the show's token American presence, had been voted to undergo the daily trial. It was something to do with gathering plastic stars from the floor of a water tank filled with eels, and he had done spectacularly well, which meant not only that they'd all had a full complement of food that evening, but after dinner—any minute now, in fact—they were also to be provided with a surprise "luxury" item. Naturally, this had put everyone in a good mood. In the afternoon, chilling out in their hammocks, Val and Roger the historian had struck up a conversation, a proper conversation, which started by being about the British weather but had then somehow turned to the coalition government and whether it really had a mandate from the voters. It had been the first real *discussion*, the first time anyone in the camp had actually talked about something important, since Val had arrived three (was it three?) days ago, and had proved so interesting that after a while everybody joined in, even Pete and Danielle; both of whom were amazed to hear that Britain had a coalition government at all, since this piece of news seemed to have passed them by last year, and indeed Val still wasn't at all sure that either of them had really grasped the concept of a coalition despite a good deal of patient explanation from Roger. Anyway, that was by the by. It wasn't a great victory, maybe, but this conversation had been a small step towards bringing everyone together, creating a more cooperative atmosphere, which Val had decided was her true role in the camp. And now she could see the result: for the first time, all twelve of them were sitting around the fire after dinner, chatting and telling stories. True, it was pretty inane stuff, but she was not really listening. She was content to let the chatter wash over her, becoming one with the other noises of the forest at night: the mysterious rustles in the undergrowth, the chirruping of cicadas, the occasional distant, plangent cry of some unknown inhabitant of the nocturnal jungle. Such a long way from Yardley! Such a privilege, when all was said and done, to be here at all! She knew now that she would always treasure this experience, whatever came of it.

Just then they heard footsteps on the edge of the camp.

"Hey up, that must be our surprise," said Pete, and rose to his feet. He went off to investigate, and came back a few seconds later carrying an acoustic steel-string guitar tied up in pink ribbon. "Look at this—brilliant!" he said. "Can anybody play it?"

The guitar kept them entertained for a further couple of hours. Val was the only real musician in the camp, and she was happy to play until her wrist was aching and the tips of her fingers felt as though they were about to bleed. They sang songs by Dylan, Stevie Wonder, Madonna and the Kinks; they crooned their way through "House of the Rising Sun," "Scarborough Fair" and "Dancing Queen." Her only respite came for a few minutes when Danielle insisted on attempting her version of "Yellow Submarine," with Pete on backing vocals. It was hard to say which was worse, her playing or her singing, and neither of them could remember the words to the verses, but everyone was feeling so cheerful by then that the whole thing was just carried through on a wave of laughter. It put them all in an even better mood than before.

Eventually they ran out of songs. At which point, Val asked: "Do you mind if I play you something that I wrote?"

Nobody minded. Everyone was eager to hear it.

"It's not the song I'm famous for. It's a new one."

"Ooh, lovely," said Danielle.

"It's not very jolly," said Val. "In fact it's quite sad and . . . sort of introspective."

"Stop apologizing and get on with it," said Roger.

"All right."

She smiled around at them all, nervously, suddenly remembering that she was addressing not just an audience of eleven friends (she thought of them as her friends now) but more than ten million television viewers. This was, in effect, the most important performance of her life. But she felt up to the task. If she could do that thing with the stick insect, after all, she could do pretty much anything. And she knew this song intimately: it was part of her body, by now. Singing it to these people would be as natural as drawing breath.

The fingers of her left hand arranged themselves to form the first chord—an F major seven, with an open A-string as the bass note—and with the thumb of her right hand she struck the six strings of the guitar with firm, tender authority.

Watch the water take me home, absence makes me fonder
Choose a path where you can go, days are getting longer

She knew at once that she had caught their attention. A great stillness had descended on the camp. The music brought everything to a halt: the passage of time was suspended. Val reached for the highest note in the melody, found it easily.

Still I try to do my best but I need your breath
As the moonshine controls the water, I will sink and swim

The two chords underpinning the word "swim" were a D minor and then a darker and more ambiguous F minor sixth. Val had been singing without thinking until this point, vocalizing the words in a semi-automatic state, but with the next lines, she realized that she could almost be reflecting on her current situation:

Turn around and look at me, in many ways I'm stronger
Choose a path and set me free, to beyond and yonder

It was true: this experience had made her stronger. Started to restore her confidence, her confidence which had been shattered over the last few years by a series of disappointments in her career and her personal life. That confidence was expressing itself, now, through the movement of her fingers on the strings of the guitar, the strength of her voice ringing out through the attentive night air. Once again it felt—at last—that she was doing what she was born to do.

The song was over. There was silence around the fire for a few moments, except for the crackling of the embers. Then the eleven campmates began to applaud, slowly and feelingly, and when the applause had died down, they hugged Val, and kissed her, and told her how beautiful the song was, and asked if they could buy it and when she was going to record it, and she could not keep herself from crying and telling them, truthfully, that this was one of the happiest moments of her life.

Alison did not think that she could bear to watch another episode of the programme by herself, in that empty living room. Remembering Selena's invitation to come over for a family dinner whenever she felt like it, she phoned and asked if she could drop by and watch the show with them that night.

"'Course you can," said Selena. "Come round about seven. We'll have something to eat first."

Just as Selena had promised, the atmosphere in her house was cheerful and raucous, with everybody crowding into the kitchen to help her mother with the cooking, apart from her father Sam, who sat at the kitchen table reading the *Evening Mail,* and her brother Navaro, who was in the living room, bent over his Nintendo DS, which was emitting a constant series of pops and beeps.

There was the latest edition of some celebrity gossip magazine on the kitchen counter, and Alison picked it up, recognizing the two faces on the cover: "PETE AND DANIELLE," the headline said. "GET THE LOWDOWN ON THE HOTTEST JUNGLE ROMANCE *EVER.*" She flicked through to the relevant article.

"I already read that," said Ashley, Selena's mother. "They don't mention your mom. I suppose they printed it before she went on the programme."

"Probably a good thing," said Alison, putting it back on the counter after a half-hearted glance. "She doesn't seem to be doing herself any favours out there."

"I think your mom's doing just fine," said Ashley, who was stirring a pot filled with some peppery, aromatic fish stew. "Takes guts to go out there and do what she's doing. I hope you're proud of her."

Over dinner they could hardly avoid talking more about Val and her Australian adventure. Selena and her family had not been following the online response, so they had no idea how vitriolic most of the reactions had been. They thought that Val had been rather harsh to Danielle the night before, but apart from that their main complaint was that she was being given so little airtime. Alison was relieved, and reminded herself that not everybody spent hours poring over the Internet. Most of the population had better things to do with their time. So perhaps all was not lost yet, for her mother. Sam asked her, straight out, how much Val was being paid for her participation, and although his wife scolded him for being so rude, Alison saw no reason why she shouldn't tell them: it was twenty thousand pounds.

"Well," said Ashley, "I thought it would be more than that, actually. And what's she going to spend it on? I hope she's going to take you somewhere nice at Christmas. Maybe buy you a few nice things to wear as well."

"I don't know," said Alison. "She'll probably spend a lot of it on studio time."

"She deserves another hit record, that's for sure. I really loved the last one. She's a very talented lady, your mom. And don't mind my husband, with his nosy questions. He's never had any manners."

"That's all right," said Alison. "I don't mind answering questions."

"I've got one," said Malikah, one of Selena's younger sisters. "Can I feel your false leg?"

At nine o'clock, they sat down together to watch the programme. Alison was nervous, but this time it wasn't too much of an ordeal: partly because Selena's family kept up such a lively running commentary, and partly because her mother was hardly in this episode at all. There was quite a jolly scene in the last five minutes, when somebody brought a guitar into camp and Pete and Danielle did an entertainingly terrible performance of "Yellow Submarine." Val could be seen singing along with the chorus: she was smiling and looked like she was having a good time. Apart from that, she was barely even glimpsed on screen.

"Ah, that was funny," said Ashley, muting the television when the news came on. "Really, that silly girl couldn't sing to save her life."

"Fuck me, she's fit though," said Navaro. They were practically the first words he'd spoken that evening.

"You mind your language, mister," Ashley said. Then, turning to Alison: "I wonder why they didn't give your mom the guitar to play? That would have been nice."

"Don't know," said Alison. "She's quite shy, my mother. I know that sounds weird, for a singer, but she really is. Very shy, in fact."

"Well, that's probably the reason," said Ashley. "But I still think it's a shame. We would all like to have heard her voice again."

A few minutes later Alison left, and Selena offered to walk with her to the bus stop. It was a cold night, enough to make their teeth chatter as they stamped their feet to keep warm and waited for the Number 11 to appear. Once again, Alison found it hard to believe that this, a few days ago, had been her mother's world, and yet now she was sitting around a camp fire in Australia with a guitar and a bunch of minor celebrities. She should have grown used to the unreality of it by now, but it continued to stagger her.

"By the way," she said, trying to put this thought aside, "I wanted to tell you something. Something about me. A little secret."

"Oh God," said Selena. "Not another one. It's not your other leg, is it?"

Alison shook her head, smiling.

"Glass eye?"

"No." But now, some undertone of urgency in her voice made Selena fall silent, waiting for the revelation. "I'm gay," Alison said finally, in a quiet, neutral way.

"Oh." Selena had been staring at the pavement. Now she looked up brightly. "Well, that's no big deal really, is it?"

"Isn't it? You sure?"

"Of course."

Alison let out a deep breath and smiled and hugged her. "I'm so relieved."

"Why?" said Selena, clasping her tightly in return. "What did you think I was going to say?"

"I don't know . . . People react in funny ways sometimes."

"They do?"

"Well, actually I've only told two people—you and my friend Rachel. But she took it so badly it's made me a bit nervous."

"Why, what did she say?"

Alison traced a careless pattern on the pavement with her right foot as she began to explain: "I've known Rachel for years. We were at primary school together. She lives in Leeds, but we've always stayed in touch. So a couple of months ago, I wrote her a letter. And then the next day, I sent her a message on Snapchat, asking if she'd got the letter. And she sent a reply, saying that she had. And then I asked her what she was doing that night, and she said . . ." (Alison swallowed hard) ". . . I mean I can hardly believe she said this, but she said she was going to be sleeping with her brother, and it was just the sort of thing I liked doing."

Selena gaped at her. "She said *what?*"

"Yeah. Being gay, for her, apparently, is just like fucking your own brother."

"Is that what she said?"

"I only saw the message for a few seconds, because that's how it works, but that's pretty much what she wrote. I asked her where she was and she said: '*With my brother. We're doing the incest thing tonight.*'"

Incredulous, half laughing and half frowning, Selena was almost lost for words: "Wow. That's a . . . pretty weird thing to say. And a weird way of saying it, actually."

"Well, it was handwritten, and, like I said, it wasn't on the screen for long. But that's what it looked like. And then she said, 'Right up your street I would have thought.'"

"Shit," said Selena. "That's harsh. Is that it? I mean, is that the sum total of her response?"

"She did write me a letter, but I couldn't face reading it. I chucked it away."

"Is she . . . is she, like, a born-again Christian or something?"

"Not the last time I looked," said Alison, and then the bus swung into view. They managed a quick kiss on the cheek—fumbled but tender—before she climbed on board.

Danielle and Val followed their guide along the jungle path. They had no way of knowing it, but it was only ten thirty in the morning. The air was already dense and sticky, and the path was heavy going.

"Can I ask you something, Val?" said Danielle, over her shoulder.

"Of course."

"It's about your song the other night—which was really lovely, by the way."

"Oh, thank you."

"I can't stop thinking about it, actually. Can't stop thinking about the words."

"Yeah? Well, that's a good sign, I suppose."

"It's just that line: 'I need your breath, Like the moonshine controls the water.' Have I got it right?"

"Yeah, that's right."

"I was just wondering . . . what does that mean, then? How can moonshine control the water? Is it just like . . . something you made up?"

Val hesitated, not sure whether this was a joke or not. She decided it wasn't. "Well no, I was just talking about . . . you know, the moon, and the tides. The gravitational pull of the moon."

"What do you mean?"

"You know—how when the tide goes in and out, that's because of the moon."

Danielle stopped and turned. Now she was the one suspecting a joke.

"Are you winding me up?" she said.

"Of course not. I'd never do that."

"*That's* why the tide goes in and out? Really?"

Val nodded.

Danielle's beautiful eyes widened. This was a revelation to her, it seemed, and a very important one.

"That's incredible. Just fucking incredible. When we get out of here," she said, turning back to resume her progress along the path,

"I want to spend a lot more time with you. *You know so much.* How did you get to know all these things?"

"I don't know," said Val, almost tripping on a creeper. "It helps if you work in a library, I suppose . . ."

In a few more minutes, they emerged into a wide clearing, where their chortling hosts, inevitably, were waiting to greet them.

"Morning, ladies!"

"We've got a nice little treat for you today."

"Yes, today we're going to do not one but *two* jungle trials!"

"But there's a twist, as always."

"Yesterday we asked the viewers at home to say who was their favourite person in the camp."

"The person with the most votes is going to do the first of today's trials, which is a pretty easy one, to be honest. It's called *The Fluffy Jungle Path of Pink Marshmallows and Cuddly Toys.*"

"Unfortunately, the person with the smallest number of votes is not going to have quite such a nice time. She's going to be entering something called *The Cave of Evil.*"

"So, are you ready to hear the results of the vote?"

They both nodded.

Val wasn't surprised, of course, to hear that Danielle was the most popular person in the camp. But it was a shock to learn that she herself had been voted the least popular. As soon as the news was broken to her, with the hosts' typical cheeky, ironic grins, her stomach turned over and she felt her legs were about to buckle. The *least* popular? How on earth had that happened? All the hard-earned confidence acquired over the last few days drained out of her. She barely knew what was happening as Danielle was led away in one direction and then she felt herself being taken by the arm as the other host (which one was it? She never could tell them apart) propelled her in the direction of a steep, intimidating escarpment at the other end of the clearing.

"Now, Val," he was saying, his voice dripping with boyish charm, "how are you with the old creepy-crawlies?"

She had no idea what he was saying, what she had just been asked. All she knew, as her eyes slowly came back into focus, was that she was being pointed in the direction of a low, narrow aperture in the rock, which seemed to lead into nothingness. There was just about room for a human being to crawl through it, and a few seconds later she was inside.

Alison stood in the kitchen, her hands over her ears. She'd been in this situation countless times before: on her own, in the kitchen, trying to block out the sounds of the TV, which Val always turned up too loud. What could be more mundane, more banal? Except that tonight there was a crucial difference: tonight, the sounds coming from the television, the sounds she was trying to ignore, were her own mother's screams of distress.

They were awful sounds. Keening, animal howls coming from thousands of miles away: from somewhere in the depths of a cave in a corner of the Australian rain forest, captured as digital information and beamed faithfully into Yardley via the television's speakers. This latest ordeal would have taken place several hours ago, of course, but that was little consolation to Alison, who was having to live through every moment of it now, in real time. Sometimes when the screams died down she could hear the chortling host intervene with comments like "OK, Val, here comes the next lot!" or "Ooh, these are nasty little fellas all right, aren't they?" But otherwise there was no respite from her mother's lacerating, inhuman screeching. How long had it been going on for, now? No more than a couple of minutes, surely. But she wasn't sure that she could stand it any longer.

"Selena!" she shouted towards the living room. "For fuck's sake turn it down."

The TV was muted and a few seconds later Selena came into the kitchen. "It's OK," she said. "It's finished. They've gone over to the adverts." She saw that Alison had been crying, and took a Kleenex out of her pocket. "Here," she said. "Let's clean you up a bit."

"Fuck," said Alison, wiping her eyes with the back of her sleeve. "That was rough."

"She didn't cope too well, did she?"

"Of course she didn't fucking cope! That would have been her worst nightmare. She's claustrophobic for a start."

The cave into which Val had been made to crawl had been no more than two feet high, and not much wider. Once inside, she had been told to lie on her back, and then the entrance had been sealed with a rock.

"She also has nyctophobia."

"What's that?"

"Fear of the dark. And entomophobia."

"Fear of . . . insects?"

Alison nodded. "The silly cow. She should have fucking . . . *told* them." She grabbed another fistful of Kleenex from the box, and blew her nose. "Were they all over her? What were they?"

"I don't know—cockroaches, mainly. And some spiders."

"Shit. She *hates* spiders."

"It's over now, Al. She's got through it."

Selena took Alison in her arms and held her close, and for a while they just stood like that, not moving, beneath the glare of the kitchen's strip lighting. Selena waited for Alison to relax, to soften beneath the embrace, but it wasn't happening.

"She was *here*," Alison said eventually. "This time last week she was here with me. A week later she's in the Australian jungle and someone's buried her alive and she's got spiders crawling into her mouth. I mean, what the fuck . . . ? What *happened* to us this week?"

Whatever it was that had happened, it was soon over. At the very end of that night's episode, the show went live to Australia, where it was now eight o'clock in the morning. It was time for the first of the celebrities to be voted off. Forlornly, Alison and Selena sat on the sofa, wielding two mobile phones and a landline, repeatedly punching in the number that was supposed to save Val from expulsion. But they were wasting their time (and money). She was, by some margin, the contestant with the fewest votes, and just a few minutes later she had left the camp and was being ushered into the makeshift outdoor studio where she would have her final interview with the two hosts. Sitting down beside them, she looked tired and skeletal. Her eyes were blank with shock and exhaustion. Her skin was grey. When the interview was over, she was directed to walk across the little suspended wooden bridge to the spot where her car and driver would be waiting. The cameras followed her as the programme's theme tune played out. To Alison, her mother looked older and more frail than ever. Her stoop was worse. At the far end of the bridge, Alison could glimpse Steve, holding out his arms in expectation. He greeted her mother with a brief, amicable hug. The credits came to an end and Alison turned off the TV.

"Well," she said. "That's that."

She poured a glass of wine for herself and another for Selena, who looked at it doubtfully.

"I should really be getting home in a minute," she said.

"Well . . . Just one more. Won't do you any harm."

Forty minutes later, the telephone rang. It was Val, calling from Australia. She was back at the hotel, crying down the line. Alison tried to comfort her at first, but it soon became clear that all her words of reassurance ("No, really, you came across very well . . . Everyone here's been rooting for you . . .") were beside the point. The point being that Steve had dumped her. Apparently, while the celebrities had been in the jungle, all their partners and guests had been taken out on organized day trips, and in the process a romance had developed between Steve and Jacqui, Pete's aunt. This afternoon they were flying up to Cairns to spend a few days surfing together.

"I've got to stay here for another week," Val said, between snivelling breaths. "What am I going to do, all by myself?"

"I don't know, Mum," said Alison. "I can tell you what you *shouldn't* do."

"What's that?"

"Go online, or read the papers."

She hung up when it became clear that her mother was too tired to speak any more. Selena had overheard most of the conversation and was already fuming with sisterly indignation.

"Has what I think just happened, actually happened?"

"Yep. I should have warned her. I should have warned her about that fucking creep. Next time I see him, I'm going to get him on the floor, and give him such a kicking . . ."

"Can I join in?" Selena asked. "I'm pretty good at kicking. I've got two good legs, for a start."

Alison gave a long, grateful laugh, and instinctively reached out to touch her friend on the cheek.

"I don't suppose you could stay the night?" she said.

Perry Barr—Handsworth—Winson Green—Bearwood—Harborne—Selly Oak—Cotteridge—Kings Heath—Hall Green—Acocks Green—Yardley—Stechford—Fox & Goose—Erdington—Witton—Perry Barr.
Shit!

Did you say that out loud? Did you scream? Why are they all looking at you?

Must have dozed off.

—Yardley—Stechford—Fox & Goose—

Same thing. Same images. Same sensations. The darkness, first of all. The knowledge that the roof is just above your head, that you can't move. And then the noises. The scurrying noises, as they empty the first load on to you, from somewhere up above, through some hole in the rock.

No sleep again last night. Not a wink. This seems to be the only place you can sleep now. But you don't want to. As soon as you sleep, you hear them again. Feel them crawling. Up your legs, inside your trousers, down the front of your shirt. Oh fuck.

—Fox & Goose—Erdington—Witton—

Two months now. Two months since you got back. Two months and no change. Nothing. Same old shit, day after day.

—Witton—Perry Barr—Handsworth—

Doctor says it's only a matter of time, a matter of waiting, but what does she know? All they do is give you pills anyway. She doesn't understand. Nobody understands, knows what it's like. "Look on the bright side," for fuck's sake.

—Handsworth—Winson Green—Bearwood—

They don't know. They think the worst thing that happened was having spiders all over you, having to shove an insect down your throat. That wasn't the worst. *Hope you get VD.* Alison was right. *You deserve to be raped.* You shouldn't have looked. Can't get rid of words like that. Twenty grand, for having shit like that poured all over you.

Not worth it. Ten, anyway, after the Australian tax people took their bit. And by the time you paid off Visa, and the overdraft . . .

—*Bearwood—Harborne—Selly Oak—*

Still, you're out of debt now. Look on the bright side. Out of debt, for the time being.

—*Selly Oak—Cotteridge—Kings Heath—*

Twenty grand. Not so bad. Not till you heard what Danielle was getting. Three hundred and fifty. Them and us. "We're all in this together." I don't think so. *"You know so much, Val."* *"When we get out of here, I want to spend a lot more time with you."* Yeah, right, you little bitch. Got my number, haven't you? So how come you never returned a single call? Nor any of the others.

Truth is, you don't belong with people like that. Stupid to think you ever did. This is where you belong. On the Number 11 bus. Look around you. Get real. *These* are your people. Ordinary people. Decent people.

—*Kings Heath—Hall Green—Acocks Green—*

Look at that old dear. Saw her yesterday, didn't you? Somewhere or other. Did she come into the library? A lot of them do, to keep warm.

No, the food bank, that was it. She was on her way out when you went in. Held the door for her. Gave you a funny look, like you weren't supposed to be there. Why not? You were only looking around. Bit of natural curiosity, that's all. Wanted to see what kind of stuff they had there. Not going to start using it. Hasn't come to that yet.

Look on the bright side.

Now why's she staring at you?

Needs someone to help with the trolley.

—*Acocks Green—Yardley—*

"Excuse me, shall I give you a hand with that?"

The woman's gaze met hers. Her eyes were pale blue, veiny, watery. Her hands were shaking as they grasped the handle of her shopping trolley.

"You're a nasty piece of work," she said at last, as the bus came to a halt, the doors hissed open, and she eased herself down the step onto the pavement. "Why don't you piss off back to the jungle where you belong?"

H. G. Wells, "The Door in the Wall" (1911):

"The fact is—it isn't a case of ghosts or apparitions—
but—it's an odd thing to tell of, Redmond—I am
haunted. I am haunted by something—that rather takes
the light out of things, that fills me with longings . . ."

The Crystal Garden

At first, after he had left the room, Laura was too angry even to think. She stood at the sash window, watching him walk back across the quad in the direction of the Porter's Lodge, and fumed silently. Projecting her own resentment onto his receding figure, she felt that she could discern arrogance in the very cut of his clothes and the angle of his body as he walked. She watched him disappear through the archway and then returned to her desk, where the first thing she saw was the cup of jasmine tea she had poured for him. It hadn't been touched. She took it out into the little bathroom halfway up the staircase and emptied it down the sink.

She had already been having a difficult day. The journal's editors had e-mailed her yet again asking when they could expect her submission, pointing out that she had missed the second deadline by more than a month. And once again she had spent three or four fruitless hours at her desk, going through her own chaotic notes, and her late husband's even more chaotic notes, trying to find the single overriding theme, the unifying insight that would draw all of these seemingly disparate ideas together. But nothing emerged.

Tim had arrived promptly at two o'clock. He was a second-year student who had come straight to Oxford from a boarding school which boasted notoriously high fees and an undistinguished academic record. He had come to see Laura to make a complaint.

When did this become a thing, she wondered? As a student, she could remember deferring to her own tutor's every word, listening in awe as little nuggets of wisdom dropped from his lips. Of course, it was healthy that students nowadays had a more spirited attitude; but still, some of them—Tim being a case in point—had gone to another extreme, regarding her as little more than a service provider, to be vigorously challenged when the service in question turned out not to meet their expectations.

"Whoever wrote that poem," he had said to her, "is not a serious poet."

"His name was Edwin Morgan," said Laura, "and he was a very serious poet indeed. I just chose to make you study one of his lighter pieces."

"But it was complete gibberish," said Tim.

"I thought we'd established that it wasn't. That was the whole point of the discussion."

Laura had got her twentieth-century group to read Edwin Morgan's poem "The Loch Ness Monster's Song," and thought she had managed to persuade them, by the end of the class, that there were fragments of sense to be plucked out of its apparently random assemblage of vowels and consonants.

"Well, I mentioned it to my mum. She said she's never heard of Edwin Morgan, and she wanted to know why we hadn't read any T. S. Eliot yet this year."

Laura remembered, now, that Tim's mother was an English graduate herself. These days she wrote historical romances, and presumably made a good living at it, as they were often to be seen at airport bookshops.

"I'm not teaching your mum," she said. "Your parents may be paying the fees, but they don't get to choose the syllabus."

It was this reference to the tuition fees, she realized afterwards, that had really made Tim bridle. She had suspected, all along, that this was at the heart of his complaint. Increasingly, channelled through the students, she was aware of the vigilant, distantly controlling presence of concerned parents, looking at the money draining out of their bank accounts and wanting to make sure that they saw a good return on their investment. What had always, to Laura and her colleagues, been a solid but intangible thing—education, the elevation of the young mind to a higher level of knowledge and understanding—had now been redefined as a commodity, something to be bought in the expectation that it would one day yield a financial return.

She was still mulling over this annoying encounter in the pub later that afternoon, as she sat sipping a large Sauvignon Blanc and waiting for Danny to arrive. On the table in front of her was a sheet of A4, upon which she had been trying, once and for all, to list the main strands of this much-delayed paper and find a way of weaving them together. So far she had scribbled:

Paranoia
The numinous/supernatural
The Loch Ness Monster, in films/books/poetry
The Monster is nearly always a fake—often at the centre of some
    conspiracy to make money out of tourists/locals
What is being sold? What is being commodified?
Some sense of awe—wonder—the UNKNOWABLE—

And only now did it occur to Laura that there might be some oblique, tenuous connection between the ruthlessly pragmatic way of thinking Tim's generation had inherited and the ideas she was trying to synthesize for this essay. Had this been the argument her husband had been trying to frame—did it explain the phrase he had kept returning to, in his analysis of all those forgotten books and films: the process he had called "monetizing wonder"?

In the midst of these thoughts, Laura looked up and found that Danny was standing over her.

"All work and no play . . ." he said, glancing down at the writing.

She half covered the words with her hand, modestly, as if he had caught a glimpse of her in nothing but her underwear.

"Can I get you another?" he asked, kissing her on the cheek. The kiss lasted slightly too long, she thought, and was slightly too close to her lips.

"I shouldn't really. I'm driving."

"Very wise. Sauvignon, was it?"

"Well, just a small one then . . ."

While he was at the bar, she wondered if it had been a good idea to meet him for this drink, when maternal duty dictated that she should really have gone home forty minutes ago, to make Harry his tea and allow Keisha, the Malaysian nanny, to finish work at the agreed time. She was too pliable, Keisha, too cooperative. She had no family of her own in this country and was always only too willing to earn extra money by staying on for an hour or two, to cover the frequent occasions when Laura decided to work late or pop into The Jericho on her way home for a glass of white wine. Usually having a quick drink by herself was just an easy way to unwind—and there was nothing wrong with that, surely?—but it was a different matter when Danny joined her. She liked him, but something about these occasions always made her uneasy. Danny was married, but he never mentioned his wife: seemed to behave, more or less, as though she didn't exist. This had never bothered Laura much when her own husband was alive; she and Danny would meet for a drink and talk about work, about research proposals, conference papers, the students, the horrors of admin and paperwork. Harmless stuff; two colleagues letting off steam about the things that bugged them. She had never really been able to have this sort of conversation with Roger; by then, his thoughts were already too fixed on the past ever to be shifted. But after his death, in any case, there had been a change in her relationship with Danny. His wife's absence from his field of reference was even more noticeable. He sat closer to her, spoke to her more tremulously, looked at her more intently, than he had used to. But why? She was still in mourning. If he wanted to have an affair, and somehow thought that she was more available than she had been a year ago, he was mistaken. And Laura believed that she had made that pretty clear, one way or another.

When he returned with their drinks he said: "What are you looking at?"

Laura's attention had by now been drawn towards a bunch of undergraduates squeezed around a corner table. There were six of them, and they all had their phones out: they were putting their arms around each other and leaning in and taking selfies while joking and swapping empty-headed banter at the tops of their voices. There were pints of beer on the table as well as vodka shots. Incongruously, a copy of the student magazine *Isis* was lying there as well. It seemed to belong to a blonde-haired student who was sitting slightly apart from the others, not quite able to enter wholeheartedly into their spirit of raucous, alcohol-fuelled hilarity.

"Just thinking what it would be like to be young again," said Laura, nodding in their direction. "Couple of my lot in there. The spotty boy, and the blonde-haired girl."

"She looks like she'd rather be in her room with a knitting pattern and a cup of hot cocoa."

"No, she's not like that. She's a bright girl. Just a bit more . . . independent than most."

"Teacher's pet, by any chance?" Danny asked, smiling.

Not rising to the bait, Laura continued (almost as if to herself): "I did that thing at the beginning of the first term. Asking each of them to bring in a favourite text. It could have been anything. Prose, poetry, drama, film. She brought in a song lyric. 'Harrowdown Hill,' by Thom Yorke. Do you know it?"

Danny shook his head.

"It's about the death of David Kelly."

He glanced across at the student now. "Interesting choice," he said. "Who is she?"

"Her name's Rachel. Rachel Wells."

"State or private?"

"State. She's a Yorkshire girl. Mother lives in Leeds, I think."

"And did she say why she chose it?"

Laura was looking at the group of students more closely. It was more obvious than ever that Rachel stood out from the others, did not feel at ease with them.

Abstractedly, she answered: "Not really. She said it brought back memories."

Laura did not much like eating lunch on High Table, but she knew that it was a good idea to do so occasionally: otherwise word would get around that you were "chippy" or "bolshie." So the next day she took the plunge, and even found herself sitting next to the Master of the college, Lord Lucrum. They were not natural dining companions: Lord Lucrum was an influential figure in public life, with close ties to the present government; but like so many powerful figures in the British establishment he had the talent of pretending to be a good listener, and of keeping his own views to himself when in company. He was a relatively young peer—a robust and well-preserved fifty-nine—and he nodded with every appearance of alertness as Laura attempted a halting explanation of her current paper on the Loch Ness Monster, and its role as a generator of income in books and films.

"Commodifying fear," he said, mopping up gravy with a slice of bread. "What a fascinating notion. Do you think that's possible, with any degree of precision? Do you think that human emotions can be . . . priced?"

"Well, that's rather outside the scope of my piece, I'm afraid," said Laura.

"Pity," he replied. "I thought you might be on to something interesting there."

Their conversation dried up soon after that, and Laura's attention was distracted, in any case, when she noticed Rachel Wells eating by herself in a far corner of Hall, the February sunshine throwing a shaft of late-winter light through the high stained-glass window onto her plate of shepherd's pie and overcooked vegetables. On a whim, Laura excused herself to his Lordship, went to fetch herself a cup of coffee and then stopped by Rachel's table. She was touched to see that she still had a copy of *Isis* magazine in front of her: she seemed to be taking it everywhere.

"Hello. A rumour reaches me that you've got a story published in there."

Rachel looked up and smiled, pleased but bashful. "That's right, yeah."

"In your second term! Well done. Mind if I join you?"

"No, of course not."

Laura sat down opposite her. For a moment or two they ate and drank in silence. Laura had her back to the wall, and could see that Rachel kept glancing up at something behind her. She craned around to see what it was.

"Oh," she said. "Him."

They were sitting beneath a large portrait, in oils, of a corpulent, white-haired man in his sixties or seventies, sporting a spotted bow tie and a suit that must have been several sizes too small for him. His face had the ruddy glow of an enthusiastic drinker but was otherwise far from benevolent, being contorted into a combative frown. He was sitting at a desk in an austere, sparsely furnished office. On the wall behind him a motto had been picked out in elegant calligraphy: it consisted of the three words "FREEDOM, COMPETITION, CHOICE."

"Who is it?" Rachel asked. "I see this picture every day but nobody's told me who it is."

"One of our more colourful fellows," said Laura. "No longer with us, sadly. His name was Henry Winshaw. He was a Labour MP, once. Then he had a Damascene conversion, like so many people, and went over to the other side. My husband, Roger, started a petition once to get his portrait taken down. He had a particular problem with that word—'Choice.' He used to claim that it put him off his food."

"I know the feeling," Rachel said. "But for me it's his eyes. They give me the creeps."

"Mm ... The way they follow you around the room. That's the sign of a good portrait, apparently."

"And the petition didn't get very far, I'm guessing."

"Hardly. Our distinguished Master up there"—she nodded in the direction of Lord Lucrum—"was something of a disciple of his, I think. I seem to remember reading they spent time on some influential committee together."

Rachel did not seem to be listening any more. She put her fork down and pushed her plate of food aside, half finished.

"You feeling OK?"

She grimaced. "I've got the mother of all hangovers."

"Ah. Yes, I saw you in the pub with your friends. Late night, was it?"

"Very. Plus, I ended up having to take someone to A & E. A girl called Rebecca. She lives on my staircase. She tripped on the pavement when we were coming back. I think she'd had one too many. About ten too many, in fact."

"Oh dear. Is she all right?"

"Yes, it was just a cut. We didn't have to wait long, and the doctors were great." Rachel seemed embarrassed by all this, perhaps worried that it was not putting her in a good light. "Sorry. Typical student behaviour, I know. And it won't help me get the Milton essay written on time . . ."

"Don't worry about that. My suggestion would be that you go and get some sleep. *Paradise Lost* will still be there when you wake up."

Rachel smiled. "OK. Thanks."

That night, sitting at home alone in the blue glow of her laptop, with Harry already deep into his second hour of untroubled sleep, Laura downloaded the online edition of *Isis* and read Rachel's story. It wasn't bad at all: a vividly imagined dialogue between a young, idealistic barrister and her client, a jaded prison officer on trial for whistleblowing. It had the ring of truth and felt experience behind it. Afterwards, Laura went on to Facebook and did a search for Rachel's name. She found her home page quickly enough, but it didn't tell her anything: the privacy settings blocked access to everything except her cover and profile pictures. Laura tried to click on the profile picture, at least, but nothing happened, and it remained the size of a postage stamp. But there was another, perhaps more promising avenue to explore: the other student she had recognized at the pub table last night, "the spotty one," as she had rather unkindly designated him. She typed his name into the search box and after a couple of false starts found herself swiftly directed to his home page, on which—as she had guessed—no privacy settings had been put in place at all. She looked at the latest messages and found—also as she had been expecting—that Rachel had been tagged in a number of recent photos. Following the link took her straight into an album called "Larking About, Monday Night."

There were about twenty or thirty pictures. Each one showed a number of students in various stages of drunken revelry, but none of them made Laura feel particularly cheerful. Rictus grins, pallid, luminescent skin and red-eye photography gave all of these young people the appearance of alien creatures, visitors from another planet who had somehow managed to colonize the bodies of human beings and learn the outward manifestation of their emotions while under the skin, at heart, lay something hollow and coldly mechanical. As for Rachel, Laura could not help thinking—as she had thought at the time—that there was something half-hearted, semi-detached, about her relationship to the rest of the group: in each image, her eyes seemed to be directed elsewhere, with a gaze that was at once far-seeing and inward-looking. The pictures were arranged in a sequence which began at the pub. In some of the earliest ones, Danny's shoulder could be glimpsed in the background—and even Laura's own left arm, once or twice. But the drinking and the photography had continued long after Laura and Danny had left, and the last few pictures had been taken out in the street, after the pubs had closed. They included one particularly disturbing—not to say pornographic—image which showed one girl (tagged as Rebecca) bent double over the pavement, apparently in the act of throwing up. Laura felt a sudden dismay that this moment, so private and so shameful, should have been not just captured in digital form but also uploaded for all of the spotty boy's friends (and friends of friends, and, for that matter, anybody else who felt like it) to see. Had the girl's permission been sought? She doubted it. Was she even aware that the picture was on public display? Laura doubted that, too.

She shut the laptop down, sat back, closed her eyes and rubbed the lids softly. There was a slight ache behind her eyes now, something she always felt even after a few minutes' computer use. One of the inescapable conditions of life in 2012.

She did not see Rachel again until the end of the week, when they had their regular tutorial meeting. It was late on Friday afternoon, and already dark outside. Once, this had been Laura's favourite time of day: the hour after dusk, when lights went on around college and the yellowish glow of standard lamps from innumerable windows threw a patchwork of violet shadows over the whole of the main quad. Recently, however—in fact, why be vague about this, it was since the death of her husband—she had begun to feel differently, and now came to dread this hour, especially on a Friday, with the prospect of a long weekend in the countryside ahead of her, with only her five-year-old son for company. This depressing thought could not be put entirely to one side, even as she did her best to concentrate on the subject of Rachel's Milton essay—or rather, its continued non-appearance.

"I'm pretty sure I can get it finished by Monday," Rachel was saying, tugging at a strand of blonde hair as her eyes roved distractedly over the contents of Laura's bookshelves.

"Really?" said Laura. "Well, that would be great. But don't rush it. Honestly. It's not a great precedent to set, but I am used to students handing work in weeks after the deadline."

"It won't be a problem," said Rachel. "There aren't many distractions at the weekend. All my friends seem to go home, for one thing."

This, Laura had noticed, was another new phenomenon of university life: students who, in years gone by, would have regarded term as a welcome opportunity to live an independent life for eight weeks now went back to see their parents most weekends, to have their meals cooked for them and get their laundry done. But not Rachel, it seemed.

"That must be a bit dreary for you," Laura said.

"Yeah, but . . . well, Mum doesn't want me under her feet. She works a seven-day week these days."

"What does she do?"

"She's a barrister."

"Ah! Is that what gave you the idea for your story?"

"You read it?" Rachel's eyes flared with delight.

"I did. And I really liked it. It's nice to read something like that which feels as though . . . well, as though the writer knows what she's talking about."

"My mum represents a lot of whistleblowers. In fact, that's more or less all she does nowadays. It's quite a growth industry."

" 'You will be dispensed with/when you've become inconvenient,' " said Laura, remembering the song lyric in which Rachel had shown such an interest. "She must see a lot of that."

Rachel, not having expected the quotation, took a moment to recognize it. "Oh yeah—'Harrowdown Hill,' " she said. "My own little obsession."

"Well," said Laura, "we're all prey to those, now and again." She smiled an unreadable smile. "Have you ever been there?"

"No. It's not far from Oxford, is it?"

"Not at all. And it's even closer to where I live. I bought a house very near there, with my husband, a few years before he died. We both liked the idea of living in a village, in the country. Thought it would be good for our son while he was still little."

"I didn't know your husband had . . ."

"Last year."

"I'm so sorry. Was it . . . ?"

"Cancer? A heart attack? No. It was an accident. A stupid accident. Or at least . . ." She tailed off. "Well, there's always more than one way of looking at things, isn't there?"

In the silence that followed, Laura made a quick, impulsive decision; and before she'd had time to think whether it was a good one or not, she heard herself putting it into words. Why didn't Rachel, if she had nothing much else to do this weekend, come and visit her tomorrow, at her house in the village? She could take the train out to Didcot and Keisha could pick her up from the station. And then, in the afternoon, they could drive out together to Harrowdown Hill itself.

Rachel seemed doubtful at first, and Laura wondered whether the suggestion sounded too morbid. "It's a really nice spot," she insisted; and then added, even more recklessly: "You could even stay the night if you wanted. There's a nice spare bedroom which hasn't been used for months."

Later that night, thinking about it soberly, Rachel knew that she had accepted the invitation more out of politeness than anything else.

The village of Little Calverton lies a few miles east of Didcot. The name itself is mysterious, since there is no Large, Big or even Great Calverton, nor is there any record of there ever having been one. It is a classically beautiful Cotswold village, where property prices are (relatively speaking) still on the low side, thanks to the proximity of Didcot power station, the massive chimneys of which rise up less than five miles away. If you can reconcile yourself to this, there are bargains to be had in Little Calverton, and houses there rarely stay on the market for more than a week or two.

"Nice country," Keisha said to Rachel, as they drove along a single-track lane between high hedgerows. Rachel did not answer, but nodded cheerfully; she was not sure, in fact, whether Keisha was referring to the surrounding countryside or to England as a whole, and did not want to appear insensitive by misinterpreting her.

"Very different from Malaysia, I expect," she said, in a non-committal way.

"Very different. But I like it. I prefer all this. I'm very happy here. Very happy in the UK. Very happy to work for Laura. She's a nice lady. She teaches you, yes?"

"That's right."

"For a long time?"

"Just a few months so far. But she's great. It's been great."

"Very nice person. Kind, generous. But sad, you know?"

"Because of her husband?"

"Because of Roger, yes."

"You knew him?"

"No. I never knew him. I came after he died."

Briefly, just as they entered the village, a few glimmers of February sunlight broke through the clouds. On their left, the hedgerow tapered away. A triangle of lawn came into view, at its apex a war memorial flanked by two tubs of early primroses. The road curved around it, and after another fifty yards or so Keisha swung the car sharply right, into a short, loosely gravelled driveway that ended at the front door of a picture-perfect thatched cottage, its buttery-yellow, Cotswold-stone walls draped in curtains of wisteria. As soon as the car engine was turned off, the silence seemed chilling, absolute.

"So, here we are. You all right with your bag?"

It seemed a silly question: Rachel's tiny holdall was three-quarters empty. She followed Keisha to the front door which, before they had even had time to touch the handle, was thrown open from inside. There, standing in the darkened, flagstoned hallway, was a brown-haired boy of about five or six, who hurled himself at the nanny and crushed her in his arms without saying a word.

"Hello, beautiful," Keisha said. "Did you miss me?"

"You must be Harry," said Rachel, reaching out to shake his hand with mock-ceremony, but he ignored her and turned back towards the kitchen, pulling Keisha after him as forcefully as he could.

Rachel was left alone in the hallway. There was a steep, uncarpeted wooden staircase to her left, and three doors at the far end of the hallway, one leading straight ahead into the kitchen, the other two closed. For a moment, the sight of these three doors gave her a flickering sense of déjà vu, but it passed before she could decide whether it arose from a real or a phantom memory. What should she do? It would feel wrong to start calling out Laura's name. She had been expecting Keisha to announce her arrival, but instead, she could see through the kitchen window that the nanny had already been dragged out into the garden by Harry, and he was trying to involve her in some sort of ball game.

Tentatively, still carrying her holdall, she crossed the flagstones in the direction of the kitchen. Pausing outside the two closed doors, she thought she could hear, from behind one of them, the muffled clicking of keys being tapped on a computer keyboard. She pushed the door open and found herself looking into Laura's study. Laura herself had her back to the door. She was working at a desk placed in front of a large leaded window, and she was wearing headphones as she worked. She seemed unaware of Rachel's presence. Through the window Rachel could see a further view of the garden—a sparse expanse of lawn rolling down towards a scruffy border which hinted at a stream beyond—making her suspect for the first time that the house and its grounds might be larger than she had thought. The sun was again doing its best to break through the clouds, throwing occasional patches of light onto the grass.

Rachel was still wondering what to do next when Laura, sensing her presence at last, swivelled round in her chair, took off the headphones and rose to her feet in greeting.

"Hello, I didn't hear you come in. Did you have a good journey? Did Keisha look after you? Where's she got to?"

"Outside with Harry."

"Come on, I'll get you some coffee."

In the kitchen, decanting coffee from a frothing, bubbling, gleaming chrome-plated machine, Laura said again: "I'm sorry I didn't hear you. I meant to have hit my word target hours ago but the dreaded e-mails intervened as usual. They never stop—not even on a Saturday. So I'm afraid I've still got a bit to do."

"It's nice to know lecturers have to set themselves word targets as well," said Rachel. "I thought that was just lazy students."

"Hardly," said Laura. "I promised myself five hundred words today. But I'll do nowhere near that, of course."

"What are you writing about?"

"Well . . . I don't really know. And therein lies the problem, of course. I'm trying to carry on with a project my husband began. I suppose you'd say it was about paranoid fiction. With particular reference to recent British sci fi. And even more particular reference to . . ." (she looked embarrassed) ". . . the Loch Ness Monster."

Rachel was surprised. "Sounds fun," she said. "But quite a long way from Milton."

"Yes, well, the faculty isn't too wild about it," said Laura, passing her a mug of treacly black coffee. "I'm sure they'd rather I just wrote the fifteen thousandth article on *Lycidas*—but . . . well, you have to go wherever your interests take you, don't you?"

While Laura returned to the study to continue writing, Rachel took her coffee outside. As she had expected, the garden was impressive, with the generous lawn dominated, at its centre, by a classical stone fountain more than six feet high, although no water was cascading today over its three lichen-encrusted tiers. Harry and Keisha were playing down by the stream and took no notice of Rachel as she found a rickety wooden bench next to a rhododendron bush and sat down on it, positioning herself carefully between the many splashes of bird shit. Now that the sun seemed to have disappeared for good, it promised to be a cold afternoon. She shivered slightly.

It was an odd feeling, being here at her tutor's house. Had she crossed a boundary by coming? Had Laura crossed a boundary by inviting her? She had not asked herself these questions before, and it was a bit late to be asking them now. Instead of welcoming her, Laura seemed to have viewed her arrival as an interruption, and for that matter the whole atmosphere of the house and the village made her feel like an intruder. The train ride to Didcot had taken only fifteen minutes and yet, thanks to the stillness and isolation of this place, the relative bustle of Oxford itself seemed already thousands of miles away. It wasn't just a question of distance, either: Rachel felt, somehow, that in the last hour she had made a long journey through time, back to some far-off, half-forgotten era in her early life. To her childhood, even? This garden certainly bore no resemblance to her mother's cramped old patio garden in Leeds; and it was at least three times the size of her grandparents' garden in Beverley, where she had also spent a good many summers. No, these were not the images that were coming to mind this afternoon, as she sipped her coffee cautiously and looked around her. But still, there *was* an unmistakable aura of childhood about this place: not a badly off, urban, South Yorkshire childhood, such as Rachel's had been, but a cosseted, Home Counties, 1950s childhood, of the sort with which Rachel was also familiar, if only in a second-hand way, through countless vintage children's novels which had been her favourite choice of reading matter at the local library when she was growing up. It was all here: the spreading cedar tree which just cried out for a tree house to be built amidst the cluster of its lower branches; the shallow stream at the edge of the lawn, traversed by a footbridge, ideal for those long Sunday afternoon games of Poohsticks; the ramshackle shed which could, without too much effort or imagination, be converted into the makeshift headquarters of a junior detective club. And above all, that fountain: looking a little derelict and melancholy now, but otherwise the perfect centrepiece for a garden which felt eerily like a stage or a film set, on which idealized vignettes of a middle-class childhood were designed to be acted out. That would explain Rachel's own growing sense of unreality, at any rate.

After another fifteen or twenty minutes, Laura beckoned her inside and showed her up to her room. It was on the second floor (she had not even realized there was a further floor) and turned out to be a low-ceilinged but otherwise spacious bedroom running the whole depth of the house, with windows looking out over both the front and the back gardens. The room should have been cosy but there was an airlessness about it, and a feeling of neglect. The books which spilled out from shelves ranged along every wall were sheened with a fine layer of dust. Glancing at them, Rachel could see that they were mainly devoted to cinema history and film theory.

"Oh dear, it's a bit cold in here, isn't it?" Laura said, laying a hand on the one small radiator. "I'll get Keisha to bring up a fan heater. And what are these doing here? They should have been moved ages ago."

She was referring to two large cardboard boxes, crammed to the brim with old VHS tapes. Her curiosity aroused by this display of antique technology, Rachel knelt down to look at the titles.

"Wow. I've never heard of most of these," she said. The first tape she had picked up was labelled *THE QUATERMASS XPERIMENT BBC 2 24.2.85/THE ABOMINABLE SNOWMAN BBC2 3.10.87.*

"Well, you're looking at my husband's pride and joy," Laura said. "Or rather, a tiny portion of it. There are thousands more—and I do mean thousands—down in the cellar. Whether that's a good place to keep them, I don't know. I can't think what else to do with them at the moment. Oh God, I've been looking for this one for *ages*."

She plucked out another tape, its cardboard case torn and patched up with Sellotape. Rachel craned over to see the title.

"*What a Whopper?*" she said, amused and disbelieving. "What on earth's that?"

"Believe it or not, this is one of the films I'm supposed to be writing about. You certainly wouldn't catch me watching it for pleasure. In fact it's hard to believe that anybody ever did. Do you think you could help me take these down to the cellar as well? I don't want them to be in your way."

They picked up a cardboard box each and began the slightly hazardous business of carrying them down the narrow, uneven staircase.

"Why are you writing about it, if it's so bad?" Rachel asked. "The film, I mean."

"Well, the plot—such as it is—involves the Loch Ness Monster. I haven't got a clue what I'm going to say about it, but in this business you always win Brownie points for digging up something obscure. Roger was particularly good at that, I must say."

And when they reached the cellar, it was easy to see why that might have been. It had been excavated to quite some depth, so that it was easy for both of them to stand upright. And it was filled with boxes: beneath the glare of the two naked lightbulbs that hung from the ceiling, Rachel could see at least thirty or forty of them, some filled with books or files or papers, but most simply crammed to the top with more videotapes and DVDs.

"Wow," said Rachel. "He was quite a collector, wasn't he?"

"Oh yes," said Laura. "Roger never did anything by halves."

They put their boxes down near the bottom of the stairs and then stood, for a while, in wordless contemplation of the scene of orderly profusion laid out before them. From somewhere in the cellar there emanated a faint, monotonous, electrical hum, which somehow seemed to accentuate the otherwise absolute silence. The light from one of the bulbs had started to flicker uncertainly. There was a damp, mouldering smell which made Rachel fear for the well-being of Roger's collection, and a piercing chill which made her shiver not just with cold but with sadness. She was keenly aware that she was looking at more than just a jumble of files and boxes. These were the last remains of a human being: all that was left of Laura's husband.

Laura's only comment was: "What a mess. I've got to do something about it soon." And then: "Come on, it's getting late. We'd better have this walk before it gets dark."

She turned and led the way up the stairs, much to the relief of Rachel, who could not get out of there quickly enough. She had always hated cellars.

On the ground floor, Laura detoured into the kitchen, where Keisha was busy loading a full basket of washing into the washing machine.

"Did you get the parcels ready?" Laura asked.

"On the table," Keisha answered, without looking up.

From the kitchen table, Laura picked up a large, eco-friendly canvas shopping bag, which seemed to be heavier than she was expecting.

"Do you think you could take the other one?" she said. "Sorry to be a bore, but this has become a bit of a weekend ritual."

Rachel grabbed hold of another bag, and glanced down at the contents: tins and packets of food, a jar of instant coffee and some boxes of breakfast cereal.

"We'll drop these off on the way, if you don't mind," Laura said, and ushered her into the hallway. They were almost at the front door when Harry came rushing up behind them.

"Mum, where are you going?" he asked, plangently.

"We're going to the food bank," she said. "And then we're going for a walk."

"Can I come with you?" he pleaded.

"No. You stay here. I thought you were playing with Keisha."

"I was but now she's busy. She says she has lots of things to do."

"Well . . . read a book, or watch a video or something." Her tone was noticeably abrupt, dismissive. Rachel looked at her in surprise.

"Oh Mum, *please.* I want to come with you."

With obvious reluctance, Laura finally relented. Out on the drive she heaved Harry into the back of the car and strapped him into his booster seat and then the three of them drove off in the direction of Didcot.

Rachel had never been to a food bank before. She had read articles about them, online and in the newspapers. But she had never been inside one.

It was a brief visit, so she only received a fleeting impression. The bank had been set up in what appeared still to be used, on other days of the week, as a café, located in a narrow side road running off the high street. People were sitting in family groups at each of the lightweight silver tables, but they were not drinking coffee: they were clutching vouchers and waiting for their parcels to be made up. Nobody bore any outward sign of poverty. Well-dressed couples waited in pensive silence while bored children sat beside them. The most noticeable thing was that nobody from one table ever seemed to make eye contact with anyone from another. The prevailing mood, as far as Rachel could see, was one of mortification: everybody simply wanted to finish their business and leave as quickly as possible. Somewhere at the back there seemed to be a store room, where the parcels were made up: these would then be carried to the counter where volunteers would match them up to the relevant voucher and call out a number. A family member would scurry up to the counter, eyes never leaving the floor, grab the parcel and then usher their partner or children out of the front door. A number would be called out every twenty or thirty seconds, and there was a constant stream of people going in and out. It was as busy as a GP's waiting room.

People glanced up at Laura, Rachel and Harry as they came in carrying their shopping bags, but soon looked away again. It was painfully clear who was a donor and who was a supplicant. Rachel had rarely felt so self-conscious. They were shown straight to the store room, and dropped off their bags so quickly that Rachel barely had time to take in the variety of food on the shelves: row upon row of tinned fruit, tinned meat, bags of rice and pasta, packets of biscuits and cakes, all marked with use-by dates in thick black marker pen. Harry, his eye-level lower than hers, stared longingly at a stack of chocolate bars in different-coloured wrappers.

"Why can't we ever *take* any stuff from the food bank?" he asked his mother as she tugged him away. "Why do we only ever give things?"

"Oh, do shut up," she said, and Rachel was struck again by the note of severity and impatience in her voice.

After that, the drive to Longworth took about twenty-five minutes. By the time they turned off the A420 on the outskirts of the village, it was quite late, and the cloud-covered sky was already darkening to a deeper grey. The village itself seemed sleepy, relaxed, perfectly indifferent to (or oblivious of) the tragedy that had unfolded there almost a decade earlier. Laura seemed to know exactly which turnings to take, and where to park the car.

"You've been here a few times before, then, have you?" Rachel asked.

"Yes, Roger and I used to come here quite often. You don't have to be a David Kelly obsessive to like Harrowdown Hill. It's a nice walk, apart from anything else. Which is why *he* took it that afternoon, of course."

They pulled in to the car park of The Blue Boar pub, a cosy, welcoming thatched building in Cotswold stone, which nonetheless appeared to be closed this afternoon, going by the dimness of the lighting just about visible through its tiny windows. Wrapping up against the now very tangible chill, the two women turned right out

of the car park and set off down the lane at a brisk pace, with little
Harry dawdling behind them, tracing a more erratic route which
involved zig-zagging from one side of the lane to the other. It was
a no-through road, and there was no traffic: any approaching cars
would have been easy to hear, so Laura did not seem at all concerned
that he was playing unsupervised. She was more worried that he was
holding them back.

"Hurry *up*, Harry!" she called, turning and frowning at him.
"You've got to keep up with us. You're making us all go too slowly."

Harry ran towards her obediently and clasped her hand. Mother
and son walked along like that for half a minute or so; then Rachel
noticed that Laura unloosed his hand and let it fall.

"So," Laura now said, "this is the lane he would have walked along,
at about three o'clock in the afternoon. And that's the hill he was
making for—look, just ahead on the left."

Rachel's eyes followed her pointing finger, towards a nondescript,
tree-covered mound in the landscape which made the word "hill"
seem somewhat hyperbolic. In the rapidly fading daylight, it did not
look especially beautiful.

"We won't be able to get into the wood," Laura added. "They've
put barbed wire around it now."

Before long the tarmac had petered out and they found themselves walking up a dirt track, overgrown with grass and bordered
with weeds and wild flowers. Harry took a stick to these and was
soon hacking them down with gusto.

"I can see why they'd do that," said Rachel. "You're right, it does
feel a bit . . . morbid, coming here."

"Why do you remember the news story so clearly, do you think?"
Laura asked. "You must have been very young when it happened."

"I was ten. I was staying with my grandparents, and I remember
them being very shocked by it. My grandad always hated Tony Blair,
so of course he was prepared to think the worst. I mean, I'm not sure
he thought he was murdered or anything, but he definitely thought
there was something strange about it . . ."

"I know, it felt very . . . *odd,* didn't it, that day?" Laura said. "But
I'm not sure I believe in conspiracy theories, and what Roger said

afterwards ... He just thought that a line had been crossed, a terrible line, and it was the shockwaves of that which were giving everyone the sense that there was something else going on, something mysterious."

They passed a sign which read "River Thames, ¾ Mile," which surprised Rachel: she had not realized that the river was nearby. Harry was starting to look cold. Another few minutes and they would be as close to the top of the hill as the path allowed, with the fatal woodland spreading out to their left.

"He had this theory," said Laura, "—Roger was full of theories, mainly I suppose because that's what he got paid for ... Anyway, this one was that every generation has a moment when they lose their innocence. Their political innocence. And that's what David Kelly's death represented for our generation. Up until then, we'd been sceptical about the Iraq war. We'd suspected the government wasn't telling us the whole truth. But the day he died was the day it became absolutely clear: the whole thing stank. Suicide or murder, it didn't really matter. A good man had died, and it was the lies surrounding the war that had killed him, one way or another. So that was it. None of us could pretend any longer that we were being governed by honourable people."

"That sounds about right," said Rachel. "But it's sad."

"What's sad about it?"

"Losing your innocence. It's just about the worst thing that can happen. Isn't that what *Paradise Lost* is all about?"

"Innocence is overrated," said Laura. "Anyone who hankers after lost innocence is ... well, I don't trust them." They had reached the edge of the woodland and were peering aimlessly into it, wanting to find meaning in its tangle of greenery and undergrowth. Harry was behind them, tugging at Laura's coat, trying to get her attention, instinctively but for no particular reason. "Look at him, for instance," she said, glancing down at her son, whose eyes met hers in a plaintive but unspecific appeal. "He still has his innocence. Do you envy him for it? He still thinks his Christmas presents are brought by a big bloke in a red suit, in a sleigh pulled by reindeer. What's so great about that?"

It was almost dark now. Putting her hands into her pockets and pulling her coat tighter, Laura started to lead the way back down the path towards the village.

"I could tell you a story," she said, "about what happens when someone longs too much for innocence."

Rachel looked down at Harry. Their eyes met and he shrugged: neither of them could guess what his mother was talking about. Rachel took his hand as they walked back down the hill.

Keisha had left a casserole in the oven for them: all Laura had to do was boil some rice. They ate in the kitchen, after which Laura went upstairs to put Harry to bed. It always took longer than she would like: when she came back down and joined Rachel in the sitting room, she found that she had managed to light a good fire, with a neat pyramid of logs already flaming on a nest of kindling wood and back issues of the *Guardian*. Now Rachel was sitting in one of the two sagging but comfortable armchairs placed on either side of the fire, her eyes fixed on the screen of her smart phone.

"This is a bit harsh," she said, looking up only briefly to say thank you as Laura put a glass of red wine down on the table beside her. "'A film that makes you want to stab out your eyes with red hot knitting needles.' And that's one of the better reviews."

"What are you looking at?" said Laura, sitting down opposite her.

"I'm on the IMDb, looking at reviews of that film you showed me earlier."

"*What a Whopper?*"

"Yes. It doesn't seem to have many fans on here. I think your husband must have been in a small minority."

"Oh, I wouldn't say that he was a fan, exactly. He knew rubbish when he saw it. But Roger responded to books and films in all sorts of different, contradictory ways. That was one of the nice things about him. And also one of the most frustrating. And of course, everything was grist to his mill as a critic. Look—I'll show you something."

She left the room and returned carrying a thick, leather-bound A4 notebook. When she opened it Rachel could see that page after page was covered with dense, spidery handwriting. It was a catalogue of films, in roughly alphabetical order, all of them glossed with Roger's fragmentary, rather cryptic annotations.

"What does he say about it in there?" Laura asked.

Rachel turned to the "W" section and soon found *What a Whopper*.

Lame British comedy, she read, *about a bunch of beatniks who travel to Loch Ness to build a model of the monster.*

1962. Sequel to What a Carve Up! *(1961)? Not really. Two of the same actors.*

*Sequels which are not really sequels. Sequels where the relationship to the original is oblique, slippery.

"What does this mean?" Rachel asked, pointing to the asterisk at the beginning of the last line.

"Ah, that means that something had given him the idea for an article," said Laura, craning forward to take a closer look. "Yeah, he was always doing that. Always coming up with ideas for pieces. When we first got married I was convinced he was some kind of genius and one day he was going to turn all this obscure knowledge into some great book, some academic masterpiece. I thought that's what was driving him. It never occurred to me that it might have been something as simple as . . . nostalgia.

"Moving to this house—that was the thing that began to open my eyes to what he was really like. I was pregnant with Harry and we had this clichéd idea that if we were going to bring up a child it would be a good idea to relocate to the country. Somewhere not far from Oxford, obviously.

"So we started looking, and then, early in 2006, we found this place. I remember the morning we drove out here to look at it. It was a pretty hard winter that year, and this was in the last week of January. The day before, there'd been a heavy snowfall, and since then there hadn't been much in the way of a thaw. Well, of course, that was what sold us, in a way. You can imagine how pretty this village looked, can't you, when it was covered in snow? And the cottage itself . . . well, it just looked beautiful. Enchanting. The owners brought us inside, and made coffee to warm us up, and showed us around the house. We were both . . . taken with it, certainly, although I wouldn't say that either of us was exactly in raptures at that point.

As you can see, it's a bit on the boxy side, and there were quite a few problems to do with damp and so on—none of which have really been sorted out. I could tell that Roger was unconvinced, was maybe having second thoughts about the whole thing. But that was before he saw the garden ...'"

Laura smiled to herself when she spoke this word, and stared, reminiscent, into the dancing flames of the fire.

"It was the last thing the owners of the house showed us. Roger and I went out to look at it together, and when we got out onto the terrace we held hands, as much for warmth as anything else, because neither of us was wearing gloves. And after a few seconds, I could feel him squeezing my hand. Squeezing it so tightly that it was actually hurting. I turned to look at him and I saw this look in his eye that I'd never seen before. It was ... it was kind of faraway and intense at the same time. It rather scared me, to tell the truth. I could tell that some weird, powerful emotion had come over him. So I said, 'Roger, what is it? What's the matter?' And he turned to glance at me, but only for a second or two, because then he turned away again and looked across the lawn and he said something. Not to me—he wasn't talking to me. He was talking to himself. And all he said, in little more than a whisper, was: '*The Crystal Garden* ...'

"It was the first time I'd ever heard him use that phrase. It certainly wouldn't be the last."

She fell silent, until Rachel felt obliged to prompt her once more: "So what did he mean by it?"

"I wasn't sure at first. It was only afterwards that he explained. You saw the fountain in the centre of the lawn? It's not working at the moment, of course. The pump stopped working a couple of years ago, and now it's one of many things that I need to get around to fixing. But it was working back then, and it formed a proper centrepiece to the garden. That was the first thing your eyes were drawn towards. And that day, I remember, it looked particularly stunning. The water had frozen, you see—that's how cold it was. So you had this cascade, this waterfall of ice, tumbling over the different levels of the fountain. It looked like some sort of chandelier in the ballroom of a fairytale castle. There were icicles hanging from all the trees, the stream itself was frozen, and the lawn was a shimmering blanket of pure white. It did look kind of . . . *eldritch,* do you know that word? It means uncanny. Otherworldly. Rather like it was made of crystal. I thought that's what Roger had meant, at first. But it turned out there was more to it than that.

"We stayed out in the garden for about ten minutes, but he hardly spoke in that time. He was wandering around in a kind of trance, walking over to different corners of the garden and then turning around to view everything from different angles. He stood beside the fountain and touched the frozen water. I can still see him doing this, such a sombre figure in his long black overcoat, his fingers stroking the cascade of icicles gently, then flicking them with his fingernails so that they sounded little notes like some far-off, tinkling musical instrument. His eyes were misted over. The owners of the house were trying to talk to us about water drainage and the cost of hiring a local gardener but Roger wasn't listening to a word. He didn't reply to a single thing they told him, until right at the very end of the tour, when he suddenly turned to them and said: 'Of course, we'll buy it.'

"I was amazed. He hadn't even asked my opinion. And he hadn't said 'We'll be making an offer'; he'd said, 'We'll buy it.' Just like that. In the car on the way back to Oxford, I was too angry to talk to him properly. Anyway, he was behaving especially strangely; he was on some weird cloud nine of his own. He never once mentioned the garden. He kept talking about the house, rhapsodizing about it as though we could never have imagined anything so perfect. Finally I cut him off in mid-flow and told him that he should never, ever do anything like that again. He didn't even know what I was talking about. When I pointed out to him that, without consulting me, he'd assured these people we were going to buy their house off them, he didn't even seem to be aware that he'd done it. And the strange thing is, I believed him. It was as if he'd experienced some sort of fugue state.

"As soon as we got back to our flat, he disappeared into the study and went online. I didn't see much of him after that, until later that evening, when he came and found me on the sofa, eating dinner. I'd ordered pizza but he hadn't heard me when I told him it had arrived. He was carrying his laptop with him and he sat down next to me and started talking.

"'OK,' he said. 'So I have to tell you what happened to me today in that garden.' I told him that was probably a good idea, and he started to explain: 'Something came back to me,' he said. 'Something I thought I might have imagined. From a long time ago.' He was struggling, rather, to find the words. 'When I was just a kid, probably aged about five or six, I saw this film. At least, until today I wasn't really sure whether I'd seen it or not. I didn't know whether it was something I'd invented, or dreamed, or misremembered, or whatever. All I know is that the memory of it—even if it was a false memory—was so precious that I'd barely even allowed myself to think about it in all that time.' He looked at me so earnestly that I almost wanted to laugh. Which wouldn't have been a pretty sight, since I had a mouth full of pizza at the time. 'I didn't know anything about it, except that it was a short film, as far as I could recall. It must have been shown mid-afternoon, in the school holidays, as some sort of filler between programmes, and it was called *The Crystal Garden*. At least, I was pretty sure that must have been the title. It's so hard to distinguish what belongs to memory and what belongs to real life. I can't remember anything about the story. I can only remember . . . an atmosphere, a feeling. A very faded print, the soundtrack filled with pops and scratches. A young boy as the hero: in one scene— the only scene I can call to mind, in any detail—he wanders into this garden, and I can remember the music on the soundtrack— there was a sort of tinkling background, some sort of tuned percussion, and over the top of that, a tune—a beautiful tune, lyrical and yearning—with a soprano singing the melody—there were no words—but again, the whole thing was incredibly scratchy, almost distorted—the recording must have deteriorated so badly . . . And this garden . . . The whole thing was made of crystal, was made of glass . . . It was a walled garden, he had to pass through a sort of passageway, a sort of tunnel in the wall to get to it, and when he came out into the garden . . . Yes, everything glittered, everything was made of crystal, all the flowers, the roses, the little topiary hedges, there were paths criss-crossing each other between the flower beds and they led towards this . . . lake, was it? this frozen pond? . . . a sheet of crystal, anyway, and this fountain at the centre of it, shimmering, glittering, just like the fountain in the garden today. The resemblance was incredible.' He paused for breath. I think this was the longest speech he'd ever made in the whole time I'd known him. His voice was quiet, but it was shaking as well. I'd never known him speak about anything with such passion. 'I'm *sure* this is real,' he resumed after a while. 'I'm sure I'm not imagining this. I *did* see that film. I know I did. I just wish I could remember more about it. It's crazy, I can't remember *anything* about the story. Nothing at all. Like I said, the whole thing is just . . . just an *atmosphere,* and the strange thing is, that the atmosphere of the film sort of . . . bleeds into the atmosphere in the room when I was watching it. It was the school holidays—it must have been the school holidays—or perhaps I was off sick, something like that—and Mum wasn't sitting next to me on the sofa or anything but she was inside the house with me, in the next room, I think, in the kitchen, getting dinner ready for when Dad came home. And it was winter, definitely winter, because there were ice crystals on the window of the living room and icicles hanging down above the window, and snow on the ground outside, or at least a frost—these details blend in, you see, they blend in with the crystal of the crystal garden; and our gas fire was on, our little old-fashioned gas fire, and it was hissing, as it always did, and giving out little pops and scratches, and again, that blends in, somehow, with the poor quality of the film soundtrack, so that it becomes even more hard to distinguish between what I've remembered and what I've imagined.'

"He tailed off, and fell silent, until I asked: 'How come you've never mentioned this before, if it's such an important memory for you?'

"And he said: 'Because I couldn't be sure if it was true or not. Not until today.'

"'Just because the garden reinforced that memory,' I said, 'doesn't mean that it makes it true. It sounds to me that what you're doing is conflating two different—' But he cut me off, and went back to the computer. 'No,' he said, 'that's not the point. The point is that seeing the garden today made me go online and start looking for some evidence. And here's what I found.'

"He passed the laptop over. I wiped my fingers on a piece of kitchen towel and took it off him. He was on the IMDb, looking at a page devoted to the filmography of some American cameraman. There was a long list of pretty undistinguished credits from the early 1940s onwards—some of them films, but mostly TV shows—and then just one credit as director, which said '*Der Garten aus Kristall,* 1937.' When you clicked on the link, it brought up a page which was completely blank except for the title of the film and the director's name: Friedrich Güdemann.

"I looked across at him and said: 'That's it?'

"'That's it,' he answered.

"I double checked. 'You've spent the last few hours searching the Internet for this film, and this is all you found?'

"'Yes. There's no other reference to it. Nothing.'

"I looked at the computer screen again. 'So it's a German film?'

"'Apparently,' he answered. 'When I put the English title into Google, nothing was coming up. So I started trying other languages, and slight variations on the title. And finally, this was what I found. It *must* be the right one,' he said, biting his lip. 'It has to be.'

"But was it the right one? This was Roger's dilemma, and it turned out to be an agonizing, drawn-out wait before he would find the answer. Already, that day, he'd posted queries about the film on the message boards of every movie website he could think of. He'd asked if anyone, like him, could remember seeing the film on afternoon television back in the 1960s. He asked for any information anyone could provide about Friedrich Güdemann, whose IMDb filmography suggested that he had moved to America in the early 1940s and anglicized his name to Fred Goodman. There was no Wikipedia entry about him, and no further references anywhere online. Having made his enquiries, Roger could only sit back and wait for some answers to come in."

"And did they?" Rachel asked.

Laura shook her head. "Nothing. Nothing at all." She sighed. "He was crushed by that. Really disappointed. He'd been convinced that in this day and age, the age of universal information, there was no subject so obscure that it didn't have its own expert online, somewhere or other. But for the time being he seemed to have drawn a blank. He kept checking the message boards, re-posting his questions and bumping the threads, but after a few weeks he seemed more or less resigned to the idea that he wasn't going to hear anything that way. He didn't talk about it much, but I knew that he was broken by it. He'd felt that he'd been on the verge of this . . . momentous discovery, and now he was back where he started."

Laura sipped her wine again. The fire suddenly gave out a sharp crackle and one of the logs tumbled out of place. Rachel looked down at the fire, and the sounds it was making, the warmth it was giving out, made her think of the infant Roger, sitting in front of his gas fire at home in the school holidays, watching this film with its ancient soundtrack of pops and crackles, his mother next door in the kitchen, preparing the family dinner . . .

"Well, life went on. In fact it became pretty busy. That year we had two life-changing events to deal with—moving house, which we did in the spring, and then the birth of Harry, which happened in the summer. Roger was . . . you know, pretty helpful about all this. He was quite involved, and for the first few months after Harry was born he was a pretty good father. Very hands-on. It seemed to be distracting him from all his other obsessions for a while, I thought, but it turned out I was wrong about that. The memory of that film was still weighing him down. The first I knew about it was when he told me that he'd been asked to contribute to a book of essays that Palgrave Macmillan were bringing out. It was a sort of Festschrift, paying homage to this film writer called Terry Worth, who'd been quite a name to reckon with in the 1990s. He'd also been a bit of a specialist on the subject of lost films, and this was the aspect of his work that Roger had been asked to write about. So of course I asked him if he was going to mention *The Crystal Garden* and he said probably not—there just wasn't enough information available to make it worthwhile. He said it in a very offhand way, so I really got the impression that he'd more or less forgotten about it, or at least put it to the back of his mind. He did say that this article was going to involve a lot of research, which didn't come at an especially good time, for me. There were about two weeks when I didn't see him at all. I was stuck at home feeding Harry, while Roger was away for days at a time down at the BFI library in London. Or at least, that's where I thought he was." She paused, stared ruefully for a moment into the depths of her wine glass, then looked up again.

"One day I got an e-mail from a friend, who'd just run into him—not at the BFI at all. He was at the Newspaper Library in Colindale." She looked quickly across at Rachel. "What's so funny? What are you smiling at?"

"Sorry," said Rachel. "It's just—I thought it might be something a bit . . . spicier than that. That he'd been having an affair, or something."

"That would have been preferable, in a way," said Laura. "At least that would have been relatively *normal* behaviour. But there was never anything normal about Roger. Only he could cheat on his wife by working in a different library than the one he was supposed to be working in. Anyway, he wouldn't have made a very good adulterer, because when he got back from London that night and I mentioned it to him, he confessed everything. Apparently he'd been going to Colindale every day to trawl through the entire TV listings of the *Birmingham Post* for the mid-1960s. I got pretty angry with him, as you can imagine, and accused him of wasting his time. To which he said: 'Ah! But it hasn't been a waste of time. Not at all. I've narrowed it down to two days.'

"'Narrowed what down?' I said.

"'The screening date. Here—take a look at *these.*' And he took two sheets of paper out of his briefcase and threw them down in front of me, like some self-satisfied detective producing his proof of the murderer's identity at the end of a film. I looked at them and couldn't see what he was talking about. They were just photocopies of two separate television listings from an old newspaper. No mention of *The Crystal Garden* anywhere.

"'Don't you see?' he said. 'Look at this one: 14 December 1966. A Wednesday afternoon. The school holidays would just have started. I'd be five and a half years old. Now look at the listings for ATV. There—look. At ten past two.' I looked at the listing and read out the title. '*Against the Wind.* What's that got to do with anything?' He sighed impatiently, as if I was some kind of imbecile. 'Don't you see?' he said. 'Look when the next programme started.' I did. It started at four thirty, but again, I couldn't see the relevance of this. '*Against the Wind,*' he pointed out, almost breathless with excitement, 'is an

Ealing film from the 1940s, set in occupied Belgium. *And it's only ninety-six minutes long.* And films run even more quickly when broadcast on television. So let's say ninety minutes. Add in even twenty or twenty-five minutes' worth of commercials, and you're still left with a big gap in the schedule. Something that would need to be filled.' He stared at me in triumph, but I just looked down with a frown, not liking the direction this was taking at all. 'And this one's the same,' he continued, 'but even better: 16 February 1967. A Thursday. Probably half-term. This time the film is *The Man Who Could Work Miracles*—an H. G. Wells adaptation, *which I know I saw round about that time.* I can remember it, quite clearly. And it's only eighty-two minutes long! Which leaves a gap in the schedule of more than twenty minutes this time. And the weather was right that week, as well—there'd been a snowfall two days before. I'm *certain* this has to be the one. Ninety-nine per cent certain, anyway. When else could it have been? I've been through all the other listings and these were the only real gaps.'

"'You've been through them *all*?' I said, incredulous. 'How long did that take?'

"'Not long,' he said, defensively. 'Just three or four days.'

"I was pretty shocked when I heard this was how he'd been spending his time, as you might imagine. But it seemed that these things went in cycles. He was all excited about his discovery for a few days, but nothing came of it. He hadn't managed to prove anything, of course. He wrote to Central TV in Birmingham, but they didn't have any of their archives from the old ATV days. No paperwork or anything like that. Anyway they thought he was some sort of crank, obviously. So once again, after a few more months, he seemed to have got over it.

"Academic publishing, as you know, doesn't exactly move fast. It took two years for that book of essays about Terry Worth to come out, and when it did, Roger's was singled out as being one of the best. It was a really good piece, I could see that. This was the tragedy: when Roger could get past his obsessions and tackle something serious, he really was a good writer. A lot of it was about a Billy Wilder film called *The Private Life of Sherlock Holmes*, which is famous for having about a third of its footage cut out before it was released. In the bits that are left, Holmes and Watson go up to Scotland and encounter the Loch Ness Monster. Roger and I watched it together one night, and I suppose that's when we both started thinking about the Monster and what it represents. The one in this film turns out to be a fake, of course. As they so often do.

"That was a good night. We sat up together for hours, talking about all these different Loch Ness films and trying to decide what they had in common. We noticed that the main characters usually take people's responses to the *idea* of the Monster—some sense of awe, perhaps, bordering on fear—and try to make a profit out of it. That's when he came up with this phrase, 'monetizing wonder.'" Laura paused, and shook her head with sad incredulity. "How long ago was that? And I'm still trying to finish the article for him. Unbelievable."

She fell quite silent. Rachel thought that some words of encouragement might be in order. "It's a good phrase anyway," she said. "You should use it as the title. But what about the other film, the German one . . . ?"

"Well . . ." said Laura, "the next thing that happened was a message. A message online, out of the blue, from someone who had finally seen one of Roger's requests for information. More than three years after he'd posted it, in fact. (Yes, that's right—because Harry was already at nursery.) And that was how he found out the whole story of the film. And it was also the beginning of the end, for him.

"This guy Chris had been browsing one of these film fan sites and just by chance he'd seen Roger's old post. So he sent him a personal message . . ." She paused to take another sip from her glass, but found it empty. "Goodness, that went quickly. Is there anything left in the bottle?"

"Afraid not," said Rachel, with a regretful glance at her own glass. "We've certainly been getting through it tonight."

"That's all right. I think it's time to open another. And while I'm doing that," said Laura, rising effortfully to her feet, "you can have a look at the thread. It's still there, on the website."

And so, while Laura opened another bottle of Rioja and poured two more glasses, Rachel sat with the laptop on her knees and read through the exchange of messages which Roger had initiated, on the forums of a site called Britmovie.

23 October 2010 18:32

Hi Roger

Sorry for the delayed reply! I have only just discovered this site and seen your queries.

First off—I have never seen The Crystal Garden but your memory doesn't deceive you. It was indeed shown in the ATV region one afternoon in the mid-sixties. This was certainly its only British TV screening and one of its very few public screenings anywhere in the world! I know this because my grandfather, Tom Ferris, was the man responsible.

It's a long story and I don't know how much information you want apart from the fact your memory is accurate. Let me know and I'll try to fill in any gaps.

Cheers

Chris Ferris

23 October 2010 19:05

Hi Chris

This is incredible. I had given up hope of ever hearing back from anyone about this (to me) mythical film, and now you have confirmed everything I suspected! To find out that I didn't dream or imagine it is an amazing moment for me. I am literally shaking in front of the computer as I type these words.

Please tell me every single thing you know about this film and its screening on British TV, starting at the very beginning.

Roger

24 October 2010 23:53

Chris

Are you still there?

Roger

25 October 2010 22:17

Hi Roger

Sorry to have left it a couple of days before replying. I can see you're pretty keen to hear about this. But it's taken me a day or two to get my thoughts together and put the facts in the right order.

So, where to start? Let's start with the director of the film, Fred Goodman, or Friedrich Güdemann as he was known before he got out of Germany in the late 1930s. Friedrich (my grandfather could never bring himself to call him Fred) came from Magdeburg, in the East. He was a young and talented DP who had worked for several years at UFA studios. But he also had ambitions to direct, and had apparently been getting quite frustrated that no opportunities had presented themselves. The only thing he'd managed to do was a tiny little film, about 8 or 9 minutes long, which he'd made over one weekend at the country house of some friends, in the middle of winter, using their little son as the main actor. As far as I know it had no real plot to speak of (you would perhaps know more about this), just one sequence of a little boy exploring the grounds of this house, making his way through this tunnel in one of the walls and emerging into a magical landscape, a garden made entirely of crystal. That's all there was to it, and yet the few people who saw the film said it cast an extraordinary spell on them. Including my grandad. It was a visionary piece of work, he said. At the very least, it was an amazing calling card. But Friedrich was Jewish, of course, and he'd already left it dangerously late to get out of Germany. When he did finally make his escape, he took the film with him—the only print in existence, on a single 16 mm reel. He pitched up in Paris and then a few months later managed to cross the Channel to London. This would be in '37 or '38. He soon got introduced to the film-making community here and found some work at Gainsborough, where he was DP on a couple of lowbrow comedies—sub–Will Hay stuff. God knows what he made of the films themselves, but I'm sure he did a good, professional job. Anyway, this was where he met my grandfather, who was designing titles for Gainsborough at the time. Friedrich asked him to do some new titles for *The Crystal Garden*—unpaid, that is. In his spare time. He thought it would be good to have an English-language version, and it was only the opening titles that needed changing—the film had no dialogue as far as I know. My grandad liked Friedrich and was happy to do him the favour. So the film was screened for him and he was quite bowled over, apparently. He said it was beautifully photographed, of course, because Friedrich was a very gifted guy, but the thing that made the strongest impression on him, funnily enough, was the music. There'd been no money to use an orchestra or anything like that, so once again Friedrich had called in a favour, and got a friend to write some music for it, and persuaded this soprano—it may even have been the same woman who owned the country house—to do the recording. Just her voice, I believe, and a little chamber group. Grandad often used to talk to me about this music and how beautiful it was, but I never heard it myself, sadly.

Well, this has already taken longer than I thought, so I'll pack it in for now and continue the story tomorrow if I get the time.

25 October 2010 22:33

Oh God yes, I remember that music. So lovely, and so sad! Like the distillation of every lament for childhood innocence that you ever heard. How did I understand that, how did I tune in to it, when I was just five years old? Or am I projecting, looking back on my five-year-old self, my eyes riveted to that tiny black-and-white screen, the recording of that music (already thirty years old) drifting out of the puny speaker on our little Ekco TV set through a quagmire, a forest of pops and crackles and distortions? And the gas fire hissing in the hearth, my mum next door in the kitchen, getting dinner ready for when Dad came home.

I think . . .

. . . I think I'm already high on the stuff you've told me, and I've had 2 or 3 glasses of wine too many while reading it, and it's always a mistake to post when pissed, so . . .

26 October 2010 22:42

Hello again Roger

I hope you didn't drink too much more wine last night, and your hangover wasn't too horrific this morning!

Anyway, I can see that this is an important story for you, and I'm sorry to have left you hanging in the air like that. It's taking me longer than I expected to tell you everything. So let's pick up where we left off.

My grandad Tom designed a nice set of opening title cards for the film and added them to the print, but I'm pretty sure Friedrich never saw them—not until many years later, anyway. In fact Grandad was still working on the film, and still had the print in his possession, when he got a telegram from Friedrich which gave him quite a shock. It was sent from a transatlantic liner and it said that a friend of Friedrich's had obtained a work permit for him in America at very short notice and he was off to Hollywood. (Along with all the other, more famous European refugees from Nazi Germany who went there in those years—I'm sure you don't need me to list their names.) And that was the last Grandad ever saw of him, as it turned out. Friedrich changed his name to Fred Goodman and after a few years in Hollywood he moved over to television and worked on a number of big shows for CBS and others. Which, coincidentally, is more or less what Grandad did after the war. He worked at Ealing Studios for most of the forties but made the transition to television almost as soon as commercial TV started up. He moved to the Midlands and worked for ATV, designing titles and captions to start with, finally ending up with a desk job in scheduling.

So that brings us to the mid-1960s. Grandad and Friedrich have sporadically—very sporadically—kept in touch during this time. A letter every two or three years. Grandad still has the print of *The Crystal Garden* and has shown it a few times at film societies and so on—at one point even offering to try and find distribution for it as a supporting feature but I don't think anything came of that. Friedrich has given him carte blanche to get it shown whenever he can—he's not interested in remuneration. And this is how Grandad one day gets his idea. The scheduling at ATV can be somewhat erratic, especially during the daytime, and the best care isn't always taken to ensure that feature films, in particular, fill the spots that have been allowed to them. Quite often ten or fifteen minutes have to be filled in, and for this reason a little stockpile of "standby" material is kept on hand: sometimes cartoons and so on, but those can be expensive to use, so more often it's cheaper material like terrible Public Information films from the 1950s. And so, Grandad decided to lend his print of *The Crystal Garden* to ATV so that they could drop it into the afternoon schedule like this if they ever needed to. To plug a ten-minute gap. And that is indeed what happened—once and once only—on the day you saw the film and it made such a strong impression on you.

So, I hope I have cleared up *that* mystery at least. It's been nice connecting with someone who remembers the film—the story of Grandad and Friedrich and this one unrepeated screening is something of a legend in my household. It's nice to know that someone saw it and, more importantly, actually remembers it.

27 October 2010 00:27
Chris
I can't believe you have left the story unfinished like this. You haven't answered the most important question of all.
    WHAT HAPPENED TO THE PRINT???

27 October 2010 21:46
WHAT HAPPENED TO THE PRINT??

28 October 2010 10:33
Dear Roger
Hm. Well, a quick "thanks" or something after I told you all that stuff would have been nice, but anyway . . .

Briefly—when the Wall came down in '89, Friedrich returned home to Magdeburg for the first time in more than sixty years. He wrote to my grandfather and asked him to send the print out to Germany as he wanted to see it again. And that's what Grandad did. More than that I don't know.

Hope this satisfies your curiosity.

Cheers
Chris

And that, it seemed, was the end of the thread. Rachel closed the laptop and handed it back to Laura, who had been watching her all this time, sipping her wine mechanically and leaning forward in her eagerness to observe her reaction.

"Well . . . ?" said Laura, after a while, when no immediate response was forthcoming.

"He certainly had it bad," said Rachel. "I hope that he didn't . . . I hope you're not going to tell me the next thing he did was go to Germany?"

Laura nodded slowly, with a sad, emphatic smile. "Of course. What else was he going to do?"

She ran a hand through her hair and took a deep breath. "Roger had a friend who lived over there. Well, not a friend, exactly—an academic colleague called James, who'd married a German woman and now taught film studies at the Freie Universität in Berlin. When Roger was writing about *The Private Life of Sherlock Holmes,* James had helped him to track down an old German TV documentary about Billy Wilder. He was resourceful and he knew his way around the key German film archives. So James made some routine initial inquiries but nothing came of them. Friedrich Güdemann had died in 2004 at the healthy age of ninety-five, but since then *The Crystal Garden* hadn't turned up anywhere. So what had become of that single print? Was it with his family—and for that matter, where *were* his family? Did he have children and grandchildren back in America? Roger sent a message to Chris asking him if he knew anything about this, but Chris was no longer in the mood to answer any of my rude husband's questions. So this was where James had to step in again.

"Well, Güdemann had been gay, apparently—that was one of the first things he discovered. When he'd come back to live in Germany he was already an old man and his long-term lover was dead. Güdemann spent his last years in Leipzig, with his sister and brother-in-law. By the time James found all this out, the brother-in-law was the only one left alive, and he was in a nursing home and not particularly *compos mentis.* James found himself dealing with this man's son-in-law, a guy in his late fifties called Horst. So we're already several steps removed from Friedrich himself by now. After putting his father-in-law in a home, Horst had sold his house and put all his effects into a couple of big storage units in a warehouse on the outskirts of Leipzig. Did this include any of Friedrich's stuff, James wanted to know? Horst wasn't sure. He'd simply taken the entire contents of the house and stored them. His plan was to go through it all whenever he had the time, but he hadn't got round to it yet.

"Now, I don't know exactly what James said to him to get him to cooperate. But, somehow or other, he persuaded Horst to let him look through the contents of the units. And as soon as he e-mailed Roger to let him know about this, Roger was on the first plane to Germany. He literally booked the first flight he could find that evening. I was sitting up in bed reading, last thing at night, when he came in and announced that he was off to Leipzig the next day. He had to get up at 3:30. I remember him giving me a good-bye kiss and saying something to me about the film—how sure he was that he was going to find it, how this was going to be the end of the search, how it would all be over and done with in a couple of days. I kissed him back and told him that I was glad. And that was the last time I ever saw him."

She tried to drink from her wineglass, but it was empty again. Her eyes seemed tired now, almost sightless.

"I'll fetch James's letter," she said. "That will tell you the end of the story."

Rachel noticed that Laura was slightly unsteady on her feet as she got up and left the room. She went into the ground-floor study and was gone for a few minutes. Rachel heard desk drawers being opened and shut repeatedly, papers being shuffled through, multiple tuts of impatience and frustration. But at last the document was found, and Laura returned, bearing it aloft in one hand while she carried a small bottle in the other.

"Brandy," she explained. "Always good to finish off the evening with a brandy. And here's the letter. Have a read of that while I pour you a little shot of brandy."

There was still a little wine left in Rachel's glass, but the brandy was added to it anyway, producing a liquid that was sickly orange in colour. She refrained from drinking it, and concentrated instead on the sheaf of handwritten sheets which Laura had given her. The handwriting was clear and firm, with a noticeable italic slant. The notepaper itself was thick, creamy yellow and expensively watermarked.

My dear Laura,

What a terrible thing it is to have to write these words. You said, at the funeral (and how beautifully you spoke to the congregation, on that wretched occasion), that I was not to blame myself for what happened. But how can I not? I was the one who led Roger to the place where he died. True, I could never have predicted what would happen there, but still—the fact remains. If it wasn't for my intervention, your husband would be alive today.

Thursday was not the time to discuss the details of his last few hours. I promised you that I would write and tell you all that I could. So I shall begin at the time that I met Roger off the plane at Leipzig.

It was a bitterly cold morning. I met him at the airport (snow had delayed his connecting flight from Hannover by half an hour) and we went for a coffee at the airport bar. He did not waste any time in small talk—he came straight to the point and wanted to know everything about our forthcoming meeting with Horst. We had plenty of time but he made me gulp down my coffee and leave. As a consequence we arrived at the storage units about 15 minutes early. It was getting ever more snowy and although by now it was late in the morning, the sky was a thick grey-black and it felt like there would be no real daylight today. The storage place was simply a large warehouse on the outskirts of town: a place totally without character or atmosphere. There was a big car park outside. We parked the car and walked inside through the snow, and bought ourselves more scalding black coffee from the machine next to the reception desk. Then we sat there drinking it and waiting for Horst to arrive. I explained a thing or two to Roger: that it had not been easy, at first, to persuade Horst to let us look through these storage cupboards in search of Friedrich Güdemann's effects. He was mistrustful of us. Until I had contacted him, he'd had no idea that Friedrich had had a career in film and television and the only reason he had agreed to meet us this morning, I was sure, was the possibility that we might be able to alert him to something among these belongings that was valuable and might be worth selling. I warned Roger that this might include the print of Der Garten aus Kristall, *if we found it, but this suggestion did not seem to worry him, but only to excite him further. "You mean—you really think it might be here?" he said, and that was his only reaction. He was so fixated on the idea of finding the film that he didn't give a thought to what might happen to it afterwards, what kinds of dispute over ownership might arise. So powerful was his need, I now realize, to see it just once again, to relive—as best he could—those minutes of far-off enchantment he had enjoyed once, as a young and carefree schoolboy.*

And what a desolate place that quest had brought him to. We were drinking our cheap, acrid coffee while sitting on a plain wooden bench, our backs to a wall. Our bench was at the centre of a pool of feeble neon light: all around us, the vast spaces of the warehouse stretched out into oceans of dense, impenetrable gloom. Corridors ran off in every direction, made up of row upon row of identical storage units, each one about four metres high and two wide. Above us were metal gantries, crossing and criss-crossing and leading to yet more storage units. I could imagine the echoing, metallic sound that footsteps might make if they pounded these walkways, but today, in reality, all was silent. A smothering and deathly silence. The only sound was the distant, sibilant trickle of music leaking out from the earphones of the guy sitting behind the reception desk. Roger and I spoke in low, murmurous undertones, as if we were in a cathedral or a library. Which I suppose we were, in a way. A library of unwanted possessions. A cathedral of the forgotten. In any case, we didn't have much to say to each other.

There was no mistaking the sound of the car when it arrived, even with its tyres muffled by the snow. We both stood up and awaited Horst's entrance. He was brushing the snow from his coat and was in a bad mood. Without saying hello to us he went to the reception desk and retrieved the keys to his two storage units. Only then did he come over and address us. I introduced Roger but he did not seem particularly interested. "You think there might be a film in one of these cupboards, right?" he asked us. "You are looking for a film." I nodded and he said: "If we find it, you cannot have this film. It's my property." I said of course, that was completely understood, and Roger said: "But we must see it. You must let us watch." Horst said something noncommittal to the effect that he would think about that, and then we set off on our quest.

Horst's units were on the ground floor of the warehouse. They stood directly opposite each other: one of them was Number 24, and the other was Number 11. The doors were painted yellow, and each one had a strong chunky padlock fitted to it. When Horst unlocked the door to Number 24 and threw it open, I peeped inside, and my heart sank. The cupboard looked much bigger than you would imagine from the outside, and it was packed from floor to ceiling with furniture and cardboard boxes. As for Number 11, it was even worse. The objects were stacked right to the very doorway, so that you could barely close the door and it was impossible to imagine what lay beyond the first stack. Sifting through all this jetsam, I realized at once, was going to be the work of many hours.

Well, I shall cut a long and difficult story short. Slowly and with great effort, we began to work our way through all the junk of Mr. Güdemann, his sister and his brother-in-law. Roger and I looked through the contents of Number 11, while Horst concentrated on Number 24: he was looking for something specific, I could tell that, I expect he was hoping to find items of jewellery or something similar. We explained to him very carefully what a can of film would look like and he gruffly assured us that we would be told if he found one.

It was long, tiring and painstaking work. Looking through the contents of the opposite cupboard, Horst had his back to us, but he still seemed to be fully aware of our movements, and was quick to call out "Be careful with that!" or "Show me what's in that box!" whenever something caught his attention. As I had expected, it was the small items of jewellery that he would always take from us and put carefully to one side.

After about an hour we were both very tired and I thought it would be a good idea if we took a break. But Roger had a feverish glint in his eyes and would not suspend the hunt, even for a few moments. I offered to fetch him another cup of coffee, but he said he didn't want one, so I just went to get one for myself.

I had been sitting on the bench by the reception desk for about ten minutes, drinking my coffee and attending to some e-mails, when I heard his cry. I have never heard such excitement, such exaltation—bordering on ecstasy—in a human voice before. "James!" he called. "James—I think I've found it!" Those were his words, but my impression was more that he was giving out a primal scream of joy. I put down my coffee, sprang to my feet and ran towards the cupboard but I had not been moving for more than five seconds before I heard a different kind of scream—the most terrible scream of fear—followed by a terrific crash. Or rather a series of crashes: three or four of them, each one louder than the last, culminating in what sounded almost like an explosion, the dying echo of which filled the warehouse like a reverberation, leaving behind it a shocking silence. In a few more seconds I was at the door of cupboard Number 11, where Horst was also standing, and where a scene of chaos confronted us. Half the contents of the cupboard were outside, in the corridor where we had been stacking them. Inside the cupboard itself was a vision of total disarray, with boxes, books, items of furniture and shattered crockery and glassware everywhere, forming a huge disordered pile, at the very bottom of which, crushed by the weight of all this junk, lay poor Roger's already lifeless body.

The man from the reception desk came to hear what the noise was and then he went straight to phone for an ambulance. Horst and I began clearing away the debris that had crushed Roger's body. We worked like demons now, tossing things to one side without looking at them, not bothering about whether we broke them or not as we did so.

I don't know what else to tell you. The medics arrived on the scene quickly and Roger was pronounced dead as soon as they looked at him.

The next few hours are a blur. I remember only one detail, *which is that in the course of digging through the junk in order to reach him, I spotted the item that he must have seen, and that must have inspired him to call out to me. It would have been at the very bottom of the pile, but in his eagerness to put his hands on it, he must have tried to pull it out from underneath, and that was what caused the huge, towering stack to tumble down. It was a metal can of the sort which might have contained a 16 mm film, and on the side of it was a label, upon which was written, in faded capital letters—more than seventy years old—*Der Garten aus Kristall.

I opened up the can. It was full of old tobacco tins, most of them containing Deutschmark coins in small denominations. Also some buttons and ribbon and needle and thread and other things for sewing.

Perhaps it's a good job he never saw that. Perhaps if he had, he might have died another kind of death.

Rachel was an early riser, and she was the first to get out of bed the next morning, although when she came down to the kitchen, Keisha had already arrived: she was making coffee and preparing Harry's breakfast. Not wishing to disturb her, and finding the thought of conversation awkward, Rachel went out into the garden.

She sat on the old wooden bench again, as she had done the afternoon before. Once again, her eyes were drawn to the silent, broken-down fountain at the centre of the lawn. It was a shame that it didn't work. Laura should really get it repaired. The garden still seemed attractive to Rachel, but no longer magical, no longer unreal.

After a few minutes Laura came out to join her. She was wearing bedsocks, and a jumper over her pyjamas, and a thick dressing gown over her jumper, and she was carrying two mugs of coffee.

They sat for a while drinking their coffee in silence.

"Are you going to get the fountain fixed, then?" Rachel asked.

"I don't think so. I think I'm going to put this place on the market."

"And move back to Oxford?"

"Maybe. Or maybe London. I've been applying for professorships."

Laura shivered, and leaned forward on the bench. It was far too cold to be sitting outside.

"The thing is," she said, "I don't want Harry to turn out like Roger."

Rachel wasn't sure how to interpret this.

"Obsessive, you mean?"

"Oh, he can obsess as much as he likes, as long as he obsesses over something useful."

"You mean, something other than the broadcast dates of old black-and-white films?"

Laura corrected her quickly. "I mean something other than the past." She sipped her coffee and gripped the mug in both hands, warming her fingers. "Like a lot of people, Roger was convinced— even if he never really admitted it, even to himself—that life was better, simpler, easier, in the past. When he was growing up. It wasn't just a hankering for childhood. It was bigger than that. It was to do with what the country was like—or what he *thought* it had been like—in the sixties and seventies."

"Before I was born."

"A long time before you were born. The culture was different back then. Very different. For Roger, it was about welfarism, and having a safety net, and above all . . . not being so weighed down by *choice* all the time, I suppose. He *hated* choice. The very thing that Henry Winshaw—and every government minister after him—said we should have more of was the thing Roger hated most. I mean, think about it. Think about that image, the one he kept coming back to, over and over."

"The crystal garden?"

"Not just the garden. Everything about the memory of watching that film. The whole . . . texture of it. Waiting for his father to come home from work—from the same place he worked for forty years. His mother in the kitchen, cooking dinner—the same dinner she always cooked on that night of the week. Can't you see how secure that must have felt? The beautiful, blanketing safety of it? Even the fact that the film came on television that afternoon and he happened to be watching it. That wasn't his *choice,* you see. Somebody else had made that choice for him. Some scheduler at ATV, or Chris's grandfather—it doesn't matter who it was, the only thing that matters is *it wasn't Roger*. The whole thing that defined that situation, and the whole beauty of it, as far as he was concerned, was passivity. Other people were making choices for him. People he trusted. He loved that. He loved the idea of trusting people to make decisions on his behalf. Not all of them. Just some. Just enough so that you were free to live other parts of your life the way that you wanted. I suppose, apart from anything else, that's one of the definitions of a happy childhood, isn't it? But Roger also thought he could remember a time when we all felt that way. A time when we trusted the people in power, and their side of the deal was to treat us . . . not like children exactly, but like people who needed to be looked after now and again. As I suppose many of us do."

"It seems . . . a bit naive," Rachel ventured.

"Yes," said Laura, crisply. "It is. Life's not like that. In fact it gets less and less like that all the time." She glanced at Rachel: a sly, rapid glance. "I know that you've noticed how I talk to Harry. You think I'm too tough on him."

"A bit," Rachel had to admit.

"But you see, I couldn't bear him to end up looking back on his childhood—back on the past—the way his father did."

And then, without another word, Laura rose to her feet and walked briskly towards the kitchen door, not looking back once: either to hide the tears that she had been withholding all this time, or simply because it had become too cold to sit in the garden for a moment longer.

William Cowper, The Task *(1785):*

Yet what can satire, either grave or gay? . . .
What vice has it subdued? whose heart reclaim'd
By rigour? or whom laughed into reform?
Alas! Leviathan is not so tamed.

The Winshaw Prize, or Nathan Pilbeam's Breakthrough Case

A "Nate of the Station" Story

1

Scotland Yard were baffled.

Or rather, they did not yet know that they were baffled. But by the time Detective Chief Inspector Capes had finished reading the e-mail, he would have a new case on his hands, and he would be baffled by it.

The e-mail had arrived two hours ago, had been forwarded from computer to computer and eventually came to the attention of "Capes of the Yard," as his colleagues insisted on calling him. Incidentally, why *did* they call him that, he asked himself, as he asked himself every day? It was a pathetic nickname. Totally without originality, and doing no kind of justice to his stature within the force. Why on earth couldn't they call him "The Caped Crusader"? He'd been dropping hints about it for months. It was the perfect soubriquet, combining a subtle play on words with a clear gesture towards his almost superhero-like approach to police work. Why wasn't it catching on?

Sipping his third black coffee of the day as he contemplated the stark injustice of this situation, he realized that his attention was drifting away from the e-mail, which he was yet to read in full:

To Whom It May Concern

Forgive me for writing to you "out of the blue" as it were. As a mere Trainee Detective Constable from the provinces, my name will not be known to you. However, two items of news from the London papers have recently caught my eye, and I wanted to make sure that their potential significance was understood by those in positions of authority at Scotland Yard.

The first of these items is the death by drowning of Michael Parr, a Caucasian male in his late twenties, on the southern bank of the Thames near Greenwich, on the 13th of last month. Mr. Parr was, by profession, a stand-up comedian. The coroner recorded a verdict of accidental death.

The second is the death of Raymond Turnbull, another Caucasian male in his late twenties, after falling from a seventh-floor balcony at a block of flats in Acton Town, west London, on the 18th of this month. Mr. Turnbull was also a stand-up comedian and, once again, the coroner recorded a verdict of accidental death.

It is my belief that neither of these deaths was accidental, and that the two fatalities are connected.

You may wonder why it is that I make this declaration with such assurance. I would be happy to explain my reasoning to you over a drink at any time and place that might be mutually convenient. In the meantime, you might acquire some insight into the methods that have already brought me some modest measure of notoriety by perusing the attached article, which was published in the features section of the February issue of *Police* magazine.

Sincerely
Nathan Pilbeam

PC Pilbeam lived in an unremarkable apartment building on Guildford's north-eastern outskirts. It was a new block, set back from the road and securely gated. You had to enter a code to gain access to the paved forecourt and then another, different code to get into the building itself. He had a two-bedroom apartment on the second floor, which looked out over a pleasant but uninspiring communal garden. PC Pilbeam lived alone and used the second bedroom as his study.

This study was distinguished by the volume and variety of the books and paperwork with which Pilbeam had filled it. Two of the walls were covered from floor to ceiling with bookshelves, which overflowed not just with the expected volumes of Blackstone's *Police Manuals* and *Operational Handbook,* but also a huge library of works devoted to history, politics, sociology, cultural theory, media studies, Marxist philosophy, semiotics, and queer studies. There were shelves filled with box files which contained back issues of journals dealing with the same subjects: PC Pilbeam was on familiar terms with most of the local postmen, who were forever arriving with copies of the latest issue of *Prospect, Private Eye,* the *New Left Review, Sight and Sound, Monocle, Diva, History Today, Searchlight, Index on Censorship* and *Intelligent Life.* He read them all, then filed and cross-indexed them on his computer using a complex spreadsheet of his own devising.

It was not that PC Pilbeam had a wide variety of hobbies or leisure interests. His ambition was to be the country's leading expert in the field of criminal investigation, and every waking moment of his life was devoted to that aim. Ever since he was a young boy, and his grandfather had introduced him to the stories of Conan Doyle and Agatha Christie, he had been fascinated by the art of detection. A modest upbringing in the suburbs of Portsmouth had given him plenty of time to nurture his obsession. Throughout the late 1990s and early 2000s, while his friends and contemporaries fell under the sway of the Internet, Nathan felt himself set apart: he was drawn, instead, to the library of books left behind by his grandfather, which after his death sat in unsorted piles, accumulating dust in a spare bedroom. Here, besides a large collection of detective stories, were the classic works of Marx, Orwell, Tressell and Shaw; essays by Chomsky and Gramsci; histories by Hobsbawn and Thompson; well-thumbed volumes bearing the names of Marcuse and Lukács, William Morris and Raymond Williams. Nathan devoured these books and was shocked that his own parents took so little interest in them, regarding them as little more than an annoying clutter which had been dumped on them to take up space in their house. His grandfather had been an autodidact, relying on the public library, the Workers' Educational Association and cheap paperbacks from

Pelican Books and the Left Book Club. Nathan decided that this was a path he would follow himself, and chose not to enter university, applying directly to the police force at the age of eighteen instead.

Nathan was now twenty-four. At the station in Guildford he was a popular figure, although his colleagues certainly regarded him as eccentric, and were prone to teasing him, both to his face and behind his back. In part this was prompted by the seriousness—not to say earnestness—of his manner. But his fellow officers were also both fascinated and amused by his approach to police work.

PC Pilbeam's theory, developed over many years' reading and thinking, was that every crime had to be seen in its social, political and cultural context. The modern policeman, he maintained, had to be familiar with, and attuned to, all the most diverse currents of contemporary thought. In a recent case of indecent exposure, for instance, he drew on the modish discipline of psychogeography (as pioneered by Guy Debord, and practised in the present day by the likes of Patrick Keiller, Iain Sinclair and Will Self), to prove that the accused could not possibly be the culprit, because the anniversary of his mother's death would have prompted him to walk a different route home on the afternoon in question, away from the public park and through the interwar council estate on which she had grown up and spent her early life. He solved another case after reading an article by James Meek in the *London Review of Books*, about the coalition government's infamous Bedroom Tax, a charge levied on council house owners with spare or unoccupied rooms. In order to avoid paying this punitive levy, some badly off married couples were pretending to be estranged and therefore to be making use of two separate bedrooms. By proving, in the case of one such couple, that this was a lie, PC Pilbeam unravelled the mystery of a burglary that had taken place in their home. If both husband and wife were indeed sleeping in the main bedroom, he argued, then the intruder's point of ingress was likely to have been the spare bedroom, and not the kitchen as they—in their fear of being reported to the authorities—had insisted. Sure enough, the spare bedroom window frame was found to be covered in fingerprints, and the thief was swiftly apprehended.

"In both of these examples," Pilbeam wrote in his article for *Police* magazine, "traditional lines of inquiry proved inadequate. The criminal does not act in a political vacuum. To understand motive, one must understand what motivates: and this involves taking into account the effect of economics and environment, culture and capital, landscape and cityscape, the politics of identity and the politics of party. To solve an English crime, committed by an English criminal, one must contemplate the condition of England itself."

It was this final sentence, read aloud by one of his colleagues, in tones half sarcastic, half admiring, to a bemused audience in the canteen one lunchtime, that had earned Nathan Pilbeam his own nickname: "Nate of the Station."

PC Pilbeam was in the middle of a few days' annual leave, but he was not exactly taking a break from police work. He had no wish to relax, in the sense in which most people would have understood the word. After sending his message to Scotland Yard in the morning, he made a brief visit to the local supermarket to buy ingredients for the dinner he intended to cook that evening for his *inamorata*. After that, he opened the package from Amazon which his overworked postman had delivered earlier.

It contained two DVDs, which bore a striking resemblance to one another. The cover of the first showed a young, tousled, slightly overweight white man wearing a loose brightly coloured shirt, untucked at the trouser. He was talking into a microphone. The DVD was entitled *Mickey Parr—Would You Credit It?—On Stage and On Fire.* The cover of the second showed another young, tousled, slightly overweight white man wearing a loose brightly coloured shirt untucked at the trouser. He too was talking into a microphone, and his DVD was entitled *Ray Turnbull—Last in the Queue—Live and Outrageous.* Nathan could remember seeing both of these releases advertised on posters on the London Underground in the run-up to Christmas last year, along with about half a dozen other posters all advertising DVDs by young, tousled, slightly overweight white men wearing loose brightly coloured shirts untucked at the trouser. For the purposes of these posters, all of these men had adopted the same slightly quizzical expressions; they had also, it seemed, all been on tour earlier in the year, and had recorded their performances for use on these Christmas DVDs.

It had struck Nathan, even then, as being an interesting phenomenon. His understanding was that none of these men were regarded as world experts in any field of human endeavour, or public thinkers possessed of radical new insight. Nonetheless, they were able to command generous sums of money and attract large audiences for their ability to comment in a casual, sometimes humorous way on various aspects of contemporary life. Occasional cutaways during the DVDs would reveal well-dressed and seemingly affluent young audience members roaring with laughter at a series of unremarkable observations about gender roles or the minutiae of everyday social interaction. In the new Moleskine notebook which he had recently bought and labelled "STAND-UP COMEDY" PC Pilbeam copied down an observation from Hermann Hesse:

> "How people love to laugh! They flock from the suburbs in the bitter cold, they stand in line, pay money, and stay out until past midnight, only in order to laugh a while."—*Reflections*

Both DVDs were about eighty minutes long. He had been watching the second one for almost an hour when the breakthrough came. He had been certain, all along, that there would turn out to be some connection between the two men, something more than the generic similarity between their acts. And now he had the proof.

Like many great men—and most great detectives, for that matter—Nathan Pilbeam had a weakness. A fatal chink in his armour.

It was not alcohol, or drug addiction. He was too young to have a broken marriage behind him, or a teenage daughter with whom to have a fraught and problematic relationship. His flaw, in fact, was much simpler than that. It was an unrequited passion.

The object of his infatuation was called Lucinda—Lucinda Givings. It was an antiquated name, and Lucinda was, in many ways, an antiquated person. This might even have been the very reason he was attracted to her. Brought up on a diet of Miss Marple and Lord Peter Wimsey, he could not believe his luck (or misfortune, depending on how he looked at it) in having stumbled upon someone whose natural home seemed to be in one of their stories, rather than the Guildford of 2013. Her speech was formal and demure, as was her manner of dress. One of her few concessions to modernity was that she sometimes used the branch of Starbucks where Nathan himself liked to go at the end of a long shift. She was usually to be found there late in the afternoon, marking her pupils' homework. After a few occasions when they had made shy eye contact and nothing more, Nathan had finally summoned the courage to strike up a tentative conversation.

Like Nathan, she was in her mid-twenties. She was extremely pretty, and determined not to show it. She wore baggy trousers and shapeless jumpers which gave away nothing about her figure (thereby allowing Nathan to imagine it all the more freely). She wore her hair pulled back and tightly tied behind her head, thereby encouraging Nathan to picture, during his fevered nocturnal fantasies, the moment when she would untie it, shake it loose and remove her horn-rimmed glasses, which would be his cue to utter the traditional words, "Why, Lucinda—but you're beautiful." She was a strict devotee of the Catholic faith. She taught chemistry at the local private girls' secondary school, where she was famous for her abhorrence of indiscipline and her unquestioning respect for the school rules, prompting students and fellow teachers alike to refer to her, behind her (long, shapely) back, as "Severe Miss Givings."

"I had Severe Miss Givings last night." That was the joke which was passed around the staff room at least once a week. But a joke was what it remained: for nobody had ever had, or was likely to have, Severe Miss Givings. Least of all Nathan Pilbeam.

Never mind. PC Pilbeam's passion was not of the base, physical sort. Nothing would have delighted him more than to gain admittance to Lucinda Givings's bed, or to welcome her into his, but he realized that this was but a distant goal, and in the meantime, to spend time in her presence was enough. Which was why he proposed to entice her into his flat that evening with the prospect of *penne alla puttanesca* and a bottle of Marks and Spencer's finest Chilean Rosé. It would be their third date, but the first time he had cooked for her; and he was hoping that it would precipitate a degree of thawing in her habitual *froideur*.

However, when she arrived, at 7:30 precisely, clutching a bottle of wine in her hand, she did not seem in the calmest of moods.

"Lucinda," said Nathan, taking her coat, "are you all right?"

"As a man," she replied, "you cannot possibly understand how fraught with stress and complication the simplest of tasks can be. On the bus over here I had to ward off the persistent attentions of a man who was sitting with his legs splayed—you know the type?— and kept saying, 'Do you want this seat, babes?' *Babes!* I ask you . . ."

"I know what you mean."

"He was your usual, casual labourer type. Paint stains all over his jeans." She shuddered. "The brazen cheek of these people! The arrogance!"

"You poor thing. Have a drink."

He handed her a glass of rosé and went to fetch some dips and bread sticks from the kitchen. When he returned, Lucinda was standing at the window. She explained that she liked to watch the autumn leaves spiralling down from the trees in the encroaching dusk. Nathan's gaze, by contrast, had been fixed on Lucinda herself. He was impressed, in particular, by her dress. It was made of some thick bottle-green material and was positively heroic in its shapelessness. For a mere arrangement of cloth to be so accomplished at not just hiding the contours of somebody's body, but even giving the impression that these contours didn't exist and must be the product of the spectator's lurid imagination was, he thought, quite a triumph of the dressmaker's art. How was it done? The more time he spent with Lucinda, the more he realized that—whatever professional heights he might go on to scale in the future—there would always be some questions that could never be answered, or mysteries solved.

Over dinner, they discussed her day at school. The calm of her lunch break had been disrupted, it seemed, by the tactless overtures of the French assistant, Monsieur Guignery, who had insisted on sitting next to her. For some weeks now he had been conducting a campaign of low-level flirtation.

"He's your usual, self-confident, French type," she explained, nibbling uncertainly on her pasta. (Nathan had put a little too much chili in the sauce.) "If it goes on much longer I shall have to complain to the headmaster."

"You do seem to be unlucky," said Nathan, "in the amount of hassle you get. And yet, I suppose it's only to be expected. After all . . ."

The compliment trailed away into nothingness, as he realized that he could not find the words to complete it. Lucinda, in any case, allowed a half-smile to tremor at the ends of her exquisite mouth.

"In my opinion," she answered, composing herself, "the trouble with all of these louche, sexually driven types is that they have too much time on their hands. Too much time to devote themselves to these . . . disturbing thoughts. It's a lack of occupation, a lack of industry. It's far more healthy for a man to be busy—like you are. That's why you're able to keep these things in proportion."

"It's true," said Nathan. "I do love my work. Never more so than at the moment."

"Why? Are you working on another of your fascinating cases?"

"It's early days yet, but I may be on to something. Two people have met with sudden deaths in different parts of London in the last few weeks, and I think the deaths might be connected. Both were comedians."

"Comedians?" Lucinda wrinkled her adorable nose. "I don't like—I mean, I would never murder one, or anything—but I've never understood the appeal of comedians."

"Well, you know, there's an old Yorkshire saying: 'Jokes is all right for them as likes laughing.'"

"But I *do* like laughing," Lucinda insisted, and to prove it, she let out a bright, tinkling, musical laugh, like a joyful *glissando* played on some distant glockenspiel. "It's just that . . . the world is so sad, and nothing much amuses me, I'm afraid, and the idea of paying money in order to get something that should be spontaneous . . . It's always seemed a bit desperate, to me. It's almost like paying for sex."

"Very true," said Nathan, who at that moment would have offered her £5,000 cash on the spot if he'd thought she would have accepted it. "But comedians are everywhere. They sell out stadiums. They pop up all the time on television. No matter what the subject—even if it's asylum seekers or global warming—every kind of public discussion has to have a veneer of comedy. Politics especially."

"I would have thought people listened to comedians to get away from politics."

"They listen to comedians to relax and escape from having to think about things too hard. Which is why it's all right to talk about politics as long as you don't say anything too disturbing. The important thing is to pick on a safe target. And when I watched their DVDs this afternoon, I realized this is what both of these unfortunate guys did. The *same* safe target, as it happens."

"And this," said Lucinda, leaning forward now that her interest was piqued, "is why you think their deaths might be connected?"

"Exactly. One factor—indeed, one name in particular—links their material, and therefore, in all probability, links their murders. It's the name of a journalist, whom they both attacked in the most aggressive and personal tones."

"And the name of this journalist?"

Nathan paused for effect, and looked directly into the measureless blue depths of her eyes.

"Her name is Josephine Winshaw-Eaves."

2

Josephine Winshaw-Eaves. Not surprisingly, Lucinda had never heard of her. She was not a great reader of newspapers, after all: especially not their online editions, where most of Josephine's rantings were to be found.

She was the daughter of Sir Peter Eaves, one of the longest-serving national newspaper editors in the country, and the late Hilary Winshaw, who had been famous, in her day, as both a newspaper columnist and a television executive. Hilary had died in 1991, when Josephine was only one year old, so she was not even a distant memory to her daughter. And yet Josephine had grown up fascinated by her mother's legacy. Her father, on the rare occasions when they had had a real conversation, was forever telling her that Hilary had been a genius among columnists, a superstar, a woman capable of taking the most minor event in public life and spinning from it 1,000 words of pure energizing vitriol. Not only that, but she had belonged to one of the most influential British families of the postwar era, of which Josephine, now, was the only direct descendant. No wonder that, from a very early age, she had carried with her a burdensome sense of her own importance.

The teenage Josephine had struggled to reconcile this sense of importance with a contradictory awareness that, as far as her father was concerned, she barely mattered at all. With the violent and premature death of his wife, Sir Peter had lost all interest in family life—if indeed he had ever had any. Increasingly, he lived at the offices of his newspaper (in which he had installed a comfortable bedroom right next to his own office) and rarely visited his Kensington home, in the spacious confines of which Josephine grew up, alone, under the desultory supervision of a series of nannies. A fiercely intelligent, articulate girl, she made smooth progress through London's private education system—Glendower, followed by Godolphyn and Latimer—before proceeding to Cambridge, where she graduated with first-class honours in art history.

Along the way, however, she made few friends. Those who tried to get close to her found her both conceited and needy. She had a tendency to make snap judgements about people, and developed a reputation for wounding and gratuitous put-downs. In this respect, at least, she was following in the footsteps of her father, who was well known for his bruising economy with words (and occasionally, after one too many brandies at the Garrick, his fists). One memory stood out in particular, for Josephine. During the school holidays, aged about thirteen or fourteen, she once had to spend a few hours with him at the newspaper, childcare arrangements for that day having fallen through at the last minute. She sat in on one of the editorial meetings and could remember vividly, for years afterwards, the way that each of the section editors, ranged around Sir Peter in a circle, had been obliged to pitch their story ideas to him. To each one, in turn—often before they had even finished speaking—Sir Peter had spat out his instant verdict: "Crap." "Bollocks." "Fucking awful." "Shit." "Bollocks—nobody's interested in that fuckwit." "Great—we need an excuse to shaft that cunt." And so on. It had been an awe-inspiring lesson in editorial procedure which had increased her respect for her father a hundredfold, and made her more desperate than ever to gain his attention.

In her last year at Cambridge she started a blog, entitled "PLAIN COMMON SENSE," in homage to her mother's column. She regularly sent Sir Peter links to the latest entries, but he almost never responded, even though she was doing her best to imitate the tone and content of his own newspaper, and to carry on her mother's tradition of ruthless, instantaneous opinion-forming. Undeterred by her lack of firsthand knowledge, Josephine began to campaign against what she called Britain's "benefits culture," which handed rewards to idlers, scroungers, loafers and cheats while "ordinary, hardworking people" (of whose silent, victimized existence it suited her to appear convinced) picked up the tab. At the centre of her phantasmagoric worldview there lay a malignant, amorphous monster called "the left-liberal establishment," dedicated to the redistribution of funds from the deserving to the undeserving, and to the general sabotage of everything that was right and proper in British civil society. The paradox of this monster was that, although Josephine knew exactly what its tentacles consisted of, she could not have put the knowledge into words. It was a slippery, evasive nexus of institutions, made up of grant-awarding bodies, human rights organizations, legal advice services, NGOs, certain branches of the Church of England and the judiciary and, of course, hovering over it all, more powerful, more insidious, more venomous than any other public body in the kingdom, the British Broadcasting Corporation itself, whose mission it was (in the eyes of Josephine and her growing band of supporters) to drip-feed a toxic daily diet of left-liberal propaganda to the nation at the taxpayers' expense.

Sir Peter was now seventy-six years old, although he showed no signs of retiring: his rampantly illiberal views and irascible personality were so closely identified with the newspaper he edited that it was impossible to imagine the two ever parting company. When Josephine graduated, he temporarily stirred himself out of his state of paternal apathy and offered her, without much enthusiasm, a platform on the newspaper's website. Josephine took it, of course, but what she really wanted was a regular slot in the print edition. But Sir Peter was reluctant to endorse his daughter's efforts to that extent. He would relent only occasionally, when a star columnist went on holiday and needed a stand-in, and when this happened Josephine pulled out all the stops. Once, seeking inspiration in the archive of columns from her mother's glory days, she chanced upon a particularly outrageous example from 1990. Hilary had been enraged by a recent court judgement in favour of a disabled tenant whose landlord had unlawfully evicted her and had railed with unusual vigour against the left-liberal establishment's skewed value system. "The landlord of this property," she had written, "was a white, middle-class, heterosexual, God-fearing, law-abiding citizen of what used to be Great Britain, and every one of those attributes was a card stacked against her. Were her claims respected? Did her point of view get taken into account? Of course not. Asked to choose between her rights and those of—to choose a scarcely hypothetical example—a black one-legged lesbian on benefits, our judiciary would inevitably come down on the side of the latter."

In her own column, more than twenty years later, Josephine set about defending the coalition government's introduction of the Bedroom Tax. But her larger point was that the climate had not changed much in the intervening decades: Britain was being dragged down by an underclass of scroungers, who lived in a "something-for-nothing culture," and Hilary's "black one-legged lesbian on benefits" could still be held up as a paragon of modern entitlement. It was high time, and only right and proper, that the government should be doing something radical to cut down Britain's welfare spending.

Sir Peter agreed with her sentiment, but he was not impressed with her reasoning. He thought that the archetype Josephine had resurrected from her mother's column was hopelessly out of date. "You fucked up your argument in the last few paragraphs," he told her. "A black one-legged lesbian on benefits? Even our readers know there's no such thing. They're only worried about Muslims these days. Put your little straw woman in a niqab and then you've given them something to worry about."

Josephine was stung. She went and looked up "niqab" on Wikipedia, and for the next few weeks turned her bile (once again confined to the online edition) on to Britain's Muslim community, bemoaning its failure to condemn terrorist atrocities and accusing the Left of giving succour to radical preachers. Meanwhile, however, Sir Peter continued to ignore her efforts, and her sense of exclusion stewed. His words "Even our readers know there's no such thing" gnawed at her soul. Why was her father so dismissive? Why did he assume that, just because he was not paying any attention to her words, nobody else was? Did he not know that her one print column, about which he had been so scathing, had been picked up by a well-known satirical quiz show on television, and mocked and vilified on primetime TV? What was that, if not a badge of honour? Within a few weeks, any stand-up comedian who wanted to milk an easy laugh from his audience had only to mention Josephine's name. What was that, if not a mark of success?

As a matter of fact, Sir Peter was aware of these developments, and he was furious about them. It was one thing not to think much of his own daughter's writing; but it was quite different when other people, both inside and outside the paper, began to make fun of her. One quiet afternoon in the newspaper's offices, a disturbing scene took place. Neale Thomson, the Deputy Features Editor, and Derek Styles, one of the few remaining full-time subs, were sitting at a computer screen watching something on YouTube. They did not realize that Sir Peter had entered the office and was standing directly behind them. They were watching a section from leading stand-up comic Mickey Parr's DVD, *Would You Credit It?—On Stage and On Fire.* It was the section where he attacked Josephine Winshaw-Eaves. The routine was not especially funny, but Neale and Derek were enjoying the feeling of behaving like naughty schoolboys, the cosy subversiveness of having a laugh at the expense of the boss's daughter, and they chuckled along enthusiastically with the live audience. The words that stopped them in their tracks came from a few feet behind them, and were uttered in the unmistakable patrician tones of Sir Peter himself; although they had never heard him speak quite so quietly before, or with such an icy note of menace.

"Right, you cunts," he said, in little more than a whisper. "In my office. Five minutes."

As Neale and Derek told the story to their ex-colleagues in the pub afterwards, it wasn't the speed of their dismissal that was so shocking: it was the undertone of quivering, barely controlled hatred in Sir Peter's voice, and the eye-watering inventiveness and cruelty of the violent acts which he swore he would arrange to have performed on them if they ever came within one hundred yards of the building or, indeed, if he ever saw them again. To say that they had touched a raw nerve would, clearly, be an understatement. A brief account of the sackings was included in the next issue of *Private Eye,* where readers were also offered a recap of some of the more colourful episodes in Sir Peter's career (a punch-up with a rival editor at a Press Awards dinner; an allegation of assault against a Kensington parking officer, which never came to court). The magazine's report concluded with one slightly sensationalized detail: the fire in Sir Peter's eyes as he dismissed the two disgraced employees was described as "murderous."

3

When he alighted upon the word, which Nathan himself had high-lighted in pale green, DCI Capes allowed himself a long, grim smile of satisfaction before laying the magazine down emphatically on the beer-stained table.

"I see," he said. "Well, that certainly puts a different light on it."

"Now—I'm not saying that we should jump to conclusions," Nathan insisted.

"Of course not."

"This is just gossip. It gives us nothing definite to go on."

"All the same . . ."

DCI Capes sat back and drank from his pint of London Pride, deep in thought. He and PC Pilbeam were seated in the public bar of The Feathers, a stone's throw from New Scotland Yard. It was an old-fashioned pub, where they had found a secluded booth, at some distance from the other patrons. The lighting was dim and their seats were upholstered in discreet burgundy-coloured leather, adding to the atmosphere of subdued conspiracy.

Nathan was delighted, of course—and somewhat astonished—that his e-mail to DCI Capes had elicited this invitation, rather than the expected wall of official silence. All the same, he was beginning to feel uneasy. His own as yet vague intuitions, combined with this one unsourced report in a mischievous magazine, seemed already to have planted in his superior's mind the certainty of a deliberate, cold-blooded assassination campaign.

In truth, DCI Capes himself was far from certain. But then, certainty was hardly a prerequisite for taking action, in the world of twenty-first-century policing. Many other factors had to be taken into consideration. One factor, in particular, was of paramount importance, and in this case, it loomed very large indeed on DCI Capes's horizon of considerations. This was the involvement of the media. It was some weeks since he had felt the gaze of a TV camera trained upon him, or had a journalist's microphone thrust under his nose, and he was beginning to smart keenly from this deprivation. To arrest a national newspaper editor on suspicion of murdering two well-known comedians would certainly bring him back into the limelight.

A few years ago, such a thought would never have crossed DCI Capes's mind. While the occasional sensational case might have called for a broadcast press conference, received wisdom held that the majority of police work was best conducted in private, well away from the media's hungry, intrusive glare. But all of that had changed now. A series of high-profile arrests of British disc jockeys and light entertainment stars of the 1970s on charges of historic sexual abuse had brought DCI Capes into direct and exhilarating contact with top journalists from television, radio and the newspapers. Better still, these arrests had brought him into contact with the stars themselves, a development in his career which he could never possibly have foreseen, and which filled him with a sort of childlike, or at least adolescent, wonder. DCI Capes was in his early fifties. When he was a teenager, many of these celebrities had been, if not heroes to him, at the very least objects of awe and curiosity. In those days he had kept an autograph book, which was filled with the signatures of second-rate TV comics encountered at the dismal seaside holiday camps to which his parents would take him during the summer holidays, and with scribbled messages ("Keep on rockin!", "Have a poptastic birthday!") from disc jockeys he had queued to meet at special local events like Radio One Roadshows or the opening of a new supermarket. Now, more than thirty years later, he still struggled to comprehend that his latest role was to be photographed alongside these same figures as they were led, grizzled, bearded and bewildered, in and out of courtrooms to testify in cases of alleged sexual assault which they (if not their victims) could barely remember. Truly, time played the strangest tricks.

But it was a few months since Capes of the Yard (a feeble, feeble nickname, he reflected, for the thousandth embittered time) had been involved in one of these cases. It was a few months since his name, let alone his face, had been in the papers. It was a few months since he had felt the power of life and death over a prominent figure in public life. He was aching to get back to it—and this was a fantastic opportunity. In this instance, show business met journalism in a heady, intoxicating cocktail. A national newspaper editor so sensitive to personal insult that it made him violent towards those who criticized his daughter. An Achilles heel that might easily—it was not too great a leap of the imagination—make him commit murder (or arrange to have it committed) when he discovered that there were comedians who had dared to pour scorn upon her for the sake of an easy laugh. Frankly, it couldn't be better. So what if nothing was certain, at this stage? Speculation and innuendo made far better copy anyway.

"So." PC Pilbeam leaned forward expectantly. "What will your next move be?"

DCI Capes pursed his lips. "It could be that this is too big for us to handle alone. We'll have to call in some specialists."

"Forensics? MI5? Special Branch?"

"No—I'm talking about a PR firm. Pott Bellinger, I think—they're the best in the business. We use them a lot to liaise with the media."

PC Pilbeam did not like the sound of it. "Before you say anything to the press," he cautioned, "I think you ought to take a look at this. It came out just a couple of days ago."

From his document wallet he produced a DVD. The cover showed a young, tousled, slightly overweight white man wearing a large brightly coloured shirt which was untucked at the trouser. He was talking into a microphone. The DVD was entitled *Ryan Quirky—Whimsy A-Gogo—Live and Loquacious.*

"Thanks all the same," said DCI Capes, sliding it back across the table, "but I'm not really a comedy fan myself. I prefer a good Britflick. Something with Ray Winstone or Danny Dyer."

"No—I mean, this is relevant to the case," said Nathan. "Extremely relevant. Start watching after forty-two minutes."

"You mean it's another attack on . . . ?"

"Ms. Winshaw-Eaves? Yes, it is. Not a severe one. Quite mild, by comparison with the others. But still, if I were Mr. Quirky, I would be checking that my doors and windows were locked before going to bed at night."

4

Looking back on his conversation with DCI Capes, Nathan could not help thinking that it had some disturbing features. It was not just his superior's eagerness to go public with the case at the earliest opportunity: PC Pilbeam was equally disturbed by his own willingness to accept at face value the assumption that Josephine Winshaw-Eaves provided the only possible link between the two murders. Perhaps there was more to it than that? Was the fact that both of the deceased comedians had insulted her nothing more than a distracting coincidence?

Above all, what was starting to alarm him was that, in drawing this premature conclusion, he had betrayed his own philosophy. All he had done, so far, was to watch three DVDs and notice that they had something in common. What they had in common was, of course, potentially very significant, but all the same, his methods had hardly been exhaustive or rigorous. Wasn't he meant to be England's first truly intellectual criminal investigator? Didn't he believe that every crime was best solved by reference to its social and political context? That cultural theory and moral philosophy could often point the way to a solution more surely than fingerprints on a window frame or footprints on a garden path? It was time to do some reading.

And so, for the next five days, PC Pilbeam rarely left his study.

He was surprised, initially, to find that so little had been written on the history and philosophy of humour. Apart from a few scattered comments from Plato, Aristotle and Cicero, the ancient writers had not found very much to say on the subject. The earliest significant commentator in the English language had been Thomas Hobbes, who agreed with René Descartes that laughter derived from pride and was an aggressive expression of superiority over one's peers. Immanuel Kant was one of the first philosophers to offer an incongruity theory of humour, asserting that "laughter is an affection arising from the sudden transformation of a strained expectation into nothing," leading to "a feeling of health produced by a motion of the intestines." Kierkegaard had broadly concurred, maintaining that comedy was born of contradiction, although in this case it was a "painless contradiction" rather than the "suffering contradiction" of tragedy. Henri Bergson, on the other hand, had gone back to the superiority theory of humour and refined it, declaring that we laugh at other people when we perceive in them *"une certaine raideur de mécanique là où l'on voudrait trouver la souplesse attentive et la vivante flexibilité d'une personne."* Only a few years after this, Freud had published his seminal *Jokes and Their Relation to the Unconscious,* proposing a theory which seemed to be the most penetrating and persuasive of all. The punchline of a joke, Freud believed, created a sort of psychic short cut, transporting us rapidly from one idea to another by a quick and unexpected route which thereby allowed an "economy of psychic expenditure," a saving of mental energy which would then be expelled in an explosive outburst of laughter.

Nathan read through all these various explanations carefully, highlighting the most suggestive passages and making detailed notes. He realized that very few commentators had specifically addressed the topic of satire or political humour, although he did come across a dismissive observation by Milan Kundera: Kundera, it seemed, looked down upon satire as a "thesis art" which sought to shepherd its audience towards a preconceived political or moral position, falling short of what he saw as the real purpose of artistic creation, which was to make people aware of ambiguity and multiplicity of meaning.

When he felt that he had exhausted the range of printed sources available to him, Nathan went online and started trawling through comedy blogs and message boards, most of them devoted to contemporary manifestations of humour. Here he found himself entering a very different world, where comedy geeks and nerds who knew far too much about their subject, and had far too much of themselves invested in it, discussed modern humour with all the unfettered passion, obsessiveness, hostility, vitriol, scatology, abuse, unfairness, aggression, mean-mindedness, rudeness, impudence and nastiness that the Internet allowed. These were people who loved comedy with a fierceness which could transmute into hatred at the flip of a coin. A joke which they had not found funny, a comedian who had not made them laugh, would be taken as a personal insult which had to be returned tenfold. A grudging reverence was shown towards a handful of the more radical comics, those who used their platform to make bitter, shocking, fundamental criticisms of society in language which put them beyond the pale for most audiences. Mainstream comedians, those who set out merely to amuse and to entertain their public with gentle absurdity, were tolerated as a harmless distraction. Real hatred was reserved for those whose work fell between these two stools: those who peppered their toothless routines with comfortable, crowd-pleasing political digressions in order to advertise their liberal social consciences. These people were attacked, pilloried and abused mercilessly by their safely anonymous online critics.

After he had been wading through this material for two or three hours, Nathan followed a link to a blog which struck him, simultaneously, as being particularly well argued and particularly unhinged. The writer seemed to be some sort of would-be anarchist/terrorist, although whether his revolutionary impulses ever carried him any further than the screen of his laptop remained unclear. There was a profile picture, but in it his face was turned at ninety degrees from the camera, in shadow, and the photograph was so out of focus as to render its subject (deliberately) unidentifiable. The blog was called *thisisyourwakeupcall* and the writer's username was ChristieMalry2.

The entry which caught Nathan's attention was headed "No Joke," and he found it interesting on several counts. It was obvious, for one thing, that ChristieMalry2 accepted Freud's theory of the basis of laughter; but he transposed it, rather intriguingly, from the psychological sphere into the political:

Freud believed that laughter is pleasurable because it creates an economy of psychic expenditure. Quintessentially, in other words, it takes energy and RELEASES or DISSIPATES it, thereby rendering it ineffective. So—what does that imply about (so-called) "political" comedy, for which Britain is historically so famous? It implies this: political humour is the very opposite of political action. Not just its opposite, but its mortal enemy.

Every time we laugh at the venality of a corrupt politician, at the greed of a hedge fund manager, at the spurious outpourings of a rightwing columnist, we're letting them off the hook. The ANGER which we should feel towards these people, which might otherwise lead to ACTION, is released and dissipated in the form of LAUGH-TER. Which is a way of giving the audience exactly what they want, and exactly what they're paying for: another excuse to sit on their backsides and continue on their own selfish, comfortable path with no real threat or challenge to their precious lifestyles.

That's why it isn't Josephine Winshaw-Eaves and her tiresome ilk who provide the greatest threat to social justice in Britain today. It's the likes of Mickey Parr, Ray Turnbull and Ryan Quirky, with their oh-so-predictable jibes in her direction which the fucking Radio-4-listening, Guardian-reading, Pinot-Grigio-swilling middle-class wankers who pay to see them in stadiums and tune in to their radio shows lap up and laugh at and then feel they have to do NOTHING except sit back with their arms folded and wait for the next crappy one-liner. Chortling along at these pathetic, woolly-minded jokes, which a blind chimpanzee could write in its sleep, gives them the perfect excuse to salve their consciences and confirm their deluded self-image as righteous combatants in a playground battle between left and right which in any case was fought and lost years ago.

I hate these fucking middle-class liberal-left comedians and so should you. It seems to me quintessential that they are all wiped off the face of this planet, or we are never going to summon up the energy to overthrow our current rotten, corrupt and soul-destroying political establishment. Down with comedy, for fuck's sake! And on with the real struggle!

PC Pilbeam read these paragraphs through a number of times. Then he bookmarked the site and also, to be on the safe side, printed out the relevant pages and placed them neatly into one of his box files. He yawned and looked at his watch. He was starting to feel that familiar ache in his eyes from so many hours staring at a screen. He was conscious, also, of another task that he needed to perform, unrelated to detective work but just as important. He put on his coat and left the flat.

Buttoning up his coat against the autumn chill, PC Pilbeam made the ten-minute walk to his local Tesco Express, where he filled a recyclable bag with tins of soup, vegetables and cooked meat. These items did not constitute his normal diet, and indeed he was not buying them for himself. He was on his way to the food bank. Normally he would have taken unused and unwanted items from his own kitchen shelves, but he didn't have any of those left. The fact was that he had learned, on the evening of their dinner together, that Lucinda Givings had started to help out at the food bank during the evenings and weekends, and for this reason he had started to visit it regularly—although so far his timing had been unlucky, and he hadn't encountered her. This would be his fourth visit in three days, and he had reached the point where he was having to buy food especially for the purpose.

And yet today—joy!—his civic altruism was rewarded, for there she was, standing behind the counter and looking as radiant, as desirable as ever. She was wearing a thick woollen jumper which would have made Marilyn Monroe herself look like a sack of potatoes, but even so, Nathan felt that he could not possibly have conceived a vision of purer loveliness, of sweeter, more crystalline beauty.

"Hello," she said, with a smile—he was sure—of genuine affection. "How good of you to come down." She began to remove the tins from his bag. "And with such generous donations!"

"I feel I must do what I can," he answered. "The terrible thing is that there should even be a *need* for places like this."

"I know." Lucinda sighed. "It's very depressing, and I'm sure there's some perfectly terrible explanation, but I don't know what it is. I'm afraid I'm not really one of those angry, political types."

Her colleague, however, a middle-aged woman in denim jacket and jeans, had definite views on the subject.

"Essentially," she said, "this is what happens when the ruling elite uses a crisis of its own making to legitimize attacks on the poorest and most vulnerable people in the country." She held out her hand. "I'm Caroline, by the way."

Nathan shook her hand, but he was not really in the mood for further conversation on this topic. His real objective was to find out whether Lucinda was busy tonight, and whether she'd like to go out with him. Turning back towards her, he casually ventured:

"I was walking past the cinema just now, and couldn't help noticing . . ." Then he stopped, and frowned. Something in Caroline's last remark had suddenly set off a strange, intriguing echo in his mind. Talking more to himself than anyone else, he mumbled: "Yes, of course. That's right. That's perfectly right."

"What do you mean?" Lucinda asked.

"What you said," he repeated, addressing Caroline now, "was perfectly right. I don't mean your comments about the economy, although I don't disagree with you there, exactly. But I'm referring to your choice of words. You said 'Essentially.' Which, of course, is the correct form of expression."

Caroline was glancing in puzzlement at Lucinda, as if silently to inquire whether her peculiar friend usually carried on in this way.

"You're not making yourself very clear," said Lucinda, trying to put it tactfully.

"I'm sorry. This is the way it is, when you've got your teeth into the meat of a case. You forget how to communicate properly. I've been holed up in my flat for days, reading and reading and reading. It's just that the last thing I read—I've realized now that there was something a bit odd about it. A quirk of expression. Whenever he meant 'essential' or 'essentially,' the writer put 'quintessential' instead. I'm sure there's nothing in it. But you can't help noticing these things, you see. Your brain starts to fixate on little details and . . . well, you start to go a bit mad, to tell the truth. Forget I ever mentioned it." Lucinda was staring at him, her eyes getting rounder and rounder. He wanted to dive into them and drown. "What I really meant to ask you," he stammered on, "was—I mentioned the cinema, and I was walking past it only a few minutes ago when I noticed—"

But once again, Nathan never managed to get any further with his invitation. This time it was the ringing of his mobile phone that interrupted him.

"Aren't you going to answer it?" Lucinda asked.

"No. Not until I've—" But then, unable to resist glancing at the screen, he realized who was calling. "Actually, yes. I'd better take this. Sorry."

He withdrew to a corner of the hall and cupped the iPhone to his ear.

"Hello? DCI Capes?"

"Afternoon, Pilbeam. Glad I caught you. Is this a good moment to talk?"

"Of course. What is it? Have there been . . . developments?"

"Not yet. But I'm pretty sure there will be, very soon. Tell me, Pilbeam, have you heard of the Winshaw Prize?"

"Yes, of course."

"Then you know that this year's winner is going to be announced next week. The ceremony's up in Birmingham. Well, Josephine is pretty much the only surviving member of the family, as you know, so she's going to be there. So is Sir Peter. But get this . . . who do you suppose is the celebrity they've chosen to present it, this year? None other than—our good friend Mr. Quirky. And he won't just be in the same room as them, but sitting right next door. I've seen the seating plan, you see. They're on table 12. Quirky will be on number 11."

Nathan let out a whistle of alarm. "An explosive situation," he said.

"I know, but don't worry. We're going to be there in force. And the reason I'm calling—well, as the person who brought all this to my attention, I think you should be there."

"But . . . but, sir, this is such an honour."

"Never mind honour, Pilbeam. I could do with your input. The dinner is on Tuesday week. Don't worry, I'll clear everything with your station, and make sure you get off for the night."

"Thank you, sir. This is . . . This is a big step for me." And then, out of the corner of his eye, he caught a glimpse of Lucinda. Watching her walk from one end of the hall to the other, her lustrous (he assumed) blonde hair pulled back more uncompromisingly than ever, her slender (he imagined) arms filled with cans of baked beans, tomato soup and spaghetti hoops, he felt himself propelled forward by waves of lust. "There's just . . . There's just one thing, sir. If I might make a small . . . official request?"

"Of course, Pilbeam. What's on your mind?"

"I was just wondering: would it be all right if I bring a date?"

5

The Winshaw Prize, by now established as the most prestigious and valuable in the country, was named in honour of Roderick Winshaw, the famous art curator, who had died on the terrible night of 16 January 1991, in the massacre which had also claimed five other members of his family.

A few months after Roderick's death, once the shock waves it sent throughout the art world had partially subsided, a committee of friends and admirers gathered to discuss how the great man's memory might be preserved. A prize was the obvious solution. But there was already a major art prize, the Turner. How could this new prize distinguish itself from its competitors?

A steering committee was set up, under the chairmanship of Giles Trending, the highly successful director of Stercus Television and owner of the Recktall Brown Gallery in Shoreditch. His first notion was that the Winshaw Prize should be the *ne plus ultra* of cultural accolades, and as such should be open not just to paintings, sculptures, videos and installations, but to novels, films, poems, ballets, operas, pop songs and even advertising campaigns. Pretty much everything, in other words. The fact that none of these things could be sensibly compared with one another would be precisely the point.

At this proposal, the eyes of the other committee members had lit up with excitement, and after many hours' enthusiastic discussion, it was decided that the Winshaw Prize, in its first year, should be encumbered with absolutely no rules and no boundaries. Accordingly, the short-listed entries for that year consisted of a book of short stories, a hip-hop single, a video of an artist writing anticapitalist slogans in letters made out of his own snot, a new strain of apple created by a fruit farmer in Herefordshire and the giraffe enclosure at Chester Zoo. This policy was continued for some time, culminating in the notorious edition of 2001, when the prize was awarded to "the distinctive smell you get when you visit your grandmother's house and open a biscuit tin which has been empty for five years."

The steering committee, however, became ever more aware that the prize had failed to capture the public imagination. It proved too challenging to interest the media in a prize which, every year, was awarded to a mere abstraction. Despite the best efforts of Pott Bellinger, the PR firm engaged to publicize it, the Winshaw Prize was far outstripped, in terms of column inches and front-page splashes, by the Booker, the Turner, the Baileys, the Costa, the Brits, the BP Portrait Award, the Carnegie Medal, the Rear of the Year and countless others. It was while contemplating this list of more successful rivals, one melancholy morning, that Trending had his second great idea. Of course! How could he not have seen it before? Later that week he gathered the other committee members for an Extraordinary Special Meeting and presented them with his proposal:

"This prize," he argued, "is meant to commemorate Roderick Winshaw and, by extension, the whole of his family. Now, when we think of the Winshaws, what do we think of? What did they believe in, above all? The answer, of course, is competition. Competition between individuals, between companies, between nations. Competition, that is, in the sense of a fight to the death. Winner takes all, loser gets nothing. And what is an artistic prize but the very distillation of this idea—and a perfect poke in the eye to all those sentimentalists who still believe that artistic creation is some sort of haven from competition. There is no such haven, in this day and age! No one believes anymore that the arts world is some sort of socialist utopia, in which different creative spirits work on their different projects side by side, in parallel and in sympathy. Things have changed, as they have everywhere else! It's a free marketplace now. Survival of the fittest, and extinction for everyone else. So let's put artist in competition with artist, let's set writer against writer and musician against musician. Let envy, rivalry, economic uncertainty and status anxiety be the new spurs to creativity! What we need to create, by rebooting the Winshaw Prize, is a sort of *über-prize*. The ultimate prize. The prize to end all prizes. Do you see what I mean, ladies and gentlemen? Do you understand what I have in mind?"

There was an expectant silence. Nobody had yet seen the logical conclusion of what he was saying.

"From this year onwards," he concluded triumphantly, "the Winshaw Prize will be awarded to ... *the best prize in the United Kingdom.*"

Around the table there was an audible gasp, at both the audacity and the simplicity of the idea. Of course! What better way to establish the Winshaw Prize's superiority over every other award in the country? From now on the Booker, the Turner, the Mercury, the Stirling and all the others would be pitted against one another, every year, in deadly competition, and there would be no need to announce the criteria for judgement, since the fundamental meaninglessness of the comparison would be the whole point, and indeed the very origin of the prize's prestige. There might well be a reluctance to cooperate on the part of the other prizes' organizers, but that was not important. Prizes would be considered eligible whether they were officially entered or not, and besides, each annual ceremony would be so lavish, so glamorous, and would attract so much publicity, that in a few years everybody would be clamouring to take part. And so, indeed, it proved. The media quickly latched on to the idea and before long the presentation of the Winshaw Prize, which took place every November, became one of the biggest talking points in the calendar of British public life. After a shaky and somewhat predictable start (it was awarded to the Turner Prize in its first year, and to the Forward Poetry Prizes in its second) the Winshaw got into its stride and went from strength to strength. The shock year in 2005, when it was awarded to the little-known Giggleswick Prize for the best flower arrangement in the BD postal area, blew things wide open, making people realize that the prize was not just open to the "big hitters" but to any plucky little independent outfit which happened to catch the judges' attention. In 2008 the prize was opened to other European prizes and in 2011, in a bold and controversial move, to

American prizes, making it a truly global and continent-spanning award. 2012 was a spectacular year, in which the Pulitzer Prize went head to head against the Nobel Prize for Physics, and yet the award was finally carried off, in a dramatic last-minute reversal, by France's Prix Médicis Étranger. Every year, now, the Winshaw prize was getting bigger, and the stakes were getting higher. In financial terms alone it was now worth one million pounds to the lucky victor. And 2013 promised to be another milestone in the prize's history.

The venue for this year's presentation was the new Library of Birmingham, which fronted on to Centenary Square in the very heart of the city. Its striking, monumental design by the Dutch architects Mecanoo proclaimed an unapologetic postmodernism, evident especially in its glittering façade, which was festooned with thousands of golden curlicues. Completed at an eye-watering cost to Birmingham City Council of some £187 million, the library had been heralded throughout the land as proof that Britain had not yet quite sunk into a state of illiteracy and philistinism, and was lauded effusively by prominent writers and other public figures, who remained unconcerned (or unaware) that the city—like most others in the country—was at the same time overseeing the closure of many smaller, less prestigious local libraries. (In fact it would soon transpire that the library itself had been far too expensive a project, and little more than a year after it opened, the City Council would announce that it needed to save £1.3 million per year on running costs, and that it had no option but to slash its opening hours and make about half of its staff redundant.) The Winshaw Prize committee felt, for all sorts of reasons, that no more appropriate venue could be found for this year's award ceremony.

Although not designed for large-scale public functions, the library proved readily adaptable for the occasion. The entire ground floor was put to use, and sixty tables were brought in to accommodate the 720 lucky invitees. The police, the security services and Special Branch all had a substantial presence: this year's guest list,

after all, included Richard Dawkins, Tracey Emin, Michel Houelle-
becq and glamour-model-turned-singer Danielle Perry, so no one
could afford to take any chances.

Security was tight, too, at the Hyatt Regency Hotel, which stood
opposite the library, and where most of the guests were booked to
stay the night. And it was on the sixteenth floor of this hotel, in a
king-size double room which commanded a fine view over the tower
blocks and arterial roads of Birmingham city centre, that a painful
scene was being played out, just one hour before the prize dinner
was due to commence. Lucinda and Nathan were having their first
argument.

"I am *so* sorry about this," Nathan was saying.

"It's so unlike you," Lucinda replied, "to engineer this situation.
To put me in such an uncomfortable position."

"I accept full responsibility. It's my own fault. I should have made
it clear to DCI Capes that we needed separate rooms. He assumed,
because you were my guest, that we would be sharing."

"And now you say the hotel is completely booked up?"

"Completely."

"Well, this is most . . . distressing. I can think of no other word."

"Lucinda, we can get through this, if you will just be brave. Look
how large the bed is . . ."

She turned to him, horrified. "You're not suggesting that we
share it?"

"Or look at this sofa. Easily big enough for a man my size to have
a comfortable night's sleep."

She looked at it appraisingly, and for the first time seemed to be
mollified. "It's true. It does look quite substantial. And it's at least
two yards from the end of the bed."

"And I've brought my sleeping mask with me. I won't see a thing."

"Do you mean that, Nathan? Can I trust you?"

She gazed at him in anxious appeal, and once again he felt that
a lifetime spent contemplating the depth and blueness of her eyes
would be a lifetime well spent.

"Of course, Lucinda. Of course."

For a moment she looked so relieved and grateful that he thought that he might be gifted a hug. But this was wildly over-optimistic. She merely nodded her approval and said: "All right, then."

"And now," he said, doing his best to conceal his disappointment, "I'm needed over at the library, so I must change into my tux, if I can use the bathroom first."

"Of course."

She stood aside to let him pass, and, within a few minutes, Nathan had changed into his dinner suit and was on his way to rendezvous with DCI Capes at the library entrance.

"For God's sake where are the fucking menus?" said Sir Peter Eaves, looking at his watch. "We've been sitting here for twenty minutes now and nobody has a fucking clue what we're going to be eating."

Helke Winshaw glanced across at him sharply. Her cousin irritated her. Come to that, he was barely her cousin: second cousin by marriage, or something like that. She was annoyed that they had been put at the same table just because of this distant relationship. He was always complaining. Complaining and, therefore, drawing attention to himself, which in her view was a strategic error when you belonged to this particular family. As for his drip of a daughter . . . well, it looked like they were going to have to sit next to each other all evening, and that was going to make this dreary occasion even more dreary. They had nothing in common. Nothing at all.

In fairness to Josephine, there were not many people in the world who would find Helke Winshaw an easy dining companion. She regarded her words, like everything else she possessed, as valuable commodities which were not simply to be spilled out in order to lubricate the gears of social discourse. On top of which, as Chief Executive Officer of Winshaw Clearance plc, she had a keen (though scarcely inflated) sense of her own importance. She had founded the company herself, twenty years ago, in memory of her husband Mark, who had died in the same massacre that had claimed the lives of Roderick Winshaw and Hilary, Josephine's mother. Mark had made a fortune from selling weapons. As a result of his efforts, many

parts of the world were now contaminated with unexploded ordnance (or Explosive Remnants of War). It was seen as touching—if
somewhat ironic—that after he died, his widow should set up an
organization devoted to clearing former conflict zones of the lethal
detritus which Mark's activities had left behind. However, she had
not done it for humanitarian reasons. It made perfect business sense
to assume that, if there was money to be made from facilitating wars,
there was money to be made from clearing up after them as well.
Helke understood all too well that ERW clearance was a ruthlessly
competitive business just like any other, and she approached it in
that spirit. She fought aggressively to secure long-term contracts in
major war zones such as Iraq and Afghanistan, since this was where
the big money was to be made. At the same time, she kept a keen
eye on smaller, independent NGOs which specialized in ERW clearance, since these outfits were often run by young and idealistic people who would energetically seek out less obvious territories which
were also in need of decontamination. Once a smaller company had
found one of these areas and commenced operations there, Winshaw Clearance would then pile in like a juggernaut, put them out
of action and hoover up the rest of the business themselves. Now,
after two decades of expansion, acquisition and asset-stripping, they
were established as the undisputed world leaders in their field, with
an annual turnover in the tens of millions. And Helke Winshaw continued to sit discreetly at the helm.

"Have a bit of patience," she said to her cousin. "What does it matter? It's only food."

"Rude bitch," Sir Peter said, leaning in close to Josephine, and whispering in her ear, "Looks like you've drawn the short straw tonight.
Try to ignore her." He noticed that his daughter's eyes seemed troubled. She was staring across at the adjacent table. "What's wrong?"
he asked.

"See that man over there? The fat one with the piggy eyes."

"What about him?"

"He's that comedian who slagged me off on his show."

"Really?" her father said. "Right. Later on, I'll have a word with
him." There was a grim note of menace to these last five words,
which bled into his next muttered question, a repeat of: "Where are

these *fucking* menus?" Looking around, he caught the eye of a wait-ress with the name "Selena" on her name tag, and beckoned her over to make his feelings known.

Lucinda left it until literally the last minute to make her appearance at table number 11. She arrived at 7:29 precisely. For Nathan, how-ever, who had been sitting there in a state of heightened alertness for a quarter of an hour or more, scanning the room for signs of villainy, it was worth the wait. For a moment, all thoughts of detec-tive work flew out of his head. As for any attempt to conceal his feelings, this was in vain. His jaw slackened and he let out a clearly audible gasp. Lucinda was wearing a plain black cocktail dress and she looked—there was no other word for it—*ravishing.*

She had arms. She had real, human, female, bare arms, com-plete with elbows and wrists, suspended from a pair of lovely pale bare shoulders. She had legs, complete with calves, shins, and knees deliciously sheathed in black nylon. She had a figure: a gorgeous, womanly figure at which none of her other clothes had even hinted before. He had already known that he was in love with her, but that love was instantly magnified and intensified a million-fold, and sup-plemented by a surging, overwhelming wave of desire which made him feel so weak that when he rose totteringly to his feet to give her a peck on the cheek, he was sure that his legs were going to give way.

"Nathan," she said, and unless he was imagining it, her voice was not quite as prim as usual; there was something almost coquettish in it, as though she was fully aware of the effect her appearance must be having on him, and was quietly relishing it.

"Lucinda," he replied. "You look . . . amazing." He prolonged the kiss for as long as he dared, relishing the cushiony softness of her cheek and breathing in the scent of her tantalizing perfume, the fragrance of jasmine with a hint of rose petal.

"Please," he said, drawing back her chair and sighing with admi-ration as she sank gracefully into it. She brushed back a rogue strand of hair and smiled shyly at the famous TV chat show host sitting next to her on the left, and at Ryan Quirky, sitting across from her on the other side of the circular table. She didn't recognize either of them. Nathan took his place beside her on the right and poured her a glass of sparkling water.

"Oh," she said. "I don't seem to have a menu."

"None of us have menus," said Nathan. "I believe our hosts have got a little surprise planned for us in that respect. And we should find out what it is in"—he glanced at his watch—"roughly ten seconds."

Sure enough, ten seconds later, a remarkable thing happened.

From the centre of each table, a circular section was removed, like a little trap door, by hands at first invisible; and through each resulting aperture a man's head appeared. Sixty different men's heads, at sixty different tables. The rest of their bodies remained beneath the tables, hidden from view. A ripple of surprise and admiration went around the room.

At table number 11, the head was crowned by a mop of red hair. The head swivelled around slowly through 360 degrees, and each of the twelve guests found themselves being stared at in turn by a pair of piercing green eyes framed by large, owl-like horn-rimmed spectacles.

"Good evening," said the head. "My name is Dorian, and I will be your talking menu tonight. I will be here all evening, to tell you about the food, and to answer any food-related questions. I'm afraid I cannot talk to you about any other subject. Nor, sadly, am I allowed to eat or drink any of the delicious items with which you are about to be presented. Don't feel too sorry for me, please, I am being well paid for my work tonight, and I will be taking home a generous doggy bag. And so, without further ado, allow me to introduce the first item on tonight's succulent *smorgasbord*. Ladies and gentlemen, prepare your palates for a selection of our chef's amazing *amuse-bouches!*"

Right on cue, a team of waiters and waitresses glided towards the table. The plates laid down in front of the eager diners contained three small, exquisitely crafted items of uncertain provenance. Dorian proceeded to explain.

"First of all, ladies and gentlemen, you have a cured-beet and Scottish salmon Napoleon with Bibb lettuce, topped with Beluga caviar and marinated in a cumquat distillation. We think you will find it both acerbic and whimsical. Next to that, you will find a cold potato-truffle soup with a hot, butter-poached Yukon Gold potato, parmesan, black truffle, and sea salt of a notorious astringency, especially garnered from the seas around the famous Kwajalein Atoll in the Marshall Islands. And last but not least, throw yourselves upon a periwig of Kumamoto oysters, served with a green apple mignonette dusted with coriander and a fennel-cilantro salad with ponzu dressing."

Wondering if the food itself could possibly live up to the sensory expectation aroused by these descriptions, the guests sat with their forks poised over their plates, their mouths filling with juices.

"Any questions, before we start?"

"Erm ... what exactly," said the chat show host, "is ponzu dressing?"

"Ponzu, sir," said Dorian, "is a citrus-based brown sauce from Japan. Not at all uncommon, I'm sure you've had it many times before. The word literally means 'vinegar punch.'"

"Thank you."

"I have another question," said Ryan Quirky. "Some oysters are known for their aphrodisiac qualities. Is this true of Kumamoto oysters?"

"Sir," answered Dorian, "it is especially true of this variety."

And with that, they began to eat. But Nathan noticed that Lucinda left her oysters on the side of her plate.

Between the main course and the dessert, Josephine slipped outside, ostensibly to have a cigarette but in reality because she could not stand making conversation with Helke for a moment longer. It was cold in Centenary Square, and her breath steamed in the air as she fumbled in her handbag, first for her packet of cigarettes and then, at greater length, for her lighter, which she seemed to have mislaid.

"Oh, fuck it!" she said out loud.

"Do you want a light?" someone said, stepping out of the shadows.

It was Selena, the waitress, who was also having a quick smoke.

"Oh. Thank you. That's very kind," said Josephine, too flustered and annoyed to feel particularly grateful.

"No problem." She offered Josephine the end of her own cigarette. "Nippy, isn't it?"

"Well, that's what you get for trekking up to the frozen North, I suppose."

Selena smiled, but said nothing to this.

"Enjoying the show in there?"

"I suppose they've made an effort. The talking menus are original, at least."

"It's given an evening's work to a lot of out-of-work actors, that's for sure."

Josephine had no wish to get into conversation with this person. This whole evening, which she had thought would be merely tedious, was turning into a nightmare. She looked around her at the unfamiliar cityscape, the steady flow of evening traffic stopping and starting at the lights on Broad Street, the groups of cheaply dressed, rather threatening (she thought) teenagers wandering backward and forward past the library, and cursed the organizers for dragging her up here. Birmingham! What were they thinking? OK, so it was a fancy building all right, but still, that didn't justify forcing her to spend a night in this dismal hellhole. She would definitely have a word with the steering committee about it at breakfast tomorrow.

"Queueing up to work here tonight, people were," Selena continued. "I was lucky to be chosen."

"Mm," said Josephine, not listening.

"My girlfriend applied, too. But they didn't want her."

"Really."

"Shame, 'cos she was hoping, with all these art people here, she might have met someone useful, you know?"

"Uh-huh."

"You write for the papers, don't you?"

"Who told you that?"

"One of the girls in the kitchen. I never read the papers these days, to be honest. Too depressing."

"Yes, well, I don't write about art, so if you want any favours you're wasting your time."

"Sure. Whatever." Selena fell silent, but not for long. "She's really talented, though."

"Sorry, who?"

"My girlfriend. She does portraits. Mainly of homeless people."

"How very fascinating and . . . worthy of her."

"But not ordinary portraits. She makes them pose to look like—"

"You're right, it is chilly out here. I think I'll go back inside."

"Look, don't get me wrong. My friend isn't looking for help. She knows there are no shortcuts. She knows you have to be tough in this business. She can cope with being knocked back a few times, you know what I mean?"

"Well, look, it's been a blast talking to you. Good-bye."

"She's a strong girl, my Alison. Very strong. I mean, you have to be, to deal with some of the stuff she's been through."

"I'm so glad to hear that. Now—"

"Only having one leg, for instance. I mean, how many people could handle something like that?"

"Great. She sounds like a real trouper." Josephine was halfway through the library's main entrance when the meaning of Selena's words suddenly came home to her. She turned round at once. "What did you just say?"

"I said she was a strong girl."

"Not that."

"And really talented."

"Did you say she only had one leg?"

Selena noticed the change in Josephine's manner. She nodded slowly.

"That's right."

Josephine came closer.

"And this is your . . . *girlfriend,* right?"

"That's right."

"Girlfriend—as in someone you . . . someone you're . . . in a relationship with?"

"We sleep together, yeah."

"So you're lesbians."

"Um . . . yeah," said Selena, thinking that she had already made this fairly obvious.

"And is she . . . like you?"

"Like me?"

"Yes."

"Well, I don't know. We're quite different personality types, really. I'm Taurus, for one thing, and she's Gemini . . ."

"No—I mean, is she black as well?"

"Ah." Christ, this woman is blunt, Selena thought. But she'd caught her interest, for some reason, and she was going to make the most of it. "Yes, she is."

"And does she have a job, your friend? Apart from the painting, I mean."

"No. Neither of us have, since we finished our course."

"I don't suppose . . . I don't suppose she's on benefits of any sort?"

"Well, yeah, we couldn't survive otherwise. There's the housing benefit, the disability allowance . . ."

She tailed off, and gave Josephine what she hoped was an appealing smile. To her surprise, the smile was returned.

"Your girlfriend," Josephine said, "sounds *absolutely amazing.*"

"Could you write something about her, do you think?"

"Yes, I think I could."

"Wow," said Selena. "*Wow.* Just wait till she hears that you said that."

Josephine held up her hand in a cautionary gesture. "No," she said, shaking her head. "I don't think you should tell her anything yet. If you can bear it, this is going to be our little secret for now." She put a hand on Selena's arm. "You can keep a secret, can't you? Good. Now—let's have another cigarette."

"You missed all the excitement," said Sir Peter, as Josephine returned to the table. "They awarded the prize five minutes ago."

"Really?" she said, stifling a yawn. "I don't even know what was on the short-list."

"Everyone thought it would go to the Hilton Humanitarian Prize this year. Either that, or the Mo Ibrahim Prize for Achievement in African Leadership."

"So which one was it?"

"Neither. They gave it to the *Literary Review* Bad Sex Award."

"Great!" said Josephine. "Another triumph for the Brits."

"Exactly. Being embarrassed about sex is one of the few things we're still world leaders at, these days."

He drained his wineglass quickly, and signalled for a refill. Josephine wondered how many glasses he'd got through while she'd been outside. She also wondered whether to tell him that, thanks to her conversation with Selena, she now knew that he'd been wrong to criticize her column that time, and soon she would be able to present him with living proof. But she decided to keep it to herself for a while longer.

"Your man made a fucking awful speech," Sir Peter said. "Didn't get a single laugh. Don't think anyone here had the faintest idea what he was on about."

"Did he mention us?"

"Oh yes. Made sure he gave the whole family a good kicking."

"The cheek! I hope you're not going to let him get away with it."

"No, I'm not," said Sir Peter. He picked up an unused steak knife from his table and began thoughtfully stroking its serrated edge. "I have plans for Mr. Quirky. In fact, I'm going to discuss them with him now."

Still holding the knife, Sir Peter attempted to rise to his feet, but he was very much the worse for drink and it took nothing more than Josephine's restraining hand to keep him in his chair.

"I don't think this is really the place to cause a scene."

"There won't be any scene," said Sir Peter, breathing heavily. "I'll tell you what I'm going to do to that fucker." He fixed her with a bug-eyed, resolute glare. "I'm going to offer him a job."

"You're going to do *what*?"

"You heard me. I'm going to take him on as a columnist."

"Oh, sit down, you're completely pissed."

"I may be pissed but I know what I'm talking about. You don't *attack* your enemies, if you really want to hurt them. You co-opt them. 'Hey, Ryan,' we'll say, 'come and join us. No hard feelings, old boy. Love your schtick. Come and do a bit of work for us.' We chuck him a couple of hundred grand a year for a thousand words a week and then everyone sees he's writing for us and thinks we can't be so nasty after all. *We* look good, and *he* looks bad. We keep him on for eighteen months and give him a couple of pay rises. By then he's lost most of his teeth and he's hardly being rude about us at all. But he has pissed off quite a few of his fans. And then we kick him out on the street—*bam!*—and watch how he copes with having his income, which in a short space of time he's become thoroughly comfortable with, slashed by about eighty percent." He smiled at his daughter and relished the way she was staring at him, open-mouthed with admiration. Sir Peter's eyes gleamed. "So now, if you'd just help a doddery old cunt to his feet, I'm going to get the wheels moving."

Josephine did indeed take his arm and raise him carefully out of his chair. Then Sir Peter started to take a few slow, erratic steps towards table number 11. Whether it was because he was becoming forgetful, or because he was rather drunk, or a combination of the two, he was still wielding the steak knife, held at a decidedly aggressive angle, as he approached the unsuspecting figure of Ryan Quirky, who was deep in conversation with a young female admirer in a low-cut dress. But Sir Peter never got as far as the comedian's table anyway. Before he knew what was happening, he felt his arm politely but firmly seized by a burly, middle-aged man flanked by four or five similar-looking guests, who blocked his path and formed a rapid, protective circle around him.

"Now then, Sir Peter," said DCI Capes. "I think it would be a good idea if you put that down, don't you?"

"What are you talking about? Who the fuck are you? Get out of my way."

"Put the knife down, and come along with us quietly, and then there won't be any problems."

The other policemen gathered around Sir Peter in an even tighter group. And then Nathan was on the scene, tapping his superior urgently on the shoulder.

"DCI Capes? What are you doing?"

"Not now, Pilbeam. We're kind of busy here."

"But, sir, I thought we'd agreed about not jumping—"

"Drop it, Pilbeam, all right? I'm taking this man for questioning. Arkwright, have you got the media room ready?"

"The media room? But you can't question him there. It's where the prizewinners are interviewed. It's full of photographers and TV cameras."

"PC Pilbeam, I shall handle this situation in my own way, thank you very much."

The other officers had by now relieved Sir Peter of his knife and were frogmarching him forward with his hands pinned behind his back. Nathan made one last appeal.

"With respect, sir, we have no case against Sir Peter at all."

"That's *enough*, Pilbeam," said DCI Capes, and there was no mistaking the note of aggression in his voice now. "Why don't you sit down, and enjoy the rest of your evening, and concentrate your energies on impressing your very attractive date?"

With that he was gone, striding swiftly to catch up with the group of officers who were already propelling Sir Peter—too befuddled to protest any further—away from the dining area and in the direction of the awaiting media representatives. A few of the diners looked around to see what was happening, but the operation had been discreet and didn't cause much of a stir. Most people were more interested in the imminent arrival of dessert.

"Nathan, dear," said Lucinda, as he rejoined her at their table, "is everything all right? You look flustered."

He was very flustered indeed, otherwise, the fact that she had used the word "dear"—the first verbal token of affection to have passed her lips in the whole of their friendship—would have sent him into a swoon of excitement. As it was, he barely noticed it.

"The case has been taken out of my hands," he said. "And I fear that DCI Capes is about to make a mess of it. And after all that work . . ." He sighed heavily. "This has been a terrible evening."

"Really?" said Lucinda. She sounded hurt. "But it's been so nice, with all these famous people here, and this lovely food, and . . . well, I thought you liked spending time with me."

"Oh, but I *do*," he said, clasping her hand earnestly.

"I mean, I know there's been that mix-up with the bedrooms . . ."

"No, it's not that. I didn't mean to sound gloomy. It's just that I had a feeling tonight—an instinct—I was *convinced* I was going to find a clue that would crack the whole case wide open. And so far . . . nothing."

"The night isn't over yet," she pointed out.

"True," he said, despondent.

She squeezed his hand. "Come on, darling. Just relax and enjoy yourself. Have another glass of wine."

Darling! He had graduated from "dear" to "darling" in the space of a few seconds. And still it made no impression on him. Abandoning the attempt to cheer him up, Lucinda turned her attention to Dorian, their talking menu, who was on the point of making another announcement.

"Ladies and gentlemen, and—as I think I may now call you—friends, your dessert is about to be served. Our chef thought you might be feeling a little full by now, so he has prepared something light for you. You will be presented with shot glasses, each containing a delicate layer of cream cheese flavoured with blueberries, a further layer of cream cheese—as frothy as a soufflé—flavoured with Meyer lemons, topped with Alaskan blueberries garnished with a Meyer lemon zest, all served on a bed of crushed all-butter Highland shortbread."

"Mmm, delicious," said Lucinda, as her shot glass was laid before her. "I *adore* cheesecake. That's what this is, isn't it?"

The question was addressed to Dorian, who admitted: "Quintessentially, yes, madam: this is a cheesecake."

And now, in an instant, Nathan was jerked out of his reverie. He looked straight across at Dorian and knew, with a thrilling but also terrifying certainty, that he was looking into the eyes of Christie-Malry2. He knew, as well, that Ryan Quirky was in mortal danger. The words from the blog came rushing back to him:

I hate these fucking middle-class liberal-left comedians and so should you. It seems to me quintessential that they are all wiped off the face of this planet, or we are never going to summon up the energy to overthrow our current rotten, corrupt and soul-destroying political establishment. Down with comedy!

How he had obtained employment at this dinner, and secured a place at table number 11, was not yet clear. What was clear, however, was that he had come here with no other intention than to commit murder. There was no time to lose.

Nathan dived under the table. The movement was quick, but not particularly elegant, since he banged his head loudly against it as he did so, thereby attracting everyone's attention. Without pausing, despite the pain he was in, he lunged at Dorian's legs and seized them in an uncompromising grip. The resulting spectacle, from the diners' point of view, was bizarre, as the disembodied head suddenly found itself being yanked downwards through the hole in the table, a movement Dorian resisted by clinging on to the edges with his hands and screaming out for help. Two or three of the guests—including Ryan Quirky—grabbed on to his arms and tried to pull him to safety, resulting in a violent human tug-of-war and, ultimately, the overturning of the entire table amidst a cacophony of shrieks and screams.

"Stop that man!" shouted Nathan, as Dorian broke free and ran for the exit. Sure enough, a barrier of security guards appeared, and Dorian found his way blocked. At the same time, DCI Capes and his henchmen came back into the room to see what all this noise was about.

"Who is this?" said the detective.

"This," said Nathan, having scrambled to his feet and made his way, panting and dishevelled, to the scene of the capture, "is your stand-up comedian murderer. And this is the weapon with which he intended to continue his campaign tonight."

With that, he opened what appeared to be a spectacles case, which had fallen out of Dorian's pocket in the course of their struggle. It contained a long syringe filled with a transparent liquid. DCI Capes took it from Nathan's outstretched hand, his face a picture of bafflement.

"I suggest," said PC Pilbeam (and he could not believe that already, so early in his career, he was using a phrase which he had always dreamed of using), "that you send this down to the lab."

Two hours later, Nathan and Lucinda were having a final nightcap at the bar of the Hyatt Regency when DCI Capes came by.

"We've extracted a full confession," he told them. "These pinkos soon crumble under pressure. No backbone, you see."

"Can I interest you in a brandy, sir?"

"Well, why not. It's been a long evening, after all. But a highly successful one, thanks to you."

"To both of us, I'd say, sir."

"All in a day's work, Pilbeam. They don't call me 'The Caped Crusader' for nothing."

He threw the potential nickname out hopefully, but Pilbeam had already turned his back to get the barman's attention, and the effort once again seemed to have been wasted. What in God's name would it take, DCI Capes thought, to persuade people to start calling him that? He gave a disgruntled sigh and took the proffered brandy glass from his junior colleague.

"So it was merely a verbal tic, was it, that gave him away to you?"

"Indeed."

"But what about his motive? How had you come across him in the first place?"

"Well, there, sir, if you will allow me to show off a little, you find the vindication of my methods. Cases like this are best approached from the intellectual point of view. The key to the entire problem lay in the history and theory of comedy. So that was where I concentrated all of my research. I began with Aristotle, of course, although sadly the half of his *Poetics* that deals with comedy has been lost. However, it's still possible to re-create something of his think—"

Fascinated as he was by PC Pilbeam's discourse, DCI Capes was distracted at this point by the appearance of two uniformed constables walking through the bar towards the lobby, carrying a couple of cardboard boxes.

"Ah—evening, Jackson," he said. "Everything OK?"

"Yes, sir," said the first constable. "The suspect is safely locked up in the cells at Newtown Station. We've cleared out his room on the seventh floor and taken everything away."

"Excellent. Find anything interesting?"

"Not really, sir. Just a few clothes and toiletries. Oh—and this book."

From the top of the box, the constable produced a battered, well-thumbed paperback: an old Pelican edition of Sigmund Freud's *Jokes and Their Relation to the Unconscious.*

Nathan allowed himself a knowing smile, and said:

"Pretty conclusive evidence, wouldn't you agree, sir?"

DCI Capes shook his head in puzzlement. He was yet to be convinced. "I rather think a syringe full of liquid cyanide will stand up better in court. I wouldn't have given much for Quirky's chances once he got that in his leg." He drained the glass of brandy and rose to his feet. "Well, I'd probably better go along with these two for now. Goodnight, Pilbeam. You've been a credit to the force this evening."

"Thank you, sir. You don't know how much that means to me."

"Keep an eye on your mailbox over the next few weeks. There'll always be an opening at the Yard for men of your calibre."

The smile on PC Pilbeam's face started to spread as the meaning of this remark sank in. Promotion ... Fast-tracking through the ranks, and a move to London ... This was the beginning of his ascent to greatness. He was on his way.

"Did you hear that?" he asked, turning to Lucinda.

Apparently she had.

"I know," she said, her eyes shining—almost mistily—with admiration and contentment. "Isn't it wonderful news? Do you want to borrow the key, so you can go and move your things?"

"What?"

"You heard what the constable said. That horrible man's been locked up, so he won't be staying in the hotel tonight. There *is* a spare room after all. So that solves our other problem!"

Which left PC Pilbeam with an entire, solitary, brandy-fuelled night to lie awake, staring at the ceiling in his seventh-floor room, and contemplating the unfathomable mystery, the frankly insoluble case that was Severe Miss Lucinda Givings.

George Osborne, addressing the Conservative Party
conference, 6 October 2009:

"We are all in this together."

What a Whopper!

———

1

My name is Livia and I come from Bucharest.

We have a saying in my country: *Totul trebuie să aibă un început.* Which means: Everything must have a beginning. So I will begin my story like this.

I have been living in London for more than five years, and my job is taking the dogs of very rich people for their daily walk. Most of my clients live in Chelsea. I used to live there myself but then the rents became so high that I moved out to Wandsworth so now every day I begin by taking a bus across the river. I look out through the windows of the bus as we cross the bridge, and from that point on, every time the bus gets to another stop I can see the signs of wealth more and more clearly inscribed in the streets and feel the air itself getting heavier with the tangy scent of money.

I get off at the Chelsea and Westminster Hospital and then walk towards The Boltons. The houses here are big and beautiful. Well-tended gardens hide behind walls which are as smart and politely forbidding as a security guard at an exclusive nightclub. Closed-circuit cameras sprout among the ivy and the sycamore trees. My first call of the day involves stopping outside one of these walls. There is a small green door in the wall and, next to it, a discreet key-pad upon which, if you possess the secret knowledge, you can enter a five-digit code which admits you to this earthly paradise. I have been coming here every day for fourteen months but I have not yet been told the code.

Instead, I have to send a text message to a Malaysian housemaid, who shortly afterwards emerges to open the door in the wall. She is accompanied by a large, bright-eyed, restless black Labrador. This is

Clarissa. She at least greets me like a friend. So now I take her for her walk. If today is a busy day I will only take her as far as Brompton Cemetery. If I have plenty of time we will go all the way to Hyde Park.

Sometimes in Hyde Park I meet Jane. I can always recognize Jane, even from a distance, by the number of dogs she will have with her. Always four or five; sometimes as many as ten. If the dogs will allow her, we'll sit at the café next to the Serpentine and drink coffee together.

Shortly after we first met, Jane told me her story. She used to work in the City of London as a trader for one of the world's leading investment banks. After a while she realized that she had hit a ceiling and would never make as much money as her male colleagues. Also the stress and the long hours were damaging her health. She left her job and spent a few weeks resting. As a favour, she started walking a friend's dog while he was at work, and then other working people started asking her to walk their dogs for them. She charged her clients £20 an hour for each dog and they paid her in cash. By walking many dogs at once she found that she could sometimes make £500 in a day—or as much as £100,000 every year, but without paying any tax. More than she had earned in the City.

In addition to this, she liked walking, and she liked dogs.

In the middle of the morning I return Clarissa to her home in The Boltons. Once again I send a text message to the housekeeper and we exchange a few words as she takes her back. As I say good-bye to the dog I wonder what kind of life she leads away from me, on the other side of the wall. I have never seen her owners. I know nothing at all about the family she belongs to. All I know is that they never seem to be at home.

But the word "home" can mean different things. Whenever I return to Romania I feel that I'm coming home but I also regard my little flat in Wandsworth as home, even though I've only lived there for a year and a half. It feels like my home because I come back to it every night to feel rested and safe, and I've filled it with objects that I love because they mean something to me.

These beautiful big houses in Chelsea are not homes in any sense that I understand. For most of the year they stand empty. Or at least, you think they are empty, but inside, there is a kind of life taking place. A phantom life. Members of staff—cleaners and cooks and chauffeurs—dust haunted rooms and polish cars in underground garages during the morning, and then gather together in the kitchen at midday to eat silent lunches. Dogs sit by windows and look out into gardens and wonder why their owners bothered to buy them in the first place. Meanwhile, the family is . . . where? The father is in Singapore, the mother is in Geneva, the children . . . who knows.

Other houses here are even emptier. They contain no furniture, no curtains at the windows, no pictures on the walls. They are always dark. In the winter, when I come back from the park or the cemetery to return the last of my dogs to its owner's house, the silence and darkness of these streets begins to frighten me. It is as if some terrible plague has come to London and everybody has had to leave but nobody has told me. Once I walked back from the park with Jane, through the streets of Chelsea, and she explained to me that people buy these houses now—rich people—and then just let them stand there, watching money attach to them like barnacles to a sunken ship.

"Think about it," she said. "A house like this may be worth thirty-five million pounds. Its value appreciates at the rate of ten percent—three and a half million every year. That's seventy thousand pounds a week. Ten thousand pounds every day. What else do you have to do, apart from buy it, and then just leave it alone? The people who own this house" (she pointed at the white stuccoed mansion opposite us in the street) "are ten thousand pounds richer than when we walked past here this morning."

I always learn something new when I talk to Jane. Sometimes what she tells me fills me with a reluctant kind of respect for the people who understand, much better than I do, how to acquire and increase wealth. Other times I think that, just as a certain famous Romanian used to suck the blood from his victims' necks, now it is money itself that has begun to drain the life out of this great city.

2

Rachel stood still and rested for a while, hands on hips, listening to the noise of the wind as it rustled the branches of the plum tree. It was one of her favourite sounds in the whole world.

It was quiet here, this breezy September afternoon. The wind rustled the branches even though the branches were laden. It had been a good crop this year. A bumper crop, that was always the expression, wasn't it? The plums were ripe: their skins powdery and purple-pink. Rachel's basket was three-quarters full even after ten minutes' picking.

It had become a ritual now, a family tradition. In the middle of September, she would come to her grandparents' house in Beverley for a few days, and one afternoon she would take out the old wooden ladder from the garage, and lay it against the sturdiest branch of the tree, and climb up to pick the plums which her grandparents were no longer strong or agile enough to harvest. For the last three years, this had been the prelude to her setting out for Oxford at the beginning of October. But the Oxford days were over now. She had finished her studies, and graduated, and was facing an empty, uncertain future, with a lovely big burden of debt to accompany her. For the last three months she had been living with her mother in Leeds, answering job adverts and sending out CVs. All to no effect, so far, although a couple of private tutorial agencies in London had added her to their books. Something would come up, she was sure. All she could do was to keep trying.

She ate one of the plums, spat the stone out, then took the ladder and leaned it up against a different branch of the tree, facing the house now. This way she could reach some of the topmost fruit.

After climbing the ladder, she could also see across the back garden and into her grandparents' bedroom, where Gran was sitting up on the bed. She had the *Telegraph* spread out on her lap but she wasn't reading it. She had her head thrown back and her mouth half open, but she wasn't asleep either, as Rachel had first thought: after a few seconds she raised herself, drank from the mug of tea on her bedside table and stared tiredly around her. She looked pale and anxious. Grandad had been ill for about a week now, with stomach cramps, vomiting and diarrhea. They both referred to it as his "tummy bug," and for several days this is what everyone had thought it was, but this morning there had been blood in his stools so Gran and Rachel had phoned the GP and on her advice driven him straight to the hospital. Grandad had been put on a ward without too much delay and this afternoon they were going to do some tests. "It's probably just a really nasty tummy bug," Gran kept saying, and Rachel wanted to believe her, wanted to believe there was nothing seriously wrong, but still . . .

The feeling she had was not strong enough to be called a premonition. It was hardly even strong enough to be called a feeling. But in the rustling of the branches as the wind brushed against them, Rachel thought that she could hear the quietest, most evanescent whisper of something momentous. It was quite different from the way that, eleven years earlier, the death of David Kelly had made her feel. That death had chilled her, even as a young girl. It had seemed not just final, but tragic and unnecessary. Whereas, the message that the wind was trying to bring her—and it wasn't necessarily about death, she couldn't allow herself to believe that, just yet—was less shocking, less unforeseen, but somehow even sadder. It had a kind of gentle inevitability about it. It belonged to the same cycle of seasons that brought rich clusters of fruit to this tree at the end of every summer.

The near-silence of the afternoon was broken, at this point, by the muffled shrilling of Rachel's smartphone as it vibrated in her pocket. Contorting herself carefully on the ladder, she managed to ease the phone out of her pocket and bring it to her ear, noting as she did so that the caller info on the screen said simply "Albion."

"Hello?" she said, and a couple of minutes later she was shimmying down the ladder and running back into the house, upstairs to her grandparents' bedroom, where she woke Gran, who had finally fallen into a doze, and said:

"Gran, Gran, I'm really sorry to wake you up, but I'm going to have to go. I've got a job. I'm going to have to go home and pack."

"Oh, lovey, that's wonderful news," said Gran, although she looked more bewildered than happy.

"I'm really sorry to leave you by yourself."

"Oh, don't worry about that."

"Maybe Mum can come and stay with you for a bit."

"I'll be fine. I can look after myself."

"Yes, but . . . waiting to hear from the hospital and everything . . ."

"Oh, that'll be all right. He's just got a nasty tummy bug. I expect he'll be coming home tomorrow. Or even tonight."

"OK," said Rachel, uncertainly. "As long as you're sure."

"It's wonderful that you've got a job, after all that waiting. Is it those tutoring people?"

"That's right. It's only for a week, though."

"Never mind. It's a start, isn't it? It's bound to lead to something else."

"I hope so. I'm just sorry I'm going to be so far away when you're waiting for Grandad's results."

"Oh, London isn't far away."

"The job isn't in London. It's in" (and Rachel found herself frowning even as she said it, since even to her it seemed so unlikely, even though Mr. Campion had been quite clear about it on the phone) "South Africa."

3

As soon as the butler showed her to her tent, Rachel realized that it was not really a tent at all. In fact, the presence of a butler should itself have been a giveaway. The servant, dressed in fez and long white tunic, said nothing to her until they reached the huge canopied space, shaded by jackalberry trees, where a king-size bed dominated the living area. Even then, he kept his words to a minimum.

"Toilet," he said, opening the door to the toilet.

"Shower," he said, opening the door to the shower.

"Table," he said, pointing to the relevant item, a handsome rosewood dining table at the far end of the decking, commanding a fine view of the swimming pool and the surrounding tents, all of which, at this hour of the day, were empty.

"This is ... beautiful," said Rachel, more or less lost for words. "Where are Mr. and Mrs. Gunn?"

"Sir Gilbert and her ladyship are on safari," said the butler. "The children as well. They will be back at six o'clock in time for dinner. They said, Relax, Make yourself comfortable."

"Thank you," said Rachel. "I will."

"I'll bring some food," said the butler. "You want wine, champagne?"

"Just water, please," said Rachel. "A bottle of cold water."

"You have water," said the butler, opening the door of the minibar. "But I will bring some more."

Before he left, Rachel wondered whether she was supposed to tip him—she had absolutely no idea of the protocol at places like this— but realized in any case that she had no local currency. She had not paid for anything so far—not the connecting flight from Johannesburg to the Skukuza aerodrome, nor the chauffered Land Rover which had brought her to the camp—nor did she have any means of doing so, apart from a Visa card with a credit limit which would probably not cover the half of it. Besides, she already felt uncomfortable, being waited on by this courteous, statuesque black man, and thought that the offer of a tip might be patronizing. It was just one of the many confusing aspects of the ridiculous situation in which she found herself.

The butler spared her any further embarrassment by leaving wordlessly. Rachel unpacked her things and then took the first of many showers (it was midday, and outrageously hot). After which, she sat on the decking, drinking her water and looking once again through the blue plastic folder with the Albion Tutorials logo, and beneath it their enigmatic slogan: "Delivering British Educational Solutions to International Clients."

It didn't, of course, answer any of the questions that were pulsing through her head. Why had she been brought here at such short notice? How long would she be staying? What were her duties supposed to be? Mr. Campion (Bill, as he'd kept telling her to call him) hadn't been able to enlighten her much.

"Don't be freaked out about it," he'd said. "These people have a *lot* of money. To you, it may seem like a big deal that they're flying you all the way out there. But to them, it really isn't. You're going there to do some work with Lucas, Sir Gilbert's son from his first marriage. For some reason Sir Gilbert took a dislike to the last tutor and hasn't renewed his contract. He says you don't need to take out any books or anything like that. I think he has something in mind that's a bit . . . more general. He has two daughters, as well—twins—by his current marriage, to the second Lady Gunn, who I believe used to be a fashion model, and is originally from Kazakhstan. I don't think you'll be having much to do with them on this trip. Just relax and enjoy it. It's not everyone who gets to go on a luxury safari without paying!"

"Relax and enjoy it." That had been the advice, but Rachel was finding it impossible to follow. She spent the afternoon lying on her bed, regretting the fact that there was no cell phone coverage in the Kruger national park, and wondering if her grandfather's test results had come through yet.

Shortly after six o'clock, the stillness of the camp was broken by the arrival of a jeep, carrying three African guides and a family of five. The guides were in good spirits as they helped the family down the high step from the vehicle to ground level. There were two pretty young girls of about eight or nine, and a tall, handsome, but slightly pale and dreamy-looking boy in his late teens. Sir Gilbert Gunn was in his mid-fifties, grey-haired and serious: Rachel recognized him from the picture on his Wikipedia page. The elegant blonde accompanying him, some twenty years his junior, was presumably his second wife, Madiana. "Don't appear too shy or backward," Mr. Campion had said, "they won't appreciate it. They only like strong people." So she bounded down the steps from her tent and held out her hand in greeting.

"Hello," she said, "I'm Rachel. From Albion Tutors. Thank you for bringing me here."

The guides dispersed, looking tired but still cheerful. Sir Gilbert, his wife and their children did not, on the other hand, seem especially invigorated by their day's activities.

"Not at all. Thank you for coming," said Sir Gilbert, giving her hand the briefest of shakes. "Excuse me while I go and freshen up."

"Was the safari good?" Rachel asked.

"There were no lions," said Madiana, brushing past her, and addressing the remark more to her husband than to anybody else. "For the third time, no lions."

"You can't just lay lions on on tap, you know," said Sir Gilbert, heading for his tent without looking back. "We saw bloody rhinos and elephants, for God's sake. What more do you want?"

"They want lions, obviously," said Lucas, the teenager, in a weary voice as he made for a different tent. Madiana and the two girls— who looked hot and disgruntled—trudged towards a third tent, the one nearest the swimming pool: this meant, Rachel realized, that Sir Gilbert's family and entourage accounted for four out of the six tents in camp. She later found out that the other two were empty, and that he had actually booked the entire camp for the week.

"Come and see me in fifteen minutes," he called back to her. "We'll have a drink and I'll tell you what I want."

"Fine," said Rachel, and returned briefly to her own quarters.

Dusk was falling as she made her way to Sir Gilbert's tent fifteen minutes later. A slow, magnificent sunset was in progress, with a shimmering ochre sun casting valedictory rays through the canopy of trees, while the cicadas sang and the night birds began their early chorus. Sir Gilbert was drinking a gin and tonic at his table and seemed to be enjoying the sunset, although, as Rachel was to learn over the next few months, he was not much given to revealing his emotions.

"Not a bad spot," was all he said to her.

"It's amazing," said Rachel.

"Been here before?"

"No. This is very much a first, for me."

"Wouldn't have been my first choice," he said. "But the kids wanted to see some animals and, you know . . . They take priority."

"Absolutely."

"So," he said, after summoning the butler and ordering a glass of white wine for Rachel, "about my son. When he's not at school he mostly lives with his mother, so I don't take much responsibility for how he's turned out."

"Which school does he go to?" Rachel asked.

"Eton. Just starting his last year there, which means he's got university interviews coming up in a few months. He's aiming for maths at Oxford. You were at Oxford, is that right?"

"Yes."

"But you didn't go to public school?"

"No."

"Good. That's what they told me. Well, the crux of the matter is this. Because of the cockeyed ideology which permeates education in Britain at the moment, Oxford colleges are under a lot of pressure to favour state-educated pupils like yourself. I believe it's called 'inclusivity.' Or 'anti-elitism.' Whatever you call it, the upshot is that boys like Lucas, who's never seen the inside of a state school in his life, have to try extra hard to make the right impression. His mother's spoiled him. I don't believe I've spoiled him, but I've certainly spent a lot of money on him over the last seventeen years, which I think is only natural when it comes to your own offspring. Not surprisingly, he's turned out cocky, arrogant and with a sense of entitlement you can spot from ten miles away. None of which would have been a problem, in the past, but nowadays, as I said, this sort of thing apparently puts people's backs up at our great centres of learning. So what we've got to do is try to knock some of it out of him. Do you follow?"

"Sort of . . ." Rachel said, although there was no mistaking the note of uncertainty in her voice.

"Well, I'll put it as simply as I can," said Sir Gilbert. "I want you to turn my son into a normal person."

Rachel would have considered this a bizarre request at the best of times. Here, disorientated after her long journey, she thought it stranger than ever, and for a moment she found herself wondering if she had somehow passed through a looking glass in the last twenty-four hours, and emerged into a parallel world where the everyday rules and assumptions had been inverted.

"A normal person?" she repeated.

"Yes. I want him to be able to open his mouth without it sounding as though he thinks he owns the world and everything in it."

Rachel took a deep breath. "OK then. I'll . . . see what I can do about that."

"You have a very strong accent," said Sir Gilbert. "What is it, Lancashire?"

"Yorkshire. You don't want me to give him a Yorkshire accent, do you?"

"No. I don't really care what you do to him. Talk to him, read to him, whatever it takes. You can start tomorrow at nine. Spend the day with him and see what you can manage."

With that, he picked up his iPad and began reading a magazine article. Rachel realized that this was his way of telling her the conversation was at an end.

The next morning, Lucas did not go on safari with the others. Nor did his father. Rachel imagined, at first, that Sir Gilbert wanted to stay behind to keep a watchful eye on their tutorial, but it turned out that this was not the case at all. He took no notice of them, and confined himself to his tent, where he busied himself with his iPad, a slim leather briefcase full of documents and a number of phone calls. (While mobile reception was nonexistent for Rachel, Sir Gilbert had brought along what seemed to be some sort of military satellite phone—a chunky piece of kit complete with retractable aerial—and he spent a good deal of the morning talking on it.)

Rachel quite enjoyed her morning talking to Lucas. She had encountered a number of Etonians at Oxford, and although they came, of course, in very different forms, she knew that there was one thing they all had in common: a tremendous air of confidence. This confidence, she had always felt, was a wonderful asset: what a great feeling it must be, to know that your wealth and education would not just insulate you against some of the worst of the world's hardships, but prepare you for a life in which your destiny, handed down as if by birthright, was to control the lives of others. But it was hardly surprising that this confidence, nurtured and encouraged by fierce parental ambition, could easily turn to unbearable arrogance, and this was no doubt what Sir Gilbert feared in his son's case.

In fact, after a few hours' conversation, she had the impression that Lucas was not so much arrogant as depressed. Maths was not his own choice of university subject, it seemed. His real passion was Classical Civilization, but "Mum vetoed that," he told her. "She says it's a Mickey Mouse subject." Maths, it had been decided instead, would better prepare him for the job in the City for which his whole education had, up until this point, been a mere laying of the groundwork. Rachel decided that what he really needed was a training in interview technique: every question that she asked him, about art, about drama (another passion), about books, about politics, produced not a thoughtful or reflective answer, but some boastful comeback about the prize he had won for an essay, or the top marks he had been given for his coursework, or the speech he had made that had won a standing ovation, or the famous author whose children he'd been on holiday with. Every reflex in his brain seemed to be geared towards competition and one-upmanship. None of this, Rachel thought, was exactly his fault, and she only really lost patience with him once, when he told her that failing to get into Oxford would be a personal disaster because it would mean "I might end up at some Mickey Mouse university with a lot of chavs." At which point she proposed that they break for lunch.

Shortly before noon—presumably having taken the same flight that had brought Rachel to Skukuza the day before—another guest arrived. He ate lunch with Lucas and Sir Gilbert, while Rachel was seemingly expected to eat by herself, at her own table on the decking of her own tent, but when the meal was over, the new arrival made a point of coming over to introduce himself.

"Hello," he said, stretching out the word in what Rachel could only assume was intended to be a flirtatious manner. "And who have we *here*?"

"My name's Rachel," she said. "I'm here to do some tutoring for Sir Gilbert and his family."

"Francis," said the man, returning the handshake. "Frederick Francis. My friends call me Freddie."

He was in his mid-forties, Rachel would have guessed. Fit and well preserved. Slight traces of grey around the temples were really his only signs of middle age. He was not unattractive, by any means, but there was something about him, something indefinable, which made her immediately want to recoil.

"You're new, aren't you?" he said. "New to the family, I mean."

"Yes," said Rachel. "I arrived yesterday."

"Staying long?"

"I'm not really sure," she replied, laughing. "That hasn't been made clear."

"Ah, yes. Sir Gilbert likes to preserve the element of surprise."

Not fully understanding this, and wanting to fill the void of silence that followed, Rachel asked: "So, have you been allocated your tent?"

"Sadly, no," he answered. "I'm going back to London on this evening's flight."

"Wow." Rachel was—not for the first time in the last two days—astonished. "That's a long way to come, just for the afternoon."

"Well, Sir Gilbert won't be in London again for a while, and I've got some things he needs to sign. They're rather urgent."

"Ah. I see," said Rachel, although she very much didn't. "You work for Sir Gilbert, then, do you?"

Freddie pretended, at least, to give this question serious thought. "Now that's a tricky one. *Do* I work for him? Or do I work for myself? Or does *he* work for me?"

Rachel wasn't interested in riddles right now. "What line of business are you in?" she asked, directly.

"Before I go," said Freddie, "I'll give you my card."

But he was either lying, or he forgot, and when he departed the camp that afternoon at 4:30, Mr. Francis left her not with a business card but with a long, appraising look from the window of the Land Rover, and an inexplicably uneasy feeling in her gut.

As it happened, Rachel and the rest of the family were not long in following Mr. Francis back to the airport in Johannesburg. That evening at six o'clock, Madiana and the twins arrived back from their latest safari, and Lady Gunn was more contemptuous of the guide's endeavours than ever.

"Gilbert, darling," she said, as the twins ran into the tent to change into their swimming costumes, "we are absolutely wasting our time here. There are no lions in this park, none at all. All we saw today were those stupid elephants again."

"I told you—I can provide you with most things. But not lions, I'm afraid."

"Then I seriously think we might as well pack up and go home."

And the next day, that was exactly what they did. They packed up early in the morning: Madiana, Rachel and the children flew back to London, and Sir Gilbert took a plane to Singapore, although whether that was his final destination was anybody's guess. Madiana did not seem to know or even particularly care where he was off to. This was one of the many things that puzzled Rachel, as she mulled over the trip during the eleven-hour flight home. She had much to think about on that flight: these last few days had been among the most mysterious of her life, after all. But amidst the dense tangle of her thoughts, the image that recurred to her most often, strangely enough, was a view of the camp itself: booked out for the rest of the week by Sir Gilbert and his family, but now defined, instead, by their absence: the swimming pool unused, the bar and restaurant deserted, the staff redundant, the very tents themselves standing empty and purposeless in the grey shade of the jackalberry trees.

4

When Rachel returned home, she found that a lot had been happening at her grandparents' house. Tests had shown up a large cancerous tumour in her grandfather's colon. He had been booked into theatre as soon as the discovery was made, and after a six-hour operation the tumour was successfully removed. But the cancer had already mestastasized to his liver, and could no longer be cured through surgery or radiotherapy or chemotherapy, the doctors said: it could only be "managed." They refused to give a prognosis, but the family all knew that cancer of the liver usually comes with a life expectancy of only a few months. For the time being, Grandad would have to remain in hospital: it would take him at least two weeks to recover from the operation.

The next day, Rachel dropped her mother off at court and then drove out to Beverley by herself. As soon as she arrived, her grandmother took her in a crooked, bony embrace, weeping quietly. Afterwards, Gran made some cheese sandwiches and they had lunch together in the garden. Rachel looked at the plum tree, still bearing a few bunches of overripe fruit, and thought about the gentle, sorrowful message that had been passed on to her by the wind whispering through its branches. She thought, too, about that camp of six magnificent tents grouped around the swimming pool in the Kruger national park, and found it hard to believe that it existed, let alone that she had been there herself just a few days ago.

She hugged her grandmother tighter than ever when she said good-bye. And then, the next morning, she received another phone call from Albion Tutors.

"You were a big hit with Sir Gilbert and his family," Mr. Campion told her, to her surprise. "Lady Gunn wants to see you tomorrow. You may be looking at a more permanent post."

So, once again, Rachel took the train down from Leeds to London. She took the Piccadilly Line to South Kensington and then, after a few minutes' walk, found herself entering a part of the city where the houses were tall and wide, with polished steps leading up to porticoed entrances, and full-length sash windows looked out over streets which once, she imagined, would have been hushed and cloistered.

Not anymore, however. The Gunns' house was located in a broad avenue called Turngreet Road, and when Rachel walked into it she was confronted by a scene more reminiscent of a building site than a residential backwater. At least half of the houses in the street seemed to be undergoing major reconstruction. There were high, solid, impenetrable hoardings around their front gardens, all emblazoned with the logos of building firms with names like Talisman Construction, Prestige Basements and Vanguard Redesign. Instead of artisans chipping away at brickwork or giving door frames a delicate lick of paint, there were gigantic cement mixers grinding away deafeningly, huge skips full of bricks and aggregate being transported on industrial hoists, fifty-foot cranes blocking the street while they hauled their massive loads of girders and breezeblocks from one place to another. Yellow signs along the side of the road indicated a series of parking suspensions whereby residents' bays had been blocked out for months at a time. Gingerly, Rachel picked her way through all this activity, nodding hello to the groups of men standing around at each of the sites, wearing hard hats and high-visibility jackets and holding low-voiced conversations in Eastern European languages. They returned her greetings with impassive stares.

Finally she arrived at what seemed to be the Gunns' house: Number 13. Like the others, it had a tall hoarding around it. This one was green, and bore the logo of Grierson Basements plc. In the centre of the hoarding was a temporary front door complete with letterbox and alarm system. Rachel had been given a phone number to dial when she reached the house. While she was waiting for the call to be answered she read the warning sign on the hoarding: "Under the Health and Safety Act 1974 all persons entering this site must comply with all regulations under this act. All visitors must report to the site office and obtain permission to proceed onto the site or any work area. Safety signs and procedures must be observed and personal protection and safety equipment must be used at all times." Another sign simply said: "No unauthorized entry." She began to feel that putting on her smartest work clothes may have been a mistake.

A voice at the other end of the line, with a slight foreign—perhaps Far Eastern?—accent, said, "Miss Wells?" at which precise moment a pneumatic drill started up behind one of the nearby hoardings, making conversation all but impossible. "Yes?" Rachel shouted into the phone, and then the voice said something indistinct and the call ended. While she was wondering what to do, and whether she was expected to dial again, the temporary green door was pulled open and the welcoming face of a housemaid appeared. Her skin was dark brown, her hair thick, black and wiry, but Rachel could not be sure of her ethnic origin.

"Miss Wells? Please, come in. She is waiting for you."

Following the maid, Rachel weaved her way past a toilet cubicle and a temporary site office, towards the front stairs of the house. She could not help noticing that the site was deserted and appeared to have been abandoned some time ago. Then they were up the stairs and had gained the sanctuary of the hallway, where calm, for the moment, seemed to reign.

Rachel was shown into a sitting room—or, as she supposed one should call it, a drawing room—which ran the length of the house. Bookshelves lined the walls, and by the window at the far end stood a grand piano with an album of Chopin mazurkas standing open on the music stand. Everything looked pristine, almost untouched.

Madiana entered the room accompanied by a large and beautiful golden retriever, who proceeded to sniff at Rachel's legs curiously and lick her on the hand. Madiana grabbed the dog by the collar and gave him a reproving slap.

"All right, Mortimer, that's enough," she said. The dog sat down beside her, panting but clearly chastened. Madiana greeted Rachel courteously but without warmth, and then proceeded to explain her business: she had decided to take on a live-in tutor for the twins, who were in Year 4 at the local prep school. She wanted them to do extra reading, extra maths, and to start learning French, Latin, Russian and Mandarin.

"You will live in this house," she said. "Faustina brings the girls back from school at three thirty. They will rest and have a snack and then you will teach them from four o'clock until seven o'clock. The rest of the time is your own."

"What about Lucas?"

The subject of Lucas, clearly, did not interest Madiana as much as her own daughters did. "He's back at school," she said. "Some weekends he will come home. When he does, you must carry on with whatever you were doing with him before. You know what you will be paid, yes? I mean, it's all agreed with the agency."

"Yes," said Rachel.

"So, you agree?"

It seemed that an instant decision was expected. In fact, it wasn't a difficult one to make.

"Yes. Of course. Thank you very much."

"Come with me. I'll show you where you will live."

Cautioning the dog to stay where he was, Madiana led Rachel into the hallway and up the main staircase. (It was one of the very few times she would ever use it.) The two girls, Grace and Sophia, lived mainly on the second floor of the house. They had a bedroom each, a shared bathroom, a study room and a large playroom equipped with everything from a table-tennis table to two PlayStation controllers and a monitor which took up most of the largest wall.

"What a lovely room for them to play in," said Rachel.

"It is not big enough," said Madiana, dismissively. "We are making them a bigger one downstairs, once these ridiculous arguments are resolved."

She did not specify what these arguments were about or who they were with, and Rachel did not feel bold enough to ask. Doubtless all would become clear.

"This is the door," said Madiana, indicating a white-panelled door in the wall of the landing, "that leads to your part of the house."

Rachel was only half listening. Passing the girls' bathroom, she noticed that the walls and ceiling were painted with gold leaf, and standing at the centre was an extraordinary item of furniture: a small roll-top bath, but not just any bath—it appeared to be a *diamanté* bath—studded all over with fake diamonds. At least she assumed (or rather hoped) that they were fake. In any case, she couldn't quite believe what she was seeing.

"You are listening?" said Madiana.

"Yes, of course."

Her new employer ushered her through the door. It led to another small landing, with narrow stairs leading both up and down. Madiana closed the door behind them and Rachel noticed that, on this side, the door was completely concealed by a full-length, gilt-framed mirror, and was also equipped with a keypad.

"You need a code to open the door from this side," said Madiana. "I will give it to you later. Down there," she added, pointing down the stairs, "is the kitchen. Where you will eat. Now, follow me."

They climbed two more flights until they had almost reached the very top of the house. There were three doors leading off the top landing.

"Faustina and her husband sleep in here," said Madiana, indicating the middle door. "This one is the bathroom you will share with them. And this is where you will sleep."

She led Rachel into a small but cosy bedroom with a sloping roof, fireplace and compact built-in wardrobe. There was just enough room for an armchair and a tiny desk which overlooked the back garden. Rachel peered through the window and was surprised to find how high the house was. She was surprised, too, to find that there was no garden as such, at the moment: just a continuation of the building site, a mess of mud and temporary planking with a square of tarpaulin laid out at the centre, covering what seemed to be a gigantic hole. Parked in a far corner, but still dominating the scene by virtue of its height, there stood some sort of piling rig. In the midst of this desolation, Mortimer was running around sniffing objects hopefully and cocking his leg against some of them, while being watched over by a dark-haired man smoking a cigarette. Both figures seemed very distant and small.

"That is Jules," said Madiana. "He does the gardening, drives the cars, things like that."

"He's married to Faustina?" said Rachel.

"Yes. You will eat your meals with them, down in the kitchen. The staff side of the house and the family side of the house are quite separate. There are doors which connect them, but the only one you will be able to use is the door with the mirror."

"Right," said Rachel. "I'll remember that."

"Good. But you will not even use that door," said Madiana, "unless you are invited."

5

And so Rachel's new life began.

Her routine, at first, was simple, and her duties undemanding. She would spend a few hours every morning in her bedroom taking an online course in Russian, and the same in the afternoon for Mandarin. In this way, at least, she hoped to stay at least one day ahead of her pupils. Then at four o'clock she would go down to the mirrored door on the second floor, key in her four-digit code, pass through into the enchanted kingdom of the Gunns' living space, and wait for the girls in their study room. Together they would work and talk for the best part of three hours, after which Grace and Sophia would go downstairs for their dinner, and Rachel would return to her bedroom. After an hour's rest, she would descend the narrow stairs again, all the way to the lower ground floor and the staff kitchen at the back of the house. There she would eat dinner with Faustina and her husband, and afterwards either stay to watch television with them, or go back upstairs to read or go online, or sometimes smarten herself up and venture outside for the evening.

The house was extremely large, and its layout was elaborate. As Madiana had told her, the staff and family living quarters were entirely separate. There were two kitchens: a small one at the back of the house, where the staff would cook for themselves, and a large one at the front, where Faustina would also prepare meals for the children and—very occasionally—for Sir Gilbert, his wife and their guests. There was a connecting door between the two kitchens, but only Faustina knew the code that would open it. Another door from the staff kitchen led to a long cloakroom, at the end of which was a further locked door. Only Jules knew the code to this one, because it opened onto a staircase which descended to the garage in the basement. Here, in normal circumstances, the Gunns would keep their four cars: a Range Rover, a Rolls-Royce, a Lamborghini and a 1953 Bentley R-Type Continental. When one of these cars was needed, Jules was supposed to drive it on to a platform in the corner of the garage which would rise up on a hydraulic lift and emerge at ground level in front of the house. Unfortunately while the building works were in progress this was impossible, and so for the time being the cars were being stored elsewhere, and Sir Gilbert and Madiana had to make do with a Mercedes-AMG which they had bought specially to tide them over for these few months and which they kept in a small additional garage two streets away: a garage which was itself valued at just under half a million pounds.

These building works were the source of the "arguments" to which Madiana had alluded when showing Rachel around the house. For some time Madiana had been insisting to her husband that their London house (one of six that they owned around the world) was not big enough to meet the family's needs. She wished to extend: but the absurd local planning regulations dictated that they could not make the house any taller, nor could they extend it at the rear, into the back garden. The only way to go, in other words, was down.

Many other households in the area had reached similar conclusions, and so ever more extensive and elaborate basement conversions had become popular among the wealthier residents of Chelsea over the last few years. The works they entailed were exceptionally noisy and disruptive, but people more or less tolerated them, largely for the reason that, one day soon, they might want to do the same thing themselves. Serious objections were only raised, for the most part, when the works threatened to do structural damage to the neighbouring houses: and this, indeed, was what had happened in the Gunns' case. A formal complaint had been lodged by the residents of the next house in the street (Number 15), claiming that since the Gunns had started digging out their basement, cracks had appeared in some of the supporting walls of their own property. The council had ordered that works should be suspended while the matter was resolved, and Madiana, who had grandiose plans for these subterranean floors, was beside herself with anger.

According to Jules and Faustina, however, there was also a much graver issue at stake. They told Rachel that the works had been shut down, not because of objections from the neighbours, but because of an accident on site. Details were sketchy, but it seemed that one of the builders had been at the very base of the shaft (then dug to about seventy feet) when a steel girder being lowered into place to complete the box frame had fallen from its cable and struck him.

"That sounds nasty," said Rachel. "Was he OK?"

Jules shook his head. "He died. That was when Health and Safety closed the whole thing down."

Rachel shuddered. She had a long-standing fear of underground spaces, and felt distinctly uneasy at the thought that, beneath the elegant, comfortable rooms of the Gunns' house, a matter of mere feet from the kitchen she used every day, there yawned this pit, this fathomless void. It seemed incredible that the only thing preventing the house itself from collapsing into it was a fragile frame of steel rods and girders. She tried to block the idea from her mind.

Rachel did not see much of the girls at weekends. If Madiana and Sir Gilbert were out of the country, the twins were sometimes flown out to join them. Occasionally Jules would have to drive them to the Cotswolds, where the Gunns kept a "cottage": actually a cluster of converted farm buildings, including a swimming pool and sauna complex which was itself twice as big as most people's houses. Mortimer, the golden retriever, would sometimes go with them to the cottage, although now and again they forgot to take him. The London house was never lively at the best of times: at the weekends, when only Rachel, the housekeeper and her husband were in residence, and the building works at all the neighbouring houses were suspended, it could be chillingly silent.

One lunchtime, after she had been living in the Gunns' house for a few weeks, Rachel was downstairs in the staff kitchen watching the television. She had made herself a sandwich and was feeding scraps of cold chicken to Mortimer, who sat at her feet, tired but content after returning from his walk with Livia, the smiling, pensive Romanian dog-walker who called at the property every day to give him his exercise.

Rachel was watching the lunchtime news, without paying it much attention. Currently there was an item about the construction of Crossrail, the big new transport project designed to connect the City of London with the outermost eastern and western suburbs, entailing a number of deep excavations across the capital which were (not unlike the Gunns' basement works) creating a lot of inconvenience for many Londoners. The report today came from Liverpool Street station, where it seemed that the construction workers had made a ghoulish discovery: twenty-five human skeletons, probably dating back to the fourteenth century and providing evidence that the current works might be taking place on the site of a burial ground for victims of the Black Death.

And then Rachel had a surprise: a nice one. The academic expert they had brought in to talk about the find was Laura Harvey, her old tutor from Oxford. She was smartly dressed in a grey pinstriped jacket over an open-necked white blouse, was wearing her hair shorter than before, and looked thoroughly glamorous and composed.

"So, Professor Harvey," the newsreader was saying, "you think that this discovery may not just be of historical value, but worth something in monetary terms as well?"

"Yes," said Laura. "Of course I'm not talking about the market value of the remains if people were to try and sell them. I'm saying that discoveries like this add to the sense of mystery which attaches to parts of London, and that sense of mystery is one of the things that attracts people here."

"Tourists, you mean."

"Yes."

"And you're part of a movement, I believe, which is tasked with the job of assigning value to phenomena such as this?"

"That's right. As members of the Institute for Quality Valuation, we attempt to quantify things that have traditionally been thought of as unquantifiable. Feelings, in other words. A sense of awe, a sense of wonder, even fear—in fact, fear in particular. Look how popular the London Dungeon is."

"*Monetizing Wonder* was the title of your book on this subject, wasn't it? But that was mainly a book about films."

"Well, London has been the setting for countless films, and the stories which filmmakers have framed around these settings are among the things which draw people here. What's been uncovered at Liverpool Street today, for instance, is strongly reminiscent of a number of famous London films. I'm thinking of *Quatermass and the Pit,* from the 1960s, in which a construction crew digging a new tube line unearths a human skeleton, among other things; or *Death Line,* made a few years later, in which a disused Underground station turns out to be housing a colony of cannibals. It doesn't matter whether people have actually seen these films or not: collectively, they are part of our consciousness. They tell us something important about London, which is that we're never quite sure what lies underneath us, beneath our feet. There is always the sense that if we dig too deeply beneath London's surface, we might uncover something sinister, something nasty. People find this a frightening idea, of course, but also rather an exciting one."

"Finally, Dr. Harvey, would you care to put a value—a monetary value—on today's discovery at Liverpool Street?"

"Yes, of course. We've developed an algorithm to produce quick and very rough estimates for this sort of thing, taking into account all the historical, cultural and literary factors, and we estimate that the discovery of these human remains today probably adds about £1.2 million to the value of London as a whole."

"Fascinating stuff. Professor Laura Harvey, thank you very much. And now—how should we cope with the problem of trained jihadists returning to the UK? We take a look at Denmark, where they are experimenting with a very different approach to this question . . ."

6

"It's wonderful to see you again, Rachel," Laura said. "Thank you so much for getting back in touch."

"I should have done it ages ago," said Rachel. "But I wasn't sure where you were working anymore. It was such a shock, seeing you on the TV . . ."

"Well, I'm a bit embarrassed about that."

"Why? I thought you came across incredibly well. So confident and articulate."

"Yes, but . . . this new public role I seem to be acquiring. I feel very ambivalent about it."

She stirred her cappuccino and took a tentative sip. They were sitting in the Housman Room, the senior common room at University College, London, on a quiet Thursday morning with not many other lecturers or research students for company. It was a bright and cheerful space, with colourful modernist abstracts hanging on the walls and autumn sunlight pooling in through a glass cupola. Sinking back into one of the comfortable leather armchairs, Laura looked thoroughly at home there. She had been on the staff at UCL for two years now, her job title—Professor of Contemporary Thought—testifying to the fact that she had started to expand her academic horizons since teaching Rachel at Oxford.

"Basically," she said, "I've done a deal with the devil. The devil in this case being Lord Lucrum. He was Master of our college, remember?"

"Of course. Is he not anymore?"

"No. He left a few months ago, to spend more time with his committees. One of which, much to my amazement, he asked me to join.

He'd actually read my book—or got someone to read it for him. Pretty surprising, in either case, since I never thought that a book of essays about obscure British films would interest anyone other than the occasional fanatic like my late husband. But I think it was the title that caught his fancy, more than anything else."

"Is this to do with that institution you mentioned in the interview . . . ?"

"That's right. The Institute for Quality Valuation—of which he's the director. Sounds pretty innocuous, doesn't it?"

"Is it not?"

"It goes back," said Laura, "to the 1980s, when Henry Winshaw was chairing a Review Board on the NHS. The idea was to privatize it, essentially, although of course nobody was going to admit that straight out. But he had this one big idea, which was that quality of human life could be valued. Priced, to use the more accurate word. So that some medical interventions are more cost-effective than others. Lord Lucrum—or David Lucrum as he was called in those days—was a relatively lowly management consultant who was part of that review. He worshipped Henry Winshaw—idolized him— and nowadays people see him as some sort of spiritual heir. He's still an adviser to the government on NHS reforms. As for this new institute, it's part of the same move to express everything in monetary terms. They want people like me—arts and humanities people—to come on board and be part of the process."

"I wouldn't have thought," Rachel said, choosing her words carefully, "you'd feel all that comfortable sitting around a table with that lot."

"I know what you mean, but I'm trying to see it from a different point of view. We're dealing with people who have *no notion at all* that something is important unless you can put a price on it. So, rather than have them dismiss . . . well, human emotion, altogether, as something completely worthless, I think it's better if someone like me comes along and tries to help them out. Makes some sort of case for the defence. So we've coined a new term—'hedonic value.' That might refer to, say, the feeling you get when you look at a beautiful stretch of coastline. And we try to prove that this feeling is actually worth a few thousand pounds; or, on the other hand, that a widow's grief might come at a cost of £10,000 a year to the economy. This way, you see, at least they'll *recognize* these feelings. At least they'll acknowledge their existence."

Rachel thought about this and said: "You know what I'm starting to think? I'm starting to realize that there are people around us who look normal from the outside, but when you start to understand what makes them tick, you see that they're not like the rest of us at all. They're like androids, or zombies or something . . ."

"Ah, yes. *They walk among us* . . ." Laura looked up to say hello to a young man who was walking past them on his way to fetch a coffee. "Jamie! Are you coming to join us?"

"Erm . . . sure. Would that be OK? I don't want to interrupt."

"Not at all. Come on over."

While Jamie was getting his coffee, she explained: "One of my PhD students. Very bright guy. And an absolute sweetheart to boot. The two of you should definitely meet."

Rachel started to tell Laura about her new job: the sudden phone call, the bewildering transition from Leeds to a South African safari park, the absurd opulence of her new home, the Sisyphean task of ridding Lucas of his arrogance, her own difficult, developing relationship with Grace and Sophia, the Gunns' glacially composed twin daughters. Jamie came to join them in the middle of her description and, like Laura, appeared intrigued by this insight into the otherwise unglimpsable milieu of the super-rich.

"So, how do they treat you?" he wanted to know. "Like an equal, or like a member of staff?"

Rachel hesitated. Not only was this a difficult question to answer, but she had just noticed something about Jamie: he was distractingly good-looking. "A bit of both, I suppose," she said, bringing her thoughts into focus with an effort. "Obviously I'm not a person they'd ever have spoken to, normally, but somehow, I don't know, there seems to be some sort of weird . . . respect going on."

"But you probably represent something very precious to them," said Laura. "You went to Oxford. You say this woman grew up in Kazakhstan and used to be a model. So, now she finds herself trying to make her way in British society, right at the top. She's got most of the stuff that money can buy, but *you* represent all sorts of other things, intangible, desirable things: tradition, culture, privilege, history. I mean, I doubt if that's how you feel about yourself, but that's probably how you seem to *her*. It's like Lord Lucrum and his committee: she sees something that exists outside the marketplace, and the only way she knows how to react is by putting a price on it. A British education—a certain sort of British education—is one of our few remaining national assets, and like everything else we're ready to flog it off to the richest buyer. I've seen plenty of that happening in my line of work over the last few years, believe me."

"I feel," Rachel said, "that there's my world, and there's their world, and the two coexist, and are very close to each other, but you can't really pass from one to the other." She smiled. "Unless you use the magic door, of course."

"What magic door?" asked Jamie.

"Well, that's what I call it. It's the only way I can get from my side of the house to theirs. It looks like a big mirror. A mirror you can pass through."

"Like Orphée," said Laura, "in Cocteau's film."

Neither Rachel nor Jamie understood the reference. Laura had to explain that in Cocteau's reimagining of the Orpheus legend, the poet was able to make his way into the underworld by passing through a mirror which turned to liquid when he stepped into it. It struck her as typical that neither of them had seen a film made in 1950 which, until recently, had been considered famous.

"I know what Roger would have thought about *that*," she said. "You don't bother to watch these great old films because you have too much *choice*. In the old days you would have watched them because there was nothing else on the television and nothing else to do."

"How's Harry?" Rachel asked, reminded of Laura's family life by this mention of her husband.

"He's fine," said Laura. "Doing well at his new school." The reply was curt: as before, she didn't seem to want to talk or even think much about her son. She dismissed the subject quickly. "Anyway, if you want to hear about different worlds colliding, you should really ask Jamie where he was last weekend."

"Really?" he said, giving her a pleading look. "Does Rachel have to hear about that? We've only just met."

"But you have to tell her what happened. It's the sweetest thing I've ever heard."

"It's embarrassing."

"You shouldn't be embarrassed. You come out of it very well. And if you're lucky, she might put it in one of her stories. When I taught her at Oxford, she wrote quite a few short stories. Very good they were, too."

Rachel blushed with pleasure at the compliment. And she was full of curiosity by now, so Jamie realized that he was going to have to enlighten her, whether he liked it or not.

"OK. So, last weekend," he began, still with palpable reluctance, "a friend of mine was getting married, and the night before we all went out on a stag night. To a lap-dancing club. Not my choice. I'd never been to one of these places before—never had to, never wanted to—so I wasn't really prepared for the whole experience. So before I know what's happening, this incredible woman, with a gorgeous figure, the kind of woman who'd never normally look at me, is sitting on my lap, more or less naked, with her arms around me, gyrating her hips, looking straight into my eyes. So I feel that something is . . . well, called for. Some sort of response. I feel that I have to say something."

"And what did you say?" Rachel asked. "You're really beautiful? 'Thank you very much—here's fifty pounds'?"

"No," said Jamie. "I can see now that those would have been good things to say. But I asked her a question instead."

He paused for a long time.

"Go on."

"I asked her if she and the other girls . . . belonged to a union."

Rachel stared at him, not convinced that she had heard correctly.

"I mean, I was genuinely interested. I wanted to know what kind of employment rights they had, and whether they were unionized. It seemed like a good kind of conversational gambit."

He looked down, apologetically, into the emptiness of his coffee cup. Laura waited to see Rachel's reaction, and before long both women were laughing: helpless laughter, laughter without end. And then Jamie, too. The readiness with which he joined them, was prepared to see the joke against himself, was adorable. Rachel decided there and then that she was not going to leave the Housman Club that morning without his mobile number.

7

At Euston station, Lucas turned to Rachel and held out his hand. For a moment she thought he had been about to kiss her on the cheek—they had just spent the whole day together, after all—but he went for a formal handshake instead. The delicate balance of the tutor–pupil relationship had to be preserved, she supposed.

"Well, thank you, Rachel," he said. "That was a very . . . enlightening day."

"Enlightening?"

"Yes. Well, I can't really think of any other word, offhand."

Rachel and Lucas had spent the day in Birmingham together, helping out at a food bank in Kings Norton. She'd had the idea earlier in the week, when she'd realized that Lucas would be with them for most of a ten-day half-term and had nothing much to do apart from his schoolwork. It might open his eyes, she thought, to come into direct contact with families dealing with food poverty, and it had been an easy enough thing to set up: choosing Birmingham more or less at random, as offering a sharpish contrast to the social and ethnic mix of Windsor, she had managed to arrange it all with a couple of e-mails.

"What I mean is," he said, stammeringly, "one reads about these places—one knows that they exist—but not everybody actually takes the plunge and visits them."

"Well, I expect all food banks are different," said Rachel, "but at least you now have a rough idea . . ."

"Well . . . I was talking about Birmingham, actually. But yeah, food banks, too, I mean, it's really cool to know what they're all about, and so on."

"Good. Well, you mustn't be late for your friends."

"No."

"Where are you meeting?"

"Not far from here. Top of Centrepoint. I'll probably grab a cab."

"Well, I bet they haven't spent the whole day making up parcels of cornflakes and orange juice and hot chocolate. Don't forget to show them the pictures. I bet they'll be impressed."

"Yeah, they'll have a right laugh, probably. I'll do that."

"OK then."

She waved good-bye and watched as his tall, loping frame was swallowed up by the crowds of commuters.

Rachel took the tube back to Turngreet Road but got out a few stops early, at Knightsbridge, wanting to walk through these quieter, emptier streets and think back on the events of the day. Try to come to terms with their strangeness. Lucas had fallen almost completely silent after their arrival at Birmingham New Street. Maybe this was down to self-preservation, because on the local train to Kings Norton, let alone at the food bank itself, his accent would immediately have attracted unwelcome attention. But Rachel was afraid there had been more to it than that. She thought again about his friends "having a laugh" as they passed around the pictures of his visit, and knew that on some level he had found the whole episode not enlightening at all, but amusing. Everything from his bottle-green volunteer's apron to the tins of fruit and vegetables stacked on the storeroom shelves had struck him, she now suspected, first as exotic, then somehow quaint and endearing, and finally comical. When they had been welcomed by Dawn, the centre's cheerful manager, he'd found her Black Country accent so hard to understand that Rachel had had to translate for him. After that, to give him credit, he'd kept his head down and worked uncomplainingly, spending most of the day in the back room making up parcels without once letting slip that in his other, secret life he attended the most famous public school in the country. Now, though, having spent the day working hard, in a less than glamorous setting, without embarrassing himself or anyone around him, he had the advantage of being able to walk away from the experience without ever thinking about it again. On the train home he'd said almost nothing, just stared fixedly at his iPhone 6, lost in some group chat or solitary amusement. She hadn't been expecting his worldview to be overturned in the space of a few hours: just hoping, perhaps, for some wondering comment, some register of shock at the discovery that, side by side with his own protected world, places like this should also need to exist. But if the thought occurred to him, he had chosen not to express it.

As for Rachel herself, she had been at the front counter, handing out the parcels themselves to downcast, monosyllabic women (they were mainly women) in return for vouchers. And that was when the strangest thing of all had happened.

"Two-four-one!" she had called out, and then, as she handed over the paper carrier, she realized that she knew the person who had come up to present her voucher. It was Val Doubleday, Alison's mother.

"Hello, Val!" she had said. "It is Val, isn't it?" There was no sign of recognition on her part. "It's me, Rachel. You know, Alison's friend from Leeds?"

Val had looked confused—more than confused. The shock of finding someone from another city, and her distant past, in this place and in this role seemed to render her completely speechless. What should have been a joyful reunion dissolved into a scene of terrible awkwardness. Rachel had asked after Alison; had received some stilted, unconvincing reply to the effect that she was "doing fine"; had scribbled her e-mail address on a piece of card and handed it over; and had explained that she was only visiting Birmingham for the day.

"I heard you were on TV a few years ago," she added. "I'm sorry, I missed the whole thing. I'd just arrived at uni and, you know, you don't really watch telly in the first year . . . Are you singing at the moment?"

Val did not answer this question. All she said, blurting out the words as quickly as she could, was: "I'm not getting this stuff for myself. It's my next-door neighbour—she's old, and she can't get out . . ."

"Of course," Rachel said.

"Say hi to your mother from me, won't you?" said Val. And then she was gone, not looking back. In fact she had not made eye contact at all during the whole encounter.

Rachel stared after her, trying to work out what had just happened. She didn't snap out of it until Dawn came out from the storeroom with the latest parcel, having finally, it seemed, found a temporary chink in Lucas's wall of silence and self-concealment.

"I *love* your friend," she said. "He's hilarious. Do you know what he called this?" She held up a jar of decaf coffee from the top of the parcel, and said, in a deadly impression of his sardonic drawl: *"Bit of a Mickey Mouse drink, if you ask me."*

8

If Lucas was proving difficult to change, the twin daughters, Grace and Sophia, presented an equal challenge. Rachel did not know what to make of them at all. They were very intelligent, she could see that. Very determined, too. They were picking up their new languages quickly; so quickly, that Rachel herself could barely keep up with them. Their prep school had small class sizes, and there were regular, weekly tests in most subjects. The twins took careful notice of the results and would waste no time in telling her whether they had come first, second or third in the rankings. (They were rarely any lower than that.) They played elaborate games on their PlayStations and watched American comedy shows on their iPads, often following the dialogue with concentration rather than enjoyment. Rachel would read to them every night at the end of their lessons but she found it difficult to choose stories that would engage them, and would often be surprised by their responses. Once she tried reading them one of her favourite stories, H. G. Wells's "The Door in the Wall." How could they fail to be moved, she thought, by this tale of a young boy who, at the age of five, finds a door in the wall of an ordinary London street, and discovers that it leads to a magical garden: a door he will never be able to locate again, a garden he will never revisit, despite a lifetime of efforts and longings? She liked to ask questions as she went along, to make sure that they understood what they were hearing: and when the little boy was first expelled from the garden, was sent back into the "grey world" of London again, and admitted, years later, that "as I realized the fullness of what had happened to me, I gave way to quite ungovernable grief," she said to them: "So—why do you think he's crying?"

Sophia's answer was hard to forget. "Because he's weak," she said, calmly.

Were Sir Gilbert and Madiana satisfied with the progress she was making with their children? It was hard to tell. For one thing, she could never be entirely sure when they were even at home: if, indeed, their London residence was their "home" in any meaningful sense. On her side of the house, there were CCTV cameras everywhere: not in her bedroom, thankfully, and not in the bathroom as far as she could tell, but certainly in the kitchen, and all the stairways and landings. The images from these cameras could be streamed to Sir Gilbert's or Madiana's smartphones and tablets wherever they were in the world, so they always knew when Rachel was in the house and when she had gone out. But the arrangement was not reciprocal. Her employers kept her informed about their own movements on a need-to-know basis, which meant, in practice, that Rachel had no way of knowing where they were at all. When they were at home, they made very little noise, and the presence of lights in the windows meant nothing, since for security reasons the lights were programmed to come on automatically at random, whether the house was occupied or not.

One evening in late November, then, it was a surprise for Rachel to catch a glimpse of Sir Gilbert as she left the house by the back door (as always) and picked her way through the abandoned builders' materials on her way to the front entrance and a date with Jamie. Her employer was standing between the Grecian columns at the top of the steps, saying good-bye to another man and shaking his hand. As the door was closed and the man descended the steps to catch up with her, she saw that it was Frederick Francis.

"Well, *hello*," he said, stretching the word again in that annoyingly flirtatious way. They hadn't seen each other since the trip to the Kruger national park.

"Hello, Frederick," said Rachel, stopping short of using the friendly abbreviation.

"Something of a mess, isn't it?" he said, surveying the jumble of ladders, drills, masonry, ironware and cement mixers that the builders had left behind.

"I find I'm getting used to it," said Rachel, pushing the temporary door open and stepping out into the street through the hoarding.

"Of course," said Freddie, hurrying to keep up with her, "you've become quite the fixture around here, I understand."

"Well, it was nice seeing you again," she said, preparing to head off down the street.

"Wait a minute. Where are you going?" said Freddie.

"I've got a date."

"Heading for the West End?"

"Soho."

"Well, Jules is going to drive me that way. We can give you a lift."

"I'd rather not."

"Oh, come on. It's a free ride. Don't be so puritanical."

In truth, Rachel needed to save the money, even if it was only a few pounds on her Oyster card. She accepted the lift, and settled with an involuntary sigh of pleasure into the deeply cushioned leather seat at the rear of the Mercedes. The leather was heated, she could not help noticing, a feature which itself was extremely welcome on this chilly winter night.

"I mustn't get too comfortable, must I?" she said. "It'd be a mistake to get used to this level of luxury."

"On the contrary," said Freddie, "I think it would be very good for you to get used to it. Everyone should experience a ride in a car like this at least once. Then they'd have something to aspire to."

"Yeah, right," said Rachel.

She stared out of the window as the car purred north, through The Boltons and across the Brompton Road. She was surprised by how clearly she could see: from the outside, the window had looked completely opaque.

"And who's the lucky man you're meeting tonight?" Freddie asked.

"Do you come to the house often?" Rachel said, not shifting her gaze from the passing houses. "Only I've never seen you there before."

"I'm very discreet," said Freddie. "Now you see me, now you don't." When this remark failed to have any effect, he added: "So . . . you're curious about me. I'm flattered."

"Don't be. This job gives me a lot of time to myself. I've got to think about something."

Discouraged by this response, Freddie fell silent.

"I did Google you, though," said Rachel, as flatly as she could.

"Really? And what did you find?"

"Mostly, stuff about a British film director. As for you—well, very little, actually."

"Just as it should be."

"I found the name of the firm you work for. But I didn't find out much about what you do."

"It's not really in the public domain."

"I did notice something, though. It said you used to work for a private bank called Stewards'. And so did Sir Gilbert, according to Wikipedia."

"Well, well. We have a real cyber-detective in our midst. That's how we met, of course. On the trading floor of Stewards'. Back in the late eighties." He sighed. "Ah, happy times." The car was paused at traffic lights, waiting to turn left into the Cromwell Road. Jules was listening to Magic FM, turned down to an unobtrusive volume. "The boss of Stewards' in those days was a man called Thomas Winshaw. A legendary figure. He treated the traders as if we were his favourite sons. The sons he never had. Gil was the outstanding one, of course. I was good, but I didn't have his flair, his nerves of steel. Currency trading was his thing. His deals started getting bolder and bolder—I mean, if we'd stopped to think about it (which we never did), he was really putting the whole of the bank's funds at serious risk, sometimes—but Thomas trusted him, he let him get on with it, and then in 1992 he put a huge bet—and I mean a really, really huge one—on the pound crashing out of the European Exchange Rate Mechanism. Which is what happened, of course. It was called Black Wednesday, because it was a bad day, for most people, a terrible day. But not for Gilbert. My God, how we all celebrated that night! We must have spent about thirty grand on champagne alone. We drank one toast after another to Thomas, who of course was no longer with us, by then. He had . . . passed on, the year before, in horrible circumstances. But that hadn't stopped us. It had just made us more reckless than ever, in fact: more determined.

"After a couple more years," said Freddie, as the car eased its way through the Knightsbridge traffic, gliding past slower, less powerful vehicles with no apparent effort, "we were both getting tired of the money markets. You burn out, in that world, pretty quickly. Gilbert formed Gunnery Holdings, and started buying and selling companies. He moved into property development. Started expanding, diversifying. He had a *big* fortune to play with, by now, a massive fortune. I was still at Stewards', stagnating a bit, getting more and more restless. And one night I met him for a drink, at some private members' club. We got pretty pissed, talked about this and that. And I realized that, even though things were going so well for him, he wasn't happy."

"Perhaps he was developing a conscience," said Rachel.

Freddie smiled. "Guess again."

"I don't know," said Rachel. "What could possibly have been making him unhappy?"

If there was any irony underpinning the question, Freddie missed it. "Well, it was quite simple. He felt that he was paying too much tax."

Rachel snorted.

"Oh, it shouldn't surprise you. It doesn't matter how generous the government is, however much they lower the top rate. If you're bringing home ten million a year, you're writing an annual cheque to the Inland Revenue for four million pounds. It's not a question of how rich you are. That feels like a lot of money. It hurts."

"My heart bleeds for him," said Rachel.

"It wasn't just him. I realized that plenty of people in his position—not that there were many Brits in London who were as wealthy as Gilbert, by this stage—were feeling the same way. So I decided that was where the future lay. *My* future, anyway."

"Tax avoidance? Charming."

"Tax management is what I prefer to call it."

"I'm sure you do. So where do you go to learn that, then? Do they send you on a course?"

"Well, I took what I thought to be the simplest and most obvious route. I went to work with HMRC for a while."

"You became a tax inspector?"

"It seemed to be the best way of learning the ins and outs of the system. You'd be surprised, nowadays, how many tax inspectors leave the Revenue and go straight into the City to set themselves up as independent advisers. But I was one of the first. I blazed the trail."

"Your mother must be very proud."

Freddie was starting to tire of Rachel's sarcasm. "This chap you're meeting tonight," he said. "What does he do?"

"He's a postgrad," said Rachel. "He's writing a thesis on *The Invisible Man*." She noticed Freddie's blank look. "H. G. Wells."

"A whole thesis," he said, incredulously, "on one book?"

"He's using invisibility as a metaphor," said Rachel, not sure why she was bothering to explain any of this, "to talk about politics. How people become invisible when the system loses sight of them."

"Sounds as though he's spotted a real gap in the market there."

"Not everybody thinks about 'the market' when they decide what to do with their lives." She leaned forward and addressed the chauffeur. "Could you let me out here please, Jules?"

The car pulled over and came to a noiseless halt.

"Well, let me know when he makes his first million," said Freddie. "I'll help minimize his tax liability."

"Lovely talking to you," said Rachel, and then she said thank you and good-bye to Jules before stepping out into the crowds of tourists clogging up Shaftesbury Avenue; relieved to find herself surrounded, once again, by people she felt she could probably understand.

9

"So, you had a nice time last night, with your boyfriend?" said Livia.

"Very nice, thank you," said Rachel, smiling, but she did not divulge any more information. She didn't feel that she knew Livia well enough yet.

This was their third walk together, and their longest. Livia had three dogs today: Mortimer, plus a pair of Airedale terriers she collected from a flat in a mansion block off Gloucester Road. They took the dogs to Hyde Park, let them off the lead near the Round Pond and then, when they had run themselves into a state of near-exhaustion, strolled over to the Serpentine Gallery. Now they were crossing West Carriage Drive and heading down towards the café. It was a bright and sunny but fiercely cold morning in early December. It seemed the only people in the park that day were women walking their dogs: they'd already come across Jane, the Queen of dog-walkers, who sometimes walked as many as ten at a time. Her dogs had been restless and unruly this morning, so they'd not had much time to stop and talk. Now Mortimer and the Airedales were looking tired and ready for a bowl of water.

Rachel was starting to like Livia very much. By training she was a musician. She played in a string quartet which gave occasional London recitals but of course she did not earn anything from this, and walking dogs provided the bulk of her meagre income. Her instrument was the cello, and to Rachel's ears, her voice itself was reminiscent of a cello, with something of its sonorous depth and melancholy richness. She spoke slowly and carefully, with a thick Romanian accent which sometimes made her words hard to understand.

"You remember that woman I told you about?" she said, when

they were sitting inside the café, in the warmth, with expensive lattes in front of them. "The one who has the same kind of cancer as your grandfather?"

"Yes," said Rachel. "I remember. You said she'd come out of hospital and was doing really well."

"That's right. Well, last week she asked me to walk her dog again. She has a wonderful Afghan hound, called William. She lives in a house between the Kings Road and the river. A beautiful part of Chelsea. The house is only small but I think it is worth several million pounds. My client, whose name is Hermione, is a member of the aristocracy, I think. She is some sort of duchess or baroness or something—I don't really understand what all these titles mean in this country. Anyway, as I said to you last time, she was told almost two years ago that she had cancer of the liver and would only live for a few months. Just like your grandfather has been told. They didn't want to give her chemotherapy or radiotherapy or anything like that. But when she went into hospital she was taken to see a doctor who said there were new drugs which could help with this condition. Not to cure it, just to make it easier to bear. So last week I asked her what these drugs were called and she told me that they were giving her one called cetuximab. And she said it had helped her a lot. It had removed many of the symptoms and there had not been many side effects. Of course, she still has the cancer, there's nothing she can do about that, but she was diagnosed two years ago now and since then her quality of life has been good, very good. She's just come back from visiting friends in Paris and now she's going to spend Christmas in Rome with her daughter."

"That sounds amazing," said Rachel.

"Are you seeing your grandfather soon?"

"Yes, I'll be seeing him at Christmas. I'm not sure whether he'll be at home or in hospital. But I'll definitely be seeing him."

"Then maybe you can ask his doctor if he can give him some of these drugs."

"Yes, I will," said Rachel. "It's got to be worth a try, hasn't it?"

10

Grace and Sophia's school term came to an end two weeks before Christmas. At around the same time, Lucas returned from Eton, reporting that his interview at Oxford had been a great success. (He would find out, in the New Year, that he had won a place at Magdalen College, Oxford, and by way of thanks would present Rachel with an expensive, linen-covered notebook from a stationer's in Venice.) Madiana told Rachel that her services would probably not be required, now, until the beginning of January, and she was free to go home.

Her grandfather had been moved to a hospice on the outskirts of Beverley. It was a functional, 1970s redbrick building, surrounded by a couple of acres of lawn which were dusted with patchy snow on the afternoon that Rachel made her first visit. Her mother and grandmother were with her. They had stopped off at the local supermarket to buy some packets of fruit salad, since Gran was concerned that Grandad was not getting enough fruit. As their car pulled into the crowded car park, in the middle of the afternoon, the December light was already beginning to fade. The thin, half-hearted snow was turning to sleet. Rachel took her grandmother's arm, feeling the sharp boniness of her elbow even through her thick tweed coat, and supported her as she shuffled slowly and carefully across the icy asphalt. It took a long time to get from the car to the entrance, with its glowing yellow light and promise of warmth: long enough for Rachel to reflect on the desperate sadness of the occasion, but also—again—its sense of inevitability. She remembered the whisper she had heard amidst the branches of the plum tree a few months earlier.

As for Grandad's appearance, Rachel had been expecting the

worst, and she found it. He was sitting up in bed, in a ward with five other patients. He was the one, without doubt, who looked most seriously ill. He had lost so much weight that his collar- and breastbones stood out starkly where his pyjama jacket lay open. His skin had yellowed horribly. He was attached to a subcutaneous drip and the smile of recognition when he saw them enter the ward was faint and effortful. Almost as soon as they pulled up their chairs and sat around the bed, the listless gaze returned to his eyes. His throat was parched and conversation seemed to sap his energy. His hand kept straying to the right-hand side of his stomach, which he would touch involuntarily even though it made him wince in pain.

Their visit lasted a slow, agonizing thirty minutes. After that it was clear that all he wanted to do was sleep.

Out in the car park, darkness had already descended and the sleet had turned to rain. They had to pay three pounds to get out through the automatic barrier.

"I can remember when parking in hospital car parks was free," was all that Gran said. It was all that any of them said.

Rachel and her mother decided to spend Christmas in Beverley. Gran did not want to come to Leeds: she wanted to stay as near to the hospice as possible, and to visit Grandad every day, however little pleasure he seemed to derive from it. Christmas day was quiet, just the three of them. Rachel's brother Nick was abroad some-where: Copenhagen, they thought, with his current girlfriend, who was apparently Danish. On Christmas afternoon they visited Gran-dad in his ward and took him a box of chocolates and more fruit. He said that he didn't want either. They gave the chocolates to the ward sister, who put them with two other, similar boxes beneath the Christmas tree in the entrance hall. The lights on the tree winked on and off fitfully, and the nurse behind the reception desk had brought in a CD player which played a party disc of carols and Christmas pop songs from a time before Rachel was born. The place had never seemed more cheerless.

This time, being in her grandparents' house was proving a strange experience for Rachel. She could not believe how small it seemed. At the Gunns' house in Turngreet Road, she had grown accustomed to high ceilings and airy, spacious rooms. Now she felt like Gulliver returning from Brobdingnag and trying to get used to normal human proportions again. The days seemed absurdly short. Darkness would have enveloped the garden by three thirty and at that point, having paid their daily visit to the hospice, they would draw the curtains, have a quick tea of eggs or beans or sardines on toast, then try to find something distracting to watch on the television. The Gunns, Rachel believed, were in the Caribbean somewhere. She imagined Grace and Sophia splashing and laughing in a turquoise lagoon while Madiana lay on a sunbed beneath the shade of a coconut tree, sipping cocktails.

She sent regular texts to Jamie. He was with his parents in Somerset. Livia had gone back to Bucharest. The days passed slowly, the hours dragged. They allowed New Year's Eve to pass without notice, let alone celebration.

It took more than two weeks to arrange a meeting with her grandfather's oncologist. Finally she was able to see him on the morning of the first Monday of January. He was a brusque, not to say inscrutable, consultant in his early forties; he received her not unkindly, but without letting her feel that the meeting was anything other than an unpleasant duty. He knew all about the drug she was talking about, and the first thing he said to her was:

"Of course you know that cetuximab is an extremely expensive therapy."

For some reason this aspect of the question had not occurred to Rachel.

"Is it not available on the NHS, then?"

"In certain circumstances it is, yes. But we'd have to apply for it through the Cancer Drugs Fund."

"Can you do that?"

"I'm not sure I could make a very strong case in your grandfather's circumstances."

"Well, how much money are we talking about?"

The doctor consulted some notes on his desk. "Cetuximab is reckoned to give an ICER of £121,367 per QALY gained."

"Can you repeat that in English, please?" Rachel said, after a shocked pause.

"An ICER," said the doctor, "is the incremental cost-effectiveness ratio of a therapy. A QALY is a quality-adjusted life-year. A service like the NHS has to keep a very close eye on its costs. To put it bluntly, not every year of human life is valued as highly as every other. You have to take quality of life into account. Whatever therapy is given to him, I'm afraid your grandfather will have a low quality of life from now on."

"How do you work that out?" asked Rachel.

"Well, he'll be bedridden, for instance."

"So?"

"And he's old."

"So's my friend. The lady I know who's taking the drug. What difference does that make?"

"Do you know this person well?"

"No," said Rachel, and then felt she had to admit: "I don't know her at all, in fact. I know the person who walks her dog for her."

"Ah. Is she quite well-off, by any chance?"

"Yes, she is. So what?"

"Well, it's possible that she paid for the treatment herself, that's all." He did his best to give her an encouraging smile. "Look, I'll put in the application. Of course, it will take a few weeks. These things always do. But we'll see what gives."

11

When she returned to Chelsea in the New Year, Rachel found that the house in Turngreet Road was much changed. Work on the basement conversion had been resumed, and the site both to the front and rear of the house was full of noise and activity.

Noise in particular. The piling rig in what used to be the back garden was working again, and all day long Rachel had to listen to its ceaseless, reverberant *boom-boom-boom*. She could even feel the ground shake with every impact. Also, from the window of her bedroom she now had a view of the pit, which lay open to the world (or at least to the neighbouring houses) like an inflamed, gaping wound in the landscape. It was, to her eyes, unthinkably deep. As well as a number of ladders fixed to its sides, there was an industrial hoist with a steel cage to take men and equipment down into the abyss and back up again. Miniature diggers had been lowered into the pit as well, and were presumably beavering away down there, with the spoil being carried back up along a huge conveyor, then along the belt through the front garden and out into the skips waiting in the street.

From the hoardings at the front of the house, Rachel learned that the building contractor had changed: Grierson Basements had been replaced by Nation Lloyd Sunken Interiors. The crew was now Romanian instead of Polish. The site manager, Dumitru, was a taciturn figure who nodded politely at Rachel whenever their paths crossed but otherwise had nothing to say to her. Like everybody else involved with the project, he wore a permanently anxious expression. Nobody, however, looked more anxious than the new project manager, Tony Blake, who spent most of every day locked up in his temporary site office, poring over the plans while still wearing his hard hat, occasionally emerging to have a nervous, conspiratorial word with Dumitru or to ring the front doorbell in the hope of a meeting with Madiana to clarify some new element in her ever-changing, ever-expanding plans.

Despite the stress and inconvenience the works were causing her and everyone in the vicinity, Rachel could not help feeling sorry for Mr. Blake. On the rare occasions he emerged from his office, he always looked so harassed, so terrified: she was constantly afraid that he was on the verge of having a nervous breakdown. One morning when she came back from the shops, she found him at the front of the house, pacing up and down between the hoarding and the front steps and visibly shaking.

"Would you like me to get you a cup of tea, Mr. Blake?" she asked him.

He took his hands away from his ears, which they had been covering in an attempt to block out the relentless noise of the pile driver.

"Hm? What?"

"You seem a bit . . . distressed. I wondered if you wanted a cup of tea."

"Tea? No, thank you. I'm fine. Absolutely fine."

He did not look fine. His face was grey, and his hands would not stop shaking.

"I think I'll get you one anyway," said Rachel. "A nice strong cup of tea with plenty of sugar."

He said nothing in reply to this, but Rachel went to the staff kitchen to make the tea and then found, when she came back to offer it to him, that Mr. Blake had returned to his office. He had a plywood desk in there, covered in architects' drawings which had been annotated and scribbled over repeatedly in different-coloured inks. They, like everything else in the office, appeared to be in a state of total disarray.

"Yes?" he said, looking up in confusion when she came in.

"I said I'd bring you some tea."

"Oh, thank you . . . Rachel, isn't it?"

"That's right."

"Well, look, if you've come to complain about the noise, there's nothing I can do. You can't dig a hole this size in complete silence, you know."

"I'm not here to complain about the noise. I brought you some tea because I thought you looked a bit upset."

She cleared a space for the mug on his desk, and set it down gently. There were two seats in the tiny office, but he didn't ask her to sit down.

"You . . . work for her, don't you?" he said, without touching the tea.

"Yes."

"Is she . . ." He swallowed. "Is she *completely* insane, do you think?"

This was the last question Rachel had been expecting to hear. "Lady Gunn, you mean?"

"Yes."

"What makes you say that?"

At last he noticed the mug, picked it up, took a tentative sip and then a longer one.

"I've worked on more than fifty basement conversions," he said. "More than fifty. All over London. But nobody has ever proposed . . . anything like this. Do you know—" He looked at her directly, urgently. "Do you know how deep we're going?"

"I've no idea," said Rachel. "It does seem a pretty big hole."

"Pretty big?" he repeated. "Pretty big? She wants one hundred and fifty feet. That's deeper than most tube stations."

"Is that . . . even possible? Wouldn't you hit the water table at some point? Wouldn't everything start flooding?"

"Oh, that happened ages ago. That's taken care of. They've installed three massive pumps. They'll be running twenty-four hours a day. You see, anything's possible, in fact. That's precisely the problem." He picked up the mug and took another sip, staring sightlessly ahead of him. "The people we took this over from quit, you know. They couldn't stand it. And a man died. Do you hear that? *A man died.*"

"Yes," said Rachel. "I heard."

"She doesn't care. It hasn't made any difference at all."

"A hundred and fifty feet is how many floors?"

"It depends how high you make them, of course. And she keeps changing her mind about that, but at the current count, there are eleven."

"*Eleven?* What does she want to do with them all?"

"That keeps changing as well. She's given me a new set of instructions just now. About ten minutes ago. Here, why don't you have a look? You should understand the kind of person we're dealing with."

Rachel sat down, finally, and drew her seat closer to Mr. Blake's desk. He scrambled around among the papers in front of him, and at last found the one he was looking for. It showed the excavation as a tall column, divided into eleven separate cross sections, each one numbered and labelled.

"Here's the first floor," he said. "That's where they keep the cars, as you know. And here's floor number two, which is going to be the children's playroom, with a full-size bowling alley. Underneath that is the cinema. Then the gymnasium. And then we have the *pièce de résistance*—the swimming pool. Which is going to take up the next three floors."

"Three floors? Why three?"

"Because she wants a diving board. A high one. And palm trees. Palm trees!" He began to laugh, almost hysterical. "We're going to have to get palm trees in there." Soon he had started shaking again, but with a few more sips of tea he managed to compose himself, and then pointed at the next level. "So now we're down to level eight, which is the wine cellar. Temperature-controlled, of course. Level nine is the vault. A secure vault. You're going to need to take a special lift to get to that one, the normal lift won't be stopping there. Level ten—well, lucky you, that's where you lot are going to be living. That's the staff quarters."

"You mean we won't be living in the house anymore?"

"Not above ground, no. You'd better forget about natural daylight, because you won't be seeing much of that when this job's finished."

"OK," said Rachel. "And what about this one?" She pointed at the lowest level on the drawing. "Number eleven. What's going there?"

"Number eleven?" He laughed. "That's the one she told me about this morning. Number eleven is new. She's only just asked for it."

"So—what's it for?"

"Nothing. She can't think of anything that she wants it for."

Rachel frowned. "So why are you digging it? Why does she want it?"

"She wants it," said Mr. Blake, "because she can have it. Because she can afford it. And because . . . I don't know—because no one else has an eleventh floor in their basement? Or she's just heard about somebody who has ten and she wants to go one better? Who knows? She's mad. These people are all barking mad." He took one final look at the drawing, and pointed again at level number 11 with an unsteady finger. "And this is the proof."

12

From: Val Doubleday
To: Rachel Wells
Subject:
23/01/2015 21:55

Dear Rachel

I've been meaning to write ever since I saw you up here a couple of months ago. Very difficult, though, to say what I have to say.

Anyway, I won't mess around. I would have liked to say it was lovely to see you but, as I'm sure you noticed, I was far too embarrassed to feel that. In fact I will be brutally honest and say that I felt totally humiliated. As you clearly realized, I was not collecting food for my elderly next-door neighbour at all. I don't have an elderly next-door neighbour. I was collecting it for myself.

Yes, I was on the television a few years ago. I took part in a dreadful reality show but I soon got through the money they paid me. Most of it was spent paying off debts and then I stupidly used the rest to pay for expensive studio time to record demos which no one wanted to listen to and got me nowhere. I was working in a library for a while but then the hours went down further and further until they let me go altogether. ("Let me go" is good, isn't it. They've even got me speaking like them.) For a while after the TV thing I was diagnosed with PTSD, which entitled me to some sick pay, but apart from that I've just been living on jobseeker's allowance and Council Tax support. It's been tough, especially this winter when I've hardly let myself put the heating on, but this was the first time I'd ever been to a food bank. I never thought I'd find myself asking a charity for free food. Thanks to you it will be the last.

Anyway, I didn't want to tell you about me, I wanted to tell you about Alison. I said she was "doing fine" but that was another lie. In fact "doing time" would be more accurate. (Sorry for the rotten joke. Sometimes I think you have to laugh just because there's no alternative.) She's in Eastwood Park prison in Gloucestershire doing twenty-six weeks for benefit fraud. They say twenty-six but really it's thirteen, which means she'll be out in a few weeks now. I won't tell you the whole story but basically she was framed by this bitch of a journalist called Josephine Winshaw-Eaves, who wrote a horrible, vicious article about her. (Link below.) It happened more than a year ago and it's been a total nightmare, the whole thing. When I ran into you again she was just about to start her sentence. Of course I told her that I'd seen you and she made me swear that I wouldn't say what had happened but as of last week I think she's changed her mind and if you felt like visiting her I think she'd like that. You can book a visit online and I'll give you the link at the end of this email too, but I expect you're probably very busy with one thing and another.

Well, Rachel, you were looking well I must say—Oxford must have agreed with you—but I still don't really understand what you were doing working in that place. Maybe I'll find out if this means that we're going to be back in touch again from now on. It would be nice to see your mum again. I often think of that crazy trip we took to Corfu together—ten years ago, was it? Happy times.

Love from
Val

THE ART OF DECEPTION

BLACK, DISABLED LESBIAN ON BENEFITS IS ACTUALLY BLACK, DISABLED LESBIAN BENEFITS *CHEAT*

by Josephine Winshaw-Eaves

Alison Doubleday is the archetypal paragon of modern entitlement. The kind of person the British left-liberal establishment cannot do enough to help.

After experiencing problems with her left leg as a teenager, she had a new, state-of-the-art one fitted by dedicated NHS staff at a hospital in Birmingham—despite only having lived there for a few weeks.

The minute she became eligible for Disability Living Allowance she signed on, and has been receiving it ever since. That's in addition to the Housing Benefit she receives for the bijou three-bedroom house she shares with her lesbian lover Selena in Birmingham's fashionable Acocks Green.

Neither of them goes out to work. Both of them claim Jobseeker's Allowance. And yet Alison already has a job—an extremely lucrative one.

As a self-styled "artist" she has created a studio in one of her bedrooms at home. Here she creates her so-called "political" portraits of homeless people.

She makes them sit for hours in poses reminiscent of the great paintings of European monarchs by the likes of Titian and Van Dyck.

"In my pictures, I try to give these dispossessed people the dignity and grandeur of the Kings and Queens of old," she says.

Needless to say, while other talented artists—whose work does not press the same political buttons—languish in obscurity, Alison's heavily ideological portraits are much sought after by London's chaterati.

At a private show of her work in Hoxton's fashionable Recktall Brown Gallery last month, her pictures went on sale with a price tag of up to £20,000. Many were snapped up by the adoring crowd of champagne socialists and North London luvvies.

And what percentage of the profits did our crusading artist declare to the authorities, so that it could be ploughed back into REAL assistance for Britain's sick and homeless?

That's right—a big, fat zero!

Alison—the daughter of failed singer and washed-up "reality" TV star Val Doubleday—was not surprisingly unavailable for comment today when we tried to contact her.

13

Faustina and Jules were from Majuro, the most populous of the Marshall Islands, a small group of coral atolls lying just north of the Equator in the Pacific Ocean. They had been working for the Gunns for a little under two years.

They were reserved, friendly and uncomplaining. If the lifestyle of Sir Gilbert, Madiana and their family seemed unusual to them, they did not comment upon it. The care they lavished on their respective charges was exemplary: Faustina made sure that the twins were clean and well presented at all times, and replenished at regular intervals; meanwhile, Jules performed exactly the same function for the cars. They rarely went out to sample the diversions that London might have offered them; all their energies were bent upon saving as much money as possible out of their earnings. In the evenings they would sit in the kitchen watching television, trying to decode the niceties of British culture from the hints that the programmes let fall. Like Rachel, like the rest of the country—like the rest of the world, it sometimes appeared—they were fascinated in particular by *Downton Abbey,* ITV's big-budget soap opera following the changing fortunes of the Crawley family in post-Edwardian England. Faustina and Jules never missed an episode, and once a week would surrender themselves to the show's high production values and its quiet, insistent, endlessly reassuring message. At the heart of this message, it seemed, was the absolute necessity of the existence of both a master and a servant class. It was understood that the master class, in particular, would always conduct itself with decency and generosity; and that although the hierarchy dividing one class from another was absolute, fellow-feeling and respectful, amicable contact between the two were not unknown. Every Sunday evening, Faustina and Jules would retire to bed having been reminded that this was the natural and indeed inevitable order of things, as much in the London of 2015 as in the troubled years between the two world wars. Whether they ever remarked upon the absence of such fellow-feeling and amicable contact in their own relationship with Sir Gilbert and Madiana, Rachel could not say.

At night, when the television was turned off, the house fell silent. In fact Rachel soon came to realize that this part of London was defined by its extremes of silence and noise. During the daytime the noise pollution from building works was overwhelming, whereas at night a profound and eerie stillness settled upon the whole area. Most of these houses had been bought as investments: there was rarely anyone living in them, and after dark, the quietness and emptiness of the streets was unsettling. One of the things that had most impressed Rachel about the rich, since she had started to know them, was their ability to disappear. She mentioned this to Jamie once, when discussing his thesis on "invisible people" in the new age of austerity. "But you shouldn't just be writing about poor people," she told him. "The rich can make themselves invisible, too."

Rachel and Jamie saw each other two or three times a week: the days varied, but Sunday was a constant. On Sundays they would meet for a late breakfast or early lunch, and then take in a gallery or museum or film screening at a Curzon cinema or the BFI. Rachel felt strongly attracted to Jamie, but he was very absorbed in his work, and for her own part, she still did not feel quite ready for a full-blown relationship: her experiences in the last few months had made her realize how much she still had to learn, not just about the world but about herself. And so, for the time being, they were taking things slowly.

It was late one Sunday morning in January, when she was getting ready to meet him at a pub in Little Venice, that Rachel's mobile rang and she saw Madiana's name on the incoming call screen.

"Rachel?" said that flat, imperious voice. "The girls need you. You have to come at once."

"Erm, sure . . ." said Rachel, her heart sinking. "What's it about?"

"You didn't tell me that the girls have a maths exam tomorrow morning."

"Well, it's only a little test, really, not an exam."

"But they don't understand these equations *at all*. You're going to have to come and explain them."

"OK." Doubtless this would mean a trip up the M40 to "the cottage." "Where are you, where do you want me to come?"

It seemed that Madiana, Gilbert and the twins were not at the cottage this weekend, however. They were in Lausanne.

She was there in less than three hours. Jules drove her to the helipad in Battersea; she texted Jamie on the way to say that she wouldn't be able to see him that day after all. From there, a helicopter took her to a private airfield just outside Oxford, where a LearJet was waiting to carry her to Switzerland.

It was her first time in Sir Gilbert's private plane (or anybody's, for that matter). The flight was, as she might have expected, intensely pleasurable. She helped herself to a chicken caesar salad from the galley kitchen and washed it down with a cold bottle of Peroni. She stretched out in one of the wide, yielding, smoothly upholstered club seats and passed the time flicking through pristine copies of *Vogue* and *Tatler*. She remembered what Frederick Francis had said when they rode towards Soho in the Mercedes together: "Everyone should experience a ride in a car like this at least once. Then they'd have something to aspire to." She could see his point. One of these days— perhaps sooner rather than later—she was going to part company with the Gunns, and after that she would never know luxury like this again. Coming down to earth would be difficult.

The eighty-minute flight went by all too quickly. They landed just a couple of miles from the city centre at another small airfield. A driver was waiting to pick her up and take her to the Beau-Rivage Palace, where Madiana and the rest of the family were having lunch. Their party was occupying two tables: a children's table, where Grace and Sophia were joined by two boys and a girl of similar age, and an adults' table, where Sir Gilbert and Lady Gunn sat with another couple, a man Rachel did not recognize, and the ubiquitous Frederick Francis himself, who gave her a little conspiratorial wave (which she ignored) as a waiter led her towards them. Both tables had a view across the empty hotel terrace towards Lake Geneva. In the furnishings and the understated conversation of the other diners there was an atmosphere of cold, clinical elegance.

"Rachel, how good of you to join us," said Madiana, half rising from her seat to shake her hand. "You're sitting with the children. Order whatever you want from the menu. All their books are ready for you. See if you can make sense of these ridiculous equations."

Thereby dismissed from the main table, Rachel took her seat next to the twins and looked quickly through the menu. She had noticed that the restaurant boasted two Michelin stars, but instead of langoustine *à la plancha* or Challans duck with beetroot confit, all of the children had asked for cheeseburgers and chips. She ordered a cheese fondue ravioli without really thinking about it, and then turned her attention to the maths. All the girls had been asked to revise were some quite simple linear equations, and she was able to bring them both up to speed within about ten minutes. She wrote out six more equations to test them and they both got full marks, so after that she was confident her job was done. She ate the rest of her meal in silence, looking out over the lake, and listened to the stilted chatter of the children: the two boys and their sister appeared to be from a Swiss family and spoke a mixture of perfect French and perfect English, but they didn't seem to have much to say to the Gunn twins, who in any case were more interested in their iPhones.

"So, did the girls finish their maths?" Madiana asked, at the end of the meal.

"Yes, no problem. They're primed and ready to go."

"Good. Well, Pascale has invited us back to her apartment for tea." Rachel thought, at first, that she might be included under the umbrella term "us," but her employer's next words disabused her of that idea. "You have three hours in which to amuse yourself. The driver will pick you up here, and then you and the girls and Mr. Francis will all travel home together."

"Fine," said Rachel. "Do you happen to know if there's a cashpoint nearby? I didn't have time . . ."

"Oh. Of course. Take this," said Madiana, handing her two fifty-franc notes. "We'll settle it up later."

Rachel thanked her, allowed a waiter to help her on with her overcoat, and then went outside to become acquainted with the streets
of Lausanne.

She walked for about an hour, at first by the side of the lake and then
through the wide, almost empty boulevards of the city centre, which
seemed modern and comfortable but completely without character.
Even though Lausanne was a lot closer to London than the Kruger
national park, and the weather was impeccably British (cold and
grey), she felt just as disorientated by this abrupt transplantation to
an unexpected country. She thought about calling Jamie, wanting to
hear his familiar voice again, but she wasn't sure what the cost of the
call would be, and didn't want to risk it.

Another ten minutes' aimless walking brought her to the Avenue
Bergières, where she paused outside the entrance to a museum. What
appeared to be a fairly modest private house opposite the Palais de
Beaulieu promised its visitors something called the "Collection de
l'Art Brut." Rachel had never heard the term before, but her attention was drawn by the posters outside, depicting strange animals
and grotesque landscapes in bright, mesmerizing colours. Venturing
inside, having handed over her money and picked up a programme,
she read the following note from the museum's curator: "In 1945,
Jean Dubuffet decided upon the term 'Art Brut' to designate a creative output by people who are self-taught, who work outside of any
institutional framework, beyond all rules and all artistic considerations. For the most part, these are solitary people, persons living on
the fringes of society or committed to psychiatric hospitals."

Even this definition did not prepare her for the surprises, the in-
finite variety, the disturbing revelations that the museum itself held
in store. For the next hour and a half, Rachel wandered through a
dream world, a chaos of surreal visions and nightmarish imaginings.
Distorted human figures were rendered in stark, primitive shapes
and outlines. Hallucinatory creatures, half man and half animal,
reared up on sheets of paper on which every other inch of available space had been scribbled over with minute fragments of text

whose meaning could be fathomed only by the artist. Fantastically detailed, wildly colourful pointillist canvases challenged the viewer to decide whether she was looking at something entirely abstract or, in some occult, coded way, representational. Weird political slogans were juxtaposed with deformed nudes or hideously lifelike faces constructed of found materials such as coral or seashells. A terrifying sculpture of an animal head boasted real, jagged and blackened teeth and a sharpened, lethal-looking horn protruding from its vulpine nose. One artist's contribution consisted of nothing but endless letters of legal complaint and recrimination, written on massive sheets of paper with no margins and tiny, insistent handwriting, the words smothering and stumbling over one another to create (as the catalogue put it) "the impression of a graphic logorrhea."

To some, perhaps, this would seem to be the world of the madhouse. To Rachel, the museum's contents felt as sane and as logical as anything she had seen in the last four months. She felt immediately, profoundly at home.

The museum housed a permanent collection, but there was also a temporary exhibition in a room to the rear. This space was devoted, at the moment, to the "Bestiary" of an artist from Barcelona called Josep Baqué.

Baqué, it seemed, had spent his peripatetic early life in Marseilles, Düsseldorf and l'Avesnois—carving gravestones, among other things—but had returned to Barcelona in 1928 and passed the remaining forty years working there as a traffic policeman. During that time, it was known that he made drawings, some of which were sought after by collectors, although, *"modeste jusqu'à l'excès,"* he always refused to sell them. Until his death in 1967, however, nobody knew the extent of his productivity: his family discovered 1,500 drawings of every shape and size, almost all of them showing mythical or semi-mythical beasts rendered in vivid colours and crude but detailed, even obsessive brushwork. Here were dragons and lizards; mutant hybrids of the horse and the flamingo; sea snakes, turtles and multicoloured fish with looks of haunted sadness in their eyes; strange insects—beetles with butterfly wings, centipedes with bulging red lips and the teeth of a hydra. And here, too, were spiders.

Rachel had been on the point of leaving the museum, exhausted by the intensity of the experience it offered, when she came upon Josep Baqué's spiders. And she looked on them, at once, with a shock of recognition. For more than ten years now, wherever she went, she had kept with her the playing card which had been given to her by Phoebe, the "Mad Bird Woman," at the foot of the Black Tower in Beverley. It was the card that Alison had discovered, discarded and lost, in the woodland one evening; one of a pair belonging to Phoebe, and which she had given to Lu, the Chinese vagrant to whom she had briefly offered shelter in that long-lost summer, the summer of 2003. The picture on this playing card showed a spider, which Rachel had always considered to be a horrific thing: standing upright on two of its legs, and raising the others fiercely in the air as if challenging someone to a fight. And here it was again. Exactly the same. How was this possible? How could this gruesome, almost stomach-turning illustration—which could be dated, according to the catalogue, no more precisely than *"entre 1932 et 1967"*—have found its way into a pack of Pelmanism cards which had once belonged to Phoebe's parents? Rachel had no idea. And yet the proof was here. She looked at this painting, framed, numbered, labelled, hanging on the wall of a museum in Switzerland to which the strangest of circumstances had brought her, and knew that she was staring at one of the icons, one of the most formative images, of her own past life. Here, taking its place among all the other works which today appeared to her as pure howls of anguish; howls of terrible beauty, born of the poverty and isolation of the dispossessed.

"These people had nothing, that's the amazing thing," she said to Frederick, as she continued to pore over the museum's hefty illustrated catalogue on the plane back to London. The reproductions of the artwork were mere distant echoes of the originals, but Rachel found herself fascinated, anyway, not by the illustrations but by the life stories of the different artists. She read of Fernando Nannetti, an electrician from Rome who suffered from lifelong hallucinations and persecution mania, but produced an enormous handwritten oeuvre carved into the walls of his psychiatric institution; of Joseph Giavarini, the "Prisoner of Basel," who shot his mistress dead, and then, in prison, spent his time fashioning beautiful statuettes out of chewed bread, the only material available to him; of Marguerite

Sir, a farmer's daughter from southeastern France who fell victim
to schizophrenia, became convinced at the age of sixty-five that she
was an eighteen-year-old girl about to marry, and spent the rest of
her life creating and embroidering a magnificent bridal dress for the
wedding that would never take place; of Clément Fraisse, who, at the
age of twenty-four, after attempting to set fire to his parents' farm
using a packet of flaming bank notes representing the family savings,
was sent to an asylum where for one year he lived in a cell measur-
ing six feet by nine, the whole of which he decorated in carvings of
incredible craftsmanship and detail. Turning the pages, Rachel read
one story after another of this sort: unimaginable cases of confine-
ment without end, illness without hope. "They had nothing, and yet
they produced this astonishing work. They created. They *gave.* They
gave these beautiful objects back to the society which had taken
everything away from them."

Freddie grunted. He was only half listening. The *Sunday Times*
business pages were absorbing most of his attention. Everything
about his posture, his indifference, his arrogance suddenly struck
Rachel and ignited in her a flame of indignation.

"Bit of a contrast," she said, "to some people I could mention. The
sort of people who've got everything but never give anything back
at all."

"Spare me the moralizing," said Freddie wearily, putting the newspaper down at last. "For your information, Sir Gilbert—if that's
who you're talking about—has already created more jobs than most
people will create in a lifetime. He employs people, he pays wages,
he spends his money in hotels and restaurants and car showrooms.
Everybody benefits from that. Everybody."

"Really?" said Rachel. "And yet he hardly pays any taxes. Thanks
to you."

"You don't know what you're talking about."

"Oh, I'm beginning to get a pretty good idea. You follow them
around the world, giving them bits of paper to sign—a trust fund
here, an offshore account there. Moving their money around to
places where the tax people can't get near it. Madiana probably has
non-dom status, doesn't she? What's the betting most of Gilbert's

companies are in her name? What's the betting he declares about the same level of income as a nurse?"

"Everything we do," said Freddie, "is perfectly within the law."

"Well, one of these days the law might change."

"Why would that happen?"

"Because people are getting fed up."

"So the revolution's on its way, is it? 'The people' are getting ready to man the barricades and dust down the guillotines? I don't think so. Give them enough ready meals and nights in front of the TV watching celebrities being humiliated in the jungle and they won't even want to leave their sofas. No, the law on this won't be changing any time soon. As it happens I attended a reception at Number 11 just the other day and had a long conversation with the Chancellor, and he very much has . . . other priorities, I would say."

"You know each other, do you?"

"Family ties. Our fathers were at prep school together."

Rachel raised her eyes to the ceiling. "Oh my God. This country really hasn't changed at all in the last hundred years, has it?"

"That's because the current system works perfectly well."

"Nobody minds the rich being rich," said Rachel. "It's just that there has to come a point where enough is enough."

Freddie laughed.

"I mean, why do they need a basement that's eleven storeys deep? Why did they need to fly me out to Switzerland when we could just as easily have done that homework tonight at home?"

"One of the things I like about you, Rachel," Freddie said, "is your modesty. I don't think you realize what an asset you are to this family. Madiana flew you out to Lausanne so she could show Pascale—who is one of the wealthiest as well as one of the snobbiest people in Switzerland—that her daughters have a private tutor who will come running at the click of a finger. You should have heard her at lunch—she never stopped talking about you. 'Oh yes, she studied Latin at Oxford University.' 'Of course she graduated with first-class honours.'"

"There's no such thing as a degree in Latin," Rachel pointed out. "I did English. And I got a 2.1."

"Well, good for you," said Freddie. "I think that's jolly impressive. Have a glass of champagne to celebrate."

But Rachel would not let the subject go. "The poorest half of the world has the same amount of money as the richest *eighty-five* people. Did you know that?"

"Of course I did," he said, sounding impatient now. "It was in all the papers a few months ago. It's a meaningless statistic."

"Meaningless? Doesn't it make you think?"

"It makes me think the poorest half of the world should get their act together."

"Really?" Rachel stared at him, looking for traces of irony, reluctant to believe that he could actually mean what he was saying. She was forced to conclude that he did. "I'll never understand you, or people like you. What . . . gives you pleasure, exactly? What do you live for?"

"I'll tell you what turns me on," said Freddie, although this wasn't quite the question he'd been asked. "Youthful outpourings of political naivety. I find those *incredibly* exciting. In fact the only thing that's more exciting is when they're delivered in a Yorkshire accent." He looked around, and gestured with his eyes towards the toilet at the rear of the cabin. "Come on, this is our chance to join the mile-high club. On a private jet! When are you going to have an opportunity like this again?"

Rachel reminded him that there were children on board, and to emphasize the fact, she spent the rest of the flight sitting with them.

The Mercedes was waiting for them again at the Battersea helipad, but, unusually, Faustina was there, too, sitting in the car with her husband. On the drive home, she placed herself between the girls on the back seat, with Rachel in the front. Freddie took a taxi home. Faustina kept both arms around the girls and hugged them tightly. Neither she nor Jules talked very much. The atmosphere was tense, uneasy.

"Is something wrong?" Rachel asked, when they reached the house. Faustina took the twins straight up the front steps, almost pushing them along. Rachel and Jules took their usual route around to the back.

"I'll show you."

Instead of using the staff door that opened onto the little kitchen, he led Rachel up the steps and into the garden. It was filled with builders' junk, as always, and there were illuminated warning barriers fencing off the massive pit at its centre.

Jules took Rachel right to the eastern wall and then pointed at something on the ground. It was a scrap of tarpaulin, covering what appeared to be some sort of animal shape.

"Mortimer," he said simply.

"Oh no . . ." Rachel knelt down, and reached out to touch the motionless bundle. "Not Mortimer." Her voice cracked and tears started to well up.

"Don't touch," he said. "Don't look. It's terrible."

"Why?" said Rachel. "Why, what happened?"

"Something attacked him. We heard terrible noises in the garden. By the time we got there, he was dead."

"But what could have attacked him? A fox? No, he could win a fight with a fox, surely?"

"Bigger than a fox. Must be. *Don't look!*"

Rachel had been about to raise the tarpaulin in spite of herself.

"It's terrible. His face—all gone. Half his body—gone. Eaten." He took Rachel by the arm and helped her gently to her feet. "Come on. Come inside for a drink. We'll tell the girls in the morning."

14

Later, Rachel would tell the doctors that was the day—the Sunday she went to Lausanne, the day Mortimer died—that everything started to fall apart, and the horror began.

On Tuesday she had booked her visit to see Alison in Eastwood Park.

Rachel had never visited a prison before and had no idea what to expect. It was in a rural setting and involved a long bus ride from the nearest railway station, alongside passengers who all wore the same closed, mask-like but apprehensive expressions. The gateway to the prison looked more like the entrance to a suburban housing estate than anything else. Rachel had brought every piece of ID that she possessed and this was a good thing because she had to show all of them before she could be admitted to the waiting area. Here, she and the other visitors were held for more than twenty-five minutes before a bell sounded and they were led into the hall.

Rachel had not seen Alison for five years or more, and their week together in Beverley back in the summer of 2003 seemed a lifetime ago. She was looking thin and her hair was cut shorter than Rachel could ever remember seeing it. It was not clear that she was especially happy to see her old friend. The visiting hall was full, and the tables were closer together than Rachel would have imagined. They both felt uncomfortable, at first, and their conversation was stilted, consisting mainly of Alison's answers to questions about prison routine.

"It's *so boring*," she kept saying. "Thank God we've got TVs in the cells because otherwise we'd go mad. Mind you, they only let you have those because lockup's cheaper than letting you out and having to keep an eye on you."

"Do you have classes and things?"

"Yeah, they're pretty crap, but they give you something to do. I've been giving a few art classes myself. Weekends are the worst. We get locked up at five fifteen. Fuck, that gets depressing."

Rachel reached across the table and clasped her hand.

"It's so good to see you again. You will come and see me when you get out, won't you?"

"Yeah, if you want me to," said Alison, uncertainly.

"Of course I do. I've missed you. We shouldn't have left it so long."

Alison hesitated a moment, and said: "Well, that wasn't exactly my fault."

Rachel frowned. "What do you mean?"

"You know what I mean," she answered; and now, as she looked across at Rachel, there was a challenge in her eyes.

"Alison, I wrote to you. I phoned. I texted. You never answered. Why not?"

"Why not?" Alison gave a quiet, disbelieving laugh. "Because . . . Because why would I want to stay friends with someone who judged me, and disapproved of me?"

"I never did that."

"Didn't you? I seem to remember that you called me a pervert."

"What? I *never* did that."

"You implied it."

"How? How did I imply it?"

Alison lowered her voice, but her tone was still emphatic as she said: "By saying that incest was 'right up my street.'"

Rachel stared at her, staggered by this allegation. "When did I say that?"

"Just after I wrote to you to say I was gay."

"I don't know what you're talking about," said Rachel. "I really don't."

Alison leaned forward, more insistent than ever. "We'd just started using Snapchat, remember? And I messaged you, asking if you'd got my letter."

"That's right. I was at Harewood House, with my brother."

"And you wrote a message back. It said you were 'doing the incest thing with him.'"

She sat with her arms folded, waiting for a response.

Rachel thought hard; tried to think back to that evening, sitting with her brother in the late-summer sunshine on the terrace. She and Alison had only just started using Snapchat, and she had barely used it since. She pictured herself writing with her forefinger . . . She couldn't remember the message she had written, exactly, but a possible explanation began to dawn on her. A smile spread across her face, slowly, grew broader and broader, and then she put her face in her hands and rocked forward, her body shaking. After a few seconds she looked up and said: "I think there's a chance, you know—just the smallest chance—that I said I was doing the *nicest* thing." Alison's mouth was half open in astonishment, so she repeated: "The *nicest* thing, Al. *Nicest*, not *incest*. Why would I have said incest?"

She looked at her friend, the corners of her mouth quivering, her eyes dancing with laughter. Alison stared back, still gaping stupidly. The silence seemed to go on forever.

Then Alison, too, put her head in her hands and her laughter became so violent that it made no sound, just shook her body like an earthquake, an earthquake that was never going to stop, and when it finally died down and she was able to sit up straight and look towards Rachel directly again, she was smiling the widest, loveliest smile, a smile that was full of warmth and affection but also relief. Enormous relief. She got up and leaned across the table and folded her in a long, passionate hug. "Oh Rache," she said, "you don't know how good it is to see you."

"You too," said Rachel.

"So shall we never, ever do that again?"

"Do what?"

"Use social media, when we could be talking to each other."

"Yes," Rachel said, feelingly. "I think that would be a good idea."

Alison withdrew to her own side of the table, laughed some more and then looked around her, taking in these drab, institutional surroundings as if she was seeing them for the first time, with a kind of wild despair.

"I hate it in here," she said. "Thanks so much for coming. I've been so *lonely*. I know I've only got a couple of weeks to go, but it's been horrible. So horrible. When I get out I'm going to find that bitch and I swear to God I'm going to tear her apart . . ."

"Josephine, you mean?" Rachel dropped her voice. "How did it happen, Alison? How did you end up in here?"

"I had this girlfriend," Alison began. "Called Selena. We were together a couple of years. A lovely girl, but a bit . . . well, not so bright, sometimes. She was waitressing one night at a big do in Birmingham where Josephine was one of the guests, and somehow they got talking. About me. Josephine heard I was an artist, and she offered to set up a private show for me in London. Selena didn't tell me who was doing it, she just said there was some benefactor who'd taken a shine to my work. I should really have been a bit more sensible, asked a few more questions. But it seemed like a such a break, you know? I couldn't believe my luck.

"I'd been doing a lot of portraits of homeless people, getting them in off the streets and painting them as if they were princes or emperors. A sort of parody of the kind of art that celebrates power and which never gets called 'political' even though it obviously is. I'd started doing them when I was at college. Bit of a simple idea, really, but I thought it worked. Anyway, this gallery was hired for the night and all sorts of celebs and bigwigs turned up. It was pretty exciting, to be honest, though I didn't make much money from it in the end. Most of the pictures were priced at five hundred quid or so, and I only sold two. Most of the guests just drank the champagne and then fucked off.

"Anyway, I know I did the wrong thing. I should have told the benefits office what I'd made. I suppose I thought I could get away with it: I'd been paid in cash and anyway . . . you know, it was only nine hundred quid. Not such a huge deal, in the scheme of things, I thought. I gave half the money to Mum because she really needed a new cooker: hers hadn't been working properly all winter. Still, it was enough for Josephine. She wrote a piece about it for her paper . . ."

"I know—I saw it. Your mum sent me the link."

". . . and then the judge decided to make a big example out of it and give me the maximum sentence. So here I am."

Once the story was told, neither of them spoke for a while. There was nothing Rachel could do to make things better: nothing she could do at all, at that moment, other than reach across and squeeze Alison's hand again. Alison didn't respond at first; and her words, when they came, were slow and faltering.

"One thing about being in here: you get time to think. Especially during those bloody weekends. I mean, there are only so many episodes of *Casualty* and *Pointless Celebrities* you can watch. So I've been thinking a lot about Josephine, and why she decided to do that to me."

Rachel shrugged. "To sell papers, I suppose."

"Sure. And it's done her no harm at all—Mum told me she's got her own column now. Weekly slot. So somebody must have liked it. But you know, why me? I know I ticked all her little hate boxes. Black? Yes. Lesbian? Yes. Disabled? Yes. On benefits? Yes. I was getting Disability Living Allowance, Housing Benefit, all sorts . . . But what had I actually *done,* to make her hate me so much?"

"She's probably just . . . fucked up herself. Had a crap childhood or something."

Alison paused, considering this, and said: "I got a lot of letters, after the story ran."

"Letters of support, you mean?"

"A couple of those, but mostly they were . . . well, horrible. Agreeing with Josephine. Blaming me. I mean, I don't really think anyone saw the fraud itself as that big a deal, so they weren't blaming me for what I'd *done,* so much. It was for . . . It was for *being what I am. Who I am.*" She smiled, took a Kleenex out of her pocket and blew her nose violently. "But there's not much I can do about that, is there?"

If Rachel wanted to know how her day could become more upsetting, she was about to find out, on her journey home.

The train had just pulled into Didcot Parkway, and she was staring out of the window at the towers of the power station, remembering the village of Little Calverton, and the picturebook thatched cottage Laura and Roger had bought there, with their dream of creating an idyllic childhood for their son. And while she was lost in

this memory, her phone rang, tugging her out of it. She answered
the call: it was Faustina, and she was dreadfully upset, almost unable
to speak through her tears.

"An accident," she seemed to be saying. "At home."

It took Rachel a while to realize that by "home" she was referring
to the Marshall Islands. It took her even longer to understand what
had happened.

"A *bomb*? In her *garden*? Oh Faustina, that's terrible ...
unbelievable."

It seemed that Faustina's granddaughter, one of her six or seven
grandchildren, had been playing in the back garden when she had
come across a seventy-year-old hand grenade. These islands had
been used as an American military base in the Second World War,
as part of the campaign against the Japanese, and there was still,
incredibly, a large amount of unexploded ordnance lying around.
Faustina's granddaughter—her second daughter's daughter, only
seven years old—had picked up the grenade and was tossing it
around like a tennis ball when it exploded and killed her instantly.

Rachel's immediate impulse was to advise Faustina and Jules to
fly home at once. Only as an afterthought did she ask: "What does
Lady Gunn say?"

"She's not answering her phone. I think she's on a plane. New
York. She's gone for two weeks. She'll organize some charity ball, she
said."

"Well, I'm sure she'd agree."

Faustina explained that the journey back home was a long and
difficult one, involving at least two changes of plane and stopovers
in Seoul or Kuala Lumpur or Manila. Even if they flew out of Heathrow this evening, it would take them about thirty-six hours to get
there. The cost was enormous: it would eat up most of their savings.
But Rachel could see that they had no choice.

"And the children," Faustina said. "Somebody has to look after
Grace and Sophia."

"That's OK," said Rachel. "I can look after them. Really. I mean,
it's just a question of feeding them and making sure they're clean
and putting them to bed. I can do that. Don't worry about it. You go
and pack, Faustina. Get ready and go."

And indeed, when Rachel got back to the house at five o'clock that evening, the housekeeper and her husband were sitting in the kitchen with their coats on, ready to depart, waiting only for her return. She embraced them both, gave Faustina a kiss pregnant with feeling, then walked with them out through the debris and saw them safely through the hoarding. They trudged off together in the direction of the nearest Piccadilly Line station, holding hands, the weight of their shared suitcase pulling Jules's body off balance to the left. Rachel went back inside and realized that the house was quieter, vaster and lonelier than ever.

She called Madiana to tell her what had happened. It was lunchtime in New York by now, and she seemed to be eating in a noisy restaurant. At the back of Rachel's mind had been the hope (the absurd hope, she quickly realized) that Madiana herself would come home to look after her children for the next couple of weeks. But she had no intention of doing that. She told Rachel that she trusted her and knew that she could rely on her, and she called her an angel and many other borderline-affectionate terms. She told her to make use of both halves of the house for the time being and to treat the place as her own.

Rachel keyed in the code to the magic door on the second-floor landing and passed through the mirror into the haunted, enchanted kingdom that was the Gunns' living space, a space that was probably big enough to house twenty people but for the moment was home only to two unattended nine-year-old girls.

It was not quite silent on this side of the mirror. The noise of the television was coming from the girls' playroom.

Rachel found them watching a rerun of *Friends* together on a satellite comedy channel. One of the female characters was explaining to one of the male characters where all the female erogenous zones were and what was the best way to bring a woman to orgasm. Grace and Sophia were watching with grave, impassive expressions; but then they never did laugh much.

"I'm sorry I'm late for your lessons today," she said. "I've been to see a friend of mine in the country. Also, as you probably know, Faustina and Jules have had some bad news and they've had to go home very suddenly. They'll probably be gone for about a fortnight."

Again, it was hard to tell whether this information really affected them in any way. Nothing seemed to get through to them, somehow: even the news that the family dog had been fatally wounded had not seemed to upset them, particularly. The more time she spent with these strange, emotionless girls, the more Rachel felt that she was dealing with two of John Wyndham's Midwich Cuckoos.

"I think we'll forget about work for the moment, anyway, I'll go down and find something we can have for dinner," she said.

Grace nodded and Sophia stuck up her thumb in approval. Rachel withdrew and went downstairs to the main kitchen, thinking to herself that even these little gestures represented a small victory.

Although the twins were cooperative and uncomplaining and didn't argue much either with Rachel or each other, the process of feeding them and making sure they bathed themselves and then reading to them in bed was still surprisingly tiring. Rachel had decided to carry on sleeping in her own bedroom but she made a point of wedging open the doors that connected the two parts of the house, and told the girls that they should come and find her, or call her on the internal phone system, if they got scared or if anything was wrong. It was almost ten o'clock by the time they were both tucked up in bed and sleeping. After that, Rachel found herself unable to settle. She kept climbing up and down the narrow staircase at the back of the house and checking that the doors and windows were locked. Faustina's sudden departure had really shaken her. That, and the terrible fate of Mortimer. That was two days ago, now. She wondered what Jules had done with the body. She went to her bedroom window, opened it and peered out into the garden. Surely he would not just have left it there? That would be too grisly to contemplate.

No, the canine bundle had definitely gone. A light breeze was beginning to stir and an untethered section of tarpaulin was flapping quite loudly. She hoped that it wouldn't keep her awake all night. It was a corner of the tarpaulin that covered the pit, or was meant to. It seemed to have come loose.

Then there came another sound from the garden. A loud, metallic clang, as if a bucket had just been knocked over. Was there something out there? In the absence of any other explanation, Rachel had still not discounted her own theory that it was some fearless, oversized urban fox that had entered the garden and attacked Mortimer. She craned her neck further out of the window and squinted towards the rear, ivy-covered wall. It was too dark to see anything for certain, but the more intently she looked, the more she suspected that there *was* something there, some wild creature, lurking in the deepest shadows.

And then she did see it. It rushed out from the back of the garden, scuttled towards the edge of the pit and disappeared through the hole in the tarpaulin. Its body was black and grossly distended, its movement was unmistakably insectile, and she was convinced that she could even make out the hairs on the last of its eight legs as it dived down into the pit, scrambling down the walls, plunging deeper and deeper into the darkness from which it had come.

15

"The thing is," Rachel said, "when I'm sitting here with you, talking like this, everything seems so normal."

"Of course it does. Everything *is* normal."

"I know. I imagined it. I'd had a really stressful day, I was incredibly tired . . . Maybe I even nodded off and dreamed it."

"Quite possibly that is the explanation. After all, you'd just seen the picture in the museum, and you'd been looking again at the card from the old pack of cards that your friend gave you all those years ago. So this creature, or something like it, was very much on your mind."

Rachel and Livia were having coffee together once again at the Lido café in Hyde Park. They had not wanted to give up on the burgeoning friendship just because Mortimer no longer furnished them with a pretext. In fact, more than ever, Rachel valued Livia's sanity, her smiling good nature, the sense of calm she always radiated with her measured advice and tuneful, cello-like voice.

"So you don't think I'm going mad?" Rachel asked, with a smile that didn't do much to conceal the sincerity of the question.

"Of course not. This is such a difficult time for you. You just need to take things easy."

"Everything seems to be going wrong at once," said Rachel. "It's just one thing after another. My gran phoned this morning. She'd had a letter from Grandad's oncologist."

"Yes? What was the news?"

"Nothing good. He'd applied to the Cancer Drugs Fund for that drug you mentioned but they turned him down. Too expensive, apparently. Oddly enough, that doesn't seem to have been a problem for your client—the Duchess or the Baroness or whatever she is."

"I'm sorry," said Livia, "I never thought about the expense. Of course, she's a very wealthy woman and might have paid for it herself. The thing is, I don't always understand how things work in your country. I'm trying to find out more about it. I thought this book might help me."

She handed Rachel the book she was currently reading, a thick, faded green hardback with no dustjacket. It was called *The Winshaw Legacy*, by Michael Owen.

"I found this in the charity shop," she said. "The Winshaws are a famous family in Britain, I think. This tells their story. Did you read it?"

Rachel shook her head. "Maybe I should. Their name seems to come up everywhere these days. My friend Alison was stitched up by one of them. She was telling me about it just the other day."

"Really? By a member of this family? Which one?"

"Josephine."

Livia's eyes narrowed. She had very striking, amber eyes.

"Oh yes. I know Josephine."

"You do?"

"She lives near here. Not far from the house where you live, in fact. I walk her dog sometimes. But nobody has seen her for a few days."

"Taking a well-earned break in Mauritius or somewhere, no doubt."

"I don't think so. The police are looking for her." She pressed her copy of the book into Rachel's hands. "Here—borrow it. Please."

"Thanks, but I'm not really in the mood for reading at the moment."

"No. Take it. You should learn about these people."

Purely because Livia was being so insistent, Rachel flicked through the pages quickly, automatically, and then put it in her knapsack. "OK, I'll give it a try," she said. "Thank you. And thanks for trying to help with my grandad. I hate to think of him suffering the way he is." She clasped Livia's hand. "You're a good friend. There aren't many people like you in my life at the moment."

"And how are things with your boyfriend?"

"Oh, OK. He's trying to get a chapter of his thesis finished. He doesn't seem to have much time to think about anything else right now."

"Well, I'm here for you," said Livia. "And the children, if you want me to take them off your hands for a while."

Rachel looked directly into her eyes, now, and felt ashamed with herself that instead of seeing—as she should have done—uncomplicated kindness there, she imagined something else instead, something ambiguous, something blank and unreadable. It was symptomatic of the way she was growing needlessly wary of other people. This job was making her cynical and mistrustful. She looked away and sipped her coffee, embarrassed.

That afternoon, she picked up Grace and Sophia from school at three thirty as always, and then, as they entered the building site at the front of the house, they found that all the Romanian workers were gathered around the site office, and some sort of crisis meeting was in progress. At the centre of it was Dumitru, the site manager, who seemed to be presenting Tony Blake with an ultimatum. The faces of the other workers were attentive and morose.

"Come on, you two," said Rachel, hurrying the twins up the front steps. "This doesn't have anything to do with us."

Nonetheless, as soon as she had ushered them through the front door and told them to go upstairs and change out of their uniforms, she went back onto the steps to listen to the argument. But the meeting was already breaking up. Dumitru was still shouting and gesturing angrily as he stripped off his high-visibility jacket, removed his hard hat, and stormed out through the door in the hoarding. The calls from his workmates suggested, to Rachel, that they were asking him to come back, but his decision seemed clear: he was quitting. Tony Blake was staring after him, tight-lipped, and brandishing an empty, clear glass bottle in his hand.

"Has he resigned, or something?" she asked a pair of workers who were standing nearby.

"Yep. He's gone," said the first of them.

"What was the argument about?"

"He was drunk."

"Well, that's what Tony says," his companion chipped in.

"You saw the bottle. This morning it was full of vodka."

"Do you blame him? Imagine having to do what he's been doing. Who would lead a crew on a job like this? It's insane. It's dangerous. This isn't a building job, it's a mining job. Why wouldn't you start drinking?"

"Fine, but if it means you start seeing things . . ."

"Seeing things?" repeated Rachel. "What sort of things?"

"Dumitru told Tony that he wouldn't go down into the pit again. He said he saw something bad, right down at the bottom." The man's companion shook his head in warning, telling him to be quiet, but he continued anyway: "Apparently when you get down there, past all the other floors, down to Number 11, there's a tunnel. They discovered it yesterday. No one had noticed it before. Dumitru went into it and crawled along for a while and saw—"

"He didn't see anything. The guy's a drunkard. Always has been."

"What did he see?" Rachel asked.

"He doesn't know what it was, exactly. He was flashing his torch ahead of him and then suddenly, right ahead of him, he saw a pair of eyes. Staring back at him. Staring out of the darkness."

Rachel felt as if her heart had stopped beating. With an effort she said: "Was it a . . . cat, maybe? Perhaps a dog fell in or something and managed to—"

"He said it was much bigger than that. Way bigger."

The man fell silent. Whether he believed the story or not, it was clear that he had no appetite for the work they were now being asked to do at this house. Meanwhile, his companion said simply:

"Dumitru saw nothing. He was drunk. There's nothing down there. It's a big hole in the ground, that's all."

16

Rachel was trapped, in effect. However much she hated being in the house at night, she couldn't leave, because she had been entrusted with the care of the children.

What she really wanted to do was pack her things, take the train north and visit Grandad in the hospice again. By all accounts he was getting weaker and weaker, and she hated the thought that she might not see him again before the cancer finally claimed him. But she couldn't move. She had to stay where she was, to watch over them, to keep guard. One night, unable to sleep, she rose from her bed at about two o'clock and sat down at the little desk overlooking the garden. As always—as she did every few minutes, during her waking hours—she looked out into the dark to see if she could see any movement around the edges of the pit, but there was nothing. The workmen had tied the tarpaulin down even more securely than before.

Turning on her desklight, she took two objects out of the topmost drawer. One was the expensive, linen-covered notebook from Venice that Lucas had bought her, as a thank-you for her help with his Oxford interview. The other was the Pelmanism card that Phoebe had given her in the summer of 2003: the drawing of a lurid giant spider that so mysteriously resembled the work of Josep Baqué. She stared at the picture for a few minutes, as she had stared at it so often, so wonderingly and so uneasily, during the last ten years. Then she opened the notebook and began to write.

❋

The paradox is this: I have to assume, for the sake of my sanity, that I am going mad.

Because what's the alternative? The alternative is to believe that the thing I saw the other night was real. And if I allowed myself to believe that, surely the horror of it would also make me lose my mind. In other words, I'm trapped. Trapped between two choices, two paths, both of which lead to insanity.

It's the quiet. The silence, and the emptiness. That's what has brought me to this point. I never would have imagined that, in the very midst of a city as big as this, there could be a house enfolded in such silence. For weeks, of course, I've been having to put up with the sound of the men working outside, underground, digging, digging, digging. But that has almost finished now, and at night, after they have gone home, the silence descends. And that's when my imagination takes over (it *is* only my imagination, I have to cling to that thought), and in the darkness and the silence, I'm starting to think that I can hear things: other noises. Scratches, rustles. Movements in the bowels of the earth. As for what I saw the other night, it was a fleeting apparition, just a few seconds, some disturbance of the deep shadows at the very back of the garden, and then a clearer vision of the thing itself, the *creature*, but it cannot have been real. This vision cannot have been anything but a memory, come back to haunt me, and that's why I've decided to revisit that memory now, to see what I can learn from it, to understand the message that it holds.

Also, I'm taking up my pen for another good reason, quite an ordinary reason, and that's because I'm bored, and it is this boredom—surely, this boredom and nothing else—that has been driving me crazy, provoking these silly delusions. I need a task, an occupation (of course, I thought I would find that by working for this family, but it has been a strange job so far, quite different from my expectations). And I've decided that this task will be to write something. I've not tried to write anything serious since my first year at Oxford, even though Laura, just before she left, told me that I should carry on with my writing, that she liked it, that she thought I had talent. Which meant so much, coming from her. It meant everything.

Laura told me, as well, that it was very important to be organized when you write. That you should start at the beginning and tell everything in sequence. Just as she did, I suppose, when she told me the story of her husband and the Crystal Garden. But so far, I don't seem to be following her advice very well.

All right, then. I shall put an end to this rambling, and attempt to set down the story of my second visit to Beverley to stay with my grandparents, in the summer of 2003. A visit I made not with my brother this time but with Alison, my dear friend Alison, who at last after so many years' mysterious distance I have found again, picking up the threads of our precious friendship. This is our story, really, the story of how we first became close, before strange—not to say ridiculous—forces intervened and drove us apart. And it's also the story of—

But no, I mustn't say too much just yet. Let's go back to the very beginning.

Rachel stayed up most of that night writing the first few sections of her memoir. She felt tired in the morning, but also strangely refreshed and energized. After giving the girls breakfast and walking with them to school, she lay down for a short nap and then started working again. She wrote throughout the day, without interruptions. Outside, all was quiet. There was no sign of Mr. Blake or the Romanian crew: she imagined that work had been suspended until a new site manager had been appointed. At three thirty, she picked the girls up from school again, and for the rest of the evening, again, she didn't give them any extra lessons or ask them to do any homework. This time, being more practised at it, she was able to get them into bed more quickly and with less fuss. By nine o'clock she was at her desk once again. Looking back across the years, remembering the youthful friendship between Alison and herself, picturing the Beverley Westwood in summer sunshine, trying to evoke the love between her grandparents when they were both still in good health, she managed to escape the feeling of dread which she knew would otherwise envelope her if she had nothing to concentrate upon except the stillness of this house and the shapeless terrors which haunted its ruined garden.

She wrote for forty-five minutes and then, at a quarter to ten, there was a ringing of the front door bell. She ran down to the nearest video monitor, which was on the first-floor landing, and turned it on. A grainy black-and-white image of Frederick Francis appeared. He was standing outside the hoarding waiting to be admitted. She buzzed him in and then went further downstairs to open the front door.

"Hello," he said, "I hope you don't mind me calling on you out of the blue."

"Not at all," said Rachel. "But Gilbert isn't here. Madiana's in New York and he's . . . well, I don't know where he is, exactly."

"I know," said Frederick. "It was you I wanted to see."

"Oh. Well, in that case . . . Come in."

She led him into the sitting room, a place she rarely visited.

"Are you going to offer me a drink?" Freddie said, sitting down on the sofa nearest the door.

Rachel could smell alcohol on his breath already.

"I'm not sure that it's mine to offer."

"Oh, come on. After all you're doing for this family at the moment, you'd be entitled to bathe in champagne every night."

"In a *diamanté* bath," said Rachel, smiling. "All right then, where do they keep the booze?"

Frederick rose to his feet and proved that he knew exactly where to find the drinks cupboard: it stood flush with the bookshelves that were full of unread eighteenth-century first editions. After a quick search among the bottles he plucked one out with an air of triumph.

"Twenty-year-old Lagavulin," he noted, uncorking the bottle and pouring two large tumblerfuls. "Almost the same age as you, in fact."

"I don't really drink wh—"

"This is more than a whisky. It's nectar." He clinked her glass. "Come on. Chin-chin."

Rachel took a sip of the leather-coloured, peaty Scotch and had to concede that it was superb. All the same, she resolved not to drink too much.

"So, to what do I owe this pleasure?" she asked.

"Well," said Freddie, "I was having a drink nearby, and I thought I might drop in to find out how you were coping, all by yourself, and also . . . Also, as it happens, I've been doing a lot of thinking about our conversation the other day, on the plane."

He had not returned to the sofa. He was pacing the room uncertainly, shooting glances of inquiry at Rachel's face as he spoke.

"Oh?" she said.

"The fact is, Rachel, that you obviously have rather a low opinion of me and . . . I'm not comfortable with that."

"I'm sorry if I gave that impression. It had just been a bit of a weird day, that's all . . ."

"I think it's about more than just one day. You hate me. You don't like what I do."

"No," said Rachel, taking another sip of whisky, and realizing that this conversation was going to be every bit as awkward as she had feared. "I don't hate you. It's true that I think your work is—well, a bit unethical . . ."

"A bit! Come off it, Rachel. What I do *stinks*. It stinks to high heaven."

She was taken aback. "OK," she said. "Well, clearly you've had something of a change of heart in the last few days. But those are your words, Freddie. Not mine."

"I thought a bit of plain speaking was called for, for a change. And yes, I have had a change of heart. And I lied to you on the plane, Rachel. I said that everything Gilbert and I do is within the law. Well, it isn't. At least one of the funds I've set up in Madiana's name could land all of us in prison. And perhaps it should."

"I visited someone in prison, this week, as a matter of fact. A friend of mine. She's doing three months for benefit fraud."

"I bet she hasn't fiddled a fraction of what I've siphoned off for Gilbert over the years."

Rachel wished that he would sit down. His pacing was beginning to make her dizzy.

"Well, these are fine words, Freddie. So what are you going to do about it?"

"I'm thinking," he said, "about going to HMRC and telling them everything. Or perhaps taking the story to the papers."

Rachel took another, very cautious sip of whisky, and allowed herself a long look at Freddie while her lips were still to the glass. Nothing about this sudden conversion of his rang true, to her ears.

"I wouldn't do anything drastic," she said. "Having seen the inside of a prison, I don't think it would suit you. And please don't turn your whole life around on my account. Whatever your ethics, I don't dislike you personally. Not at all."

"Really?"

"Really."

"Because it may surprise you to learn that your opinion means a lot to me."

"And why would that be?"

And suddenly he was upon her, pressing her up against the bookshelves, causing her to spill the rest of her whisky on the floor, his lips crushing down on hers, the full weight of his body bearing down on her. "Because you are . . . so . . . fucking . . . gorgeous," he said, between heavy, alcohol-soaked breaths. "Because . . . I can't die happy . . . until I've got inside your pants . . ."

"Get *OFF* me!" Rachel shouted, and pushed him away with a force that sent him reeling across the room. He toppled against the grand piano, steadied himself, and then for a few moments they stared at each other. When he made no further move, she pointed at the door. "Get out. Get out now."

It seemed that he was about to obey her. He wiped his mouth and started making for the door, but as he was passing beside her he made another lunge, grabbing her around the waist this time and throwing her to the floor. Now he was on top of her and she was pinned to the carpet.

"Get *OFF!*" she screamed again, and just then a child's voice said, "Rachel?" and they both looked towards the doorway, in which Grace and Sophia were standing, side by side, wearing their matching pyjamas and looking rumpled and sleepy.

Averting his eyes from the children's questioning gaze, Freddie staggered to his feet and went over to the mirror above the fireplace, where he straightened his tie and smoothed down his hair. Rachel was still on the floor. The impact of the fall had bruised her and for the time being she didn't think she could get up.

"Are you all right?" Sophia said, and they both came forward and held out their hands to help her.

Without another word, or so much as a glance in their direction, Freddie left the room and strode across the hallway towards the front door. They heard it open and then slam shut.

In a slow, painful movement, Rachel rocked herself into a sitting position, and then stayed that way for a while. Grace and Sophia knelt down on either side of her and put their arms around her. It was this display of sympathy, above all—so unexpected, so unlooked-for— that gave her the strength to raise herself finally, and stand upright.

"Come on," she said. "Let's get you back into bed. I think we all need another bedtime story, don't you?"

"Aren't you going to say good-bye to Mr. Francis?"

"No," she said. "I think he knows the way out." And then, holding hands, the three of them slowly climbed the stairs to the second floor.

Freddie certainly knew the way out. But he was in no hurry to leave. For ten minutes he stood in the Gunns' front garden, next to the temporary site office, and tried to calm himself, breathing slowly and heavily, his breath steaming into the night air. It was a clear night, cloudless and starry. The moon, three-quarters full, threw antic shadows across the paving slabs, the patches of dried-out mud and cement, the temporary planking. The disorder of the builders' materials seemed to suit his own deranged state of mind. He felt no immediate inclination to pass through the door in the hoarding. The thought of hailing a cab and making the journey home sickened him.

At first, when he became aware that he was being watched, his reaction was surprisingly calm. He did not know where the creature had come from, or how it had crept up on him so silently, and for a moment he pondered these questions in a mood of dispassionate curiosity. It dawned on him only slowly that he was in mortal danger; and not just that, but that he was about to die in the most grotesque and unbelievable way. The eyes, the two high, widely separated, beady amber eyes, gazed at him with fixed malevolence. The creature's legs were long and double-jointed, rising at their apex to a height taller than Freddie himself. The belly, the huge, distended belly, was covered with short hairs which in the moonlight appeared to have a greenish hue; it sagged heavily against the ground, an obscene sac containing vast, revolting liquid secrets.

The creature's legs quivered and twitched as it readied for the pounce.

Only now did Freddie start to back towards the wall. But with the third or fourth step he tripped and fell, so that he was prone and supine as the spider advanced towards and over him, its legs thrashing and scuttling, the stomach dragging itself across Freddie's shins, knees and thighs, then over his torso before finally settling on his face, so that the entire vile, colossal weight of the thing was pushing down on him, the stench of it, the thick, coarse texture of the body forcing the gorge up to his throat and sending him quickly, irresistibly into a swoon from which he was never to recover.

17

"What a whopper!" bellowed Grace.

"What—a—whopper!" echoed Sophia, at half the speed and in a much deeper voice, and, swept up by uncontrollable laughter, they both started rolling around on the playroom floor.

The credits and the title music came up on the screen all too quickly and they started shouting:

"Oh, Rachel, can we see it again? Please, Rachel!"

"Just the last scene, Rachel . . . *please!*"

Who would have guessed it, Rachel thought, as she rewound the DVD about three minutes. Who would have guessed that of all the things she could have shown them, it would be this terrible, creaky, inept, black-and-white British comedy film from the early 1960s that would send them into such paroxysms of delight, breaking down the final barriers of icy composure which they had maintained in front of her for so long? She had only bought the DVD two years ago because Laura had mentioned it to her as forming part of her researches: warning her, at the same time, that watching the whole thing would probably destroy her will to live. But the last scene, at least—or rather, the final gag—was a miracle of audacious stupidity. After ninety tedious minutes of joking around with fake Loch Ness Monsters, the real monster (itself about as dreadful an example of low-budget special effects as you could imagine) reared its plastic head out of the water and uttered the three immortal words that Grace and Sophia found so hilarious, and which they were now repeating over and over again, trying to imitate the monster's droll, deadpan voice as they waited impatiently for the scene to restart.

"One more time," she said. "One more time, or we're going to be late for the train."

It was Sunday morning, and for the second week in a row she had cancelled her regular date with Jamie. Not, this time, because she had been brusquely summoned to a foreign country to help with ten minutes' homework. No, this time she had made the decision herself (and had arranged to see him tomorrow during the girls' school hours instead) because she was determined to get them out of the house for the day, and to take them not to a museum, gallery or gourmet restaurant, but somewhere where they might have some mindless, uncomplicated fun. Chessington World of Adventures seemed the obvious choice. It wasn't the easiest place to reach by train, but that in itself was part of her plan. She wanted to show them that not everybody in the country travelled in a chauffeured limousine. Other modes of transport were available.

In any case, they ended up having a glorious day. Grace's favourite ride was the Scorpion Express; Sophia inclined towards the Rattlesnake. They both enjoyed getting soaking wet on Rameses' Revenge, and they emerged looking pleasantly shocked, dazed and dizzy from the Dragon's Fury. For Rachel, most of the time was spent standing with them in queues, or watching them on rides and trying to take photographs while they whizzed past on some roller coaster or carousel. A few months ago, she would never have imagined that this was how she would choose to spend an entire Sunday. But there was a reward at the end of it, and it was a precious one: by the time they returned to Turngreet Road, the twins were more animated and talkative than she'd ever known them, and they both promised her that it had easily been the best day of their lives so far. They had loved everything about it, even the terrible junk food and the crowded, severely delayed train ride home. In fact, sitting opposite them in the packed carriage and watching the bright-eyed curiosity on their faces as they looked around at the other passengers, enthralled by the novelty of finding themselves in contact with this mass of ordinary humanity, Rachel wondered whether this hadn't been their favourite part of all.

The next day she went to see Jamie in Crouch End, where he shared a house with six other students. He paid almost £200 a week, for which he was given sole occupancy of a tiny bedroom on the second floor. All the rooms in the house—including what used to be the sitting and dining rooms—had been turned into bedrooms and rented out, so Jamie rarely ventured out of his own bedroom unless it was to go down to the kitchen and make some instant coffee or microwave himself a meal. His bedroom was just about big enough to hold his single bed and the child's dressing table which served as his desk.

"I can only stay a couple of hours," Rachel said, explaining that she had to be back in Chelsea to pick the girls up from school. It was annoying, then, that Jamie proposed watching a film, and would not be talked out of it, all the more so because the film was *Ghosts,* Nick Broomfield's dramatization of the Morecambe Bay cocklepickers' tragedy of 2004, which he needed to watch for the latest chapter of his thesis.

"Why are you always thinking about work?" said Rachel, who after the stresses of the last week had come with an entirely different purpose in mind.

"It's only ninety-six minutes," said Jamie, checking the back of the DVD box. "We can do something else afterwards."

Despite herself, Rachel could not help finding it an absorbing and upsetting film. It followed the misfortunes of a young Chinese illegal immigrant forced into ever more insecure jobs within the food industry, in order to pay back money to the "Snakeheads" who had smuggled her into the UK. Rachel found that the story had a strong resonance with her memories of Lu, the Chinese worker Phoebe had looked after for a few days back in 2003. It was an odd coincidence to be watching a film that so clearly reminded her of this episode now, just when she had spent the last few days attempting to set it all down on paper. When the film was over, Jamie sat at his desk and started making notes.

"Do you have to do that now?" she said. "I've got to go in like . . . half an hour. Forty minutes tops."

"Just a minute," said Jamie. "There are *so* many things I'll need to say about that film. Really I could start a whole new chapter about it."

He scribbled rapidly in his notebook for another two or three minutes, his brow so furrowed with concentration that he did not even notice what Rachel was doing behind his back. When he turned to speak to her again, he found that she had stripped off her clothes and was stretched out beneath his duvet.

He put his pencil down.

"Wow," he said. "I didn't know . . . I mean . . ."

"Come on, then," she said. "Are we going to do it or not?"

He pulled off his shirt and slid in beside her. Rachel put her arms around him and planted a long, moist kiss on his mouth.

"I was attacked last week," she murmured, as Jamie's hands began to glide over her body. Immediately he stopped and pulled back.

"What?"

"This guy came round to the house and . . . tried it on with me."

"Guy? What guy? Who was it?"

"Someone I know. A friend of Gilbert's."

"Did you report it to the police? Did he hurt you?"

"He probably would have done. But he didn't get very far."

Jamie pulled away even further, sitting upright and staring down at her angrily.

"Tell me his name."

"No. Why?"

"Tell me the bastard's name."

"Then what are you going to do?"

"I'll go and smash his face in."

Rachel tried hard, but couldn't refrain from giggling.

"Come off it. You?"

"Yes, me."

She reached up, put her arms around Jamie's shoulders, and pulled him back towards her.

"That's very touching, sweetheart, but it's the last thing I want."

She kissed him again.

"What do you want instead?" he asked.

"A bit of tender loving care would be nice," said Rachel, taking his hand and placing it carefully between her legs.

They made love twice: the first time being slow, and gentle, and deeply satisfying, the second being much more fierce and urgent.

Then, just as Rachel was about to reach her second climax, Jamie's mobile phone rang. To her amazement, he leaned over to answer it.

"What the hell are you doing?" she said.

"I'm sorry," he said, "it might be important."

"Fuck that," she said, biting him frantically on the neck. "This is important."

But still, Jamie craned over and glanced even more closely at the name on the screen.

"I'll have to get this," he said. "It's Laura."

He picked up the phone and answered the call. Furious, Rachel flopped back on to the bed, panting heavily, more with frustration than anything else. She had been on the very brink of orgasm. She couldn't believe that he'd abandoned her at that precise moment.

She ran her hands through her hair and then down the side of her neck, feeling the sweat that had gathered there. For a while she was too agitated to take any notice of what he was saying. Then she became aware that Jamie and Laura were making some kind of arrangement to meet tomorrow evening: there was mention of a train journey. Then Jamie was asking her about someone who should, it seemed, have been joining them, but had gone missing. "Well, when did anyone last see him . . . ?" he was saying. Rachel could hear Laura's voice at the other end of the line and could tell that the conversation was going to continue for some time. That was as much as she could tolerate. She got out of bed, clutching the duvet to hide her nudity, and pulled on her clothes as quickly as possible. By the time Jamie had finished his call, she was fully dressed and standing at the bedroom door.

"Where are you going?" he asked, looking genuinely surprised.

"Back to work," she said. "Where are *you* going?"

"Me? I'm not going anywhere."

"Tomorrow, I mean."

"Oh, that . . . Laura's asked me to go up to Scotland with her. Didn't I mention that?"

"No, you didn't."

"It's this committee she's on. They're going on a jolly to Inverness."

"*Inverness?*"

"The Scottish Tourist Board have asked them to come up and put a price on the Loch Ness Monster."

"How completely ridiculous. And you're going because . . . ?"

"She thinks it'll be good experience for me. You don't mind, do you?"

Rachel said nothing. Jamie frowned.

"A strange thing, though," he said. "Lord Lucrum, the head of the committee . . . Nobody can find him. He seems to have gone missing."

At any other time, Rachel might have found this interesting. At the moment, though, she was far too discomposed, both physically and emotionally, to give the subject even cursory thought.

" 'Bye, then," she said. "And thanks for showing me the film. It was great."

And before leaving, she gave Jamie another kiss on the mouth—one which already foretold, in its briefness and politeness, the death throes of a relationship which had scarcely begun.

18

The silence had returned. As soon as the girls went to bed, as soon as their television was turned off and their friendly chatter came to an end, that was when the silence entered the house, climbing the stairs and wreathing its way into every room like a trail of mist.

Rachel tried to ignore the silence. Tried to pretend it wasn't there. She turned on her computer and streamed some music. She Googled the Morecambe Bay cocklepickers and, after reading some old news stories about them, added a final few paragraphs to her memoir. Still she felt horribly apprehensive and uneasy. Every muscle in her body was taut with anxiety.

While she was online, she did some more browsing and read some of today's newspaper stories:

HELP FIND OUR JOSEPHINE, one headline said.

Thinking that there was a distant, subtle noise outside, out in the garden, Rachel turned off the music and opened the bedroom window. The restless, eternal hum of London was all that she heard. She looked out into the night. She looked down at the pit. There was nothing. No sound. No movement.

The recent death of a seven-year-old girl on the Marshall Islands could have been averted, an expert has claimed.

Chris Baxter, operations director of SafeSpace Ordnance Removal, a small NGO which has been working to raise awareness of the dangers of unexploded WW2 ordnance on the tiny group of islands, said that the area where the girl was playing should have been cleared by now.

"Our programme of clearing this area was 70% complete," he

said. "Unfortunately our operation was closed down when one of our competitors, Winshaw Clearance, was chosen to complete the contract. As of today, my understanding is that Winshaw have yet to commence any operations in the area."

The CEO of Winshaw Clearance, Helke Winshaw, was unavailable for comment.

A flapping noise reached her from the garden. It looked like the corner of the tarpaulin had come loose again. How had that happened?

A rustling noise, a scuttling. Like legs on loose gravel.

All in her mind. All imagination.

Fears are growing for the safety of Lord Lucrum, chairman of the Institute for Quality Valuation, who has not been seen for ten days.

The flapping of the tarpaulin was more insistent now. Rachel decided that she would have to go outside and check on it. She tiptoed quickly down the first flight of stairs, not knowing why it felt so important to be quiet. The mirrored door was wedged open, as it had been for the last few days. She slipped through it and peeped around Sophia's half-open bedroom door. The twins had both chosen to sleep in the same bed, for some reason, their arms wrapped around each other. She could hear their gentle breathing.

Down two more flights of stairs, and into the staff kitchen. She turned on all the lights. Then, very carefully, she unbolted and opened the kitchen door. The cold night air rushed in at once, confronting her, encircling her. She stood on the threshold, not crossing it yet, listening for the tiniest of sounds, her head cocked, as tense as a hunting dog sniffing for a hint of its prey.

She stayed like that for twenty seconds or more, until there was a sudden, unexpected noise which in the stillness of the night seemed deafeningly loud and almost made her jump in the air. It was the buzzer at the front door.

Clutching her heart, Rachel rushed upstairs to look at the nearest entryphone screen.

In her haste, she had omitted to do two things. She did not close the back door properly. And although, while standing in the doorway, she had looked all around her, she had not looked down. Had she done so she would have seen, a few inches from the ground, a thin length of silvery cord, sticky and glistening, stretched across the doorway like a tripwire, then twining itself around a drainpipe and disappearing back into the pit.

She did not recognize the two callers at the front door, but when she went down to speak to them they both produced identity cards proving them to be detectives. One of them looked to be in his early fifties; the other seemed much younger, about twenty years younger.

"My name is Detective Constable Pilbeam," the younger one said. "And this is my colleague, Detective Chief Inspector Capes."

"Otherwise known as the Caped Crusader," said his companion, with a hopeful smile.

Rachel returned the smile, even though she found this rather an odd remark.

"Come in," she said, and led them into the sitting room. Neither of them took off their coats, but they both sat down on the nearest sofa and seemed ready to make themselves comfortable.

"I didn't know they called you that," DC Pilbeam said to his colleague, in an undertone.

"What?"

"The Caped Crusader."

"Well, they do," he answered sharply.

Rachel wondered whether she should offer them a drink, then decided against it. It would have been a friendly thing to do, but they probably weren't allowed to drink on duty.

"Who does?" said DC Pilbeam, apparently unwilling to drop the subject.

"Mm?"

"Who calls you that?"

"Everybody."

"I've never heard them."

"I wonder," said Rachel, growing impatient, "if you'd mind telling me what this is about."

"Ah. Yes." DCI Capes sat up straight, and adopted a formal tone of voice. "We're speaking to Ms. Rachel Wells, I take it?"

"That's right."

"And you are employed as private tutor to the daughters of Sir Gilbert and Lady Gunn?"

"Yes."

"Good. We're here to make some routine inquiries about a missing person. Would we be right in thinking that you're acquainted with one Frederick Francis, Senior Partner in the firm of Bonanza Tax Management?"

"I know Mr. Francis, yes. Is he the person who's gone missing?"

"Mr. Francis has not been home for several days, and nobody has seen him in that time. His friends are growing concerned. Does this come as a surprise to you?"

"That he's gone missing, or that he has friends who are concerned about him?"

DC Pilbeam smiled. DCI Capes didn't.

"Please, Ms. Wells, this could be a very serious matter."

"What's it got to do with me anyway?"

"Last Thursday evening," said DC Pilbeam, consulting his notebook, "Mr. Francis was having a drink at the Henry Root bar around the corner. He got into conversation with one of the ladies behind the bar, and told her that he was coming round to this house. To see you. She said that at this point in the evening, he was rather the worse for drink." He looked up. "Did he visit you that evening?"

"Yes," said Rachel, "he did."

"At what time?"

"About quarter to ten."

"Would you mind describing the encounter?"

"Well, there was nothing very special about it," said Rachel, suddenly feeling nervous and evasive. "We . . . had a drink together. Talked about this and that."

"What was the purpose of his visit, in your view?"

"He'd heard that I was here by myself, looking after the children, and he was—concerned about me, I suppose. Where did he go afterwards, do you know?"

"What time did he leave?"

"Probably about five to ten."

"I see. So it was a very short visit. Surprisingly short, one might say."

"Yes, I suppose it was."

"And did you see Mr. Francis leave the premises?"

"No. I heard him leave by the front door. But after that I took the girls back upstairs."

"The girls? So they were witnesses to his visit as well?"

"Yes, they were."

"But if I understand you correctly, you can't actually say for certain that Mr. Francis left the premises at all."

"Well, I think I would have noticed if he'd been hiding here for the last week."

"This short conversation you had with him," said DCI Capes, "was it . . . friendly, amicable?"

Rachel nodded. "Yes, I'd say so."

"You didn't argue, at all? There was no quarrel? No . . . lovers' tiff?"

"He was *not* my lover."

To emphasize this point, Rachel had raised her voice, but at the same time it cracked and broke. She sank down into an armchair and put her head in her hands. DC Pilbeam immediately leaped up from the sofa. He crouched down beside her and put a comforting hand on her knee.

"Ms. Wells, are you all right? You seem rather distressed."

"Oh, I'm . . . Not really . . . I don't know, I'm fine . . . It's just . . . It's this house," she said, fighting back tears. "I hate it here. At night it's dark and lonely and I start to imagine all sorts of strange things. And I get worried about the girls. So worried about them. I worry that they're not safe."

"Why would they not be safe?"

"I don't know. There's some . . . danger here. I'm convinced of it."

"Is that what you thought when Mr. Francis called?" said DCI Capes, from across the room. "That he might pose a danger to those girls?"

DC Pilbeam shot him a warning glance: he did not seem to like the slightly aggressive tone of this question. His own voice was much smoother and more reassuring.

"Ms. Wells," he said, "I'm going to tell you a little bit more about this case, and why we consider it so important."

Rachel wiped the tears away from her eyes, and nodded.

"The fact is that Mr. Francis is not the only person to have disappeared recently in this vicinity."

"Oh?"

"DCI Capes and I suspect that his disappearance is linked to five others, which have all occurred in the last few weeks. First of all, Ms. Josephine Winshaw-Eaves, the newspaper columnist. Then Mr. Giles Trending, the CEO of Stercus Television. Then Philip Stanmore, a director of Sunbeam Foods. Then Helke Winshaw, CEO of Winshaw Clearance plc. And also Lord Lucrum, head of the Institute for Quality Valuation. Mr. Francis is the sixth person to have disappeared. One thing that all these people have in common is that they either lived, or were last seen, within a few hundred yards of this street."

DCI Capes added: "But that's not all they have in common."

"Indeed not," said DC Pilbeam, rising to his feet and beginning to pace the room. "But this is where the theories of my colleague and myself diverge."

"My *junior* colleague," said DCI Capes, "is a remarkable young man. He believes that in order to solve a crime, you have to look at it from the political angle. Using the word in its broadest sense, that is. I have to say that in the past, his theories have produced impressive results. So that's the approach we intend to take in this instance."

"All the same," said DC Pilbeam, "as we've learned from past experience, we must be careful not to jump to the first and most obvious conclusion, even if it looks as if—"

"There is no mystery, Nathan, about what these six people have in common. Just because *I* was the one who found out the link—"

"What is the link?" Rachel asked, butting in before their argument spiralled out of control.

"It's perfectly simple," said DCI Capes. "All six of them were pres-

ent at a reception held last month at Number 11, Downing Street."
He turned to DC Pilbeam with a challenging gleam in his eye. "Well?
Isn't that so?"

"Yes. Absolutely. I don't deny it. But I still think we should look
beyond that . . ."

"Beyond that!" said Capes, in a scoffing tone. "To what? What *else*
is there?"

"There is something else," said Pilbeam. "There is the Winshaw
family itself."

"Not them again!" said Capes. "How many times do I have to
point it out to you? Only two of these people are members of the
Winshaw family, and one of those only by marriage."

"True," said Pilbeam. "But look at the other connections. Mr.
Trending heads the steering committee of the Winshaw Prize, established in honour of Roderick Winshaw. Mr. Francis began his career
as a trader at Stewards' Bank, as a protégé of Thomas Winshaw. Lord
Lucrum used to work—"

"—with Henry Winshaw, on the committee that started disman-
tling the NHS," Rachel said.

"Quite," said DC Pilbeam, so absorbed in his own reasoning that
he barely noticed where this contribution had come from. "And
Philip Stanmore's Sunbeam Foods—"

"—is the biggest member of the Brunwin Group, established by
Dorothy Winshaw in the seventies and eighties."

"Exactly!" Pilbeam turned to his colleague. "Don't you see? You
have to dig deeper. Have you read that book yet? The one that I lent
you?"

"Which book?" said DCI Capes.

Pilbeam raised his eyes to the ceiling. *"The Winshaw Legacy,"* he
said, "by Michael Owen. Everything you need to know about the
family is—"

He broke off, his attention suddenly caught by an object placed
on top of the grand piano. He went over and picked it up. It was a
book.

"But . . . this is extraordinary," he said. "This is the very book I'm
talking about. How . . . ? What . . . ?"

Rachel reached out and took it from him, her hands shaking.

"I've been reading this," she said. "A friend of mine lent it to me the other day."

"I see," said DC Pilbeam, taking a step back, and eyeing her very differently, with a new closeness. "And that, I suppose, is why you are so familiar with these connections I was making?"

"Yes," said Rachel. "I suppose it is."

"Interesting," said DC Pilbeam. "Very interesting." He was staring at her now, so intently that she was obliged to look away and blurt out, in a strong but quavering voice:

"I have nothing to do with Mr. Francis's disappearance. Or any of these other people. I've got nothing to do with *any* of this. I shouldn't even be in this house. I don't belong here."

Her lips trembled and she fell silent. But this time it was DCI Capes, rather than his younger colleague, who took pity on her and, rising to his feet, said in a kindly voice:

"Of course you have nothing to do with it, miss. We know that. Take no notice of him and his theories." He tapped his colleague on the arm. "Come on, Pilbeam. It's time we were off. And listen to me, for a change: I've already cracked this case. Have a look at the guest list for that reception, and your suspect will be there. Number 11 is the key, I tell you. It's as simple as that!"

The men were gone. The house was silent again.

Rachel went back to the sitting room, opened the Gunns' drinks cupboard and took out the bottle of twenty-year-old Lagavulin. It seemed wasteful to use such a rare and valuable whisky simply to steady her nerves, but such considerations did not weigh with her anymore. She poured herself a tumbler at least three-quarters full and sat on the piano stool, drinking it slowly and methodically. From time to time she looked at the book on the piano and wondered how it had got there. She did not remember bringing it down here, but she knew her behaviour was becoming erratic and forgetful.

She had almost finished drinking the whisky when she heard a noise in the hallway. A swift, busy rustling, as of legs upon the marble tiles. She stood up and walked slowly across the room. She stopped before reaching the doorway, listening. Then, very slowly, very carefully, she crept towards the doorway and peeped round it.

The hallway was empty.

The hallway was empty, but something had changed. It took Rachel a few moments to realize what it was. On the staircase, something had been twined around the banister. Rachel stepped forward, relieved now, assuming that the children were playing a joke on her: they had stolen downstairs and wrapped a ball of string or a washing line around the uprights. But no, as she came closer, she thought that it didn't look like string. It was thinner, and more silvery. She reached out and touched it and it stuck to her hand.

Shaking the thread loose, Rachel followed it down the hallway until she came to the stairwell that led down to the family kitchen. At this point, her way was blocked, and this time, there was no mistaking the obstruction. It was a giant web, made of the same glutinous, gossamer thread.

Rachel stared at the web in horror, but soon, not knowing where her own strength or courage was coming from, she found herself reaching out and tearing at it with frantic, clutching fingers. It stuck to her everywhere: her shoulders, her legs, especially her face, but finally, panting with effort and revulsion, she had broken her way through it. She rushed down the stairs and into the kitchen, which was in darkness. Hollow with dread at the thought of what she might see, she flicked the lights on.

Nothing there. She ran back up to the hallway, then upstairs to Sophia's bedroom. The girls were still asleep, blameless, angelic. Through the mirrored door, back into the servants' half of the house, then all the way down the narrow staircase, and into the staff kitchen. Here, threads and webs had been strung up everywhere. The very air was thick with them. Rachel forced her way through them—a particularly tough thread got caught in her mouth, and she bit through it, almost gagging at the bitter, poisonous taste—until she reached the knife drawer, which she threw open, extracting the biggest, sharpest, most lethal carving knife she could find, fully ten inches long.

She turned and faced the back doorway. The door was open. How could that have happened? If it had been her doing, then she'd been very careless.

A particularly thick and elaborate web had been woven across the doorway, but she slashed her way through it somehow, then ran straight out into the garden and towards the corner of the pit where the tarpaulin had been loosened. In the distance, a siren wailed, grew louder and closer, then faded into the distance: a reminder that elsewhere, not far away, normal life was still in progress, bringing home to Rachel the nightmarish unreality of her own situation.

The single thread that led down into the pit itself was as thick as a rope. She sawed away at it for a few seconds and it snapped with a satisfying twang. Then Rachel lifted the tarpaulin and peered inside.

She could see nothing. Just a yawning void; a bottomless pool of blackness.

She stared harder. Perhaps she could discern some outlines. A platform, was it, down there? Scaffolding? Was that an immense ladder fixed to the wall? Impossible to say.

She must have stared into the darkness for three minutes or more. The handle of the knife grew moist with the sweat from her palm. And then, at last, she did see something. Way down in the depths of the shaft, more than a hundred feet away, two pinpricks of light suddenly appeared. A pair of eyes. Whatever the eyes belonged to, it had seen her, and it was staring back at her.

Rachel met the creature's distant gaze and held it. She stopped breathing. She clutched the knife more tightly. She felt herself mesmerized. She couldn't move.

And then, at the same distance, at the very bottom of the pit, two more amber pinpricks appeared. Then two more, and two more, and then four more, and a dozen more. Soon Rachel knew that she was being watched by at least fifty pairs of eyes.

Still she did not move. She could not force herself from the spot until the eyes themselves started moving. In response to some sort of collective will, the creatures stirred themselves and smoothly, silently, with unthinkable agility, they began to swarm up the sheer walls of the pit. Their progress was swift and inexorable. In just a matter of seconds they were only fifty feet away. The eyes came closer and closer, never diverting their gaze from Rachel for an instant.

Then, and only then, did she scream. She screamed and ran: ran back to the house, where she slammed the kitchen door shut, bolted it, ran to the staircase, closed that door behind her as well, then hurtled up the stairs, up to the ground floor, the first floor, the second floor and the mirrored doorway that led through to the other half of the house.

Before passing through it for the last time, she turned and looked out from the landing window. The spiders were massing in the garden, overturning the builders' tools, scuttling over the garden walls, breaking down the trellising. And some of them were trying to get into the house.

Rachel ran into Sophia's room and shook the twins awake.

"Get up! Get dressed!" she shouted. "We've got to leave, *now!*"

The girls tumbled out of bed drowsily and rubbed their eyes.

"What? Where are our clothes?"

"No time! Put your dressing gowns on."

They struggled into their dressing gowns. Grace got her arm caught in one of the sleeves and realized she was trying to put it on inside out. Sophia fumbled for ages in her attempt to knot the cord at her waist.

"Follow me," said Rachel.

She grasped Sophia's hand, and Sophia grasped Grace's hand, and in that way she tugged them out of the bedroom and onto the main staircase. Their way was blocked by two dense, glistening webs, which she slashed to the floor with a couple of strokes of her blade.

"What are you swinging that knife around for?" asked Grace.

"Why do you even *have* a knife?" asked Sophia.

They reached the main hallway and Rachel threw open the front door. Three spiders were gathered at the foot of the steps, barring their path to the door in the hoarding. They were huge, and their swollen bodies shone in the moonlight, burnished with lurid green.

"Keep back," said Rachel. "We have to get past them."

The girls waited at the top of the steps, while Rachel descended, step by step, her knife outstretched. The creatures never took their small, vicious, bulbous eyes off the blade. When Rachel lunged out at them they hissed, reared up on their two back legs, but gradually backed off.

"Now!" Rachel called to the girls. "To the doorway! Run!"

Grace and Sophia tore down the steps, through the mass of builders' rubble, past the site office and waited panting by the door. Rachel
joined them, walking backwards, the knife still outstretched to keep
the monsters at bay, then switched the electronic latch and shoul-
dered the door open. They were out in the street.

"Where are we going?" said Sophia. "I don't want to go anywhere.
I want to go back to bed."

They were out in the street, but they were not safe. The creatures
were here as well. In their loathsome droves they swarmed, milling along the pavements and carriageway, spreading destruction in
their path. They clambered onto cars, overturning them, toppling
the massed rows of Range Rovers, Porsches and Jaguars. They ran
up the walls of the vast, arrogant houses, tearing into brickwork,
smashing glass. Property was their first target; after that would come
people. The moon was at its fullest and everywhere Rachel looked
she could see the green bodies of these vile, mutant insects, crawling
across white stuccoed walls, rearing up triumphantly at the summit
of chimney stacks. The night air erupted with shrill, deafening noise
as a symphony of burglar alarms began to play up and down the
street.

"Hurry!" she shouted to the twins. "We've still got time!"

Grabbing Sophia's hand again, she began to drag them both
along, breaking into a sprint. Miraculously, the hideous, rampant
creatures would back off and allow them to pass whenever they were
approached. And so the thing that finally stopped them in their
tracks, at the end of the street, was not a spider at all, but a human
obstruction: a man. DCI Capes, standing at the corner, who seized
Rachel in a rugby tackle and brought her to the ground, while DC
Pilbeam wrested the knife from her grasp.

"It's all right," one of them was saying. "Calm down. It's all right
now. Everybody's safe."

They held her like that, pinning her to the asphalt, until her
breathing had subsided into a calmer, more regular rhythm, the din-
ning of the burglar alarms had faded away, the spiders had retreated
to their subterranean home and Rachel realized that, apart from the
sobbing of Grace and Sophia, the world was now empty and silent.

19

Alison was not thinking about anything in particular. She sat in the armchair at the bay window, watching the sunlight throw elaborate shadows across the curlicued red-and-yellow patterns of the old-fashioned carpet. It was odd how well she remembered this carpet, given that she hadn't seen it for more than twelve years. The house itself hadn't changed much. Beverley hadn't changed much, for that matter—except for Number 11, Needless Alley, which, it turned out, had been shorn of its leafy aviary, and was now home to a prosperous, well-dressed family, who had tidied up the garden and fitted a new front door and repainted the window frames. What had become of Phoebe? Nobody seemed to know.

Rachel's grandmother seemed cheerful enough on the surface—could not have been more delighted, really, to welcome Alison and Rachel back to her home, even if just for a day—but there was no escaping the fact that her husband's absence now filled every room, settled everywhere like a film of dust, in a way that his presence never had. Gran herself, under the strain of this absence, had almost buckled, become wraith-like. She passed through doorways, from kitchen to living room, from bathroom to landing, as silently as a ghost. Even now, as Alison sat in the sunshine daydreaming, she did not even notice that Gran had entered the room, and quietly settled herself on the sofa. Not until she heard her say:

"Rachel was telling me that your mum's had a stroke of luck."

Startled, Alison turned round. "That's right."

"What happened?"

"Well . . ." After telling so many people, so many times, over the last few weeks, Alison still found the story hard to believe. "She was coming home on the bus one afternoon, just like any other day, when the phone rang, and it was this woman she'd been on TV with. Danielle Perry. She's a sort of singer, actress . . . I don't know what you'd call her really."

"I know who you mean," said Gran. "She's ever so pretty."

"And she said she wanted to record one of Mum's songs. The one she'd heard her sing in the jungle when they did that show together. 'Sink and Swim.' So that's what she's done. And it's selling really well. In the charts and everything."

"I'm so glad," said Gran. "Will she make some money out of it?"

"Yeah, she already has. Quite a bit in fact."

"Everybody deserves a bit of luck now and again. Jim used to do the Lottery, you know. Every week. He never won a thing." She was looking at the chair in which Alison was sitting, but it was as if she didn't see her at all. "I can picture him now, sitting right there, crossing out the numbers. That was his favourite chair. His favourite spot."

Alison started to get up. "You can sit here if you want, Mrs.—"

"No, don't be silly. You stay where you're comfortable. Enjoy the sunshine. Best time of the day to sit there."

She was perched on the edge of the sofa, clutching a mug with "World's Best Gran" written on it, a Christmas present from Rachel long years ago.

"In the mornings, too. Always sitting there, he was, when I came down. He was waiting for the paperboy, you see."

Alison nodded, and smiled. She didn't know what to say.

"That was how the day used to start," said Gran. "I'd come down. Put the kettle on. Make the tea."

She smiled, faintly. The recollection seemed to warm her.

"Then the paper would come. He'd get it first. I'd make some breakfast, get him his cereal. Then we'd have it in the kitchen together.

"Then he'd go on his computer. He loved his computer. That was the best thing he ever bought. He'd do the letters, and the bills, whatever needed doing.

"I'd stay downstairs, while he was doing that. Start the crossword.

"Middle of the morning, we'd have another cup of tea. Together. In here. That was his chair, the one you're in. Then I'd go out to the shops.

"We had lunch in the kitchen. Just soup, normally. Tomato for me, mushroom for him. He'd put the radio on. Always wanted to hear the news at one o'clock.

"Then if the weather was good, we'd go out in the garden. He was proud of the garden. We never had a gardener, never had anyone to help. Right to the end, we'd do it ourselves. Trim the borders and keep the hedge tidy.

"Then he'd come inside for a sit-down. That chair where you are now. He always knew where to catch the sunshine.

"I'd want to watch television later on. Quiz shows and things. He didn't like them so much, so he'd go back upstairs, on his computer. We weren't in the same room, but I always knew he was here, always knew he was in the house.

"Dinner at six. We never had it much later than that. Neither of us liked fancy food. Fried mushrooms were his favourite, he'd like anything with them. Just mushrooms on toast, we'd have sometimes.

"We never agreed what to watch on television. He liked the news, current affairs, anything political. I liked plays and comedy programmes, something to make you laugh, but they don't make such good ones anymore, do they?

"He had a whisky at night, just before he went to bed. There was no harm in it. He only ever had the one. It helped him sleep.

"He went to bed early. Always in bed before eleven. He'd put the radio on, not very loud. I think he just liked to listen to the voices. I'd be down here. Still trying to finish the crossword, probably. I couldn't hear anything from upstairs, but it was enough. It was enough just to know he was there."

She fell silent. Hunched over her mug, she wasn't crying, but she looked frail, and tired. The afternoon sunlight fell upon her face, finding wrinkles, illuminating the folds of skin at her throat.

Alison stood up and walked over to her. She put her arms around her, felt the brittleness of her bones beneath her jumper, leaned in, saw the whiteness of her scalp through the thinning, frost-coloured hair. She kissed the top of her head, a gentle, lingering kiss.

"Rachel was calling for you," Gran said. "I think she needs your help."

Rachel was sitting at the top of the plum tree, her face tilted towards the sun, enjoying the warmth of its rays upon her face. She loved sitting amidst the branches of this tree—had loved it ever since she was a child—with its view over the neighbouring gardens, the tidy patchwork of suburban life laid out beneath her, and in the distance, the monumental, greyish-cream towers of the Minster.

She looked down when Alison approached and said:

"About time too. Where've you been?"

"Chatting to your gran. Are you all right up there?"

"Very comfortable actually."

"You're not supposed to exert yourself."

"I'm fine. I've been fine for ages. I wish everybody'd stop worrying about me."

And it was true. Rachel was looking healthier than she had looked for many weeks. She'd been living at home with her mother in the months since her discharge, and she was rested, and she was happy again. She had put it all behind her.

"Come on, then," said Alison. "Those plums aren't going to pick themselves. Chuck them down and I'll catch them in the basket."

"Right you are."

Rachel reached across to the furthest bunch. There had been another wonderful crop this year. They were purple and luscious, perfectly ripe, with soft powdery skins.

As she plucked the first one, a spider ran out from beneath it. She held out her arm and allowed it to scuttle along the pale skin of her underarm until it had reached the neighbouring branch, where it ran off to safety. Rachel watched it disappear between the cracks in the bark. Then she threw the plum down to Alison.

"Here, catch!"

They continued like this, throwing and catching, throwing and catching, for a minute or two, until Alison stopped and said:

"Do you miss Jamie, Rache?"

"A bit." She threw down another plum. "What about you, do you miss Selena?"

"A bit."

"Well, if you ask me," said Rachel, "we're better off single."

"Too right," said Alison. "You know what, though?" she added, a thought having just occurred to her. "Perhaps we should be a couple."

"You and me?" Rachel laughed dismissively. "Dream on," she said. "This lady's not for turning."

"Suit yourself," said Alison. "I don't fancy you anyway."

Rachel laughed again, and plucked one more plum from a bunch of four. She took the fruit, rubbed it clean against her T-shirt and bit into it. The juice was deliciously sweet in her mouth. It was the taste of her childhood; the taste of home; the taste of autumn sunshine.

20

My name is Livia and I come from Bucharest. I have been living in London for more than five years, and my job is taking the dogs of very rich people for their daily walk.

But that is not all.

Strange things have happened in this part of London. Six people disappeared, and they have never been found. The police keep making enquiries, looking for connections. They came to interview me. But the real connection between these six people is something that they have never noticed.

They all had dogs.

I am Livia, and I come from Bucharest. I have lived in London for five years, and I know not just its streets, but also its secret places, above ground and below. None of these places is deeper, or more secret, than the place beneath the tall house in Turngreet Road, eleven floors beneath the ground, beneath the wine cellar and the vault and the swimming pool where the palm trees grow.

There is a tunnel. And beyond the tunnel there is a room. And there they hang, in the dark. Each one wrapped in a cocoon of silver threads. Watched over by the vengeful creature with the amber eyes.

My vengeance takes many forms. My body takes many forms.

We have a saying in my country, by the way: *După faptă și răsplată.* Which means, measure for measure, or the biter bit.

If you understand the saying, you will understand my nature. I am not merciful. I am not just. I cannot be tamed. I attack whomever I want, and whatever I want.

I am not angry. I am anger itself.

You may feel pity for my victims. That is your choice. You may place your sympathies with them, or with me. That is your decision.

In the end, I believe, we are all free to choose.

ACKNOWLEDGEMENTS

The section of this book entitled "The Crystal Garden" was inspired by the piece of that name by Harold Budd, recorded on his album *The Pavilion of Dreams* (OBS 10) in 1978.

Michele O'Leary, Andrew Hodgkiss, Ralph Pite, Philippe Auclair, Georgia Powell and Vera Michalski all assisted me with valuable background material. My heartfelt thanks to them, but above all to Louise Le May, for letting me take her beautiful song "Sink and Swim" and put it at the centre of Val's story.

A NOTE ON THE TYPE

This book is set in Minion, a typeface designed by Robert Slimbach and produced by the Adobe Corporation specifically for the Macintosh personal computer and released in 1990.

Typeset by Scribe, Philadelphia, Pennsylvania

Printed and bound by Berryville Graphics, Berryville, Virginia

Designed by Betty Lew